**Coming soon from Adriana Herrera
and Carina Press**

American Fairytale

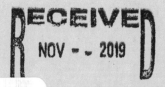

For the Dreamers.

AMERICAN DREAMER

ADRIANA HERRERA

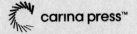

carina press™

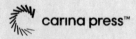

ISBN-13: 978-1-335-00687-5

American Dreamer

Recycling programs
for this product may
not exist in your area.

www.CarinaPress.com

Printed in U.S.A.

AMERICAN DREAMER

"The future belongs to those who believe in the beauty of their dreams."

— *Eleanor Roosevelt*

Chapter One

Nesto

"So, this is it? You're really taking off to that wilderness upstate."

I looked up from where I was trying to shove another gigantic container into the back of my food truck, and saw Camilo, one of my three best friends, walking down the sidewalk wearing oversized sunglasses and holding an enormous cup of coffee.

Late as always.

He was supposed to be here an hour ago, but could he manage to make it on time to help me literally pack up my entire life? No.

"What the fuck, Milo? You're an hour late, pendejo! I've been waiting on you since seven a.m. You know I'm on a schedule, man. I can't have this truck sitting here all morning!" I cringed thinking of everything I needed to get done in the next twenty-four hours.

"We need to be on the road by nine if I'm going to be ready for the gig tomorrow. I shouldn't have let Mamí talk me into opening this thing the day after getting up there."

Milo looked at me shaking his head, then put down

his coffee and crossed his arms over his chest like he had all the time in the world.

"Chill out, you'll be fine. Your mother already has your food order waiting at the commercial kitchen she found you. As soon as we get in, she'll be deploying people to make sure you're ready to go. Besides Juanpa, Patrice, and I will be there tonight to help too. Don't worry so much, pa. It's only like a five-hour drive. We'll be there by two, tops."

I took a deep breath, because I knew arguing with Milo would probably mean I'd either get going even later or that he'd get himself so worked up he'd crash my damn car on the interstate.

"Dude, can you be at least a little sympathetic? This is a big fucking deal for me. I'm moving out of New York City, my home since I was six years old, to try and get a food truck business going upstate."

I reached over for another container and huffed in exasperation. "If I had a beard and a man bun I'd be a cancelled show on Food Network."

Milo's face softened, and he started chuckling while he finally got his ass in gear and walked a box to the truck. "You're so over the top sometimes. But okay," he said, raising his hands. Palms out. "It's only a six-month trial, you can always come back. Your truck is doing fine here. It's not like you're going out of business or anything. People love those burritos."

He grabbed his coffee and drank deeply before continuing with his pissy pep talk.

"I mean, true, it's hard to make a living out here with all the competition, but your food sells well. You've been killing it at Smorgasburg when you're down in Brooklyn. Those hipsters go crazy over your shit."

I shook my head forcefully at his words as I slammed the back doors of the truck closed.

I stepped away from the vehicle, taking a long look at it. Emblazoned on the back was the logo for my business, *OuNYe, Afro-Caribbean Food* in huge bold black font on a red background. The black and red contrasted with the flags of the Dominican Republic, Puerto Rico, Cuba, Haiti and Jamaica painted over the entire truck.

To name my business, I used a word from the Yoruba language. Which had been spoken all over the Caribbean by our ancestors, the West Africans who were brought there as slaves. *Ounje* is the Yoruba word for nourishment, and I'd decided to play a bit with things and put the NY right at the center.

The two worlds that made me merged into one word.

OuNYe was my baby. I put my blood, sweat, and tears into getting this idea off the ground. Street food filled with the flavors of the Caribbean. My roots and those of Juan Pablo, Camilo and Patrice, my three best friends. The food we had grown up with and had been our connection to where we came from, while our families tried to make a life here in the Big Apple.

Now I was taking one last shot at making my living from it.

I looked over at Milo, who was still gulping down coffee. "I've been doing this for two years, and I need to be able to make a decent living. I'm not going to be sweating it out for the rest of my life, to barely break even. If I can't get it off the ground like I want to in Ithaca, I'm done. *Se acabo*."

Milo clicked his tongue like it was taking every ounce of patience he had not to hit me upside the head.

"Oh my god, you gotta stop. You've agonized over

this move for a year. You'll be doing business like gang-busters up there. You're gonna kill it. You know white people love 'ethnic' food wrapped in a tortilla."

He held up his hands with his index fingers hooked together, ready to start pulling out the receipts to shut down my bullshit.

"First of all, the concept is awesome, and your food is delicious. Second, there isn't any Caribbean food anywhere up there. Now stop whining before I lose my temper with you! I've had like three sips of this coffee and you know better than to aggravate me when I'm not properly caffeinated."

I could only laugh, "You're an idiot."

This is why I knew Milo and the guys coming along for the drive up was a good idea. Because despite the fact that he was salty as fuck sometimes, the guy could give a hell of a pep talk. I walked to my Prius, which Milo would be driving up to Ithaca, met him by the driver's side door, and handed him the keys.

"Here, don't drive like a fucking maniac. I texted you the address where we'll stop for lunch. There's a truck stop so we can park. Patrice and Juanpa already left in J's truck. They'll meet us there. Again, do not drive while reading something on your phone or text the guys while the car is moving."

"Pshh, you're being mad extra today." Milo blew me off. "Stress is not a good look on you, pa." He scrunched his face, pressing the point as he got in the car. "See you in a couple of hours." I stepped back and watched him set up the Google maps on his phone and drive off with a little wave.

I went back to stand by the truck and looked around one last time. It was a beautiful Sunday morning in

New York City. The sun was shining and it was going to be a perfect spring day.

People in this corner of Manhattan, right up against the Hudson River, were already buzzing past me, heading to jobs and lives. Going after their little piece of the American dream. I choked up because this felt final, like it would never be *my* New York City again. This place was not just where I lived, it was part of my DNA, and I was convinced I would never feel at home anywhere else.

After twenty-seven years of calling this place mine, I was leaving.

I took one last look at my surroundings and inhaled the smell of fresh coffee and hot oil from the empanada cart down the street. I stood right off Broadway, on 155th street, Boricua College on my right, Trinity Church Cemetery on my left, and the Hudson straight ahead. This had been my neighborhood for almost eight years, and I was going to miss it. I was going to miss all of it.

I sighed as I made my way back to the truck and climbed in. I got the map up on my phone, pushed down my sunglasses, and started the truck.

I was ready.

I was going after my dream, to pursue my passion. As I headed out of the city, I looked out and said a silent "See you soon."

If it didn't work out in Ithaca, I'd be back soon enough.

I was a son of New York City, and she would always have me back with open arms.

The day ended up being perfect for a long drive. Just a bit before two p.m. I took the exit for Ithaca and began to feel the nervous anticipation of what was to come. I was adventurous when it came to travel or trying new things, but not with my livelihood.

Immigrants didn't fuck around with a steady stream of income. If you were making a decent living, you worked your ass off to keep it on lockdown.

Pursuing your passion? Risking everything on a dream?

That was for people with trust funds, not a Dominican kid from the Bronx.

While I coasted down the rural two-lane road that led to my destination, I thought about what this move meant. It'd been terrifying to leave a good and secure job to try my luck in something so unpredictable, and where the chances for utter failure were sky-high. Sure, I was confident in my skills, in my food, but I knew there would be a long way down if I failed.

This was not just a side-hustle anymore. I was going all-in with my business. It felt big, like it could change everything.

Before I got to my mom's, I decided to stop at the gas station where I was going to park the truck for lunch services, and check out the location. I was low on gas too, so I could kill two birds with one stone.

Navigating one of the many hills of Ithaca entering downtown, it was like I was seeing it for the first time. I drove by houses painted in bright colors and narrow streets full of trees laden with flowers. It was so green and quaint here. I wasn't sure how I'd fit in, being so used to the fast pace of the city.

I turned the steering wheel of the truck and wedged into an empty spot next to a pump. I jumped out and glanced around, taking in the location. I couldn't help the grin that broke out on my face. Of course my mom would somehow manage to find me the best possible spot in town. It was right by the public library and all around were commercial buildings. There would be a lot of foot traffic during the week.

I kept looking around as I filled the tank and didn't notice the car that drove up on the other side of me. It was a small, green Subaru hatchback with a Human Rights Campaign sticker on the back window. The guy who jumped out was gorgeous. He had the blondest hair I'd ever seen, and was wearing tight jeans and a black NPR t-shirt.

For some reason his shirt struck me as hilarious, and as he was pushing up his Ray-Bans to look at the screen on the pump, a laugh burst out of me. He turned around with a startled expression, probably looking for the jackass laughing at him for no reason. The intensity of his blue eyes, and the way his mouth pursed and then turned up into a smirk like he wasn't sure if he should get pissed or laugh too, made the laugh die in my throat. He was so pretty, and currently looking at me like there was something seriously wrong with me.

I put my hand up in an attempt to apologize for my bizarre behavior. "Sorry, man. Ignore me. I'm just a bit punchy from a long drive."

He didn't respond, just kept staring me, looking confused. I quickly finished up, and almost left without saying anything. But at the last second decided not to be an asshole and called out, "Have a nice day" before jumping in the truck.

I sent a quick text to my mom to let her know I'd be at her place soon and pulled out of the station. As I drove, I mused that if the blond was a sample of the men running around town, I'd need to look into some socializing opportunities. Then I remembered I was here to run a business, not to get laid.

I needed to get my head in the game and remember if this plan didn't work out my only prospect at the moment was going back to TPS reports and coming up with ways to make fro-yo sound "a little more urban."

After a few minutes navigating my truck through the tight residential streets of Ithaca I turned onto my mom's block and saw her waiting outside.

She was wearing a flowing white linen shirt, her long salt-and-pepper curls falling down her back. As a boy I thought she was the most beautiful woman in the world, and that was still the case. These days she was embracing the natural look; had given up wearing makeup and relaxing her hair.

I parked the truck in the empty space in front of her house, which I knew she must have been guarding furiously all day.

"M'ijo! You made it," she yelled out as I walked over to her. "Look at you, so handsome. Your hair is getting long, papí," she griped as she gave me a bear hug and kissed both my cheeks.

"Mamí, you look gorgeous. I like this blouse. Very Stevie Nicks."

Complimenting her on her clothes and how great she looked was first and foremost.

She smacked my arm but the big smile on her face gave her away.

"Muchacho, Stevie Nicks is a lot older than me!"

She pulled on the hem of the shirt as we walked, as if only now noticing what she was wearing. "Besides, this old thing? Your Tía Maritza got it for me at some hippie clothes sale she goes to. You know how she is, goes overboard, buys too many things, and then I end up with half of them!"

I raised an eyebrow, because she was just as bad as Tía Maritza with the shopping.

"You two are hilarious."

She put her hand around my waist as we walked up the sidewalk. "Tell me about the drive. Did you have any trouble?"

I was thinking how much I'd missed having my mom and sister close by, when a pinch on my arm got my attention. "Sorry, Mamí. Drive was good," I said as we got to the door of my mom's little house.

One thing was certain, even if things flopped with the truck it would be nice to have family close again. My mom moved up to Ithaca eight years before. She wanted a more sedate environment for my little sister Minerva to go to school, and decided to join Tía Maritza and Tío Tonin who'd been here for years. I'd been out of college and working then, so I stayed behind. I looked down at her smiling face as she ushered me into the house.

"Good. Come in your sister should be home soon, and your tíos are on their way over. We're all so happy you're here, papí." I got another squeeze.

"The guys are inside," she said, trying her best to look grumpy, and failing completely. "They've only been here for fifteen minutes and Juanpa's already eaten all my food."

I just grinned down at her. "Don't even front like you're mad, Mamí. I know you love having a house full of people."

She looked up at me with a blank look on her face, as if she wasn't sure what my point was. "Nesto's home!" she called while she went for another hug.

I loved seeing my mom in her home. She'd busted her ass as a single mom for so long to give us a good life. She'd kept us out of trouble and was an amazing role model, but it all came at a cost.

She never stopped. She worked hard, and always knew what was up with school, with friends, and on the block. All while going to night school, and sending money home to help the family back in the DR. If anyone deserved to slow down and smell the roses, it was Nurys Maldonado.

We stood by the door arm in arm and then my mom waved toward the kitchen. "Let me go start some coffee." She gave me one last peck on the cheek before she hurried off.

I spotted Milo sprawled on the couch messing with his phone. "Did Milo do anything to my car?" I asked my mom, who was already in the kitchen.

Mamí smiled in Camilo's direction while she bustled around. "Car looks fine to me, but you know Milo. As soon as he got here he started moaning about getting lost three times and cursing out Juanpa and Patrice for not picking up when he called them."

I looked over and saw my friends filling my mom's living room. My brothers. I wouldn't have them just a few subway stops away anymore. I tried to shake off the feeling of unease the thought brought me and focused on all the stuff we needed to get done before they went back to the city.

But before I could get to them, my uncle and aunt were barreling into the house making a fuss over me, and talking over each other asking about the truck.

"Nesto! M'ijo. Look at you. You look more like your

abuelo every day. Doesn't he, Nurys?" my aunt asked my mom as she engulfed me in a tight hug.

Tía Maritza was a slightly thinner and older version of my mom. The same bronzed skin, the curly hair, tall and curvy. She didn't look a day over forty-five, even though sixty-two was just a few months away. She and Tío Tonin had been married for almost forty years and still looked at each other like they were high school sweethearts.

"What's good, Tío? You letting Tía Maritza feed you too much of that platano?" I asked, patting the little bulge around his waistband.

He laughed heartily as he went in for a bear hug.

Tonin as always had a big smile on his face, and at sixty-five his dark brown skin was still free of any wrinkles. My uncle had always been like a father to me. He taught me by example how a man should act toward those he loved. I hoped when the time came, like him, I could be the type of man who put his people first.

"It's good to have you home, mi muchacho. Your mother's been putting the pressure on us all week getting everything ready for you. We've been talking up the truck in town too, people are excited for the Caribbean burritos."

"That's good, man, I need to sell a lot of them if I'm going to make rent!" I said, clapping his back as he moved to put his arm around Tía Maritza's shoulders.

"Tía, you're looking younger every year." She preened and gave me another kiss.

"We're so happy you're here, papí."

"It's good to be here. How's Pri doing? I haven't seen

her in a minute." At the mention of my cousin, my aunt's face shone with pride.

"She's great. She may be here tomorrow. Hopefully you can see her."

"Definitely." I nodded and looked over at the guys who were lounging on my mom's furniture. Juanpa's stank face told me he probably heard us talking about Priscilla.

He was ridiculous.

Those two had a love/hate thing going on since we were kids, and apparently they were back to hating each other.

"Yo, are you bums just going to lounge over here all afternoon? We got shit to do!"

Juanpa squinted up at me while he sipped some kind of Frappuccino looking thing.

"I'm taking a break, son. I just drove five hours hauling all your shit out here. Let me enjoy my independent coffee shop beverage, pa." He lifted his cup. "They got a drive-thru barista situation in town. This shit is fire. They need to open one of these places in the city."

He looked so happy sucking down on that straw.

"Okay, man, drink your sugar bomb first, but we need to unload your truck before you leave tonight." Juanpa went back to focus on his drink and doing something on his phone and just nodded, already distracted. I looked over at Milo who was hunched over, looking at something on Patrice's laptop.

"What did I tell you about calling people while driving my car, man?"

Patrice shook his head and grinned as he typed, but knew better than to try and make a joke about Camilo's driving. Milo flipped me off, looking like he was about to curse me out, when I saw my sister Minerva coming up the path to the house.

She was so tall, and was looking more like Mamí every day. She was just a few inches shorter than my six feet two by now. We didn't have the same dad, but everyone said we were identical as babies, same light brown skin with a tint of red. Whenever we ran or laughed too hard our whole faces flushed. Her hair was straighter than mine, and my eyes were a lighter brown, but we both had our mom's face. Full mouth, broad nose and thick eyelashes. Minerva's were so long they looked fake.

She was gorgeous, just like Mamí.

I went to meet her by the door and as soon as she walked in, I picked her up and twirled her around a couple of times.

"You're getting too pretty, baby sister. It's a good thing I'm here, Mamí!" I yelled over my shoulder. "We can start working on the protective fence around the house this weekend. Got to keep the boys away!"

"Stop it! You're so extra, Nesto." She hit me on the shoulder, laughing. "What's wrong with you? Put me down."

"What, you're too big for your manín to pick you up?" I asked, squeezing her tight. "So, are you dating? What's his name?"

I crossed my eyes, making her laugh again.

"Stop it. *Loco.*"

"She had this gringito following her around like a puppy all winter," my mom said, walking out of the kitchen.

"He was here all the time, hanging around with

a mopey face, and Justin Bieber hair, trying to read poems in Spanish."

She clicked her tongue and gave my sister her patented "pobrecita" face, which was half "I feel bad for you" and half "but really I should be mocking you."

"I didn't have the heart to tell him to stop coming over," she teased Minerva, who was giving her a death glare with the intensity only a sixteen year old could produce. My mom kept going though. "He sabotaged himself enough with that haircut and bad Spanish."

We all cracked up while my baby sister silently gave me and the guys the finger as she sat on the couch. Before my mom and Minerva got into something I decided to get people back on track, because the clock was ticking.

"Okay, mi gente," I said clapping my hands together. "What's the plan? We have a lot to get ready if I have the truck scheduled for a lunch service in town tomorrow." I flashed a smile at my mom who was standing at attention.

"Mamí, I stopped by the gas station and that spot is going to be lit." She beamed with pride at my comment. "You said you had all the food at the kitchen, right?"

"That's right. Everything's there ready to go."

The "I told you so" face Camilo was flashing my way did not go unnoticed.

I looked at my watch and saw it was only 2:30 p.m. "Excellent. We have plenty of time to get all the night before food preparation done. Milo and Juanpa, since you guys are driving back tonight we should go to the kitchen and get all the stuff in J's truck unloaded now."

Everyone nodded and people started getting up and ready to get going as I talked.

"I can get my clothes and stuff moved into the studio with Patrice tonight since he's here until tomorrow. The woman I'm subletting from texted today and said I can go into the apartment anytime. She left the keys with you, right, Mamí?"

She patted her bag, which was already slung on her shoulder.

"Yes, I have them here, I can't believe you aren't staying here even one night."

I had to nip the guilt tripping in the bud.

"Mamí, you know it'll be easier for me. The studio is in Trumansburg, right by where I'll be parking the truck overnight. It's closer to the commercial kitchen space we're renting. It just makes sense for me to be up there."

She sighed and came over to pinch my cheek.

"Yo se, yo se. I just wanted to spoil you a little bit. Anyways, I took the week off so I can help you with the truck, m'ijo. Tía Maritza will also help until you hire some people."

Mamí was already headed for the door but called over to my sister who'd gone back to her room for something. "Minerva, vamonos, are you playing with that thing on your phone that gives you rabbit ears again?" She turned around to look at me. "She spends all day making faces at that thing!" She rolled her eyes, while the rest of us lost it, then went back to yelling in the direction of Minerva's room. "Vamos, muchachita! We need to help out your brother, and you have school tomorrow."

Minerva hustled out, looking flustered. "Ay, Mamí, why are you yelling? I'm ready." My sister hiked her thumb at me, as she walked to the door. "Vamonos, Ernesto."

That was it, my people were ready and so was I. The Ithaca chapter of OuNYe was finally off and running.

Chapter Two

Jude

It happened again. Misty Fields, that menace from fundraising, picked through my lunch. This morning I'd made a specific pattern with the blueberries on top of my salad *and* counted them, so I could tell if my food had been tampered with.

I'd checked it before I stuffed it in the fridge, and even labeled it with my name and the date. Now half of the blueberries were gone and the label looked like someone peeled it off and then tried to smooth it over. I sighed as I put the lid back on the container before shoving it back in the fridge. This what was my life had come to, psychological warfare in the break room.

I hurried back to my office and slumped in my chair located behind the circulation area of the Tompkins County Public Library. I was the Youth Services Director here and shared an office with my coworker Carmen, who shot me some serious side-eye as soon as I walked in, letting me know she was aware of exactly what was going on. I fiddled with the mouse on my desk as the sound of an IM hitting my Skype chat pinged and a message from Carmen popped up.

BiblioCarmen: Did that bitch eat your lunch again?

Jude_Fuller87: 100% definite yes. Half of the blueberries were gone. I even looked to see if they had sunk down to the bottom, but no luck. Someone picked through it and possibly tampered with the label. Who eats salad without dressing, Carmen? She's sick.

BiblioCarmen: Her shit's gotta be pathological. Who DOES that? And it's just your food she fucks with, because she knows you're meticulous with your meals. You don't see her messing with the frank and beans Bill brings every single day. *shudders* It's so messed up. You should call her on it Jude.

Riiight. That was not going to happen.

I was not the most confrontational person in the world, but I had a hard time keeping my mouth shut around bullies. Misty Fields was a *bully*, and she seemed to have a gift at pushing my buttons, except I could not let her get to me right now. Misty was the grant writer for the library and knew she had me by the balls for the foreseeable future. I was a week away from taking another shot at getting my dream project approved by the board and she could totally mess with my plans.

I looked over my monitor at Carmen and rolled my eyes at her before starting to type a response.

Jude_Fuller87: You know I can't piss her off right now. She's got half the board eating out of her hand, and the rest are clueless. If she says it's not viable for this year's fundraising efforts, I'm screwed and will need to sit out for another year. They're not exactly open to new projects right with all the cuts from the state.

I heard her sigh from across the room.

BiblioCarmen: I know. I KNOW. She's just so annoying and evil. I mean someone touching your food is practically psychological torture for your borderline OCD ass.

Jude_Fuller87: She's evil, I agree, but we have to bide our time. We need the mobile library project operating next school year. The need is there, most of the kids in the rural parts of the county never come out here, and the stuff that's available in the schools is not enough.

BiblioCarmen: I am 100% with you, and you're right we just have to wait until we have our book truck, and then we can run her skinny ass over with it.

I couldn't help it, I cracked up and made the "stop it" sign with my hands. She smiled and went back to typing.

BiblioCarmen: Let's blow this place off and take our lunch out. Did you see the new food truck parked at the gas station? It's covered with practically every flag in the Caribbean, which makes me so excited I could cry. Unless it's some poser from Brooklyn, which would be tragic. I did see a guy by the truck when I was walking in this morning, and he is fiiiiine. Had them Latinx vibes, so we'll get lunch and a view.

I'd been distracted listening to a podcast when I was walking into work, and must have missed the truck, but

I perked up at the mention of Caribbean food. I wondered if it was the same truck the sexy weirdo from the gas station had been driving.

Did his have flags on it? I couldn't remember, I was too distracted by the gorgeous stranger laughing at me. That interaction had been bizarre, even for Ithaca. One does not expect someone so hot to all of a sudden act like a lunatic.

Not that it mattered if it was the same guy. A, he was probably straight. And B, lusting after men I most likely couldn't have was not on my to-do list. However, for Carmen, hard-staring at hot guys was like a competitive sport. If anything, she'd at least do or say something hilarious.

Carmen waggled her eyebrows at me and I rolled my eyes in response, then gave her a thumbs-up. I opened the file with my proposal for the board, and got to it. I could at least channel the rage over my desecrated salad by making some progress.

"All I'm saying is someone at some point needs to call Misty on her bullshit," Carmen complained as we pushed out of the library and onto the sunny street.

"Since she lost all that weight people treat her like she's some sort of mystic. If you ask me she's the same old bitch she was before, except now she's fucking insufferable."

"This is true," I concurred as we waited to cross the street.

Carmen huffed before launching into another Misty rant. "She goes out of her way to shame people about what they eat, and acts all superior about her workouts as if anyone who isn't running eighteen miles a day like she does is a lazy slug." The look of disgust on her face would have been hilarious, except she was one-hundred percent right.

Misty was awful.

"Did you see that poor intern walking out of her office just now? I think she made her cry because she brought a donut into work. Ugh, she makes me so mad."

"Well, it won't be me calling her on any of it. At least not while I'm trying to get this project approved," I reminded her as we got closer to the gas station where Carmen spotted the food truck earlier.

Carmen's answer was another exasperated sigh, but I could tell she was already off of Misty and on to figuring out what to eat. From where we stood I could see the front of the truck with the awning up, looking ready for business. It was definitely the same one from the gas station, I remembered the black logo with a red background.

"This is the truck from yesterday," I said to Carmen, who was busy inspecting the scene. I noticed a chalkboard hanging to the left side of the window, with what looked like a short menu. There was a respectable amount of people waiting to order already, a good sign for a brand-new place. We quickly walked over and took our place at the end of the line.

"So, what are we getting?" I asked Carmen as she stretched her neck to look at the menu.

"Let me check what they have. It's so sad that this is the most exciting thing that's happened to me all spring."

She started reading and after a few seconds clapped her hands and did a little happy dance. She was wearing a bright yellow shirt dress, which looked amazing contrasted against her dark brown skin. Her mahogany curls streaked with blonde highlights bounced on her shoulders as she moved.

"Oh my god, please let this be legit! There's Dominican food on the menu, Jude!" She grabbed me by the shoulders with a big smile. "Do you know what having real Caribbean food in this frozen tundra would mean for me? Oh man, I wonder if the owner is Dominican. He kind of looked Dominican," she said, tilting her head to the side.

I laughed at her because Carmen was always on the hunt to spot a fellow Dominican, and yet never really made an effort to befriend any of the ones who lived in town. She said it was like having a fire extinguisher, it's reassuring to know it's there, but you don't need to carry one around all the time.

"It does sound promising. I wonder if they'll have more options in the future. I think I'm going try the Lupe. I love Cuban black beans. Should we get the tostones? Yumm. We can share," I said, getting excited for the food. "The smells coming from the truck really are incredible."

Carmen bobbed her head giddily next to me as we moved up the line.

"Yes, yes, yes. Imma get the Mayimbe. They have a *Dominican* burrito, Jude." She pointed toward the menu again and gave the guy in front of us, who was now openly eavesdropping on our conversation, a thumbs-up.

"I already fucking love this guy for naming the burritos after badass Latinx singers. If the mastermind behind this is the hot guy I saw this morning, it is going to be a *very* good summer for us, Jude!" She broke into another happy dance.

"I don't know if I'm ready to declare this the 'best summer ever' just yet, but if the food's good and they're here for a while it will be a nice addition to our lunch repertoire." Carmen didn't respond, and was now trying to get a photo of the menu with her phone.

I left her to it and looked over at the guy taking the orders in the window. Although he was good-looking and possibly Latinx, he was not the guy from the gas station.

I pointed in the direction of the window, and gently nudged Carmen to get her attention.

"Is that the guy you were talking about? It's not the same one I saw yesterday."

The man had to be in his thirties and was very handsome. His face looked like it was carved from ebony, and he was so big I was surprised he could fit in that truck. He had long locs tied up into a knot on top of his head and he was wearing a white t-shirt that said, *More Amor, Por Favor.*

Very attractive, but not dead sexy like the guy from yesterday.

Carmen finally looked up from her phone. I assumed she was reporting our new food discovery to her husband.

"Umm," she said as she gave the guy a long look. "Uh, no that's not him. Although this one's pretty hot too."

She got closer and after a second leaned back with her mouth pursed. "Maybe this truck is run by part-time models, because damn."

She may have been on to something.

Carmen talked as she glanced in the direction of the service window. "The guy I saw was about the same age, same height, but not so bulked up. More of a swimmer's build, short black hair, fine as hell. But nope, looks like he's not here."

I lifted a shoulder and glanced toward the truck again, before I turned to Carmen. "Maybe he just came to bring the truck up here, creep people out at the gas station, and has headed back home."

Carmen laughed distractedly at my lame joke, still in the midst of an intense text exchange.

"Does Ted want us to get him something?"

Carmen and her husband, Ted, were both foodies and got extremely excited about any new food offerings in town. He was from Kansas, but had lived all over Latin America for years before *and* after he met Carmen. He also spoke perfect Spanish and was a devoted enthusiast of all Latin cuisine.

"No, he's at a luncheon with some guest speaker, but he's asking a million questions about the burritos and wants to try them ASAP. I told him he's got to come down from that ivory tower once in a while and join us for lunch."

Ted was a professor at Cornell, and spent a lot of time on campus. Although Carmen made sure he took a breather from the scene up there as much as possible.

"I'm sure this truck will be at the Ithaca Farmer's Market at some point this summer. If not, we can ask them where they'll be. They probably have a Twitter or Instagram account where we can keep track of them." She nodded again, her eyes focused on what she was tapping on her screen.

The line was moving pretty fast and soon there were only three people in front of us. There was music playing in the truck and I could hear Spanish coming from the back.

After high school I lived in Honduras for a year and my Spanish got pretty good while I was there. Over the years I made an effort to practice it as often as I could, so I still could speak and understand it pretty well. I was too far away to make out what they were saying, but was loving the music coming over the little speakers they'd set up at the counter. Some of my favorite artists were Latinx singers, so when a song I loved came on, I bobbed my head along with the music. I must have gotten distracted by the song, because when I looked up, I came face-to-face with "gas station guy."

My heart almost leaped out of my chest when I saw him grinning at someone inside the truck. If possible, he looked even better than the first time I'd seen him.

I felt a nudge on my shoulder as I stood there gaping.

"Oh shit, that's the guy."

I was having trouble making words, so I didn't answer Carmen. It seemed like he was taking over for the other guy, who I saw walking away from the truck with a backpack on his shoulder. When I stepped up to the counter he didn't see me right away, but as soon as he turned around, his eyes lit up with recognition.

"Wow, three times in less than twenty-four hours. I had a feeling I'd see you again, Mr. NPR."

He gave me another once-over as he took a pencil out of his apron pocket and held his pad up, ready to take my order. Like I wasn't going to ask about the supposed second time he'd seen me.

"Three times? When did you see me a second time? Also, it's pretty rude to laugh at people for no reason. Creepy, actually."

He threw his head back and laughed, then winked at me like that could fix it.

"I did say I was sorry. I wasn't laughing *at* you, it was just, when I saw your shirt, it sort of sunk in I was in Ithaca."

"Sure, that makes total sense," I said with an eye roll.

He pointed in the direction of the library. "I saw you walking in there this morning, while I was setting up."

The grin he was flashing in my direction was activating all sorts of feelings in my body.

"I'm a librarian."

His eyes twinkled at my incredibly vague answer, then gave me an appreciative look. "I wondered."

I was not totally sure what was happening, but I wasn't going to hold up the line to continue awkwardly flirting with him, even if he was a smoking hot, very tall man.

"Never mind." I waved my finger in the direction of the menu and tried to give him a businesslike look. "Could you please tell me about these? There are a lot of things I love happening here, but I've never had them in a burrito."

He flashed me a devastating smile and said, "I thought you'd never ask." He rubbed his hands together as he talked, making the muscles in his arms bulge.

"All our burritos are inspired on Afro-Caribbean flavors. *El Mayimbe,* I named after Fernando Villalona, my mom's favorite merengue singer."

Getting the rundown of a burrito menu *should not* be this erotic.

"On that one we hit you with white rice, Dominican style red beans, beefsteak *Criollo* with sautéed onions, caramelized sweet plantains, *Mi Abuelita's* slaw and avocado slices."

Carmen let out a squeal from behind me at his description.

"If you want to go with Cuba, you want *La Lupe*, which is named after *my* favorite Latina singer." He preened at that. "It's comes with killer Cuban black beans, Cuban shredded beef, caramelized sweet plantains, and hot and spicy pickled onions."

He smiled again and leaned on the counter a little bit when he was done. I was already sweating and hadn't even ordered my food. "We also have the tostones topped with queso crema, cilantro pesto and sweet-and-sour pickled shallots."

This time I could not help myself and a moan escaped my mouth. "I love tostones."

That rakish smile he kept flashing at me was going to be my undoing.

"That's what I like to hear. We also have a sweet corn pudding with a passion fruit glaze for dessert. It's a small offering, but these are some of our most popular items and a great intro to our food."

He lifted an eyebrow at me in question. "So, did I tempt you with anything?"

If only you knew, "gas station guy."

I nodded and tried once again to sound unaffected. "Definitely, everything sounds delicious. I'll have the Lupe and an order of tostones. Oh, and the Yerbabuena lemonade."

He kept staring at me with a weird smirk on his face, like he found me infinitely entertaining. After a second he started jotting down my order.

"Excellent. Can I get your name so we can call you when the order's ready?"

I widened my eyes at his perfectly reasonable question. This elicited yet another semi-filthy smile.

I had no idea what he found so damn amusing. "It's Jude."

Carmen stepped up to give her order after shooting me an amused look, and immediately asked, "Can we do this in español or what?"

"Claro, aquí se habla español."

Another wink.

I was starting to wonder if he had a condition.

"¡Excelente!" Carmen gave him a big smile and proceeded to tell him what she wanted in rapid fire Spanish. When she was done she jerked her thumb over her shoulder, "Just put my order under Jude's name." She held up her phone at him. "I need to make a call, so he'll get mine too."

Liar.

He beamed at her, and gave me a thumbs-up.

"It'll be ready in a few, guys."

With that he turned his attention to the next people in line.

Once we were out of earshot Carmen started talking excitedly, her hands all over the place. "See! I told you he was Dominican! I knew a man so fine could only be produced in the DR. He sure was staring you up and down too. You're so funny." She cackled and shook my arm. "And of course he thought you were adorable. Oh man, if the food's good we're making this a regular stop."

I angled my head in genuine confusion, because

adorable was *not* what I'd been going for. Finally, my brain came back online, and there were questions.

"Wait, how did you find out he's Dominican? You were only standing there for like thirty seconds."

"Oh Jude." She shook her head, looking at me like I was an idiot.

"I got a full report! His name is Ernesto, but everyone calls him Nesto. The truck is his, he drove it up from the city yesterday, and is planning to be here for five or six months. If the business does well, he may stay longer. His mom lives here. She works for Cornell. Has other family here too, they came up from the city like ten years ago."

"Wow, you're good."

"You know I don't play," she said smugly.

We stood by the truck while we waited for our food. From my spot I could see Nesto taking orders, and the easy way with which he interacted with the customers. He had such a striking smile, and he was generous with it too. He used his whole body when he talked, his hands, his shoulders, even his eyebrows. Leaning in to say something funny with a conspiratorial look in his eyes, like he was sharing a secret, or throwing back his head and putting both hands out as a laugh exploded out of him.

It was like watching life happen. I wanted to get close, feel what it was like to have all that joy and passion directed at me.

Be the reason for it.

From my side, I heard Carmen click her tongue. "Oh man, you is staring, and staring *hard*. Don't blame you, he's gorgeous. It's just not fair. Who looks that good in an apron? He was giving you the look, though. This could have some potential."

I rolled my eyes at Carmen's comment, because I was not going there.

Thankfully I heard my name called to pick up our order, before Carmen could go on one of her "you need to go on a date" tirades. So, I turned and started walking, then yelled over my shoulder. "Can't talk now. Gotta get our lunch!" Ignoring the grumbling in Spanish directed my way.

When I got there Nesto was holding a white paper bag, and giving me his radiant smile. I pointed at the black trucker hat he was wearing, which I'd noticed earlier had a tiny pride flag pinned to the lower right corner.

"Nice hat."

"Thanks." He smiled and waved his pen in front of his neck. "I like your bowtie. I noticed it this morning."

He cringed at that. "That sounds a little creepy doesn't it?" A husky laugh escaped his lips and I tried to ignore the shiver running through my body.

I probably should have said something, but instead I stood there taking inventory of his delicious body. His shoulders were obnoxiously wide and muscular. The red t-shirt with the OuNYe logo he was wearing could barely constrain all of it. I moved my eyes back up and almost sighed.

He really did elevate the jeans and t-shirt ensemble.

When I realized I'd probably been staring a bit too long, I stuck my hand out for the order. He lifted an eyebrow, clearly aware of what I'd been doing.

Dammit.

He grinned handing me the bag. "Here you go. One

Lupe, one Mayimbe, and two orders of tostones. I gave you an extra one for Carmen, because she said you'd probably eat them all yourself."

I gasped, and turned to give her a murderous look.

"I would not! She's one to talk!" I pointed at her and yelled, "Traitor!"

He threw his head back, and laughed again.

God that laugh. It could change my life.

Nesto was still grinning at my flustered fidgeting. "She's trouble, that one. I can already tell. Dominican girls, you gotta watch out."

Another smile.

This was getting out of hand. He leaned down on the counter and said in a low voice, "I hope you enjoy my food, and that we see you back soon, Jude." The way he said my name made me tremble. "We'll be here for lunch, and at the Farmers Market on the weekends for the next few months."

He grabbed a card from a pile next to the napkins and condiments and handed it to me. I was almost surprised not to see sparks fly when our fingers touched. For a moment we both stood there, the tips of our fingers grazing as we held the little piece of cardboard between us before letting go.

He lifted his hand in a wave. "So stop by again, all right? I have more burritos for you to try. See you soon, Jude."

Between this man and the smells coming from the bag, I was starting to feel a little overstimulated. I was just about to say thank you and walk off when an insane impulse came over me.

I leaned up closer to the counter, so I was on my tiptoes, then looked straight at him and said, "Si no te veo a ti primero, Nesto."

I winked and walked off with my heart pounding out of my chest and giving him the best ass shaking strut a boy from Canandigua, NY, could manage. Behind me I heard Nesto whistle in my direction.

The image of his surprised expression after I blurted out my best attempt at flirting in Spanish, made my face split into a huge grin. By the time I got back to Carmen I could tell Nesto must've done something behind me, because she was cackling and had a look in her eye like an interrogation was coming.

"Got the food. Let's go."

I didn't let her talk, pulling her toward the library.

We could debrief about my lust-induced outburst there.

Chapter Three

Nesto

I stood there watching Jude walk off toward the library after tugging Carmen by the arm.

His Spanish was great, and totally caught me by surprise. And damn his ass was fine. He knew it too.

I was thinking Jude and his ass were going to be a serious monkey wrench in my "total focus" plan for the next six months when I heard my mom chuckling in the back.

"What are you laughing at?"

"At your face when that rubio hit on you. His Spanish is pretty good!"

Of course my mom overheard.

"Damn, Mamí, it's like your ears get supersonic or something if there's a man I can even remotely think of dating in the vicinity."

She would probably be telling me to ask him out within the next few minutes. I'd been here for less than twenty-four hours and she had already started on me about finding someone. How I was "too good and handsome to be alone," and "any man with good sense would want me for a partner."

"I'm not gonna lie, he is pretty, but I kind of have my hands full at the moment," I exclaimed, waving said hands around.

"Ay m'ijo, I'm not saying marry him, just ask him out for a drink. He's a good dresser too. I like that, formal," she said, giving me a disapproving look. "Not wearing jeans and t-shirts everywhere like someone I know."

As soon as she talked about his clothes my mind drifted to Jude again. His outfit had been pretty fly. Slim gray chinos, which did wonders for his ass, navy boat shoes, and a blue cardigan over a white shirt. But what made me take notice was the chartreuse bowtie completing the ensemble. He'd looked like a fashion magazine's version of a sexy librarian. I snapped out of it before my mom started making fun of me for "day-dreaming about the gringo."

When I turned I found her looking at me like she had every single one of my numbers. "Mamí, it's like seven hundred degrees in this truck. I have to dress like this or I'll die from a heat stroke."

"Pssh, you're Dominican, you were born in one-hundred-degree heat with one-hundred-and-ten percent humidity." She waved me and my whining off. "This is nothing, people wear coats in Santo Domingo when it's this cool out."

It was seventy-six outside and the truck was steamy, but I laughed, because she wasn't lying.

"En serio, m'ijo, don't get so focused on the truck you forget to live your life. You can have some balance." She bumped my shoulder as I tried to grab something from the shelf behind her.

"You forget sometimes, papí. You're such a good man, so serious and hardworking, but you also need some love. Someone to carry the burdens with you. Don't be like me, sweetheart."

I really looked at her then, her hair in a sweaty bun, with grease all over her hands, decked out in one of her many OuNYe t-shirts, and I felt so much love for this woman.

My mother, my biggest supporter, my rock. Taking vacation time from work to come sweat it out with me in this truck, because it was my dream. Emotion swelled inside me and I got closer to give her a hug.

"Mamí, at my best, I could only dream of being half as strong and badass as you. You're my hero." I leaned down and kissed her forehead.

"Then listen to your hero and ask the cute blond guy out," she said, playfully poking her finger into my chest. "Winter nights in Ithaca can be lonely and cold. And watch your language."

I pinched her cheek and conceded, "Okay, okay, mujer! I'll ask him out when I see him, it's not like it's a hardship."

"Don't worry so much, m'ijo, you'll see, this truck will be doing great business in no time."

I shook my head at her, because my mother's optimism and certainty I could do anything never waned.

"You'll have your own restaurant in town by the end of the year."

"I don't know about all that. But one can hope, right?"

"I do know. Listen to your mother and keep doing what you're doing, and you'll see."

We started working in silence again. We'd gotten the last few orders out, closed up for the day and were cleaning up. Scrubbing and putting things away before we drove the truck out to its overnight spot. I was whistling to some old-school merengue playing on the speakers when I heard someone come up to the back door of the truck.

"Hello?"

I turned around and saw a woman standing by the back of the truck. She was wearing one of those work-out outfits people don't actually workout in, and she was giving me and the truck stank face so intense I got scared she'd melt the paint off the damn thing.

I smiled at her and she just glared back with her arms crossed against her chest. Her blonde ponytail so tight, her eyebrows were almost flush against her hairline. She was probably in her fifties, and had clearly been to the Botox dealer in town.

Oh man… I did not have the energy for any of this. Nothing good could come from this lady seething by my truck like I owed her money.

I stepped down to where she was standing and did my best to look friendly. "I'm sorry, the lunch service is over for today. I can give you our card so you can follow us on Instagram. We update our location and menu every day."

She did something with her face I think was her attempt at a smile, but it came out more like a grimace. Then she flicked her hand at me, dismissing the information, stretching her neck trying to look past me.

"I'd like to speak to the owner, please."

Oh, it's like that, is it?

I extended my hand out to her. "That would be me, Ernesto Vasquez. How can I help you?" I snapped those syllables too, no diluting my name to *Ehr-nais-tow Vas-quays* today.

Nope. *ErrrrrrNESTO Vas-QUEZ* in motherfucking *ES-pañol*.

She looked at my hand like it would bite her, then stepped back.

"So, are you moving through town or something? I'm with the city council, and saw your truck here selling food when I walked by earlier. I just want to make sure everything's in order." She tipped her head to the side like she wasn't sure I could understand her. "That all the documents for your business are in place."

Whaaaaaat the fuuuuuck?

I tried very hard to control my temper before I answered her. Because this woman at the very least was implying I was running my truck without a permit, or at worst that me, the truck, the food and the whole fucking rig were here, what? Illegally?

I was about to clarify for her I was a U.S. citizen if that's what she was referring to by "documents," when my mom came out of the truck. She stopped for a second, and seemed to know or at least recognize the woman. Then she started walking up to her with the smile she only gave people right before going full-blown "Bitch, I'm Dominican!" whenever anyone tried to fuck with her kids.

Before my mom got in the lady's face, and the impending verbal bloodbath unfolded before my eyes, I got my ass in gear, and blocked Mamí's path with my hand.

"Ma'am, are you a sanitation inspector? Otherwise, I have my permit to operate this truck and my insurance and licenses are in order."

I pasted a smile on again, and tried to be courteous and polite, to show this rude fucking woman what it meant to behave like a human being. I knew my face was definitely not friendly at this point, but I was done with this. "Like I said, please stop by sometime to try our food. I should get back to cleaning the truck before we drive it out."

I turned around, grabbed my mom's hand and left the lady down there looking pissed as we stepped back into the truck.

I hoped this was the end of it, but my brown ass had been around the block enough to know this lady and her meddling would probably be back.

Jude

"Oh my god, Jude Eugenio Maria Fuller! What did you say to him before you walked off? He was blushing and fanning himself!"

I laughed as Carmen and I hurried to the library with our lunch in hand. "Stop giving me random names in Spanish, Carmen! It's weird!" I shrugged, in answer to her question as we power walked back to the office.

"I may have flirted with him a little." I blushed at the thought of how bold I'd been. "When he handed me the food he told me they'd be around all summer, and hoped to see me soon. I don't know but something just came over me. I leaned up to the counter and told him, 'If I don't see you first,' *in Spanish*. He has a very strange effect on me." Carmen gave me a confused look and I couldn't blame her, I was confusing myself.

"Maybe it was because he gave us extra tostones. You know how much I love them."

"Riiiiiight." One of her eyebrows raised so high, I feared it would pop right off her head. "It was because he gave you deep fried plantains. This is great. You need to be a little more spontaneous. If you ask me, you should come back on Friday and ask him out for a drink! He said he wants to see you."

"Yeah, buying his burritos, not at the bar."

We walked into the library and headed straight for the break room.

"I'm spontaneous all the time. I go out with people. I just don't date-date. I certainly wouldn't say no to a drink with Nesto," I said as I pulled food out of the bag.

I even winked to give the whole thing a lighthearted effect. But pursuing something with Nesto felt dangerous to me. Like I would not be able to keep my usual walls up with him. And where was I even going with this line of thinking? I'd seen the guy twice and exchanged maybe twenty words with him, ten of which were me ordering a burrito.

I shook my head and smiled at Carmen again, hoping to get her off this topic. "A man that hot is certainly a lot more than I can take on right now. Nope, I will eat his delicious food and I will stare at his even more delicious body, but that's all for me."

I even attempted another laugh, but it came out like I was in pain. "The dating thing is just not something I do well, so I stay in my lane."

As we sat down with our food, Carmen started talking again.

"Babe, you can't possibly know if you're not good at it when you have only ever had one serious relationship, which ended sort of horribly. All I'm saying is to try. You don't have to be so lonely."

I lifted my head from unwrapping my burrito with what I knew must have looked like a very brittle smile and powered on.

"Who says I'm lonely?" It's funny, you said something enough times, and it started sounding like the truth. Even when the words felt like they would choke you. "C'mon, you know I don't like to talk about this stuff, Carmen."

I patted her hand, ignoring the frustration on her face. I knew she wanted to see me happy, and was convinced a relationship with a man was part of the equation.

But it was *my* life.

"No. Look, Nesto seems nice and is objectively beautiful. *And* if you ever let me have a bite of this burrito, we'll find out if he can actually cook. I have a lot in my life." I waved my hand around the room. "I have friends, I have a job I love. I'm happy like I am."

After a few seconds of tense silence Carmen finally relented.

"Okay, I hear you, you're a grown ass man, and you do whatever you want."

I gave her a grateful look and grabbed my food, "Thank you. I'm not really interested in a romantic relationship, that's all."

"Okay, hon, let's dig into our burritos and talk about what you can do to get the board eating out of your hands instead."

I sat up in my chair, nodding. "Now, that's definitely a conversation I'm open to, as soon as I have a couple of bites of this."

I inhaled the foil covered bundle. "Smells so good."

We unwrapped the burritos and took huge bites at the same time. After a few seconds we both moaned.

They were delicious, the rice and beans, the spicy

beef, with the sweetness of the plantains and the tangy crunch of the onions were the perfect combination.

Figured. Not only was Nesto physically perfect, but he was also a burrito genius.

"I could probably eat this every day for weeks," I said through a mouthful of goodness.

Carmen dipped her head in silent agreement as she took another huge bite. For the next few minutes we ate in silence, alternating between bites of burrito and the tostones, which were golden, crispy and delicious.

I glanced up when Carmen put down her half-eaten burrito and mournfully said, "Please tell me I can go back and try the Lupe on Friday. I already told Ted he could meet us there for lunch."

I tried to keep a straight face when I saw the look of complete agony on hers. Anyone else would think she was trying to be cute, but I knew she was dead serious. I loved her for being willing to sacrifice herself and not go back for more burritos if I asked her.

"Please, these are too good to let my issues keeps us from going back. I'll just make sure I don't have any more outbursts." I pointed at my own burrito. "There's no way I'm depriving myself of food this amazing."

If I tried really hard, I could almost convince myself my eagerness for lunch Friday was just about the food.

Chapter Four

Nesto

It'd been a long-ass day.

It was hard to believe I'd only been in Ithaca a little bit over twenty-four hours. After dropping my mom off at home I decided to take a walk, hoping to tire myself out before doing the twenty-minute drive to Trumansburg. I was physically exhausted and emotionally worn out, but felt too wired to go back to the studio and get in bed.

I strolled down a quiet street, wishing I could call one of my boys to come out for a quick one, and debrief them on the events of the day. But I was on my own, my best friends were all back in New York City, and I didn't know anyone of drinking age other than my mom and my uncle and auntie, so I was screwed.

I shifted my thoughts from my sad social life to review the day again. Sales had gone much better than expected. One of the best days I'd had all spring.

Then there was Jude.

A smile broke out on my face thinking about his corny Spanish pickup line, and how salty he was about me laughing when I saw him at the gas station. Which only reminded me of the bullshit with that woman and my good mood sank.

Mamí recognized her from benefits and other events on campus, and said she was some rich lady who always gave her catering staff a hard time. She'd been ready to go on a full recon expedition about the woman, but I told her to not go overboard.

What could this person even do?

We had all our shit straight. What we needed was to keep our heads down, and not get caught up with distractions. Mamí hadn't liked it, but she'd agreed to leave it alone.

After a few more minutes of walking around aimlessly, my thoughts drifted back to Jude.

I wasn't looking to get involved. My last relationship went down in flames, because running the truck was not exactly conducive to keeping boyfriends. And with the timeline I'd set for myself here, the grind would be even more intense than usual. Jude seemed like a lot of fun though, and fuck, I needed a little fun in my life.

My mom was right. I had zero balance right now.

I lived and breathed for OuNYe and at some point, it was going to be a problem. I might actually ask Jude out for that drink the next time I saw him. If anything, I had to admit he'd been the first guy who caught my attention in a very long time.

I was mulling over Jude and all the things I needed to prepare for the Farmer's Market, when my phone buzzed with a text. I pulled it out of my pocket and grinned when I saw the message.

Hey primo! I just stopped by Tía's and she said you'd just left. I'm having a drink with Easton if you'd like to join us.

It was from my cousin Priscilla. She was a police detective downstate, but came up pretty often to see her parents. Easton was one of her best friends and an assistant district attorney in town. He was also very much out and proud. He was an okay dude, and I quickly realized, someone who could help out with my pathetic social life.

I texted back after figuring out where I was.

SI! POR FAVOR. I'm just walking on Buffalo, by The Commons. Close?

After a second the three dots popped up on the screen.

We're at Ophelia's. Just go to MLK and walk away from Commons, it'll be on your right. You're five minutes away.

I quickly fired back.

See you in five then.

I turned back toward MLK Street, already feeling a hell of a lot better. Making my way to meet Pri, I tried to stop my rambling mind and appreciate my surroundings.

After years of coming to Ithaca for holidays and summers to see my mom and sister, the place was pretty familiar. Though I always enjoyed my visits here, I'd never given it much thought as a potential place to live. Now I was looking at these streets through a new lens, sizing it up as a potential home base. Nothing would

ever come close to New York City. It was useless to
even try to compare.

This place had something though, it was like the people here *wanted* to be here. I could appreciate why my
mom loved it. It was quaint and eccentric at the same
time. The kind of place where you'd walk by the window of a cozy little bookstore, then look more closely
to find a display of the latest BDSM erotica.

As I walked up the street to the bar, I saw a rainbow
flag proudly fluttering in the evening breeze. Above
the maroon doorway was the sign for Ophelia's Cos-
mic Lounge.

I stepped in and immediately decided it would be
my favorite bar in Ithaca. It was decorated in a fifties
theme, with lots of chrome and vinyl and a blue-and-
white checkered floor. There was a little stage to the
far-right end of the room with musicians setting up,
and Xenia Rubinos's "Mexican Chef" was playing on
the speakers.

I looked over at the bar and saw the menu on the
wall featured cocktails with names that made me laugh
out loud. It was not a very big place, could not fit more
than forty people, but almost every seat was taken and
everyone looked and sounded like they were having a
great time. Of course Pri would come through suggest-
ing an awesome place.

I scoped out the crowd trying to spot her and Easton,
then saw them sitting at the end of the bar talking to a
very pretty bartender, with tattoo sleeves on both arms
and a gorgeous head of auburn hair.

As I started walking toward them, Pri saw me and
waved furiously. She stood up when I reached her and

offered me her cheek to do the Dominican kiss and hug combo. I picked her up instead, making her squeal.

"Nesto! Chacho, stop. Jesus, you do *the most*. What's wrong with you?"

I laughed, putting her down. "Aww, come on, prima. I haven't seen you in so long. You looking fly. Love that dress."

She preened and smoothed the front of her dress, which had about twenty colors and three different patterns. On anyone else it would have been too much, but it looked great on her. Pri was the perfect combination of her parents, she had deep brown skin like my uncle, and my aunt's gorgeous curly brown hair and hazel eyes. She had curves for days too, but the most beautiful thing about her was how she carried herself.

Totally confident.

She was also a total badass and killing it at life in every aspect.

"You just missed J, cuz. My boy was up here yesterday, helping me move." I almost lost my shit at Pri's side-eye when I mentioned Juanpa.

"Why would I care where Juan Pablo is, Nesto? You know I don't mess with fuckboys."

I grinned at her and decided not to push since she could most definitely kick my ass. I turned so I could say hello to Easton, who was looking at us with an amused expression. When I got to him he stood up and we did the compulsory dude backslap thing.

"Ernesto, good to see you, man! Why didn't you tell me you were coming up? Pri said you're planning to be here for a while."

I sat down on the stool between him and Pri, running my hand over my fade. I smiled at Pri, who looked like she'd forgiven me for mentioning her sworn enemy, before replying to Easton.

"I let my mom convince me to try and get the truck going here. She said the food truck scene was starting to blow up and I should bring OuNYe up for a while, since there wasn't really any Caribbean food around." I grimaced a bit, still feeling out of sorts about my decision to come here.

"I did a bit of research and decided to give it a few months. If I crash and burn, I'll fuck off back to the city—"

Just then Priscilla spread her arms out and yelled.

"Wait let me introduce you first!"

She waved her hand between me and the bartender.

"Nesto, this is my friend Marty, he's the best bartender-slash-hairstylist-slash-aspiring-kindergarten-teacher in Ithaca. Marty, this is my cousin Ernesto, the man who is about to set the Ithaca food truck scene on fire."

The three of us laughed at Pri's introductions and I extended my hand to Marty. "Nice to meet you. So, what do you recommend?"

I pointed at the cocktail menu on the wall behind the bar.

"I'm thinking about the Beetarita."

Marty nodded in encouragement. "It's really good, the beet syrup is homemade and the tequila we use is really nice."

"Sounds good, man. Hook me up."

Easton raised his glass at Marty and the bartender took it with a wink. I wondered if there was anything going on between them.

Easton was a very handsome man, a bit older than me, late thirties, but he looked like the cover of a Ralph

Lauren catalog. Perfect bone structure, jet black hair and green eyes, with a body like whoa. He was also filthy rich. Pri told me his family almost disowned him when he decided to join the DA's office after law school instead of going in on the family business. Not to mention, coming out publicly the first day on the job. The guy was legit.

Pri looked at me and smiled like she knew the kind of math I was doing. I tipped my chin at her and pulled her stool a little closer so we could talk.

"It's so good to see you, cuz."

She squeezed my knee as she sipped her wine, and in that moment, I felt more settled than I had all day.

We all sat there quietly watching Marty mix my drink, which looked very much like beet juice. When he was done he slid the glass over and grinned at the look on my face. "I promise it'll be delicious."

"Okay, Imma trust you on this one, Marty."

I lifted it up to get a closer look then tipped it in Pri and Easton's direction.

"Here's to life saving texts from your favorite cousin."

Pri laughed and clinked my drink with her wineglass.

"I was hard up when you texted, was just going to buy a six-pack and drink alone in the studio I'm subletting."

She gave me a sympathetic look. "I got your back. So, tell us how things are going. I know how much you love talking about yourself."

"I do not," I said, feigning offense. Then I turned to Easton who was laughing at Pri's antics. "Like I was saying, I'm just trying things out here for a bit. It's going pretty well so far. I have a few potentially steady gigs. Ergos, the new B&B in town, wants me to park there on Fridays nights."

Pri perked up at that. "Ooh, I love that place, and it's crazy busy! They don't have a kitchen, so you would do good business there."

Easton nodded at that. "My friend owns it. He's been doing very well. It should be a good place to get your name out."

"Yeah, it sounds promising, and I also have an invitation for the wine and beer festival in July."

"Nice, they're going all out for that." He made a face. "My family's winery is the main sponsor, and I can tell you, when they get behind something, they go big."

Pri scowled at the mention of Easton's folks. From what she'd said there was still a lot of bad blood there, and I was not about to touch family drama, so I steered in another direction.

"One weird thing did happen today. We were doing our cleanup after the lunch service when this woman showed up at the truck. She said she was with the city council and wanted to make sure 'all our documents were in order.'"

I loved Pri, for the stank face she made when I said that.

When I looked at Easton he was frowning too, which confirmed my suspicion this lady was full of shit.

"So, this person just came to your truck and asked for 'documents'?" he asked, making air quotes.

"Yup."

"That's concerning. Even if she were part of the city council, she has no right to go around harassing business owners. I wonder who it was. There are only four women on the council, and for the most part they're too busy to be trolling local businesses."

Pri scoffed. "Easton, you know this town is full of busybodies. She probably isn't even on the city council."

"Maybe. They're usually happy to see any business drawing customers to downtown, though. Did she say her name?"

I shook my head, "No, man. I got so heated, I kind of cut her off and got back in the truck. I knew I'd lose my temper, and I didn't need some white lady—"

I cringed realizing what I'd said.

"Sorry."

Easton waved me off. "No worries."

"Anyway, I didn't need to get accused of assaulting her or some shit on my first day out, you know?"

"I hear you." Easton paused for a second, as if something had occurred to him. His face immediately turning cold. "If the woman *was* a city council member than it was either Misty Fields or Deborah Muir, and between those two I can almost guarantee it was Misty." Pri scowled in agreement.

Easton gave her a pained expression and turned to me again. "Deborah is too busy running the biggest architecture firm in town to go around checking on food trucks. Misty, on the other hand, works part-time at the library and spends the rest of her days trying to avoid her husband."

"And shit-stirring," Pri added.

"Right." Easton put his hand under his chin as if trying to work out what she'd been doing at my truck. "I heard she was still trying to make Tab, that's her son, run some grilled cheese food truck. If she's trying to intimidate people, it's because they're competition for Tab. Which is highly inappropriate."

After a pause he added, "If she bothers you again, let me know."

Pri sighed. "That woman is such a bitch. See, this is the small-town bullshit I don't miss. White Plains is not exactly a metropolis, but it's too big for this kind of fuckery."

Easton assented, his brows furrowed. "Lack of meddling townies is certainly one of the pros of city life. That and low-maintenance fuck buddies. God, I miss anonymous, uncomplicated sex."

Pri and I laughed at his agonized expression.

"I toast to that." I took another sip from my drink wondering how much of a problem this lady was going to be. "Thanks for the info, man. I'll definitely let you know if she comes around again. Thankfully she didn't show up until after we were closed, so at least she didn't start up drama in front of customers."

I glanced over at Pri who looked like she had something on her mind. "Okay, enough serious talk. Now, tell me about this guy Tía Nurys wants you to marry so she can get some blond grandbabies."

I almost choked on the Beetarita. "Holy shit yo, once again, the Dominican information distribution channels put *The New York Times* to shame."

She shrugged. "This is factual information."

"My mother is ridiculous."

Priscilla and Easton busted up at my flustered reaction.

"Look, there was this cute blond guy who came by the truck today. His name is Jude, I think he works at the library. He actually had a Dominican woman with him,

Carmen, I think. She was fly. Anyway, he *was* very attractive and did a little flirty thing with me in Spanish."

I laughed at how intensely Pri, Easton and Marty were looking at me. Like they were hanging on my every word.

How boring does shit get in this town?

"I mean he's hot, no question, but I'm not here for that. I need to get my business going, and dating is not part of the plan. So, Mamí's going to have to wait on the blond grandkids."

Now even Marty was laughing at me.

Pri was not giving up easily, though. "I think I know him from the gay potluck." She turned to Easton. "You know who I'm talking about right?"

Easton raised an eyebrow, and took a long drink of his bourbon.

What the fuck was that?

"I know Jude, what there is to know anyway. He's a bit mysterious." He looked up and squinted at me. "He's been in town a few years, but I haven't heard any gossip about him. No love triangles or falling outs, which with the gay rumor mill on steroids we have over here is quite rare, let me tell you."

Pri and Marty let out a heartfelt "Word" in response to Easton's comment.

"I've only talked to him a couple of times, but know quite a few guys who've tried with him and haven't gotten very far. The word is he doesn't date. Not sure what that means." He lifted a shoulder. "In any case he's a nice guy. Always polite to everyone, really funny."

Pri looked like Easton had just told her she'd won the ten-million-dollar Powerball.

"This is very promising. *Very*," she said, as she gave me a thumbs-up.

This was getting out of hand, I had to get Pri off of this.

"Sure, he seems cool, but again, I can't get distracted. I'm not interested in fucking around with random dudes."

Right as I was done with my statement and feeling pretty good about my focus and determination I saw Jude and Carmen walk in. They had their heads together and looked like they were discussing something serious. I was about to try and distract Pri when I heard her inhale loudly, and then felt a hard pinch on my arm.

I slapped her hand away, glaring.

"¡Coño! Pri, you gonna rip my damn skin off? The hell?"

"That's him!" she said in the loudest whisper ever.

"I know that, but like I said, I am not here for that." I made my point by taking a big gulp of my Beetarita, keeping an eye on Carmen and Jude as I swallowed.

I probably would've sounded more convincing if on my way here, I hadn't been daydreaming about asking him out. I wasn't even sure why I was being so salty, it wasn't like there was a rule I had to be a monk to run a food truck.

Easton widened his eyes as he finished up his drink.

"I'm almost sad I have to get back to the office. This is certainly about to get interesting."

He stood up and slapped my shoulder. "Good to see you, man. I'll be in touch."

"Same here." I nodded. "Come by the truck some time."

"Will do."

He gave Pri a big hug and a kiss, and walked toward the door.

Carmen, who was standing with Jude talking to the tall man who'd come in after them, saw Easton heading out and then looked at the spot he'd left at the bar. It took her a second, but as soon as she recognized me, she started waving her hand so hard her wrist looked loose. She gave the man the "I'll be back in a second" hand signal, grabbed a slightly apprehensive-looking Jude by the arm, and came over to where Pri and I were sitting.

I refused to look at Pri as they came closer, but could hear her giggles just fine.

"Hey! Look at you, only in town for a day and you already know one of the best spots! We just got out of work and needed to get a drink." She turned toward the man she'd been talking to and waved him over. "My poor husband had to come down to pick us up."

She pointed in Jude's direction. "This one was working late and I was catching up on a ton of paperwork, so we kept each other company."

I looked at Jude and smiled. "Four times in two days. It's got to be a record, even for a small town."

He lifted a shoulder and gave me a bored look. "It all happened within the same four-block radius...so."

"Oh, snap."

Thank you, Priscilla.

For some reason his saltiness made my pants tighten a little around the crotch area. I felt an urge to get up and smack his ass, just to see what he would say. He looked even sexier than this afternoon. His clothes were a little rumpled, his hair messy like he'd been grabbing at it, and his lips were red like he'd been biting them.

I was staring.

Again.

After a moment Carmen's husband, whose name was apparently Ted, walked up and she proceeded to make introductions. She immediately started telling him about her work troubles and asking Pri what she was drinking. Pretty soon the three of them were engaged in conversation, which left Jude and I staring at each other. For a second I was unsure of what to do, because he was standing there silently, as if waiting for me to come out of my mouth with another asinine comment.

I was not one to push myself on a guy if my attention was unwanted. So I was about to turn around and try to wedge into the conversation with the other three, when I noticed Jude making himself look away from my general direction. He'd let his gaze land on my face, and then run his eyes up and down my body. After a few seconds he'd catch himself and look somewhere else. He actually jumped a little, like he was telling his eyes to stop it with the staring. It was fucking adorable, and it gave me the push I needed to put a lid on the last ounce of common sense I had left for the evening. Before I knew it, I was standing up and moving toward him.

As I reached him, I took a moment to relive the speech from a few minutes ago when I told Priscilla about my priorities, and all the reasons why getting involved with someone was not in the master plan.

I took a deep breath and told the me from before to go fuck himself, because I was going to talk to this guy, hopefully buy him a drink, and let the evening take its course.

Chapter Five

Jude

Shit!

He caught me.

Nesto saw me running my eyes all over him, and was now standing right in front of me flashing a smile which was having an unnerving effect on my knee joints.

I glanced at him, feeling more than a little mortified, and lifted my hand in greeting. "Hi."

"Hey."

Oh God. His voice was actual sex. I was so out of my league right now.

He smelled so good it was addling my senses, like cedar, lemon, and man sweat. He had on a long-sleeved gray t-shirt that looked super soft to the touch, and the jeans he was wearing were molded to his strong thighs and ass like they were painted on. I would *not* whimper.

I had more self-control than this.

I tried to focus on other things which were not his body, but looking at his face didn't help at all. His closeness was doing things to my insides, and his skin was perfect. Light brown with a rosiness on his cheeks, like he would flush in the heat…or when he was turned on.

At this hour he was showing a bit of scruff too and it made his lips stand out even more. His mouth was… big. His lips broad and fleshy. I could probably suck on them for hours.

I closed my eyes for a second to try and tamp down everything that was happening inside me. When I opened them again he was looking down at me with a wicked expression, as if he knew exactly what was going through my head.

His was such an arresting beauty.

Not just pretty or handsome, but striking. Like every single part of him was made with the utmost intent. The more I looked at him, the more I got the feeling starting up something with Nesto was not going to allow for my usual surgical extraction. This man could make my simple, fastidiously structured life, very messy.

I kept looking up at him, at that perfect mouth, and I let myself drift in a fantasy where I could freely walk up to Nesto and kiss his lips. Touch his chest, run my hands up his neck and face. I imagined he was mine, and the warmth the image brought almost sent me running. I came back to reality when I felt a hand on my forearm and heard Nesto's raspy voice close to my ear, asking,

"So, can I buy you a drink?"

I snapped my eyes open, intensely aware of the spot on my arm he was touching. I was overwhelmed by him, his face, his smell, his voice. I had to count to three and breathe before I could answer his question.

Do I want him to buy me a drink?

My usually honed instinct for depriving myself of anything I desired too much didn't seem to want to kick in. So, I smiled at him and nodded. "Sure. I'll have a Negroni."

He grinned, looking impressed with my drink choice. "Nice. I approve. I'll be back in a minute."

I gave him the "no worries" hand signal and proceeded to talk myself down from whatever social anxiety rabbit hole I was about to go into.

It's only a drink, it's not a date. It isn't anything.

As I watched him move up to the bar, I took a deep breath and forced myself to pay attention to my body for a second, grounded myself in the moment and listened to what was playing on the radio. It was something funky and soulful and I focused on the sound for a few seconds, breathing slowly.

I turned my head to see where Carmen had gone and noticed she was still chatting with Ted and Nesto's cousin. I knew she was keeping them entertained so Nesto and I could talk. I should have been annoyed at her blatant disregard for my request she not meddle in my love life, but the feeling never came.

And what is the big deal anyway?

I let men buy me drinks all the time. I let them kiss me. Occasionally even more than that, why was I making such a big deal out of this?

Because I want it too much.

This man could trip up my world.

I observed Nesto chatting with the bartender as he waited for my drink, and marveled at how relaxed he looked, how comfortable in his skin he was. His face open and his eyes clear. I wondered what it took to make someone move through the world with that ease.

We were so different. It had taken me months to be brave enough to go out for a drink with people from the office. He'd just been here a day, and he was taking up space like he owned the place. And yet, his mere proximity made me feel more alive and present in my body than I had in years. After a minute he strutted back from the bar with a triumphant smile, handed me my drink and tipped his glass to mine in a toast.

"To small towns and random encounters."

I tipped my glass to his. "Cheers."

After I'd had a sip of my cocktail, I looked up at him. "Thank you."

He waved his hand like it wasn't a big deal and smiled. "No problem, I can sympathize with jobs that go way past five p.m. Were you able to get all your work done, or will there be more late nights in the library?"

Okay, so he was going with work talk. *That* I could handle.

"Unfortunately, it looks like I will have quite a few more nights like this, at least for the near future. I'm working on a project I want the board to approve, which at the moment is not looking likely." I grimaced, thinking about Misty and how happy she'd be to see me fail. "If I get my wish and can move forward with it, there will be a lot of work getting it off the ground. The project is sort of my baby, so I will have to do a lot of it myself."

Nesto nodded, looking interested. "What's the project? Or is it like a secret campaign which can't be discussed until it's launched?"

"Not a secret at all. Actually, the more buzz the better," I said, taking another drink. "It's a mobile library for youth. A book truck, if you will."

He laughed. "I like the idea already!"

I tried not to get too distracted by the perfect teeth he kept flashing at me and powered on with what I was saying. Keeping my face neutral, so I didn't come off as a total spaz. Talking about this always got me excited. Being a part of getting the project going was one of the most exciting parts of the job when I started at the library three years ago. Finally I had an opportunity to get the board to give the go-ahead. Unless Misty messed it for up for me, of course.

Before I started, I glanced up and Nesto's encouraging smile got me talking. "The idea is to get books and other services from the library to children and teens who are out in the more rural parts of the county. Our library is amazing, and there are very nice smaller ones in most of the towns, but we still have gaps in what kids can get out there. There's also the issue of the libraries being run by people *from* the towns."

Nesto nodded like he got where I was going.

"Checking out a book about something taboo or potentially embarrassing in a library where the entire staff know your parents can be a big barrier for kids in vulnerable situations. We just have a lot more to offer here in the big library. My hope is to make what we have in town available to all the young people in the county."

When I stopped talking I realized in addition to Nesto's, I had gained the attention of Carmen, Ted and Priscilla.

Carmen was giving me her "Proud Mom" face and Nesto had a weird smile on his, like what I said happily surprised him. The others looked interested in the topic too. Of course, now I was feeling self-conscious and wanted people's attention to be focused elsewhere.

I cleared my throat and wrapped it up. "That's the gist of it."

"That sounds like a great project." Nesto said, "Where

I grew up, in the South Bronx, it's very urban, but it's essentially a book desert. No bookstores, really."

Suddenly he looked serious, eyebrows furrowed. "But we could walk to the library center to get what we needed and it was a lifesaver for me and my friends."

The thought that Nesto understood why I wanted this project so badly spread a warm feeling through my chest. When I finally spoke it was low and a little breathless. "That's exactly why I want to make the mobile library happen."

He beamed at me and continued his story. "When there was something we were too mortified to ask our parents, we would do a group trip to the library after school and do our own research." He took a sip from his glass, looking adorably self-conscious. "There are some conversations one can't have with a parent, no matter how cool they are, you feel me?" He grimaced at this and we all laughed.

Carmen piped in from the stool she was perched on at the bar. "We'd wanted to get the project off the ground for years before Jude joined the library, and no one could get a viable plan going. But he said he would do it on his interview, and he came up with an awesome proposal," she gushed, kissing me on the cheek.

I pulled away, feeling a little mortified from all the attention. "Stop it, Carmen, it's not like we're giving them all scholarships. Besides we don't exactly have a green light. I could get shot down again." I was pretty sure I was red in the face.

She looked over at Nesto. "He's too modest, he's done amazing things with our youth programs since he started with us. If anyone has a chance of getting this approved, it's Jude," she said, wagging her finger at me. "We lucked out to get him!"

"I'm pretty impressed so far," Nesto said, as he shot me a conspiratorial look and stepped a bit closer to where I was standing, the warmth of his body sending tremors through my own.

He put his mouth against my ear and whispered. "So, you bring the books and I bring the Caribbean to all corners of the Finger Lakes, huh? I like that plan."

At this point I wasn't even sure *what* my body was doing. I was hot and cold with shivers running through places. Apparently being close to Nesto made my body think it had the flu. Something like a mix between a gasp and a laugh escaped my mouth, which sounded pretty hysterical to me, even in my disturbed state, and I prayed Nesto's drink was stronger than it looked.

I came back from my inner ramblings and noticed he and I were back to our own devices while Ted, Priscilla and Carmen continued to solve the mysteries of the universe. So, I got my shit together and decided I was going to make conversation.

"Tell me about these friends you went to the library with." Nesto, who had been looking at me with worry, immediately smiled and relaxed his shoulders.

This was clearly the right thing to ask. He shifted his body as he talked, turning all his focus on me.

"Oh, those are my boys. My best friends. We grew up together in the Bronx and we're still pretty tight. There's Juanpa and Patrice, those two I knew from the day I moved to the neighborhood. Juanpa's grandpa was our landlord, and he and his family lived across the street from us." He shook his head and smiled.

"Patrice and his mom lived a few blocks away, but

we all went to the same elementary school. The day my
mom and I moved in, I went outside to scope out the
block and found them fighting over what to do with the
five dollars they'd earned doing yard work for Juanpa's
grandpa."

As he spoke I had to work hard to keep my eyes on
his face. There was so much of his body I wanted to
take a closer look at.

"They had me break the tie between Italian ices or
Bubble Tape, and we've been close ever since. Camilo
we didn't meet until the summer before eighth grade
when he and his mom came up from Miami and moved
to the neighborhood."

I nodded as Nesto talked, even smiled, trying to
show him how much I wanted to hear all about the
people in his life.

"Patrice's mom knew them from when they first
came to the States from Haiti. So Patrice brought Milo
around and the bossy little shit has been trying to run
our lives since. They're the inspiration for OuNYe.
Juanpa's dad is Puerto Rican, Patrice is Haitian and
Camilo's folks came from Cuba and Jamaica, and me
and Mamí came from the DR. The GA Crew," he said
with a wistful smile.

"What does the GA stand for?" I asked.

He laughed, and shook his head. "Umm, evidence
that despite our running our mouths and fronting
like we were hardcore, we're just big nerds. GA is for
'Greater Antilles.' The biggest islands in the Caribbean-
Hispaniola, the island the DR and Haiti share, Puerto
Rico, Jamaica and Cuba."

I looked at him and smiled. The affection for his

friends, and the obvious pride for who he was and where he came from were pretty damn sexy.

"Will you miss them while you're here?" I asked, curious.

"Sure, I mean, we've been apart before. Juanpa and Camilo left the city for college. Juanpa went to USC in Cali and Milo to Temple in Philly. Patrice and I stayed local. I went to Fordham and he did his thing at Columbia. Dude is still there finishing up a PhD." The admiration for his friend's accomplishment was clear in his voice. "Anyway, after college everyone made their way back home. It's been good, having them close all this time. I'll miss them a whole lot, but I think we're all at the point where we're looking for what we want to be, you know?"

I was nodding again. "I definitely know."

My body kept reacting to Nesto. Everything he said was charged with such passion. Like he meant every word.

His face turned serious for a moment. "We've been working, doing our thing, and now we're feeling like we want to lay down roots, figure out what we want for the long run. Or I don't know, maybe that's just me." His smile was rueful, like he was a bit unsure of what he meant by that. "They'll come and visit, though. They actually drove up yesterday to help me move, but they went back already."

I nodded, remembering Carmen said his mom lived in town. I was about to ask a question about her when my very meddlesome best friend and Priscilla moved closer.

Carmen looked like she was about to do something I'd regret, so I braced for it.

"Hey, babe, so Ted is beat and has to head to the city early in the morning for a talk he's giving down there." With that she turned to Nesto. "So we were wondering if you could give Jude a ride. He doesn't have his car today and we were going to take him home, but Pri mentioned your sublet's in Trumansburg. We figured it wouldn't be too much trouble," she finished, looking infinitely pleased with herself. Standing next to her, Ted had the resigned expression of a man who knew when to just play along.

Pri looked like she was waiting for her turn to deliver her line, and as if on cue, stretched up to give Nesto a kiss on the cheek. "Hey, primo, so I'm going to get a ride up with them since I left my truck up on campus. I'm so glad I got to see you before I went back."

Nesto looked like he knew exactly what those two were up to, but obliged his cousin with a kiss goodbye. We waved them off as they walked out of the bar. Nesto sat back on the stool and pulled me by the hand, so I was standing over him.

"So I guess we've been left on our own so we can proceed to fall in love and fulfill their plans for us, huh?"

I laughed and shook my head. "Carmen is incorrigible."

"Priscilla is no innocent either, believe me," he said as he finished his drink.

Nesto cleared his throat, took my empty glass, put it on the bar and sat up. He grabbed my hips tight and looked up at me with a smile. I stepped closer into the vee of his legs and when I pushed against him, I felt him harden.

"So, am I really taking you home?" The hoarseness

in his voice was incredibly hot and for once I quit trying to hold back. i looked at him, not hiding how much
I wanted him at all.

"Lead the way, Ernesto."

Chapter Six

Nesto

All Dominican men think with their dicks. I usually got pretty pissed off whenever I heard people say that, but holy shit, today I was repping on that particular stereotype like a champ. Jude had me thirsting after him something fierce. He'd only been in the bar for thirty minutes and I was already rock-hard, and trying to scope out a dark corner I could drag him into.

I tried to get my shit together, since we agreed I'd take him home, but with him leaning into me, pressing his hard cock right into my belly, I couldn't seem to get my ass off the stool.

He was standing so close to me, our bodies were touching at various critical points. His breaths were coming faster and his skin had this flush, which was making all the blood in my body rush down to my nether regions. I stood up, bent my head to tell him something and resisted the urge to run my tongue along his ear, instead, in a voice I knew sounded filthy I said, "Let's go then."

I felt a shiver run down his body at my words, but he grabbed my hand and pulled me out of the bar. I turned around to wave at Marty, who was looking at us with a knowing expression. Once we were on the street, Jude stopped and smiled up at me. "Where to?"

I took a deep breath, because I was seriously tripping. For a moment I blanked and could barely remember where I was, much less where I'd left the car. I shook my head, trying to clear the sex fog taking over my brain.

"I'm on Buffalo and Cayuga, just a few minutes."

He nodded and started walking. As we made our way down the street side by side, I felt so connected to him, like our bodies were in sync. I impulsively grabbed his hand, and kissed it. He gazed up at me and shook his head as I released it.

"You're a bit of a romantic, aren't you?"

I shrugged. "Not usually. If anything, I'm a bit aloof. Maybe it's Ithaca. Everything is so much slower here. Not so frantic. The idea of a leisurely walk is not so absurd."

"The biggest place I've lived in is Rochester," Jude said, as we walked. "Which isn't all that big compared to New York. I can't imagine being a kid there. I grew up near Canandaigua, about sixty miles northwest from here. It was pretty small. The big city we went to for shopping only had like ten thousand people. Ithaca is practically a metropolis. I think that's why I decided to buy a place in Trumansburg. It's smaller. Feels more familiar."

"I get that," I answered. "It's small enough you can get to know your neighbors, but you got everything you need."

"Exactly."

It seemed like we'd shifted gears from the intense

flirting, which was all right with me. For a moment there I was feeling reckless.

This was good. Regular conversation was very good. I didn't need to get naked within twenty minutes of buying a guy a drink like a fucking scumbag.

"I was born in Santo Domingo, which is the capital of the DR. It's huge, almost three million people. Then I moved to New York when I was six and have been there ever since. I've travelled all over, but I've never lived anywhere this small." I laughed. "Can I tell you a secret?"

He nodded solemnly like he knew I was about to share something I wouldn't easily admit to. "It's so quiet in my apartment I couldn't fall asleep last night. I had to put on some talk radio." I covered my face with my hands. "I actually put some right-wing nut job on. The angry rambling helped me settle down."

He clicked his tongue at my mortified expression. "Poor city boy, can't deal with small town life. You're going to be bored out of your mind within a week."

"Oh, I don't know about that. So far things have been pretty interesting." I squeezed his hand again. He squeezed mine back, but kept walking in silence. I wondered if I'd said something wrong, but before I could ask, he started talking again.

"So where in Trumansburg is your apartment?"

"Right on Main Street. You know the old school laundromat? The one with the weird posters."

He nodded. "Yes, I do, and they're not just weird, they're completely inappropriate. There's one of a guy punching himself in the face because he forgot fabric softener."

"Yeah, they're pretty fucked-up. Anyways, I'm in one of the apartments upstairs."

Jude turned his head to look at me. "We're neighbors, then. I live just a block away. The little blue house next to the church."

"Oh, I know exactly where that is." I bent my head and whispered, "Hey, neighbor."

He bumped my hip and said, "Welcome to the neighborhood, Nesto."

We'd reached the spot where I parked, so I stopped and pointed to my Prius. "This is me."

Jude made a move to go around to the passenger side when I pulled him to where I was standing. I was leaning on the car door facing the dark sidewalk, and he stepped up to me, pressing his body to mine. He looked up, and I bent my head so our lips were almost touching. My heart was beating so hard, my head was throbbing. It was like for the last hour all my body wanted was to get as close to Jude as possible.

"Jude, dame un beso." The words came out like they were from somewhere deep inside of me. He closed his eyes and pushed up so his lips were just centimeters from mine, and I bent my head to meet them. Just as our lips grazed, a car drove by breaking the spell. He gasped and turned his face, hiding his eyes from me. I pulled his chin, and the look on his face was so fragile, like he was scared of what he'd almost done.

"Are you okay?"

He groaned and shook his head. His eyes tightly shut. "This was not part of the plan." But even as he said it, I felt him press closer to me. It was like his body and his mind were waging a war on what to do about me.

He wasn't the only one in that dilemma.

"What wasn't supposed to happen? Kissing me? We don't have to." I tried to lift his chin again, but instead he pushed his face into my chest.

After a moment he spoke, his words muffled, "I'm a mess."

I took a chance and tightened my arms around him, unable to hold myself at a distance. "You're not. You're great and running into you was the best part of my day." He raised his face to look at me. His eyes were brighter, and a tiny smile was lifting up the sides of his mouth. I could feel his pulse racing as fast as mine.

This moment felt entirely too intense.

I spoke into the silent night, hoping to lighten the moment. "Besides I'm glad at least one of us has some sense. My mom lives like two blocks away. She would not be amused to find me necking in the street."

He gave me a full smile then, and it was like the fucking sun. His voice sounded more like himself when he spoke. "I wouldn't think so."

I pressed our foreheads together for just a second then pushed off from the car and clicked the key fob to open the passenger side door for him. "Let's get you home."

I was getting uncomfortable with the long silence as I drove down the dark two-lane road leading to Trumansburg. Second guessing everything I'd done in the past twenty minutes and wondering if I'd pushed Jude too far. When it was obvious he wasn't going to initiate a conversation, I blurted out, "For the record, I don't usually move this fast."

Jude responded in an amused tone. "For the record, I don't either…mostly."

I laughed. "Okay, fair enough, I don't *usually* move this fast."

Even though I was sure we were both suffering from a bad case of blue balls and feeling a little awkward about the turn the night had taken, the mood did lighten after that.

"So was your first official day as a small business owner in Ithaca everything you hoped for?" Jude's tone was neutral, but I could detect a hint of humor.

He was such a contradiction, at times so reserved, like he wanted to blend into the scenery, but he was funny. He had a fire in him too, I'd seen it when he talked about his book truck.

I cleared my throat, trying to decide if I should match his tone, but instead I surprised myself by saying something I hadn't shared with anyone. "It was a good day, but I'm still stressed about whether I did the right thing by coming here. In the city the competition is hard, but at least there I knew what I was up against." I glanced over at Jude and he was looking at me with concern and I felt like a jackass.

Way to kill the fucking mood, Ernesto, because unloading on a guy you barely know would totally make him want to see you again.

"Sorry, I didn't mean to spill my feelings all over you." I sighed again. "I guess I'm just tired."

His eyes widened like he didn't expect me to apologize. "No that's fine, and I get it. It's such a big change, and I can imagine it was a major decision. What made you finally want to do it?"

I glanced over at him, a little surprised at how interested he sounded. "Are you sure you want to hear about all this?"

He gave a sharp nod. "Yes."

Jude's interest in my business, my story, did something to me. "Well, I'd fantasized about the idea of owning my own business, making food I love, for years. But that was as far as it went. It took my mom finally reminding me of who I was."

At the mention of my mom Jude's face lit up. He was so into me talking about my family. I couldn't remember anyone being this curious about my roots. Most guys I dated would tune out as soon as I started talking about this stuff.

"One night, after I'd sat on her couch and talked for hours about how my job was killing my soul, and whined about wishing I was making food for a living instead, she looked me in the eyes, and gave me her 'se acabo' face." He laughed at that and I winked at him, feeling warm all over. "She told me, 'Nesto, you were the boy who held my hand and told me not to worry when we sat on that plane to come here and I sobbed for the whole flight. The little kid who walked into the classroom on the first day without knowing a word of English, and told me, 'You can go, Mamí, I can handle it from here.' Baby, we're immigrants, we don't just take chances, we know what it's like to leave everything behind and start over. If this is your dream, then go make it happen."

I heard Jude give a deep sigh like he understood exactly how important what Mamí had said to me had been.

"So, I went for it. I did culinary school on the weekends while working full-time and after I graduated, I quit my job and used a whole lot of my savings to open my truck."

For a moment he hesitated as if he was looking for what to say in response. "It's really great how supportive your family is, Nesto. It must be nice to have them close by again."

I kept my attention on the road, but the yearning in his voice made me wonder what he wasn't saying.

I smiled thinking of my mom and how she'd gotten on my case about asking Jude out. "It's not easy running a business on your own, having them to help out makes a huge difference."

"I'm glad you have them."

I wanted to ask about that longing in his voice, but suspected it would shift the mood in another direction.

"I hope someday I can repay my mom for everything she's done for me and my sister. My dad was a bum, he wasn't really around by the time I was born, and Minerva's dad." I shook my head. "He was a nice guy, but not exactly looking to be a family man."

I pursed my lips, thinking on how hard it was sometimes to take on something that felt so big on my own, and how my mom had done it for so long. I couldn't even imagine what it would be like to rely on someone other than family for help. To have, as my mom told me this afternoon, someone to help carry my burdens with me.

"I'm sure she's glad to help you."

I jerked my head at the sound of his voice and muttered quietly into the space between us, "I know she is."

We made small talk for the last few minutes of the drive and before I knew it we were pulling up to his house. Jude lifted his hand pointing ahead. "That's me."

I stopped right in front of his driveway, and turned my head to get a good look at it. It was so pretty from outside. It was a little colonial, painted navy blue with gray shutters. His garden was in full bloom with lots of tulips and daffodils.

Having lived in the city my whole life, I never envisioned living anywhere other than an apartment. But seeing Jude's house, I got an image of myself walking up the pathway and opening the door to find him there waiting for me curled up on a sofa.

And *that's* when I knew I needed to get my ass to bed, because this had to be some sort of exhaustion induced delusion. I was already moving myself into the guy's house, and we'd known each other for ten hours. I turned off the ignition and looked at Jude. "I had a great time tonight. I feel like we have some unfinished business, but I don't want to be too much of a thirsty motherfucker and invite myself in."

He laughed, leaning over to kiss me on the cheek. "You'll get an invitation. Eventually. I had a nice time too, Nesto. Thanks for the ride."

With that he got out of the car and walked up to his door. Cool, calm and collected. Meanwhile I felt like a hot mess, and was going home to jerk off until my hand went numb. I sighed and rested my forehead on the steering wheel. I had a feeling this would not be the last time Jude would leave me panting.

Chapter Seven

Nesto

"Mr. Nesto! I think we lost Ari!" I turned my eyes from the road for a second to look at the passenger seat and saw Yin, one of my two brand new employees, with his head and half of his torso sticking out of the truck window.

"Yin! Put your seat belt back on and relax. He's right behind us." Yin was highly concerned his partner in crime, and my other new staff member, Ari, would be somehow lost forever in the fifteen miles between Trumansburg and Ithaca.

I'd given Ari my car to drive this morning after he handed over his brand-new New York State driver's license, and assured me driving in Ithaca was child's play for someone who learned to drive in the streets of his hometown, Kinshasa, the capital city of Democratic Republic of Congo. Having gotten my first driving lessons in the South Bronx, I could relate and decided to entrust him with my Prius. Yin on the other hand, spent his teenage years in a Thai refugee camp and did not trust motorists or roads in the slightest. He kept craning his neck to look behind us trying to make sure he didn't lose sight of Ari for too long.

I laughed and tugged on his seat belt. "He's fine. He has the directions on his phone, he probably got caught up in the traffic light behind us. And just call me Nesto, the 'mister' makes me feel old!"

Yin smiled and nodded, but didn't look very convinced. After a moment he sat back down to review his checklist. I hired Yin and Ari the day after I contacted a friend of Pri's who worked at a local nonprofit, which helped refugees and immigrants with job placement. I'd called her up, told her what I needed and she informed me I was in luck, because she was looking to place two young men with experience in food service who were fresh out of a course in food hygiene and preparation. I told her I would love to talk to them, but that I was gay, and was not going to hide it, so if it was an issue I'd rather not get their hopes up.

She happily let me know these two young men had been referred to her by the LGBTQ youth center in town. So, I met them at a local coffee shop that afternoon, we talked for a bit and I hired them on a trial basis. They'd been with me for over a week now, and so far, it was the best business decision I'd made in Ithaca. I had never seen two people more excited to come and work their asses off for fourteen bucks an hour.

Yin, who had worked at a restaurant in Thailand for years, after his family left Burma, was a born food truck man. He could work in any space, no matter how small or hot it got in there, and he was militant about organization.

Today was our first time at the Farmer's Market, and he showed up at the kitchen at the crack of dawn looking impeccable in his OuNYe t-shirt and jeans, which I suspected were dry cleaned for the occasion. He had a clipboard in hand, with a comprehensive checklist of everything we needed to get the truck ready for the market. Under *that* list he had one with everything we needed to get the truck *out* of the market.

I liked the kid, but damn, he did the most.

"Looks like we have more than two hours to set up before market opens, since we'll be there before 7:15 a.m.," he said with a nod.

As we drove out of Trumansburg I tried very hard not to stalkerishly look at Jude's house to see if I spotted him, but like every other time I'd driven by his place this week, if he was in, I couldn't tell from the street. I sighed inwardly and put my eyes back on the road. The guy completely ghosted on me after the night I saw him at Ophelia's over a week ago.

I mean it's not like we were going steady or anything, but I thought we'd had a moment. I'd at least expected him to come by the truck and say "hey" or something, but *nada*. He was totally out of sight. Carmen stopped by the truck a couple of times to get orders way too large for one person, but things were so busy I didn't get a chance to ask her about him.

I didn't even know what the hell my problem was. I was the one who usually felt smothered. Always complaining the guys I got involved with didn't get my business came first. I should be glad Jude wasn't making a big deal out of things. Instead I was driving by his house every night like a hard-up loser, sticking my neck out of my car trying to see if his lights were on.

I sighed again and turned my head to find Yin glaring at me.

"Sorry, you're right, we're totally good. We should be able to get everything done with time to relax a bit before we start. My mom and sister are coming to help too, they'll be there around eight a.m."

Yin nodded and kept going over his list. He was a cute kid, short and skinny. With big brown eyes and a sassy haircut. His family had fled Burma when he was nine years old, and after almost ten years in a refugee camp they had been relocated to Ithaca. When I hired him, he informed me in very formal English he wanted to be a nurse. I'd only known him for like a week, and was already rooting for him.

We drove down the last stretch of road along Cayuga Lake as we made our way into Ithaca. The clear blue water surrounded by dense forest was a stunning view even this early.

You could already see the sailboats out there.

We exited the road and made the turn into the market at exactly 7:15 a.m. The grounds swarmed with vendors preparing for the first day of the season.

I turned to Yin who was perched on the edge of his seat looking at all the people buzzing around. "Right on time. Just like you said."

"Right on time." The satisfaction in his voice made me laugh. This kid was too fucking precious.

The Farmer's Market in Ithaca was an institution, people came from all over the region to shop here on weekends. It was one of the city's main tourist spots, and the location was certainly part of the attraction. The place was called Steamboat Landing, right on the edge of Cayuga Lake. This morning as we drove by we could see the Cornell women's crew team gliding along the water.

The market was set up in a T-shaped open-air structure with wooden stalls. Customers could enter and keep going down a corridor, which led them to the pier, or go left or right to walk through the offerings in the market. They had produce, fresh flowers, food, art, local wine, cider, clothes and even music. It was quite a scene, and I was excited to have OuNYe as part of the season's offerings.

We navigated the parking lot and looked for our spot among the stalls.

"Yin, what's our number again?"

Yin checked his notes and confirmed, "B-18." After a few seconds we spotted it. I maneuvered the truck, so the back side was flush against the opening of the stand and quickly got off. Yin jumped out as well, and started getting things in order like I'd shown him. Ari drove up a few minutes later and parked the Prius in a spot close to us.

"See, I told you, he was right behind us." Yin blushed as he watched Ari park the car.

Ari walked over with a strut, like he had just stepped out of a Ferrari, a big smile on his face.

"Boss man, that little car makes no noise. I had to stop like three times to check it was still running," he said, shaking his head.

I laughed and threw my hands up. "I told you it did that!"

"I like cars that make noise," Ari complained, a grin still on his face. "How else will people hear me coming, so they can get out of the way?" With that he turned to the other member of the OuNYe All-Star Team.

"Yin! Where's the checklist?"

Ari was the complete opposite of Yin physically and

in personality. He was a strapping young man, with ebony skin, over six feet tall and ripped with muscle. He had come to the U.S. from the Congo seeking asylum, but had been detained at customs because of some "issues" with his visa. He ended up in limbo, stuck in an immigrant detention center for almost two years. He'd been finally released the previous winter with a "Whoops, guess your papers were fine after all."

He was already working two jobs and going to community college. His goal was to be a human rights lawyer, and despite the hell he went through to get here, he was the sunniest person in Ithaca. You could not keep him down. I watched them both run around thinking once again this Ithaca experiment was turning out to be an excellent idea.

"Okay, guys," I said to them as they unloaded the truck. "Make sure we keep everything needing refrigeration in the truck." I thought better of it and waved my hand toward the place in the stall we were going to prepare the food. "Actually, why don't you two get the grill down and I'll work on getting the truck connected and powered up." I pointed at the spot it should go in as I pulled out cords.

"After, we'll work on the menu. We have three burritos today and the yucca fritters with the mojo aioli, plus the two juices. Let's get moving." We got busy, getting containers with the prepared ingredients set up, working together and joking around as we went. We were going fast and would be set to go well before the first customers started roaming the market. I was trying to get the truck hooked up to the electricity when I heard someone calling for me.

"Hi, there. Are you the person responsible for OuNYe Afro-Caribbean Food?"

I called out a "that'll be me," my attention still on what I was doing, and not so much on the guy asking questions.

"I think there's been an issue with your application, and unfortunately you're going to have to move your truck. We seem to be missing some of your paperwork." I got up in a rush from where I was crouching and turned around to see a frazzled older man with a clipboard.

I attempted to speak in a normal manner a couple of times, but in the end what came out of my mouth was a loud growl that sort of sounded like "What are you talking about?"

As I walked up to him, my body tense, I hoped I didn't look as pissed as I felt.

"I'm sorry, I'm not sure I follow." I made a conscious effort to unclench my fists and relax my shoulders, because this dude looked like he had the Ithaca PD on speed dial. I spoke in the most cordial tone I could manage. "I have copies of everything I submitted to your office, and my season vendor pass. It's all in my truck, I can go grab it."

The man looked even more put out, and started glaring behind him like he was looking for the person responsible for all this. "Oh, you do? That's funny." He stared back at his clipboard and looked up again. "The copy for your approval must have been misplaced then. If you have the original it would certainly help. I apologize for the inconvenience, this is very unusual."

As he said that he turned around *again*, looking even more annoyed.

I huffed and went to the truck to get the papers.

I thought this Farmer's Market was supposed to be organized. I had to apply for a spot almost a year ago. What was this bullshit about them losing my papers?

As I walked back to the man with all my documents in hand, I was glad for my control freak ways and hoped this was a fluke, because I did not have time for this. Not to mention that not being able to do the market over the summer and fall would essentially destroy my plans for the next six months.

I handed over my copies and the pass which clearly read "Season Vendor" with the year and the name of the business.

"Is this what you need?" I said, unable to keep frustration out of my voice. "I mean, I talked with Jim yesterday and he confirmed I was good to go, so I'm not really sure what the issue is."

The man looked at my stuff, sighed heavily and handed them over.

"I'm so sorry about this, Mr. Vasquez. Everything's in order, you can carry on setting up." He gestured in the direction of the truck. "I will make a note on your file and try to look through our documents and see if I can locate your original application. If I can't find it, I'll just make a copy of what you have. Hope you have a great first day." He shook my hand and gave me another mortified look before walking off like he was about to go ream out whoever made him come over here to look like an asshole.

This was the second time in two weeks someone had come to my business and hassled me about whether I had my shit in order. I really hoped this was a coincidence, and had nothing to do with the woman from the first day, but I was not naïve enough to completely rule it out. I sighed and turned back to see Ari and Yin looking spooked. I was still pissed, but had way too much to do to dwell on the last five minutes.

So I did what I always did. I got to work.

"What's good, A?" I asked Ari as he hustled back into the stall and quickly started putting on his apron.

"There are twenty people in line and we've served almost a hundred! It's not even noon yet!"

Ari was obsessively tracking how many people we served since yesterday. It was Sunday, our second day in the market, and sales were ridiculous.

Yesterday we sold out of everything, and today was looking the same. People were loving the food and the concept, and wanted to know where we'd be during the week.

I was feeling good and absolutely not sweating that so far Jude was a no-show at the market.

Nope, I was focused on selling burritos.

"M'ijo, we need two more Marleys with the chicken, one with Jerk tofu and another batch of the yucca fritters," my mom yelled from the front.

"Ta' bien, Mamí. Yin is finishing up the fritters for this order. We'll start another one in a minute."

My mom was kicking ass taking orders, and my sis was rocking getting them ready and chatting up customers with Ari. In the rear Yin and I were like two machines getting the food ready. We deep-fried pork belly, grilled chicken, and rolled burritos nonstop.

As I worked I could hear Ari just a few feet away at the counter answering some questions for a client in his lilting soft voice. "Yes, the Manno is our burrito inspired by Haitian cuisine. It comes with Djon Djon rice, which is made with black mushrooms. Griot, pork belly cubes marinated in bitter orange and oregano, which is braised and then deep fried. It also comes with Pikliz, our homemade Haitian spicy slaw, avocado slices and yucca straws. It's my favorite one, although they're all delicious!"

"Oh, I think I'll have that one," the client said excitedly. "And I'll take one Lupe too, and the yucca fritters, they look so good. What's the sauce?"

"The sauce is a mojo aioli, it's very nice and tangy. I can give it to you on the side if you like."

"Perfect, thanks so much. I'm so excited for this, I've never had Haitian food before!"

Music to my ears.

The day moved fast, but by two in the afternoon things were slowing down, and it was my turn to man the counter while my mom and sister took a break and walked around the market. I was grabbing a bottle of cold water for myself when I saw Jude walking up to the stall with some guy.

I tried to act cool and not let my desperation show too much, but damn he looked good today. He was wearing red chinos and a tight navy t-shirt. His hair messy, like he hadn't bothered with it this morning. It was all I could do not to walk up to him and drag him home so we could finish what we'd started by my car. I knew this was not exactly keeping with my "no distractions" plan, but fuck it.

I stood up with a grin as he walked up to the stall. I looked him up and down with appreciation, sniffed and flexed my shoulders. I was being a scumbag, this was a fact, but I wanted to clue in the fucker with him that he had competition. Before Jude or I could get a word in, the guy extended his hand and introduced himself.

"Hi, I'm Raj, and I was brought here under false pretenses," he said as he flashed me a smile. Jude sputtered behind him, getting redder by the second.

I fake-laughed as I gave him a firm handshake. "Oh, yeah? How's that?"

I could be friendly. Nobody needed to get their head snatched off, yet. I glanced over at Jude who looked like he was bracing for whatever this dude was going to say. I noticed he was looking at the guy more like an exasperated older brother than a boyfriend, and I relaxed a little bit.

"Well, I thought we were coming here to check out a new food stand. I was not informed there would be amenities." The last line he delivered with a pointed stare in the vicinity of my biceps.

I laughed for real this time. This kid was funny.

"Well, we aim to please here. It's good to see you again, Jude." I threw in a wink. That first day at the truck I'd noticed those got me a reaction every time. "You ready to try something new? We have the Lavoe today, our Puerto Rican burrito. Have you ever tried guandules?" Jude still looked a little unsure, but he came up closer. Was I coming on too strong?

Probably. Fuck.

"Looks like you've sold out of some stuff already," he said, while still looking at the board. "That's really great, Nesto." His voice was so earnest, like me selling a bunch of pork and chicken burritos completely made his day.

"Thanks, we've had a good first weekend." That

blond hair and shy smile combo was going to be the end of me. I could not stop staring at him.

"I'll try the Lavoe," he said with a nod. "I've had pigeon peas at Carmen's and really like them."

From next to him Raj quipped, "I'll have that too, with the tofu instead of pork, though." I gave the order to Ari, and leaned over the counter to flirt a little more with Jude, while Raj chatted up Yin on the other side.

"So, how's your weekend going? You're looking fresh. I like that shirt." I was shameless, but hey, nobody needed to know I'd been driving by his house with my car windows down all week.

He looked at his chest like he'd barely noticed what he had on before turning those gorgeous blue eyes on me. "Oh, I'm good. Raj's here visiting from the city for the weekend, so we've been doing the rounds. Wine tasting yesterday, market today. He leaves this afternoon, so we had to pack it in." He blushed and then flattened his mouth. "Sorry I've been MIA, work has been crazy. Our grant writer is a total nightmare, and I needed to work with her all week getting my proposal for the board ready."

I shook my head wanting to reassure him. "No problem, I know how it is. Things have been busy for me too, as you can see." I extended my hand toward Ari and Yin. "I even hired new people."

He looked at them and smiled. "Looks like they're working out well."

"They are. Listen," I said, leaning in a bit more. "I'm glad you came by. I was meaning to stop in by the library this week to ask if you wanted to get a drink tonight."

His eyes widened a bit, and he looked like he was

about to say yes, but then he scrunched his face and shook his head.

Dammit.

"Actually, I'm going to Carmen's for dinner." At least he sounded kind of bummed out. "It's sort of an ongoing thing. I eat with them every Sunday." I was disappointed, but didn't want to get pushy. I got the feeling the Sunday dinner invitation at Carmen's was a big deal to Jude.

I didn't need to guilt him because I was a scrub who had nothing going on other than stuffing burritos and hanging out with my mom and sixteen-year-old sister.

"No worries. Maybe another time, then?" I said, while focusing on getting their order packed, not wanting him to see my disappointment at his refusal, the intensity of it surprising me. After I made sure everything was in the bag, I handed it over, trying for a smile.

Raj grabbed the bag and gave Jude a look before inspecting the contents, then off-handedly said, "Jude's totally free if you want to do a late drink, they're usually done by eight at Carmen's." He stopped and held up his hand, giving Jude some side-eye.

"I did grad school here, moved to the city in January. I was part of the Sunday night dinner crew for a while. He can be at your place by eight thirty, right Jude?"

Damn, Jude's friends were mad nosy, and pushy. After glaring at Raj, Jude turned to me and the agonized look on his face made my stomach sink. I almost took the invitation back, then a tiny smile appeared on his face. He fidgeted with his phone before answering and the wait felt like years.

Finally he spoke, his voice unsure. "Let me think about it, okay?"

I shrugged, trying to give him an out if he wasn't really into the idea. "I mean only if you're up for it."

Raj rolled his eyes. "I'm telling Carmen about this."

Jude turned to his friend red in the face. "Raj!"

"What?" Raj asked looking slightly contrite. This whole thing had turned a lot heavier than I intended and I needed to chill. I wasn't trying to embarrass Jude. Maybe I'd made more of a thing out of that kiss than he had.

"Look, Jude—"

Before I finished he started tapping his phone and said, "Let me make sure I have a number for you, and if I can make it I'll let you know."

I knew he had it, because I'd given it to him at some point on the drive home the other night, but I wasn't going to get offended because he didn't remember every second of the evening like I did. So I just parroted my number again and he nodded. "Yup, here you are."

I dipped my head once, keeping my lips shut. He knew what I wanted.

Raj was about to say something when I noticed the woman who'd come to my truck that first day making her way down the aisle to my stand. As soon as Jude spotted her his face changed, his gaze turning stony as she smiled and came up to him.

"Hi, Jude, are you enjoying some of the new ethnic offerings at the market?"

Jude didn't smile back and just pointed to the bag in Raj's hand.

She glared at it like it was full of shit, then looked up at me. "I didn't realize we'd have more Spanish food available at the market this season. You'd think one taco stand was enough."

I again tried to control my face because this fucking woman clearly came all the way here to disrespect me, and I was not giving her the pleasure of seeing me lose my cool.

"My food is Caribbean, not Spanish, but yes, we'll be here all season."

I grabbed a flyer from a stack on the counter. "Here you go, in case you lost the one I gave you the other day."

She glanced at my hand and nodded without taking it. "Right, well we have the critically acclaimed gourmet grilled cheese stand on the other end of the aisle."

Jude's eye roll when she said "critically acclaimed" was epic. I almost laughed in her face, but decided to ignore her. After a second she turned back to Jude.

"I'll see you tomorrow in the office. We have to talk about the proposal again. I'm just not sure how we'll manage that first year of funding. So many startup costs, I wouldn't get my hopes up too much."

Great, so this must be the monster grant writer Jude had mentioned. This lady was a nuisance. I'd bet anything she had something to do with that bullshit about my application yesterday. I had to give it to Jude though, he was cold as ice. The nod he gave her was barely an acknowledgement.

"Sure, Misty, we can talk then." He turned around and gave me a shy smile, then waved at Ari and Yin who were just staring quietly as the scene unfolded. Raj gave us a little wave as well, and walked away with Jude. I stood there seething, because I hadn't even had a chance to properly say goodbye to him.

Why was this woman hell-bent on messing with me?

Misty looked after them, her face murderous, then turned to me. "Don't get too comfortable. I've seen half a dozen of these ethnic places come and go. People in this town don't have the palate for your type of food."

She said the word *food* like she meant to say *trash*.

I leaned over and turned my head toward the grilled cheese stand, which was as empty now as it'd been all day. "I've had lines thirty people deep all weekend, and I've been checking out the competition in the market. I didn't even know there was a grilled cheese stand, you know," I said, as she glared at me. "Since I'm only paying attention to the places which actually have customers." I knew taunting this lady wasn't a good idea, but fuck her and her bullshit.

She sneered, then turned around and walked off without saying a word.

If she thought she was going to intimidate me, she had another thing coming. She wasn't the first bigot to try to make me feel two feet tall or to tell me to go back to where I belonged, and she wouldn't be the last. I had every right to be here, and had the skills to stay where I was.

If anything, now I had something to prove.

Chapter Eight

Jude

It was eight p.m. and so far I'd avoided dealing with the drink invitation from Nesto by sitting on Carmen's couch, obsessively going over my proposal for the board. I knew Misty said what she said at the market because she was pissed I'd been at Nesto's stand, and not buying her son's disgusting food. But I also knew she was petty enough to actually mess with my project out of spite.

Critically acclaimed.

She was delusional; those sandwiches were barely edible. The only reason she could even keep the stand at the market was because she went around intimidating people using her husband's name. She'd also totally ruined the moment with Nesto.

Of course she had, because her superpower was killing fun.

Nesto looked so good too, sweaty and delicious in his red tank top. I honestly didn't know what happened to my body when I was around him. I felt completely out of control. I wanted to kiss him, run around, just everything. And god that night at Ophelia's.

I hadn't had anyone turn me on like that, ever. Those hands, so big and rough. When I pressed against him and felt that hard cock my brain almost short circuited. Even through my clothes his heat was overwhelming. I wanted to melt into the sidewalk, or worse, beg him to fuck me right then and there.

This was the reason I'd avoided running into him after that night. Because I knew that as soon as I saw him again, it would be hard to resist him. Nesto made me want too many things I didn't trust myself with. I knew if I was alone with him again I was going to want more, and the possibility was giving me pause, which meant a drink with him would probably end in disaster.

Dating was always such a mindfuck for me. Things had ended disastrously in my last relationship. Since then, any time I got close to anyone I felt like a pawn in some game. Like it was just a matter of time before I'd get dropped for something or someone who mattered more. Nesto had already gotten so deeply under my skin, I knew pursuing something with him would only lead to heartache.

"Jude!"

Carmen's terse voice startled me out of my fretting, making me jump up and almost drop my laptop. "Carmen, why do you need to yell like that? I'm five feet away from you."

She was standing by the couch, holding a plastic container of the braised short ribs and polenta she made for dinner and tapping her foot like she was about to lose her patience with me.

"Here's some food you can take with you to Nesto's. Now get your skinny ass off my couch, and over to his house before this gets cold and he can't appreciate my mastery of the short rib," she said, thrusting the tub at me.

I backed up without taking it. "First of all, I haven't even decided if I'm going to do this drink. Second, I am not showing up there with a tub full of meat."

She shook her head at me, widening her eyes more and more with each swivel. "Don't start with me, Jude. You're taking this food, going over to his place for a drink and hopefully some sex. I don't even know why you need to make this so difficult. Take him the food! Who doesn't want free short ribs?"

I squinted at her, trying to convey just how over-the-top she was being at this particular moment. "Someone who makes and sells food for a living? He probably has tons of stuff to eat at home already."

"Wrong." If possible, her eyes got even wider. "You've seen Chef's Table, people who cook for a living have no food at home. He probably only has condiments in his fridge. You'd be doing him a huge favor. Also, who's not into a beautiful man bringing him a late-night snack?"

I pursed my lips before answering. "That sounds really seedy."

She just waggled her eyebrows at me.

I don't even know why I argue with her.

"Exactly. Besides, what are you even doing right now? Sitting on my couch, working. Please tell me you didn't let Misty freak you out. Don't let her intimidate you."

I took advantage of a potential distraction and changed the subject. "Speaking of Misty, she was in rare form at the market today. I ran into her while getting some lunch at Nesto's stand and she was so rude to him." Just thinking about how she was looking down at Nesto got me heated all over again. "She's so ridiculous about her son and that stupid food truck. She thinks she's in a war to the death with everyone in town trying to make a living selling food. Her son's business is failing because his sandwiches suck," I said, exasperated.

Carmen was looking at me with a scowl on her face. "That woman is too fucking much. I bet you she was seething because Nesto's stand was busy. I hope he didn't let her get to him."

"He looked pissed, but he was polite to her. I left him with her standing there fuming, but he seemed to have things under control."

Carmen shook her head in disgust. "She's something else, and I would love to bitch about her more, but I know what you're doing," she said, pointing a finger at me. "I'm not letting you distract me. We were talking about you taking this food to your future boyfriend."

I should have known she wouldn't be deterred for long. She handed me the container and then went over to the couch to stuff my laptop in my bag, because the word "boundaries" wasn't even a concept for her.

"Let me know how it goes. And don't worry too much. He'll love the food! Dominicans are suckers for a man who can cook!"

I threw my hands up as she zipped up my bag. "I didn't make this though, and I'm not sure about the drink, Carmen," I said, standing there like an idiot until she almost physically pushed me out the door.

"He'll appreciate you have friends who cook, and you're making too big of a deal out of this, Jude. It's just a drink, hon." She looked at me like she had no clue what to do with me.

It wasn't unfair though, because I *was* making way too big of a deal out of this. Why couldn't I have a drink with someone I liked?

I deflated and turned to open her door. "Fine. I'll go."

She immediately perked up. "Finally! I was starting to think I was going to have to take matters into my own hands and go to his truck tomorrow for a chat."

"You wouldn't."

"Ha."

I let her have the last word, because goading her was not going to help, so I walked to my car, trying to text Nesto one handed. I was going to do this. I wanted to see him and that was the end of it.

Jude: Hey, so I'm just leaving Carmen's if you're still up for that drink.

I got a response almost immediately.

Nesto: Yes! You know where I am. My place is the first door on the left.

Jude: Great, I'll see you in twenty minutes. Warning: Carmen made me take some leftovers to bring you.

Nesto: That's perfect. I've been trying out new sauces for the truck, and haven't made any dinner yet. *smiley face with tongue sticking out*

I typed a See you soon and got in my car.

I was still not sure if this was a great idea. I had too many feelings already. Regardless I powered up the car and drove toward Trumansburg and Nesto.

* * *

I walked up to Nesto's apartment clutching the container of ribs and polenta for dear life. When I got up to the landing I saw him standing by the door in only basketball shorts, grinning like he knew exactly the effect his naked torso would have on me.

I scoffed. "You're evil."

He laughed, then touched the tip of his tongue to his upper lip. Every time he did that my stomach dropped down somewhere by my feet and the urge to kiss him was practically unbearable.

He stepped aside as I passed by, eyeing me up and down as I walked in.

"Glad you made it. You look good, Jude."

"You've said that."

"It bears repeating."

For fuck's sake.

His sublet was a pretty spacious loft, the side facing the street was one big glass window. I could see my house just down the street and the woods I ran in just beyond. There was a small couch, a desk area, and what looked like a sleeping space behind some curtains in the left corner. The person who lived here must like photography because there were beautiful scenes from local parks all over the walls.

"This place is great," I said, handing him the container from Carmen.

"It is, I lucked out, and the rent is less than half of what I paid for my place in the city." We stood in silence for a moment and then Nesto nodded toward the kitchen area. "I have wine and beer, both local," he said with a grin.

"Wow, embracing the 'Eat and Drink Local' movement already."

He shrugged. "I adapt quickly."

"A valuable life skill. I'll have a glass of white if you have it. If not, a beer."

"I have a chilled rosé."

"That sounds great."

With a nod, Nesto went to the fridge to get our drinks. After a minute he handed me my glass and sat on the couch with the container. He immediately dug in, taking a big bite of the ribs. He chewed a couple of times and then put his head back, sighing contentedly.

"This is great. Thanks so much." He gave me a little smile and stabbed another bite of meat. "Tell Carmen I may have to steal this recipe for the truck. I was too tired to stop at the store on the way home, so I figured I'd order something, but nothing delivers after seven p.m."

"Nope, it's one of the downsides of living out here. Nothing like the city, or even Ithaca." I was trying to make conversation, but Nesto shirtless was a distraction. He had turned down the lights in the room too, so he was half in shadow. His chest was sculpted and deeply tanned, it looked like brushed bronze. He also kept running his hand over his left pec and every time he did, my eyes would follow his hand's movement. I tried to make out the tattoo he had there, but his hand blocked my view. He had other ones, two quotes in fine black cursive font, one on each forearm. I'd read them the night at the bar, when he pulled back the sleeves of the shirt he'd been wearing.

I sat up on the other end of the couch and pointed at them. "Tell me about your tattoos."

He finished swallowing, placed the container on the table, and extended his arms out, palms facing up. "Well, these two are lyrics from a song my mom used to listen to a lot when I was a kid. It's from a Spanish artist, his name is Joan Manuel Serrat. It's from a song called *Cantares*."

I read out loud, running my fingers over the inked words as I went. On the left, *Caminante no hay camino,* and on the right, *Se hace camino al andar.* "Walker there is no path, you make the path as you walk."

I looked up at him and smiled. "I love that."

"It's pretty much our family mantra. You just keep going. You make the way." He said it with a nod and ran a hand over his chest again.

Looking at his skin, I remembered how warm it felt under my hands when I'd touched it. The craving to reach out, feel him under my fingers, made me shiver. We sat there silently for a few moments as Nesto ate. When the container was half full, he stood and put the lid back on before putting it in the fridge.

He came back to the couch and sat closer, so our bodies were almost touching. He took a sip of his beer, and then leaned in. He asked in a husky whisper, "Where did you learn Spanish? I've been meaning to ask, but every time I see you my mind starts running in a million directions." The rueful smile on his lips made me want to kiss him so badly.

I looked down and thought of giving him one of my usual evasive answers. Those unnecessary walls I always put up to avoid having to say too much about myself. My usual "oh just in school" answer seemed disingenuous now, with Nesto so close, his skin brushing mine, and his eyes full of interest.

"I lived in Honduras for a year after high school. I learned there mostly, but over the years I've tried to practice, so I don't lose it. Watch movies, read and listen to music in Spanish. Stuff like that."

"Did you do a study abroad program?"

I almost said yes, but again for some reason I didn't want to go down that road with him. To lie by omission or agree with whatever he was saying to avoid getting into my family baggage.

"No, I went on a mission trip through the church my family went to growing up. They, ah, have an ongoing program there and sometimes younger members of the congregation go for a few months, or even a few years to help with the projects they have."

His eyes widened at my explanation, like he wasn't sure what to make of what I said. "Oh wow, that sounds pretty intense."

I shrugged uncomfortably, not sure how to proceed. "Working for the church wasn't great." I wondered what he would think about the way our church moved in on the locals, bribing poor families to join the congregation with food and then tried to brainwash them once they were in.

"I loved the people I met though, and travelling around Honduras and some of the other countries in Central America was amazing. Learning Spanish was also one of the best things I've ever done. It's been so useful in my work." I couldn't help but smile remembering the people I'd met there.

"It's also kind of magical, knowing Spanish. Feels like I have an in to a universe people who don't speak the language miss out on, you know?"

His face lit up as I talked and he looked at me with curious eyes. "Oh. How's that?"

"Well, I get to experience books, music, artists, I otherwise wouldn't. Like reading Borges in the original language, listening to musicians who only record in Spanish. It's a whole other world."

His face glowed from my words. "I know. I always think about what it would be like for those people who look at our brown skin and only see interlopers, to actually learn about all the treasures we've brought with us. Our colors, our words, our songs, our stories even. Because most of us, we want to share them, we want them to be part of this place too."

An impulse moved me to put my hand against his face. I tried to imagine what it would be like to have people dismiss you out of hand because of the color of your skin, or the place you were born. To have to put up with people like Misty diminishing your entire culture as unimportant. He was so beautiful, and his face looked so open, so earnest. I almost told him I wanted to hear all of it, to know him. I almost said, "*I* want you here" even though it felt sort of ridiculous.

After a moment Nesto took my hand from his face and kissed the palm. Just a brush of his lips, but the sensation moved through my body like thunder. I trembled, knowing what was about to happen. I looked at him and tried to focus on the conversation, when he leaned down and kissed me. Just grazing of lips again, but the effect was fire running through my veins. Every part of me lit up when Nesto was near. He pulled back and whispered softly in my ear, "Is this okay? Can I kiss you again?"

I nodded and pushed in closer, turning so I could wrap my arms around his neck. He pulled me so I was leaning on him and started kissing me again. This time a lot hungrier, with tongue and teeth. Our ragged breaths were the only sound in the room as we frantically bit and sucked on each other's lips.

His skin was so hot under my hands, and there was so much of it to touch. I had forgotten what it could be like to be overwhelmed by the feel of another body. How their closeness and their breath on you could make yours catch. He groaned and moved us again until I was lying under him on the couch.

"Ever since that night at Ophelia's I haven't stopped thinking about this mouth." He ran his hand down and brushed against my hard cock as he looked at me with an intensity that made me burn. "I wondered how you'd taste."

The idea of having his mouth on me made mine water. All I could do was nod and moan as his hand slipped under my shirt up to my chest. He took my nipple between his fingers and pinched, then he ran his teeth and tongue up and down my neck making me gasp.

"Nesto."

"Lift your arms, baby." I did and he pulled my shirt over my head. I was panting and shivering as he touched and kissed everywhere.

"I wanna see what you have for me here," he said as he ran his hand over my crotch, and I nodded frantically, wanting him to get on with things. My reluctance from earlier floating away with each touch.

"Tell me how much you want my hands on you, Jude." He ran his teeth over my neck, nipping at my collarbone.

I heard myself speak in a breathless voice. "Just keep touching me. You feel so good."

"I bet you'd like it if I played with your balls, maybe I'll wet my finger and play with your hole." My body jolted like I'd been shocked. He gave me a dirty look as he undid my fly and squeezed my cock. I was so hard I was afraid I was going to come any second, but still I couldn't speak. I opened my eyes to let Nesto see how good he was making me feel.

"Mmm you're wet and hard for me, papí." He started stroking me off, all the while moving his tongue inside my mouth and sucking on my lips as he went.

I returned the favor by nipping on that mouth, which was becoming an obsession. His lips felt so good on my skin, like I would feel them for days on every spot they touched my body. As he moved his hand faster, running his thumb over the head of my cock, I felt my orgasm build, panting out short breaths as he stroked me.

"God, you look so hot like this. Fuck my hand, baby, come on." He pushed up so he has kneeling in front of me, and kept jerking me off with one hand while he brought the other one up to my mouth, pushing his thumb inside. I sucked on it hard, and after a moment he popped it out and brought it down, right under my balls. He just grazed my hole and my orgasm hit, my vision going white and that sweet liquid sensation flooding my ass and groin. I gasped as a shudder ran through my body.

I opened my eyes to see Nesto looking at me, his face hungry.

"Your eyes look so blue right now," he said as he got his cock out of his shorts and grabbed himself. With his hands covered in my come, he started stroking. As he thrust into his hand, he moved his hips fast, circling them in a tight grind. I imagined him working himself into my body in the same way, and a whimper escaped my throat.

I moved my hand up to where his was on his chest and touched it, then up to his face and put my thumb in his mouth. He sucked it in and groaned, then closed his eyes and threw his head back, lost to his pleasure. After a few more strokes, he doubled over, a look of exquisite pain on his face. When it was over, he slumped on top of me and turned to kiss me again. For a few minutes we touched lazily, running our hands all over each other. We were a mess, but I didn't want to move.

We shifted around on the couch so he was wedged against the back, looking down on me, as I lay my head on the armrest. He was beautiful, his skin flushed with red, and his lips swollen from my kisses. In that moment everything about Nesto seemed amplified to me, like my senses had woken up for his skin.

He was running his hand over my chest and suddenly said, "Tell me more about Honduras."

I didn't want to ruin the mood by talking about some of the sad things that came to mind, so I stayed quiet as I thought of what to say.

"Honduras was beautiful and a little heartbreaking, but mostly beautiful."

He hummed as I touched the tattoo on his chest. It started at his rib cage and took up most of his left pectoral muscle. It was a forearm that ended in a half-open hand, holding up a beating heart, right over his real one. The heart bore the stars and stripes of the U.S. flag, and another flag I supposed was the Dominican one, its colors also red, white and blue. They blended into each other, so it was hard to tell where one started and the other one ended. Beautifully done with red, white and blue drops dripping all the way down the arm.

"Tell me about this first, it's quite something," I said as I ran my fingers over it.

He put his hand over mine and came down pressing our mouths together, like we couldn't move on to the next thing until he'd kissed me.

"You don't like talking about yourself very much. I'll let you get away with changing the subject...for now." I groaned and he laughed. "I got this one done with the guys. We all have the same one, well theirs have their own flags. We got it from the same artist, the year we all turned twenty-one."

I ran my hand over it again, admiring the art and his strong, proud body. "Why did you guys decide to get it?"

He smiled as he touched his chest on the spot where the tattoo was. "We were all in college back then and talking a lot about how hard it felt to navigate our worlds sometimes. We were American, but we had this other side to us too." When he spoke, his eye blazed with passion.

"It always seemed like for one to thrive the other one needed to be left behind. What we wanted was for them to blend. We were American, but our skin, our names, gave us away as strangers. Our struggle was in whether we could find the balance of feeling like we belonged here without letting go of our roots."

He grimaced then said, "When all you hear is how your people are criminals, or that they're only here to mooch off the government, it can be hard to lift that side up, you know? But our parents came here with nothing and worked hard. Gave us good lives. We *had* to be proud of that, of them. So, we got the tattoos to remind ourselves we were always both."

"You *should* be proud." I certainly understood what it was like to feel as if you were being pulled in two different directions. Once again my mouth started moving before I could think of what I was saying.

"Our church was really conservative and our pastor was horrible. He used his pulpit to spew out the most bigoted vitriol. Every Sunday we sat there hearing him rant about whatever group of people or thing he'd decided was the latest menace threatening *our way of life*." I shuddered at the memories of him shouting about AIDS and how people deserved to die, but Nesto's warm and steady hands on me kept me talking.

"He spent hours up there bellowing about sin and retribution. After I realized I was gay, I'd sit there sick to my stomach, hating myself and listening to him talk about all the ways in which I was an abomination."

I felt Nesto's head shaking above mine. "God that sounds awful. I'm so sorry you had to go through that."

I tipped my head up to look at him and his eyes, which usually sparkled with humor, were full of concern. I lifted my hand to touch his face again. "Thanks for saying that. I was terrified people would find out about me. That's why I decided to go to Honduras. I thought if I got away for a while then maybe I could breathe, you know?"

Nesto nodded silently and squeezed his arms around me.

How could he feel this familiar, this comforting already?

"I got there and just the distance from all of it felt

like such a relief. Even though the missionaries who ran the church down there were even more intense than the people in our home church, at least I could travel and get to know Honduras. Safety is an issue down there, not just for tourists or expats, but everyone. Especially young people in poor families are so vulnerable."

I sighed. "Being there helped me gain a lot of perspective about what was important, and of how many choices I actually had. It's also so beautiful there. Some places so lovely they took my breath away." I exhaled, worn out from bringing back things I hadn't thought of in so long.

"Sounds like you were dealing with so much all on your own, Jude. That takes a lot of courage."

I scoffed remembering those times. "I didn't feel very courageous back then. I didn't come out of the closet for a long time after I left Honduras, but when I got back, my perspective had shifted. I was sure I wasn't the issue. The problem was how our church and our community chose to look at the world. Like something scary we needed to either control or keep at bay. I was afraid of losing my family, so I stayed, until I couldn't anymore. But I knew there was nothing wrong with me."

Nesto's arms were tight around me as he spoke. "You're fucking right about that. You're amazing, and I can't tell you how glad I am you took pity on me and came over tonight. I don't think I could take one more Netflix binge with my mom and sister." I could tell he knew how drained I was from this conversation and was so grateful for his attempt to lighten the mood. I looked up at him again not bothering to hide the smile on my face. "I'm glad I came over too, although Netflix with your mom and sister sounds nice."

He gave me that cheeky grin that made my knees weak. "It is, but this is better."

I didn't respond, just nodded and pressed against him, because with the way I was feeling I was going to say something ridiculous.

I felt weightless in Nesto's arms, like I could let go of all my hang-ups.

"You feel so good," Nesto said in a husky voice and sighed. "I wish I didn't have to get up so early."

Immediately I started trying to dislodge from him.

"No wait, I'm not throwing you out. You're good right here. Stay."

I turned and kissed him on the cheek. "I have to get going too. I have a million things to do this week. I'm starting to stress that my project may not get approved."

He raised his eyebrows like I'd said something outrageous. "What? Of course it will. I was ready to fund it myself after hearing you talk about it." I turned around to face him and after I put my t-shirt back on, he moved in to kiss me again. He licked into my mouth, his tongue silky against mine.

It was so easy to give in to the way Nesto made me feel.

After a few more kisses, I pulled back and sighed. "It's very hard to focus when you do that."

He laughed and brushed my lips with his thumb. "That mouth of yours is hard to resist, next time I'd like to see it around my cock."

I groaned and my skin felt hot, I knew I had to be turning red. "Next time." I sounded breathless.

I gave him one last kiss and stood, starting for the

door. He followed and gave me a squeeze when we got there.

"Hasta la proxima," he said with a nod. "I'll text you tomorrow, maybe we can have a drink after work?"

I wanted to and I almost said yes, but the intensity of my desire to see him checked me.

I smiled anyway to soften my answer. "Maybe. It's so busy right now."

His eyebrows dipped, a vexed expression on his face. He wasn't the only one. I wanted to backtrack, not close that door completely, even though I still wasn't sure what I was doing with Nesto. "Text me tomorrow. It might not be as crazy."

His shoulders relaxed at my offer. "Okay, I will." He leaned down to peck me on the cheek and I slipped out of his apartment.

As I got to the sidewalk I looked up and saw him watching me from his big windows. He lifted his hand in a wave and I returned it, smiling up at him. I started walking, waiting for the feelings of unease from a moment ago to return, but instead what I felt was anticipation, and *that* should have scared me. I made my way home, waiting for the guilt that usually accompanied my attempts to get close to someone to sink in.

The feeling never came.

Chapter Nine

Nesto

Man, I was in over my head with this gringo. Who gets that worked up over leftovers? I was standing by the window, watching him walk home and feeling things I had no business feeling for a guy I barely knew. But when I saw him standing in my doorway, looking so unsure, I just wanted to drag him inside and wreck him. He was so skittish, he pulled back as if he needed to keep himself in check. and I wanted to know why. What hurt was he protecting himself from?

There were no two ways about it, Jude was going to be a distraction.

As I went back to the couch my phone started buzzing on the coffee table. I looked down and saw Camilo's face on the screen and grinned. Those fools were probably half drunk and wanting to rag on me for fucking off to the *campo*. I took the call and Milo immediately appeared in the center of the screen, with half of Patrice's face on the right, and Juanpa's behind them.

"What's good, pa? You staying out of trouble up there in the boonies?" Juanpa shouted, taking the phone from Milo and commandeering the call.

"¡Dimelo tiguere! Where you fools at?" I said, unable to control the grin taking over my face.

Milo piped in from behind, pushing on Juanpa's head. "Uh, forget our location for the moment and tell us why you have sex hair and a hickey on your neck." His face was in a hilarious sneer. "Jesus, you're a skank, you just got there!"

Juanpa grinned, shaking his head. "Damn, it's true though. You've been there for like a week, and you're already going through them frat boys up north."

"You two are extra as fuck. What's a grown ass man like me going to do with a frat boy? And where did Patrice go? He didn't even say hi!"

Milo rolled his eyes. "You know him, control freak. He went to argue about the bill."

Milo had his curly hair in a man bun thing, and was wearing thick eyeliner around his eyes. His tight military-green shirt was unbuttoned so low I could see the top of his chest piece. Seeing his tattoo, exactly like mine, but with the colors of the Jamaican and Cuban flags sent a wave of homesickness through me.

I missed my friends.

I noticed they were in a familiar rooftop bar, and then saw Milo looking to the side. He was giving someone off-screen some serious "papi, come here" eyes. That paired up with the eyeliner and shirt could only mean one thing.

"Holy shit, J, did you two let Milo drag you to The Americano again so he could thirst after the bartender he fucked last summer?" I shook my head hollering. "No loco. No."

Milo flashed me the finger, his face still turned the other way, and Juanpa bared his teeth in our friend's direction. "He promised us dinner at Chop Shop but we let this pendejo drag us here instead, and we still haven't eaten. You know how he gets. He's been eye-fucking the dude for the last hour, but has he gone to talk to him? No. Every time the guy tries to get his attention he turns around and ignores him. It's a fucking drag, man."

As Juanpa ranted Patrice came back into the screen, his ebony skin contrasting with Juanpa's light brown complexion. As usual he bypassed our banter and went straight to the point.

"Nesto, are you already diverting from the plan to get laid, mi hermano?" He shook his head, looking half amused and half disappointed. "How's the truck doing? Do you need us to come up and help again?"

Patrice's long locs were in a half knot. The stark features of his face and the small stud on his nose giving him a fierce appearance, his serious expression softened only by the tiniest tilt of his lips.

I was about to assure him I had my shit together over here when Milo came back on the screen, pushing his way in. He was at least a head shorter than Patrice, so he must have been on his tiptoes. "Of course, just tell us when to come up if you need anything and we're there! Are you doing okay? How are Nurys and Minerva?"

I saw Juanpa nodding behind him in assent, he was working his Drake doppelganger thing tonight. With two huge studs in his ears and a black Hood by Air sweatshirt that said *Anonymous, Everything You've Heard is True*, in big white font. His fade looked fresh too, that line up so sharp it could give you a papercut.

All of us were so different, how we carried ourselves and how we approached things, but we would do anything for each other. I swallowed hard and opened my mouth before I started bawling.

"It's all good, man. Great, actually. Things are going smoothly with the truck other than a few annoying run-ins with some white people foolishness." I shook my head, not wanting to get into the Misty thing.

"Hey actually, there is one gig this summer I'll need help with, if you can make it. It's a beer and wine festival in a few weekends. OuNYe will be a vendor. They're expecting to have a few thousand people coming through, so if you punks are up for it, I could use the free labor."

Camilo was nodding his head furiously as I talked. "I'm in. I love it up there in the summer. It was too short when we came up with you for the move." Then he looked at the other two. "And I'm sure these losers have nothing going on."

Juanpa rolled his eyes. "Can you say anything without some sort of insult, Camilo? You're so fucking abrasive."

"Ooh are we using our Big Boy words today, Juan Pablo?"

"Fuck you, Milo."

"Can you two shut up?" Patrice muttered.

"Okay! Okay! Calma pueblo. No fighting. Damn, y'all are mad salty tonight. See what you did, Camilo?" I said, pointing at Juanpa's scowl. "You got Juanpa in the hangry zone, pa. You need to get him some food before he hurts somebody."

Milo opened his mouth probably to curse me out, but I cut him off again. "Now back to what we were discussing. The gig's in a few weeks. I'll send you guys the details when I get them. I miss you knuckleheads."

Milo's face softened and nodded. "Sounds good.

We'll be there." Then casually he slipped in, "Tell us who gave you sex hair, though. We can still see the hickey." He took the phone from Patrice and went to sit down.

"I want a full report." I could see him primly crossing his legs like he had all the time in the world. Milo never changed, a hopeless romantic, eager to hear someone, anyone, was struck by lightning and found love overnight, so he could hold on to the wish he'd be struck someday too.

"It's just a little thing right now." I could've said more, told them about what had been going through my head before they called. But for the first time ever I didn't share every detail with my friends. I felt protective of what I was feeling for Jude, and I didn't want to give it away to be deconstructed or examined.

I shrugged, going for lightness. "We'll see how it goes. It's a guy from town, he works at the library close to where I have the truck during the week. Turns out he lives just down the street from the place I'm subletting. So, he came over tonight...things happened."

Juanpa chuckled while Milo cut his eyes at me. "Of course you'd move into an apartment where you can get some culo delivered right to your doorstep. Figures."

Laughing, I teased, "Some of us are just that good, besides it's about the only thing a motherfucker can get delivered out here, for real." They cackled at that. "He's a nice guy, though. Really funny. And, man, the dude is a blanquito, like W-H-I-T-E, but his Spanish is mad good. He came to the truck the first day, and flirted with me like a fucking pro, all in Spanish," I said, unable to suppress the grin on my face.

Milo's face got soft again. "Aww that's sweet. He sounds great."

Patrice piped in from the side. "Don't get distracted, Nesto. You left here with a plan."

Juanpa rolled his eyes again. If he kept it up he was going to give himself a seizure. "Damn, P, you got no chill, man. Why do you have to be so damn intense all the fucking time? He just said the dude was hot, he didn't say they were eloping to Niagara Falls or some shit. You need to take it down a notch, my man. Fuck."

Patrice just gave him the stone face and looked back at me on the screen. They really needed to get Juanpa some food, though.

"Just making sure Nesto keeps his head on straight up there."

Patrice was right. I came here with a plan and I needed to stick to it. "Nah, it's okay. He's right. But it's nothing serious at the moment, and the business comes first. Full stop."

Patrice nodded as he ignored Milo's stank face. "Good."

Juanpa took the phone away from Milo and said, "Okay, tiguere, we gotta bounce. It's getting late and I have to be at the stadium ass early. Unlike the student here, or the social worker I need to keep regular hours."

Juanpa was a physical therapist for the Yankees and had a hectic schedule during the season. I was surprised he was even out on a Sunday this time of year. Patrice being a PhD student had a lot more flexible schedule, although he worked every day, at all times, and was an anxious mess whenever he wasn't. Milo was our activist, and worked for a local nonprofit, which provided services for survivors of domestic violence.

They were all very busy, but Juanpa never wasted

an opportunity to flex about the job with the Yankees. Couldn't blame the guy, for a boy from the Bronx, bragging rights were in order. That didn't stop both Patrice and Milo from cursing him out though. I laughed at their antics before we all said our goodbyes.

I ended the call feeling a little melancholy for my friends and the life I would give up if I decided to stay here in Ithaca. I felt unsure about everything. What was I doing here? Why was I leaving a life which fit me so well for something that could fail?

For some reason Jude's face kept coming up as the answer to all those questions. But I tamped that shit down immediately because it felt stupid and too fast. We barely knew each other, and as I'd said to myself and other people a million times, I was here for other reasons.

Then why did things going well with Jude seem to feel just as important as OuNYe succeeding?

Jude

There was a lot of brown skin flashing on the screen of my phone, and I went for it so fast I almost spilled coffee all over my desk.

"Shit!" I yelled after I knocked over an empty water bottle and bumped my desk chair. After settling down, I opened the screen and saw a text from Nesto, it was pointless to try to hide my smile as I read.

Looks like I got marked up last night, wonder how that happened...you better hope my t-shirt covers it or it's payback if I see you tonight.

The image was a shot of his chest, right on his collarbone above his tattoo there was a little red bruise, it wasn't very big, but it was definitely a bite. I tried to overlook that "if" on his message glaring at me like a beacon, and responded, chuckling as I typed.

You must have the wrong person. I have no idea how that got there.

I was grinning like an idiot staring at the three floating dots as Nesto typed his message.

I'll make sure to fill you in on how this sort of thing happens then. I'm still up for that drink if you change your mind.

Why could I not just say yes? I had nothing going on tonight. I could meet him for a drink. I could see him again.

It's what I wanted.

I'm not sure. I have a packed day today, but I'll text you when I leave the library.

The heat on my face and the churning in my stomach, as I waited for the rebuff I was sure would come was a twisted comfort. Because a man like that didn't need to beg anyone for a drink.

Those three dots lingered for what felt like hours, and by the time the bubble with his message appeared on the screen I was lightheaded from holding my breath.

You just let me know. I'm here. Have a good day Jude. <3 TTYL

Dammit.

You too.

I closed my phone and sat there for a minute, feeling mildly nauseated with dread and anticipation. I tried to think back to a time when anything had felt this inevitable, this important, and I came up blank.

Three years after keeping myself at a safe distance from anything involving messy feelings, Nesto was making me want to be bold, and that terrified me.

I returned from my thoughts, and saw Carmen staring at me with a funny look. She came over and sat on my desk with her arms crossed. "Okay, spill. What's all this grinning, then frowning, then staring into space looking spooked about? I know at least some of it must be Nesto. How did it go last night?"

Her pushiness truly knew no bounds.

"Yes, some of it was in fact Nesto. Last night was nice." I cleared my throat.

"Ooooh." She nodded with a smirk, like I said something very scandalous. "*Nice*, huh? I assume by that you mean sex."

I blushed again and looked away. Because even though I was thirty years old, it was still pretty embarrassing to talk about sex with other people, even my best friend.

"Well, I wouldn't say *full on* sex, but we kissed and fooled around a bit. It was good, he's attentive and gentle, and very intense." I groaned, closing my eyes.

"It was amazing and I can't stop thinking about him, which is a problem because I'm not really looking to get involved. He wants to go for another drink tonight, and I don't know." I squeezed my eyes shut and let out an agonized breath. "I don't think this is a good idea."

I could tell she was about to go on a monologue about my stupid self-imposed love drought, but I wasn't doing that this morning, so I held up my hand before she started. "I know what you're going to say. I can lecture myself inside my head if you like, but I need to get back to work, and so do you." I turned toward my keyboard, smiling placidly. Carmen would just have to keep her opinions to herself for now.

"Oh, no you don't. Don't do that shit where you pretend everything is fine, but you're actually a ball of anxiety. Hon, what's the harm in getting to know him a bit? Besides—" Carmen stopped talking and looked up, her face immediately going icy.

"Hi, Misty. Can we help you with anything?"

Great. The final nail for the coffin carrying my Nesto afterglow had arrived.

I sighed and looked in the direction of the door and saw her walk in. She was in her usual workout-chic attire. How she got away with wearing yoga pants to work seventy-five percent of the time was a mystery to me. Today she was wearing a top in a particularly vision-searing shade of orange.

Misty was in her fifties, with skin so fair you could see the veins. She was one of those women who fought a hard and bloody battle against aging, and it showed. Her face was tight and stretched from all the work she'd gotten done, and she was always talking about her workout routines and beauty treatments.

She was married to one of the big real estate developers in the area, and as she regularly let us know, she worked for the library as a favor. She was good at her job, I gave her that, but it came at a cost because she antagonized everyone.

"Hi there. Working hard I see." She flashed us both with a smile that made my entire body shudder. "Carmen, I was surprised I didn't see you getting lunch with Jude yesterday at the new 'ethnic' truck he seems to like so much."

She used air quotes for "ethnic."

"It looked like it was doing a lot of business. Too bad there are like three Mexican places in town already; they should enjoy the business while it lasts."

Carmen immediately objected. "It's not Mexican food, Misty. It's *Caribbean* food, which is nowhere near the same thing. Have you even eaten there yet?"

She made a face like Carmen just asked her if she liked eating dirt. "Oh no, I'm not really into foreign foods. I like more authentic American fare."

I spoke up, trying to keep the edge out of my voice. "OuNYe's food *is* American, Misty. It's made in this country, by people who live here. That's what American is."

She produced another one of those shark smiles. "So inclusive," she quipped, her voice dripping with condescension. "You two are certainly well-informed. I tried to talk to the man who works there when he first came to town. Being on the city council I need to make sure everything is above board with people doing business here."

God, she pissed me off so much.

She knew perfectly well Nesto was the owner of the truck. He hadn't mentioned she'd asked about his documents. How the hell did she think that was okay? She probably justified it to herself because he was brown, and to her all brown people were "illegals." I knew I shouldn't get in her face because of the mobile library project, but this was too much.

I got up so we were at eye level. "If you mean Nesto, he doesn't work there, he *owns* the truck. As far as I know he has everything in order to operate his business. Actually, the truck has been doing great and he's already getting requests to work the summer festivals. You saw it yourself at the market yesterday."

Her eyes widened when I mentioned the festivals because her son probably hadn't gotten a single invitation.

"You certainly seem to know a lot about him, Jude," she said, giving me a sour look.

"He's a friend, and also very serious about making his business take off here in Ithaca, so I expect you'll be seeing his truck around for a while."

Behind me Carmen said, "We're trying to work here, Misty. So unless you have something you need." She moved her hands in a shooing motion in the direction of the door.

"Oh no," she said, still glaring at us. As she started for the door she looked at me. "Just checking in. I saw you sent out a draft of your proposal first thing this morning. Hopefully it'll work out for you this year. It's so hard for the board to figure out what to prioritize; they need a lot of guidance."

She was threatening me. She was letting me know she wasn't above interfering with my project.

"I'm pretty confident in what I sent them. I'm looking forward to hearing their thoughts."

"Of course," she interjected, her voice heavy with animosity. "Well, I have to get going. I'm meeting with Martha. I need to remind her we need to be cautious about the new projects we take on this year, with so many of these funding cuts, and all." Our Executive Director was not gullible enough to shelve a project just because Misty told her to, but the way she looked at me when she said it sent a chill down my spine. "See you guys later. Don't work too hard." With that, she turned around and left.

"Damn, but that woman is a bitch, is she actually threatening you about the project because she saw you hanging out with Nesto? What the hell is her problem?" Carmen asked exasperated.

I shook my head, stunned by how vile Misty could be. "You know she thinks she's living in a *Survivor* episode. She's probably scheming how to fuck with Nesto too because he's 'competition.'"

I went back to my desk, feeling out of sorts from the confrontation with Misty. "The level of privilege of that woman is unreal. She's pissed because people are doing better than her son, yet he opens the truck when he feels like it, and when he does, serves shitty overpriced food. But in her mind, he's still entitled to do better than people who are working their ass off. How do people even get like this?"

Carmen sighed wearily. "Being rich and mean certainly doesn't help matters. It's typical," she said, crossing her arms, her face sullen. "Misty is at all the fundraisers, talking about the plight of this minority or that vulnerable group until her tongue falls out. But only as long as those people stay in their place, as her 'good person' talking points. As soon as she personally has to make space for any them, all of it goes out the window and she's back on her homestead guarding her shit to the death."

I nodded, feeling exhausted. "Too true."

"Black and brown people causes are extremely nice on a tote bag, or for making you feel better than your country club friends on Facebook. But actually seeing them as human beings who should get to have the same things you do? Oh no, fuck that shit, there's not enough to go around."

I let out a long breath. "This all makes me so damn tired."

Carmen just looked at me sadly. "Babe, at least you still get to walk into all this in your white skin. The rest of us have to go out there in our melanated armors, and suck it up while working five times harder to get a tenth of what she got just for breathing."

I came over and hugged her, she was usually the one going for the hugs, but dammit I needed one. "Well, if there was any happy left after my make-out session with Nesto last night, this little interlude with Misty killed it dead." I pouted while Carmen gave me a tired smile as we pulled apart. "I'm serious, Carmen, I don't want to be a reason for Nesto to get on her radar. Misty is petty and mean. I should cool things off with him."

Carmen looked at me with disbelief. "Are you serious?"

I shrugged, feeling stupid that Misty got under my skin like she did. "Maybe, I mean, there's nothing going on between us really, and I don't want to make problems for him."

"Babe, you're not. You won't. Nesto is perfectly capable of looking out for himself and no matter what she thinks, Misty doesn't actually run this town." She tilted her head in the direction of the street where Nesto's truck was probably parked at that very moment. "His food is excellent and he works hard. He'll be fine, and so will you for that matter. The board will see the light."

I gave her a grateful look. Her unrelenting optimism went a long way to calm my self-doubt in moments like this. "Okay. Maybe I'll meet up with him for a drink after all, but just as friends."

She rolled her eyes at my "just friends" statement but still clapped her hands like I'd told her the best news ever. "Good for you. Don't let her mess with your happy." She walked back to her desk and pointed at her monitor. "I'm in an ass-kicking mood, so I might as well tackle this proposal to get the bilingual social worker for the library I've been begging for, and may finally get."

"Go for it. I'm going to try and do some work and not worry about the board hating my proposal."

Carmen gave me a distracted thumbs-up, already focused on her work. I sat down at my desk and before I talked myself out of it, texted Nesto.

Maybe tomorrow?

His response came within seconds.

You just tell me what time and where. I'll be there.

My face heated again and I felt my lips stretching into a wide smile.

I will.

I hoped the Misty interactions would be at a minimum this week, but mostly I hoped both Nesto and I stayed off her shit list.

Chapter Ten

Nesto

"Did you tell me to meet you at a bowling alley?" I gripped my phone and grinned like an idiot as I made my way to meet Jude.

"Yes, I did. It's less than a five-minute walk from both our houses and they have a great bar."

I felt a warmth radiating through my chest just from hearing his voice. After his brush-off yesterday, I'd almost given up on seeing him again. Then I got a message from him almost at five asking if I wanted to meet up. I hadn't seen him since he left my house Sunday night. Only two days, but it felt longer. With the phone pressed against my ear, I covered the few hundred yards from my building to the bowling alley. The desire to see him practically propelling me to the door.

"I'm about to walk in then. See you soon." I ended the call with a flutter in my chest. I was hungry for the sight of him. To touch him. More excited than I'd felt about anyone in a long time.

I walked into the bowling alley and looked around. I knew the place had only been open a couple of months. It had a retro vibe, which seemed to be a theme around here. Lots of gleaming wood and chrome. I glanced around and spotted Jude sitting at the bar, sipping a pint of dark beer. He was wearing a red-and-white gingham shirt with gray slacks. His blond curls rumpled, like they always seemed to be at the end of the day.

I stopped for a moment to look at him. He was reading something on his phone, his face serious, totally focused. He seemed unaffected by the people talking around him, the music coming from the speakers or the sounds of bowling balls crashing against the pins.

He was a peaceful and quiet presence amongst all the noise and movement. I probably would've stood there for ages, just watching him, but as if he could feel my eyes on him, after a few seconds he glanced up and saw me. The smile that broke out on his face when he did lit me up. I knew I probably had a carbon copy of it on my own face as I walked toward him.

When I got to him I put my hand under his chin, tipping his head up before I leaned in for a kiss, without giving it a second thought. He seemed a little startled when I pulled back and I felt like a jackass. What if he didn't want people to see us kissing? Maybe he wasn't out in town. Maybe he didn't want this at all.

I didn't have the right to do that and I rushed to apologize. "I'm sorry, I should've asked if it was okay for me to kiss you."

"It's okay." He looked down as a blush worked itself up his neck, making me want to maul him.

"I don't know what it is about you, Jude Fuller. I can usually keep my shit together when I like a guy, but when I see you all I want to do is get my hands on you." I sounded flustered even to my own ears. I expected him to come back with a salty reply like he usually did, but he just sat there quietly. There was something a little off, like he was holding himself back. The idea of losing the closeness we'd had a few nights ago made me uneasy. I rushed to say something that would bring back some of the comfort we'd had.

"Also someone owes me, since they left this on me the other night." I pulled on the neck of my t-shirt and exposed the skin where I had the little bite mark. Jude's neck and face went bright red, then he took a big gulp of his beer and turned so he was facing away from me.

"Like I said, I have no clue how that got there." I could see the small smile he was biting back, and it was like the sun was coming out after total darkness. His shoulders relaxed and I could tell he was a little pleased with himself.

"You're a bad influence, Ernesto Vasquez." His tone was easy again and the warmth in my chest from being the one to bring that out in him was a revelation.

I needed to calm down before I really did something reckless and pushed him too far. So, I turned my attention to getting a drink and figuring out our plan for the evening.

I pointed to his beer. "What are you having?"

It took him a moment to react, but then he picked up the glass and offered it to me. "It's a chocolate stout. Local of course." The smile he gave me was radiant, sharing an inside joke. I didn't respond, caught off guard by how much I already felt for Jude.

I cleared my throat and turned to the bartender. "I'll have what he's having." She winked at me as she grabbed a pint glass. "You got it."

After I got my drink I stood next to him leaning in

close. I'd gone home to change after work, but I'd worn one of my OuNYe hats.

Had to stay on brand.

Jude pointed his glass in the direction of my head.

"How did the truck do yesterday?" He looked so serious, like my answer really mattered to him.

"Good. The B&B wants us to do dinner there twice a week now, instead of just Fridays. I met with them today to get it all on paper. They said they're trying a few different trucks, but want to find a few to be there on certain nights for the long-haul, which would be great."

He looked so pleased. "That's awesome, Nesto. Sounds like you'll be busy this summer."

I took a sip from the pint the bartender had handed me and nodded. "They're really ramping up the ads for the festival too. I think it's going to be good."

Jude nodded in agreement. "They've been advertising for months. It's going to be a huge event." He paused then, as if considering something. After a moment, he looked straight at me, his expression serious. "If you need an extra hand, let me know. I'd be happy to help."

There was that reckless feeling again.

"Thank you, I might take you up on that."

His cheeks reddened at my words. Jude's shy little smiles were going to be hell on that master plan.

We stood there in silence for a second and I wondered if he was as affected as I was. I wanted to ask him, *are you feeling this too?*

But I veered into safer waters. "Enough about me. How was work?"

His face darkened at that. "It was fine." He exhaled like he was thinking of something annoying, and I wondered if it was that woman.

"Anyone bothering you at work?" He shook his head, clearly not wanting to get into it.

"Oh just Misty being Misty. She didn't bother you at the truck again did she?"

"No. I hope she'll just move on to something else, and forget I'm there."

He looked like he wanted to say something else, but instead, jerked his thumb toward the restaurant area. "Do you want to get something to eat?"

I was trying to think of a way to get whatever he'd been about to say out of him when he spoke again. "Or we could do some bowling."

I laughed, throwing my hands up at the suggestion. "I'm up for it, but you're going to have to show me. I don't think I've ever been bowling, not that I can remember anyways."

Jude's look of horror was hilarious. "What? How is that even possible?"

I shrugged, grinning at his bemused expression.

"I don't know, I assume there are bowling alleys in New York City, but I've never been to one."

He grabbed his drink and stood up with purpose. "Well, we need to remedy this right now." I turned around to leave some money for our beers and followed him to the bowling shoes counter. That's when I remembered why I didn't bowl.

Deadass, I didn't fuck with corny-looking used shoes.

"Jude, I don't know if I'm down with wearing those," I said, pointing at the shelves. This time he did laugh at me.

"You're wearing socks, it's fine."

"Okay, but just for the record, my people don't mess

with shit that involves hauling forty-pound balls while wearing rented shoes."

Jude chuckled like I wasn't being totally serious, and I had to admit I was feeling pretty good about myself.

I liked making Jude Fuller laugh.

Jude

"Okay you've swiftly kicked my ass at bowling for a solid hour and now I need to eat." Nesto's grin gave away that even though he really was terrible at bowling, he had fun. Not that he was even trying to learn. For the most part the last hour involved me bowling and him finding excuses to touch me. I tried not to get into my head too much about what was going on between us. I knew at some point he would go back to fully focusing on his business, and I would go back to being alone. But for now, I'd enjoy his presence. Anything beyond that felt too perilous to consider at the moment.

"Damn, I know I suck, but you don't have to look so torn up about it." I looked over my shoulder at Nesto and I could tell he knew whatever I'd been thinking about, it wasn't his bowling.

He was trying to make me laugh. Even after only a couple of times together Nesto cared enough to know when I needed a distraction or a word to get me out of my head. I shook myself off and tried to get back the lighter mood we'd had just a moment before.

"Well, your bowling is sort of astonishing in its horribleness. I kinda want to keep watching."

A bark of laughter came out of him and he pulled me close again. Not for a kiss this time. Just to touch, talking to me as he ran his hands over my arms and shoulders. "I *am* hungry though." He seemed so content just from being with me. "You want to order something here?" He looked up at the clock on the wall behind us, then smiled. "Actually it's still early. If you don't mind waiting like an hour, I can make us something at my place."

The idea of Nesto cooking for me made my stomach flutter.

I wasn't the best of cooks. I could follow a recipe, but it wasn't something I was very good at. But I loved home-cooked meals. It was one of the things that I'd missed the most after having to leave home, and why I was so grateful for dinner at Carmen's house every week.

I thought of my sister Mary, and the Sunday meals she'd prepared, of my whole family eating together. Then I remembered the last meal I'd had with them and felt like someone had punched me in the gut. I glanced up and saw that Nesto was looking at me worriedly. I felt small and stupid for still getting so upset about things with my family. The conversation with Carmen from that first day I met Nesto came back to me.

If I wasn't up for dating, if I didn't mind being alone, why was I here with him? Why did I keep coming back? Because he was a good man and he looked at me like he wanted me.

Hadn't I earned the right to have that?

"Jude."

Nesto touched my elbow, his fingers only lightly on me, as if he was afraid to startle me.

"We don't have to do that if you don't want to. We can—"

I cut him off because I didn't want him to think even

for a second any of this was about him. "No, actually that sounds great. I don't usually eat until later, anyway." The tension in his shoulders relaxed, making my own apprehension subside.

"What do you want me to make for you?"

"Spaghetti and meatballs?" He seemed surprised at the speed and intensity of my answer and I cringed at my weirdness.

"Okay, I can do that. I actually have a couple of hacks for that. We'll be eating in no time. Just need to stop by the store to get a few things."

I nodded as we finished putting on our shoes and returned the bowling ones. "I might have some of the stuff we need at my place. We can just go there, if you don't mind."

"Sounds good. So why spaghetti and meatballs?" he asked with a big grin. "You had that answer right at the tip of your tongue."

I wondered what would happen if I told him about that last Sunday dinner with my family. Would my answer wipe that smile from his face? Would my baggage send him running?

I didn't want to know that right now.

I *did* want to be here with him, and tonight, I didn't feel like lecturing myself on all the ways this could go wrong anymore.

I turned to him, letting myself go with the feverish feeling his presence gave me. "It was my favorite when I was kid." He smiled at that, his eyes shining and curious. I could tell he wanted to know more. Hear about my family, *my people*, as he would say.

So, I told him.

"My sister made it all the time for Sunday dinner. It

just occurred to me it's been a long time since I had it."
I stopped there and started walking toward the door,
not looking back to see if Nesto had more questions.

He caught up with me just as I walked out to the
parking lot.

"Hey, what happened back there?"

I turned around and Nesto was standing up straight,
his brows furrowed.

I shook my head. "Sorry. I think I'm just a little tired."

And overthinking, oversharing.

"I was worried I'd said something to offend you,"
he said. "I don't want to push you, Jude. If you're not
comfortable with being more than friends." He took
my hand and squeezed it, his face still serious. "We
can do that."

He looked down at me and his smile was a little sad,
but so genuine. "I don't want to mess up with my only
friend in Ithaca. How about it, neighbor? I'll make you
the best spaghetti and meatballs you've ever had, and
we'll work on getting some more of those smiles out
of you tonight."

Friends.

I could do that. Friends, felt safer.

"Okay," I conceded.

The corner of his mouth tipped up. "How about
neighbors who kiss on occasion?"

All I could do was push up and oblige.

He grunted as he tongued into my mouth, tasting
me. We pulled back at the same time and I shook my
head, grinning. How did he do that? Make everything
okay again with a kiss.

"There it is. I'm going to make it my mission to keep
you smiling, neighbor."

"I thought your mission was getting your business to be a success."

He looked serious for a moment, then whispered, "I told you, I adapt."

Chapter Eleven

Jude

"Hey! How did you get in here?" I asked, startled.

I must have missed the knock because I looked up and Martha Jackson, our executive director, was standing in front of my desk.

I lit up when I saw her, despite my day not going great so far. I'd been in an email back and forth with Misty since I'd gotten in to the office. It was almost five o'clock and she was still asking me questions. She was nitpicking every single line of the budget for the mobile library, with the excuse of needing to answer questions for the board. I knew they were deciding on the project next week, so I was trying to go with it.

"I knocked. But you were very focused on whatever you were doing." She had such an easy manner and was generally a great boss, so I tried not to let her see my irritation.

"No worries, come on in. What's going on?" Martha was one of the most impressive people I had ever worked with. She was originally from New York City and had relocated to Ithaca over twenty years ago. She started as a professor at Ithaca College, but after a few years decided to leave academia to work in the community. I respected and valued her opinion of my work very much. She rarely popped into my office at the end of the day for a chat though. So whatever she wanted to tell me was probably important. I just hoped it wasn't bad news.

"So don't freak out okay," She looked so serious, that all I *could do* was freak out.

"You're kidding, right?"

She did smile then and sank down on the chair in front of my desk.

"What is it?" I knew I sounded like a wreck, but after a day of dealing with Misty, I was a bit on edge.

She sighed and dropped her head backward. She looked weary and pissed, which did nothing to calm my nerves.

"I want you to pitch the project to the board next week."

I must have been hearing things, because she could not be telling me to stand in front of the board and do a presentation with a week's notice.

"Pardon?"

She put her hands up at what I knew must be the horrified look on my face. "I know that public speaking is not your favorite thing."

I balked at her major understatement. "Not my favorite thing?" Wow. My voice could go really high. "Martha—"

"I'm not sure what's going on with Misty, but she's dead set against this project."

I tried very hard not to look murderous. Of course this had to be some bullshit she started.

"You know I want this to happen, Jude, but it's not

up to me. The board decides on new projects of this size." She leaned in and looked straight at me. "They need to hear from you. I trust they won't be able to say no once they see your passion and all the work you've put into this."

I was trying to keep my cool. Because this all came down to Misty interfering with my project for sport. She didn't give a shit about the budget. This was just more of the same harassment she seemed to live for.

I took a deep breath before I answered. I was not letting Misty's scheming take this chance from me. If it took standing in front of the board, and pleading my case. I would do it.

"Of course I'll do it, Martha. You know I'm willing to do anything to make this happen."

The relief on her face made me smile despite my nerves. "Great. Thanks. I think it will make a difference. I don't know if it'll actually get us the votes when need, but it can't hurt." She waved a finger at me. "Tom White is the one to convince because he can sway the others. He also has the ability to come up with funds."

I nodded, remembering Tom was a high-up executive in one of the local banks. "Okay, I'll keep that in mind."

She shook her head again. "I honestly wonder sometimes if Misty is worth the aggravation. She's a good grant writer and has amazing connections in town, but I feel like I spend a third of my time dealing with her issues with people."

I didn't say a word, but she could see my face, and my scowl had to be epic.

"I'm not going to put you on the spot, but if she's giving you trouble, please tell me, Jude. I value you and the work you do here."

"Thank you for saying that." I was so tempted to rat her out. To tell Martha that Misty had been harassing Nesto for weeks. That she showed up at his truck almost on a daily basis to bother him, but I didn't because he'd asked me not to. "Everything's fine. I'll be ready for the board next week."

She didn't look too convinced about my "Everything's fine" but she stood up. "Okay, excellent. I'm sorry for dropping this on you without warning, but I want the mobile library operating next school year, and if anyone can talk the board into it, that's you."

I gave her a real smile then. Martha's confidence in me meant a lot.

"I'll give it my best shot."

She got to the door and turned around before walking out. "I'm certain you will. Go home. I don't want you pulling all-nighters over this. You could do this pitch in your sleep."

"I'm glad you think so, and that I have a week to prepare."

Once Martha left, I felt a trickle of panic starting to run up my spine when the screen of my phone flashed with a notification. I picked it up, and I saw it was a message from Nesto.

Up for a neighborly dinner tonight?

Just seeing his name on the screen made my stupid heart flutter. We'd been doing this "neighbors with benefits" thing since that night at the bowling alley. Nesto would show up with groceries or text me, asking if I wanted dinner, and we'd hang out, make out.

Spend time together, without ever saying what exactly we were doing.

Every time we saw each other I seemed to end up re-negotiating some physical or emotional boundary with myself, which only months ago was uncharted territory. At some point I would probably need to figure this out, but today, with this board thing pending, my nerves were fraught and the thought of seeing him felt like everything I needed. I was about to respond with a yes, when I noticed the date. I frowned, since it was a Thursday and he usually had dinner service at the B&B.

Aren't you at Ergos tonight?

I saw the three dots pop up and then disappear four times before a text finally appeared.

Can I call you?

The unusual request and the message made my stomach sink.

Something was wrong.

Nesto

"What's going on?"

I'd been on pins and needles for hours but three words from Jude and it was like someone undid all the knots I'd had tightened around my chest all day.

"Ergos called this morning to tell me they didn't need me to do dinner service this week." I sighed, trying not to get worked up again. "So, I'm free tonight. If you're up for a neighbors' dinner." I cringed at my naked desperation, because we both knew, "neighbors' dinner" was just code for him taking pity on me and letting my thirsty ass come over.

When Jude spoke I could hear the worry in his voice. "Did something happen?"

I shook my head like he could see me. "I don't know, and I'm trying to not read into things. They just said they wanted to try different trucks and they'd call me in a couple of weeks. Things were going well in the few weeks I've been there. I could barely keep up with the demand." I breathed through my nose, and closed my eyes. Cringing at what I was about to say and how humiliated I felt. "When I drove by tonight on my way back from the bank I saw the gourmet grilled cheese truck setting up."

I could hear Jude exhale, and I knew we were both thinking the same thing.

Misty.

"Maybe they just want to give other businesses a chance, you said they were trying out different places. They'll call you again, no one is serving better food than you in this town."

Eventually, I would have to face the fact that whatever Jude and I had going on was a hell of a lot more than neighbors being friendly. Today I'd talked to my mother, to the guys who called to check in, I even talked to Pri, they all tried to cheer me up and got nowhere. A minute of talking to Jude and I was feeling like a different person.

"Thanks for saying that, but tell me about your day. We always talk about me. Are you up for dinner?"

This time he was the one to sigh. "Sure. I'm still at my office though. My boss just told me I need to pitch my project to the board, because she's not sure if she can convince them to approve it on her own."

I almost scoffed at that. "No fucking way. If they pass on your book truck they're fools."

He chuckled, making me feel ten feet tall. "If only I could get you a vote on that board. She thinks Misty's been convincing people the project is too expensive. I hate public speaking, but I don't have a choice." His voice hardened and I felt my face heating up.

"Fuck, why is she like this? I don't want to even think she had anything to do with me getting dropped from Ergos, but that's a hell of a coincidence. She won't be able to keep getting away with this shit. People will eventually catch on. Besides, you'll blow them away, babe. Don't worry."

I heard a gasp over the phone and bit back a curse. I'd kept the endearments to a minimum, but occasionally I slipped up. We were okay like this for now. Just friendly neighbors.

If I told myself that enough times, maybe I'd actually believe it.

"When do you want to come over?" The need in Jude's voice set off every nerve in my body.

"I'll stop to pick up some stuff to make dinner. Is an hour okay?"

I could already taste his mouth, my hands tingling from wanting to touch him.

"One hour."

When we ended the call, the tension in our voices was palpable.

I needed to think about what was happening with Jude meant, but this Misty woman seemed hell-bent on running me out of town. I was feeling lost and scared for my business, and tonight I wanted some comfort. The only thing that'd made sense this entire day was the thought of driving to Jude's little house and sinking into those blue eyes for a while.

Chapter Twelve

Jude

"Is that you, neighbor?"

"Yes, I'm back," i called out, a smile already forming on my face from finding Nesto in my house. Tomorrow I was going in front of the board to pitch them my project. Nesto, knowing how much I'd worried over the past week, had texted me about coming over. I said I'd leave the door open for him, and he responded by saying he'd have food ready for me when I got back.

We were still doing our "we're just neighbors" thing. Except after that night he lost his dinner service gig, the boundaries were getting more blurred every day. There were moments I felt like I was playing with fire letting myself depend on Nesto like this, but I couldn't walk away yet.

If I was going to be a fool, I'd be a fool for him.

I distracted myself by looking around my living room as I cooled off after my run. My house was a small colonial, which I'd decorated in a mid-century style. There was a lot of art on the walls. Some I'd picked up while travelling, and others were prints of pieces from my favorite artists. I never envisioned having a man in my home when I moved to Ithaca. Back then all I wanted was space. I'd relished the freedom of picking out colors for the walls and furniture I loved without having to think about whether my family would think it was too "prissy" or get on my case about my "weird" tastes.

I looked at a print of a Maine landscape by Marsden Hartley I'd hung right above the couch. Right across from it, and above my little mantle was my favorite piece, a large print of Kerry James Marshall's *School of Beauty, School of Culture,* which I bought after seeing his show in New York a couple of years ago. It was a scene at an African-American beauty salon, an explosion of colors and textures. It was busy and beautiful, and I loved it.

I was musing on how nice it was to be able to display it without having to give anyone an explanation, when Nesto called from the kitchen again, his voice brimming with humor. "Are you gonna come in and say hi? Or am I just here to make you food?"

Nesto was loud.

He didn't walk into the room I was in to tell me something. He would just holler from wherever he was, calling out what he wanted to say.

He could have an entire conversation like that.

He'd laughed when I told him if he wanted to keep communicating while in separate rooms, we'd have to get walkie talkies. I'd asked him how his voice could stand it. He just smiled and shrugged then said, "I'm Dominican." Which I was learning was the explanation for quite a few things.

I smiled as I walked into the kitchen and ran my

hand across his back while I opened the fridge, looking for a cold drink.

I was hot and sweaty, but feeling calmer about work,
and so pleased to find Nesto making himself at home.
As I stood in front of the fridge chugging water I felt
him walk up to me and wrap his arms around my waist.
His chest against my back, strong arms tightening as
he nosed my neck.

"Mmmm, hombre y sudor. My favorite."

I leaned into him, closing my eyes. "I doubt a fra-
grance called 'Sweaty Man' would do very well in the
market, but I'm glad you find my funk pleasant."

He bit my ear before whispering, "You know I do."

There it was again. That thrill Nesto's touch gave me.

"Have you always been this keen on making meals
for people who live by you?"

He laughed at that. "I lived in my last apartment
for eight years, and I don't think I said more than five
words to anyone in that building." His lips grazed my
ear as he spoke, making me tremble. "This is all you."

"I'm flattered." My words came out on a gasp and
I let myself sink into him again. In the last couple of
weeks, I'd shed a lot of my usual reluctance about having people in my space, and little by little, Nesto became a constant presence in my home. Where in the past
others set my inner alarm bells blaring, his easy, unde-
manding ways had been met with very little resistance.

It was so simple with him, no complicated explana-
tions or weird games, he just said what he wanted and
asked if I would be up for it too.

"I'm making a green curry with some halibut I got
from my fish guy today, is that okay?"

"Sounds wonderful, thanks for cooking. You're

going to spoil me." He shook his head with his face in my hair. He was almost a head taller than me and a lot bulkier, which he was a bit too fond of. He liked using his height to wrap himself around me.

I turned around pushing up on my toes to kiss him. He smelled like the garlic and ginger he used for the curry, and I wanted a taste of him. I bit his bottom lip and then sucked on it.

My addiction to Nesto's mouth only got worse the more access I had to it, and I never wasted a chance to kiss him when he was close. He licked into my mouth and groaned. As we tangled our tongues, he let his arms fall down behind me, grabbing my ass and squeezing tight. I tried to get closer, feel more of him against me.

I was wondering how much further we could take things before dinner was done, when a timer went off somewhere. Nesto groaned and pulled back.

"I guess the rice is done," he said, pushing our foreheads together before turning toward the stove. "Why don't you take a shower? I'll finish up here and walk next door to get some beer."

I nodded, reaching up to give him another kiss. "I'll be done in ten minutes."

I started walking toward the bathroom and turned to look at him. He was watching me go with a small smile on his face.

I stepped into the shower, hoping whatever it was we were doing, we could keep going for a while longer.

"You're going to kill me with food." I put my spoon down after having one last bite of delicious curry, and rubbed my belly. "Is there anything you can't cook perfectly?" I asked.

He laughed at my feigned annoyance. "Lots of things. I seriously struggled with the more complicated French techniques when I was in culinary school."

"So how *did* you get into cooking? I mean you've told me about culinary school and starting the truck, but you never said how you got interested in it."

He finished chewing and leaned back in the chair. "Well my mom and all my friends' moms are amazing cooks. They made the traditional dishes from back home all the time. I was always around people who showed their love by feeding me." He smiled softly, like he was picturing those times. "But what made me want to make food for a living was one of the schemes the GA moms came up with, to keep us off the stoop after we started high school."

I laughed at the mention of the GA crew, which earned me a wink from Nesto.

"By the time we started high school the part of the Bronx where we lived was still pretty hot. 'Stop and frisk' and 'Zero Tolerance' were still alive and well in our part of the city. If you were black or brown, in our neighborhood, walking with a frown was enough reason to end up shoved onto the hood of a police car." He pursed his lips at whatever he was remembering, and I felt so angry for him, but I didn't interrupt. I wanted to hear his story without making it about me.

"So my mom got nervous about us hanging out on the corner with nothing to do after school while she was at work. The guys and I were too old for after school or anything like that, and sports only kept us busy a couple of afternoons a week. So, the moms decided to find us jobs we could be at for a few hours every day until they got home."

He smiled in the way I noticed he only did when talking about his mother.

"My mom was the ringleader of course, but she got Juanpa, Milo, and Patrice's mom in on it too. Pretty soon they were out pounding the pavement, offering us up to whoever owned a business and wanted to take on four surly punks as projects for the school year."

"Your mom is something else."

His eyes twinkled at that. "She really is. I ended up at Mr. Battaglia's. He owns a fresh pasta and ravioli shop his grandfather opened in the thirties. It's right on Arthur Avenue in Little Italy. He sells to the local restaurants and specialty stores in Manhattan. Everything is handmade, and let me tell you the old man is a pain in the ass. Meticulous about how the pasta is made. If it leaves the store with his name on it, it better be fucking perfect." He shook his head with a fond expression on his face.

"Mr. Battaglia taught me to be passionate about making good food the right way. He was like a father to me, more than my own ever was." Nesto rarely talked about his father who'd never really been in his life.

"But the most important thing he taught me was to be proud of where I came from, of my roots. He always told me to hold my head up high, because I had a lot to offer this country. That people like him and I built this place." He was leaning forward as he spoke. His wide shoulders almost parallel with his knees, vibrating with emotion. "He got on me about not letting the negativity I heard about Dominicans out on the street or in the news get to me. He was and still is a great mentor and friend."

I could see the respect and admiration on his face. "Sounds like Mr. Battaglia means a lot to you."

"He does. When not a lot of Italians would hire Dominicans, he took me in and treated me like family. Man, I loved being in that shop." Nesto felt everything so intensely. When he told a story, he did it with his whole body.

"I ended up working for him all through high school and most of college. He's still in the shop too, he's like eighty-five, but no one can talk to him about retiring. All the guys ended up liking their jobs too. In the end my mom was twenty steps ahead of us. Like usual. Those jobs kept us off the street and out of trouble."

His eyes got serious for a moment then he picked up his beer and took a long sip. "There are a lot of guys we grew up with who weren't as lucky. And that's my story about how I got into cooking."

I smiled at him. "I love hearing you talk about your mom and your friends. You have such incredible bonds with them, you light up telling those stories." I didn't mean to sound wistful, but I did. I couldn't help it.

He reached over and grabbed my hand, like he was going to ask me something. So far he'd been respectful of my weird silences whenever we talked about family. He'd stopped asking about them after a couple of uncomfortable moments, like that first night he offered to make dinner. Suddenly I felt frustrated with myself. I wanted to be more open with Nesto, to tell him about my life.

After I left home I'd been so resentful of all the time I'd wasted hiding my sexuality from my family. Sometimes the regret I felt for the lost time could make me forget there had been good times too. But now, here with

Nesto, I thought about some of those happy memories, and found I wanted to tell him about some of the things which shaped my life.

"My sister Mary was the one who got me into reading. She wanted to be a writer, but my dad was dead set against any of my sisters going to college." I frowned, remembering his lectures about a woman's place being "in the home taking care of their families."

"He was barely okay with them finishing high school. Mary especially never had a chance, she was the oldest, and basically ran our house after my mom got sick. But she loved books, she always read to us. She walked my brothers and sisters and I to get books at the library every week."

Nesto squeezed my hand as I spoke, his eyes focused on me.

"Once I caught the reading bug, I never looked back. The library was a haven for me. After I realized I was gay, I practically lived there."

"Oh Jude."

I shook my head remembering those days. How lonely I'd felt, how much I yearned to someday find a safe place, a safe person I could be myself with. There with Nesto, I felt so close to that refuge I'd longed for.

"When I felt like I was going to lose my mind worrying about what would happen if my family found out, I went to the library and read about other places, other people, other ways of thinking and living. It was such a comfort just to know the world was big and there was probably space out there for someone like me. It pulled me out of a lot of dark times. That's why the mobile library is such a big deal to me," I said, my voice wobbly all of a sudden.

Nesto stood up and walked around the table where I was sitting and pulled me up for a hug.

"See? This is what happens when I talk about myself," I said in a shaky voice. "Weirdness."

He shook his head and squeezed me tighter. "It's not weird, babe. I'm just glad we both had people in our lives who cared enough about us to give us things to be passionate about. You had books, and I had the shop and my friends. We're lucky." He turned my face around to kiss me. By this point he knew his kisses were a sure way to distract me. I immediately responded, wrapping my arms around his neck, sliding my tongue into his mouth.

His body was warm and felt so solid against me. I didn't want to do anything to mess with this, with him being here. I didn't want to go too much into my family issues. I wasn't sure someone with one as supportive as his could understand how messed up things got with mine.

He pulled back, his eyes hungry, like he could devour me. I'd never had someone look at me with so much want. Like he was barely able to keep his hands to himself. I pushed up and gave him another kiss, and he squeezed me hard. After a moment, I let go, and turned around to pick up the dishes from the table.

He groaned in protest, calling after me in a whiny voice. "No, where are you going? Come back."

I laughed and shook my head. "If we go down that road we won't clean up and we both have early days tomorrow."

He pouted as he started to help bring dishes into the kitchen. "You're too good. Ven aca, dame otro beso," he said, pulling me back for one last kiss.

"I'll help you with these before I head out. I have to get the food prep done early because I have lunch service by the library, and I have to get everything ready for the festival too. There's a lot of hype already, the organizer I talked to today said they were expecting about a hundred charter buses with people coming from all over the state. Since I don't have the B&B gig anymore, I'm hoping this weekend will get us some new clients. Are you going to be able to come and help?"

"Yeah, I want to be there for you." At my words, Nesto stopped what he was doing and looked up at me. The intensity in his eyes made the moment feel a lot bigger than I intended. Unsure of how to react, I cleared my throat, and got busy cleaning up dishes as I spoke. "I've been hearing a lot of buzz about it too. Everyone at the library is going."

Nesto didn't respond right away and he kept his eyes locked with mine. When he spoke his voice was almost breathless. "I'm glad you'll be there," he said as we worked together to clean the kitchen. "It's an all-hands-on-deck kind of thing. Yin and Ari will be there, plus my mom and sis, and as of this afternoon Juanpa, Milo and Patrice confirmed they'd come up for it too."

I smiled at how happy he looked talking about his friends, even though I felt a little nervous about meeting them. "That's great that your friends can come."

"They've helped me at events before, so they know what to do. My mom will be happy to hear you'll be there." He looked at me with a mischievous smile because he knew the mention of a conversation with his mom would freak me out. "She's been asking about you. Said she hasn't had a chance to talk to you yet!"

"It will be nice to see your mom again," I said, blushing.

He laughed. "Riiiight, I can hear you freaking out inside your head from here." He bent and kissed my hair. "You'll be fine. She's mostly harmless."

I rolled my eyes. "Oh, that helps."

He winked like I was being silly. "Don't worry. I promise she won't get on your case. As far as she knows, you're my very awesome neighbor who I've been hanging out with a lot." Ouch. That one hurt, more than I thought it would. Then I reminded myself that this way we could just stay like we were. No complications.

"Okay, let's get the rest of this stuff cleaned up. I have my meeting at 7:45 a.m. sharp." Nesto made a sympathetic face at the early meeting time. "We scheduled it so the board members who have to be at their own jobs before nine could also attend. Between the meeting being at the crack of dawn, and Misty, I want to be at my best tomorrow."

At the mention of her name his face hardened. He shook his head in disgust as he started the dishwasher.

"That woman is a piece of work. I don't know if she's a bigot, or just bored, but I'm going to lose my patience with her one of these days. Yesterday she stopped by right in the middle of the lunch service to interrogate me on whether I got my ingredients locally." He shook his head, his mouth flattening.

"I laughed in her face, because seriously. I told her, 'Lady, I source locally as much as possible, but I would have a hard time finding plantains and yucca at local farms don't you think?' And the fucking nerve too. Her son buys his shit at Costco and she's coming to my business when it's full of people to try to show me up. You'd think she'd leave me alone now that her son has the Ergos gig, but no." Since they'd asked Nesto to stop coming, we'd seen the grilled cheese truck there on his regular nights. "It's like she won't be happy until I close up shop and leave town."

Nesto worked so hard, and he was so good at what he did. As I looked at him, leaning on my counter, his usually happy face ashen with worry, I felt dread too.

I didn't want him to leave.

I walked over to him, put my arms around his waist and tried to keep my voice steady when I spoke. "Why didn't you tell me about that?"

He lifted a shoulder. "I don't want you getting into something with her and then her coming for your project even more than she already has. I can handle it, Jude."

I wanted to push, beg him to let me help him with this. "I wish you'd let me tell our director about what she's doing. She already asked me once if Misty had a problem with me." He opened his mouth to say something, but I held my hand up. "I didn't say anything to her."

He exhaled loudly and closed his eyes for a second in a gesture I now knew was his way of grounding himself when he was exasperated.

He leaned his hands on the counter for a few seconds, then lifted his head and sighed. "I've got to get going and talking about Misty will just get us both worked up. But I'll see you tomorrow, right? You have to come and tell me how the meeting goes. Even though I know you're going to kick ass."

"I wish I had your confidence. I'm a wreck in front of people."

He shook his head. "I don't believe you. You'll have them eating out of your hands like you did to me when you told me about the project the first time."

I pulled back a little and narrowed my eyes. "That's because you wanted to get into my pants."

He touched his tongue to his top lip, and it was all I could do to not go in for another kiss. "Okay, that might've been a part of it, but I also think your project is legit and it will be an amazing resource for the kids. There's no way the board won't see that too."

"Unless Misty decides to hijack the meeting and wrecks the whole thing."

He grimaced at that. "I'm sure they're not that gullible. Besides, I know you can stand up to her."

Chapter Thirteen

Jude

"You're cut off. No more caffeine for you." Carmen grabbed the coffee mug on my desk and walked away with it. It was only seven-twenty and I'd already had three cups, which was not a good move on my part. Too much coffee and I were not a good mix.

Carmen shook her head at me. "Hon, you totally got this. I've never seen someone prepare this much for a presentation. You got great feedback from the board when you sent them your proposal. I know it's nerve-racking, but you're going to do great."

Rationally I knew she was right, but I was still nervous. "I feel like if I screw this up, I won't get another chance." I sat at my desk, trying to slow down my mind. Above my head I heard Carmen sigh and walk quickly to close the door to our office. She didn't say a word, letting me work on calming down.

After a minute I opened my eyes and felt more relaxed. Carmen was right. I was prepared. All I could do was go in there and do my best at making a case for my mobile library. Just as I was about to gather my stuff to start walking to the conference room, my phone vibrated with an incoming text. A message from Nesto popped up on the screen.

Good luck in your meeting. You got this!

I sighed and smiled as I quickly texted back a thank-you then I stood up, feeling a thousand times better.

Carmen laughed as she walked with me. "So I get up at the crack of dawn to go get you the good coffee and a sandwich, and you're still a mess, but one text from Nesto is all you need to get your head in the game," she scoffed. "Malagradecido."

I laughed as we walked into the conference room. "How am I ungrateful? I said thank you like ten times!"

"Just saying, my sandwich didn't get you smiling like that."

"Duh. Here, help me put out these packets with the handouts in front of everyone's chair. I'll set up the PowerPoint. People are going to start to come in any minute now."

"Fine, but I'm going to have to talk to Nesto about this."

I rolled my eyes at her and pointed to the table indicating she needed to get to work. We got everything arranged and were sitting down as the first board members and Martha walked in with Misty not too far behind.

As soon as Martha saw me, a big smile appeared on her face. "Jude, I'm so excited for this presentation."

I stood up to say hello and smiled at her gratefully. "Thanks, I hope the board likes it."

She shook her head at me, her long silver locs bouncing around her head as she did. "I don't think this board has ever met with anyone as well prepared as you are."

"Stop worrying," she teased as Tom White came up to us. Martha turned to him as he joined us. "Tom, have you met Jude?"

"Yes, I have," he said, extending his hand. "It's good to see you again, I'm looking forward to hearing from you today. I've been pretty vocal about my apprehension on taking on any new projects this year, but I'm curious about your book truck idea. My mother was a librarian in the town I grew up for more than forty years. When I told her about this project, she made me promise to keep an open mind."

"Thank you, sir," I said distractedly, as I caught Misty glaring in our direction from the other side of the room.

Jesus.

What was her problem?

Martha looked at her watch and turned to address the rest of us.

"Good morning, everyone, thanks for being here this early. I hope you all availed yourself of the lifesaving coffee and bagels," she said, getting a few laughs.

"We have a few things to address today, but the first order of business will be to hear from Jude Fuller." She beamed, extending a hand in my direction.

"As you all know, Jude joined our library three years ago as the youth services director. Since he took over the position he's grown our program exponentially. Last year we had over twenty thousand books for children and youth checked out of the library, and over five thousand children came in, to participate in the programs and activities we offer. We also began our ESL classes for parents, as well as a homework assistance program for lower income children."

She looked at me with a smile, and shook her head. "But of course that is not enough work for Jude." This got a few more laughs around the room. "He has a bigger project in mind which he'll talk to us about today. So, I'll give him the floor."

I stood up quickly and moved to the front of the room with my heart feeling like it was going to burst out of my chest. I quickly fired up the projector, scanning the crowd, which with the exception of Misty and a couple others, seemed interested in what I had to say. I hoped my nerves weren't too obvious as I looked down at my chambray shirt and pressed chinos, suddenly nervous about being underdressed.

I cleared my throat, took two deep breaths and launched into my presentation.

"Good morning, thanks for being here so early. Today, I want to talk to you a bit about the youth in the rural areas of our county, and how more access to our library services could impact their lives. If you could please open your packets and go to page three…"

The whole thing was over in fifteen minutes.

"Any questions or comments?" I asked as I looked around the table. There were eight board members present and about five library staff, including myself. Most of the room looked engaged, and there were more than a few smiles.

Tom White leaned forward, his face serious. My pulse raced as he opened his mouth and all I could think was "please don't destroy my dream."

"Thanks for the presentation, Jude. I appreciate you taking the time to give us some examples of how projects like this have worked in counties similar to ours."

He looked around the room as he spoke. "I'm the first to admit I haven't been very receptive to using funds for new programs next year, but Jude made some really great points in his presentation and I think we need to reconsider."

I sagged with relief and when I turned to Martha, she gave me a very discreet thumbs-up, as Tom continued talking. "I think this project would be of great service to the more isolated parts of the county. I make a personal commitment to explore funding possibilities through Cayuga Trust."

He smiled at what probably was a very grateful expression on my face and continued, "Given the current state of the world, I think it's more important than ever to make sure our young people have access to books and information that open their eyes to our larger world." There were several nods and words of agreement at that.

"Thank you, Tom," I said, my voice cracking a bit with emotion.

Another board member who I knew was one of Misty's cronies spoke next, and I prepared for what I knew would be a very different take on my presentation. "This is all very nice, but it seems to me like it's a lot of effort and money, just so people can get books delivered to them. I mean this is why kids these days are the way they are, everything gets handed to them."

I smiled and tried not to get defensive. I had prepared for this kind of response and knew what I needed to say.

I tried to maintain a placid tone while I spoke. "Thank for your comments, Miss Winters. I think the best way for me to respond to that is by sharing a story."

I looked around the table, trying to make eye contact with the more friendly faces, before I shared something

I never talked about with strangers. "I grew up not so far from here, in Canandaigua, and the public library for me, like for many of the kids in our community, was a lifeline. For a kid growing up in a very conservative family, in an isolated little town in Upstate New York, realizing I was gay was terrifying, but I had the library."

I tried to keep my body relaxed as I spoke, opening up was not something that came easily for me, but I would do whatever I needed to do to get my project approved.

"I found stories of young people like me, books which told me being gay was normal and it didn't mean eternal damnation. Even if I could not safely talk with anyone about what was happening with me, reading about it made a huge difference. But it was not only myself I learned about. I read about the civil rights movement and Stonewall. I read about immigrants and what their work did to build our country. I learned to love myself and understand the place I lived in, in large part thanks to my local library."

From the corner of my eye I could see Martha nodding in agreement with my words, giving me the push I needed to finish saying what I wanted to say.

"So I agree with you that we should challenge our young people to be more proactive in working toward the things they want, but I also believe if there's a kid out there isolated and hungry to read, then it's our job to put a book in their hands."

I glanced over to the woman who had asked the question and saw she was looking at me with contrition. I was about to go sit down when a few of the board members nodded and started applauding. Martha and Carmen joined them with big grins on their faces.

"Well, thanks again for giving me the opportunity to talk about the mobile library today, and if you have any questions please email or call me. I'm sure you know by now, this project is something I love to talk about."

Before I could make my escape, Misty started talking.

"This was a nice suggestion on how to spend our resources over the next year, but as the grant writer, I would like to remind all of you how limited funding will be. I think the project to renovate the old conference room into a space we can rent for events as a source of income takes priority over anything else. No matter how much of a feel-good story it is." She looked around the room then, her face getting angry when no one seemed to agree with her comment.

I was about to respond, when Martha began to speak. "Thank you, Jude, for your wonderful presentation. Misty, I appreciate your input; however, the board already decided your conference room idea would have to wait until next year. I know you're aware of this, but if you would like further clarification, we can discuss it…at another time. Now, moving on."

With that, I made my departure and did not even attempt making eye contact with Misty, knowing she would be furious. As soon as I got out of the meeting, I grabbed my phone to text Nesto while power walking back to my desk.

But before I could, Carmen snatched the phone from my hand. "Wait! Let me give you a congratulations hug for killing it in there before you get all lovey and shit on your phone." She grabbed me and hugged me hard.

"I'm so proud of you, friend. You even got personal. You were a star, and fuck Misty, and her bullshit." She rolled her eyes in the direction of the conference room. "I can't believe she's so tone deaf she couldn't tell her comment wouldn't go over well."

I squeezed her back. "I have no idea if this will make a difference, but I gave it my best shot. Thank you. For the moral support and all the help with this project. I'm not even going to waste my breath on Misty. I just hope this doesn't get her so pissed off she does something to Nesto."

"Now you're being paranoid. What can she possibly do to Nesto?"

Famous last words.

Maybe I was being paranoid, but Misty was a very sore loser.

Carmen kept talking as I fretted about Misty. "I'm gonna go get some more coffee. That grocery store swill Misty brought did nothing for me. I'll bring you some herbal tea, because you have a twitch in your eye right now that's a bit worrisome," she said, waving a finger in front of my face.

I gave her a light nudge and took my phone back, calling after her as she walked away, "My eye is *not* twitching." I immediately opened my text app and sent Nesto a "thumbs-up" emoji.

A few seconds later my phone pinged.

Nesto: I knew you'd kill it. See you tonight? I can only stop in by for a bit, because this festival shit is getting out of control, but I want to congratulate you in person.

Jude: Yes. I'll be home.

I realized I was standing against the door of my office, with my phone clutched to my chest, a stupid smile on my face. Just texting with Nesto made me so happy I was silly. It was a strange feeling for me. To be carefree with a man, it almost felt like happiness…and I should have known it wouldn't last with Misty in the building.

I saw her coming out of the conference room and walking straight toward me. She was probably coming to say something horrible about the meeting. Usually at this point I would just turn around and go to my office to avoid getting into something with her, but for some insane reason I just stood there as she approached me.

"I guess congratulations are in order," she said sourly. "The board certainly seemed to think your project was worthwhile."

I lifted a shoulder in response.

"Big weekend for you, a good outcome at work and I heard the festival is going to be massive. Your Spanish friend should do a lot of business." The tone with which she said that last part made the hairs on my neck stand up.

"For the last time, Misty, he isn't Spanish. He's *Dominican*. Why is it so hard for you to remember that?" This time she gave *me* a raised shoulder for an answer. She was looking a little too smug, given how hard Martha had shut her down in there.

"Besides why do you care about Nesto's truck so much anyway?" For a second she almost looked flustered, but then went back to her usual sneer.

"I don't care about it in the slightest. My only concern is that there aren't any people coming into town serving bad food."

"Bad food? Misty, what are you talking about?"

Another shrug, then she straightened as she started

to walk past me. I couldn't help the worry niggling me as Misty walked away.

She was up to something, I was sure of it.

Nesto

I thought I was intense when I was going after something, but Jude could give me a run for my money. I was still laughing about his text as I drove into town, headed for the truck. He had worked on that presentation day and night all week and was still surprised it went well.

He was something else.

It was a shame we wouldn't have time to see each other very long tonight. We still hadn't talked about where things were going with us. He knew my goal when I got here was to get OuNYe profitable enough so I could stay here permanently. And that was still the plan, but I'd never really talked to *him* about it. I'd had some setbacks, and couldn't afford too many more of those, but things were mostly on track. And if I was honest with myself, I had to admit, I wasn't just invested in the business succeeding. I was also invested in what I had with Jude.

He still had his hang-ups though, so far we hadn't moved too much past making out. I knew at least part of it was my dumbass "hey neighbor" idea, but it was more than that. He'd only share little pieces of his past or his family. Sometimes I wondered if it was because there was a chance things with OuNYe could go south. He was so invested in my business too. He'd been so supportive from day one.

I never really paid much attention in my past relationships but for the first time, I felt like I was the one who wanted it more. I was willing to adjust my plan just to see where things could go with Jude, but I wasn't certain if he wanted that too. What I did know was that at some point soon, I'd have to ask. I had feelings for Jude I could no longer ignore, and I needed to be sure if it was the same for him.

I didn't want to make promises I couldn't keep though. I needed to have something solid to offer, before I asked him to take a chance on me, and OuNYe simply wasn't there yet.

I was lost in my thoughts when I heard a call coming through the Bluetooth, and tapped the screen without realizing it could potentially be the answer to a lot of my questions about the future.

"Ernesto Vasquez."

"Ernesto, hi, my name is Harold Sheridan. I got your number from one of the attendants at your truck when I stopped there a moment ago. I'm a business investor here in Ithaca, and I've been following your food truck since you opened it in town this summer. Some of my business associates assure me your burritos are the most exciting thing to happen to the Ithaca food scene in years."

Okaaay, things had been going well, but I had no clue business people were *discussing* me. I recognized the last name Sheridan though, it was on half of the buildings in town, so this was certainly interesting.

"I appreciate you saying so, sir," I said, unable to hide my bemusement.

"Let me cut to the chase since we're both busy men." He was all business, but he sounded friendly enough. "I'm looking to expand into the restaurant business, and right now I'm interested in taking a closer look at some of the most popular food trucks in town, to see if any fit with the concept I have in mind."

What did that mean? Did he want to open an actual brick and mortar restaurant? I was so fucking confused right now. But it occurred to me if he wanted to see OuNYe in action, the festival would be a great opportunity.

"I'm not sure what you have in mind, Mr. Sheridan, but we'll be one of the vendors at the wine and beer festival on Seneca Lake this weekend. It may be a good place to experience our food and see what we can do."

He made a sound of approval on the line and my pulse sped up. "That's ideal actually. I was already planning to go to the festival. I can't say for sure when I'll be there, but I'll stop by sometime this weekend. Mind you, at this point I would just like to come sample food, observe, and speak with you for a bit."

"That's fine. I'll be there all weekend from ten a.m. to closing. I look forward to meeting you, Mr. Sheridan."

"Call me Harold, and likewise. Have a good day, Ernesto."

I hung up the phone realizing I had arrived at the spot I usually parked across from the gas station when Mr. Sheridan's words started sinking in. I wasn't sure if this would end up going anywhere because the dude had been pretty vague, but holy shit this could be *it*.

I pushed the button to turn off the car and pulled out my phone. As I was dialing I realized I'd been about to call Jude.

Out of all the people in my life who would be ecstatic to hear my news, and would cheer me on like Mr.

Sheridan had actually offered to open a restaurant with me, the person I wanted to tell first was Jude.

Just as my poor brain was about to explode from all the mind-blowing shit I'd dropped in there in the last five minutes my phone started ringing. I looked at the screen and saw it was Juanpa.

Dude did have good timing.

I picked up after the first ring. "Where are you, motherfucker? You better be on your way to pick up the other two, I have important shit happening tomorrow. So please don't tell me you're flaking out on me."

I heard Milo screeching from somewhere. "We're already on our way!"

Juanpa's annoyed voice came on a second later. "Camilo, what have I told you about wilding out when I'm driving? We're on the GW right now, do you want to die or what? You need to cut down on the caffeine, son."

Patrice's calm voice came through the speakers next. "Does everything need to be a three-ring circus with you two? Nes, we're leaving the city right now. We'll probably stop at one of the outlet malls since J seems to *need* something at the Gucci outlet." Patrice's aggravation was kind of funny. "So we'll be there around five. Where do you need us to go? We'll be ready to help the minute we get there."

Only my people would drive five hours each way to come and work like dogs for free an entire weekend.

"I don't know what I'd do without you knuckleheads. Just text me when you're close. Most likely I'll be at the kitchen prepping for tomorrow. By the way, Jude's going to help over the weekend too, so if you fuckers could try not to scare the shit out of him, I'd appreciate it. I don't mean you, Patrice."

At the mention of Jude I heard Milo making kissing noises on the phone, because he was a twelve-year-old.

"Oooohh, Jude! We can finally meet him, and get the deets from the source, since you've been cagey as hell every time we've brought him up, and none of us buy the 'you're only friends' bullshit."

"Yes, you'll meet him, and I haven't been cagey. I just said we were keeping things casual. Lots of balls in the air right now, doesn't make sense to get serious." Which was a complete lie since two minutes ago, I was figuring out how to stay in Ithaca so I could be Jude's boyfriend.

"On other news. I just got off the phone with one of the major business guys in town and he's coming to the stand this weekend to try the food and meet me. He said he's thinking of opening a restaurant in town and may be interested in OuNYe."

There was a moment of silence and for a second I worried the guys would be bummed out because it could mean I wouldn't be coming back to New York any time soon. But before I had a chance to react, I heard an explosion of cheers and whoops.

"That's right! My boy is going to be a restauranteur." That was Juanpa.

Milo was yelling in Spanish while Patrice tried to get a word in.

"That sounds promising, Nesto. I knew your business would do well, the hard work paid off, mi hermano."

These fools were going to make me bawl in my car. "Thanks, Patrice, I appreciate that, man."

Milo's voice came back on. "I'm so proud of you, Nesto. Someone with your heart and talent couldn't stay unnoticed for long." Fuck, Milo was always the one who made me cry.

"Thanks, guys, you know OuNYe is not just mine. It's ours."

"Of course, we know, man," Juanpa said, his tone serious. "We'll see you in a few."

We signed off and after a second I got my shit together and realized I was late. I would have to call Jude later.

What a morning.

This day had gone so fucking awesome so far. Things were looking up with the truck and I was feeling good about Jude too. I didn't think anything could bring me down.

That was until I got out of the car and saw Yin running toward me, a look of complete panic on his face.

Chapter Fourteen

Nesto

"Mr. Nesto! Did they call you?" Yin shouted as he ran into traffic trying to get my car.

"Yin, watch out," I yelled as I dropped the crate full of cups and napkins I was pulling out of the passenger seat and jogged to meet him at the corner. He looked completely freaked out. When I got to him, I saw he was holding his phone out to me like he wanted to show me something.

"The lady said we couldn't open the truck until she saw the inside. That someone made a complaint about our food, and she needs to do an inspection." His face was splotchy like he'd been crying and his voice wobbled on the last word.

"What complaint? Yin, I haven't talked to anyone about an inspection. Can you start from the beginning? Who came? Was it the blonde lady who stopped by asking where we got our food?"

If Misty had come here to stir shit up again, I was the one who would file a complaint for harassment, but Yin shook his head. "No this was a different lady. She said she was from the Sanitation Department." Yin sounded more distressed with every word.

As I listened I tried to figure out what was going on. I saw Ari crossing the street, his face in a grimace. Yin looked up at him and gave him a shaky smile, then looked back at me. "The other lady, she was here earlier, but she didn't say anything to us. She just stayed for a minute and left. The inspector came like five minutes later."

At the mention of Misty, Ari's already serious face became thunderous.

"I'm still not sure I follow, guys. This person was going to call me? She said we couldn't open until when? We have lunch in a couple of hours and the festival all weekend." I started pacing in front of my car. This was not good. Mr. Sheridan was coming to try the food at the festival. What would I say when he showed up? "Oops, we got shut down because someone got sick from the food."

Ari and Yin looked at me like they weren't sure if I was going to yell at them, so I tried to chill out before I scared them. "Guys, I'm not mad at you, but we need to figure out how to reach this lady. Did she leave a number?"

Ari nodded, and pulled out a card from his pocket. "She said you should call her."

"Okay," I said, taking the number from him and gestured toward the truck. "You guys just go back, take the drinks with you too and put them in the fridge. Hopefully this woman can come do the inspection this morning and we can move on with our day."

This whole thing was very suspect. An inspector had come to look over the truck like a week ago and everything had been perfect. So what could this even be about?

"Fuck." I slammed my hand on the hood of the car, making Yin jump back, and Ari flinch.

"Sorry, guys. I'm a bit frustrated right now." I deflated when I saw their reaction. I did not need to scare the shit out of my employees on top of everything else. "Don't worry, we'll figure it out. I'll be there in a minute."

When they started toward the truck I got back in my car to make the call. After two rings a woman picked up. "Muriel speaking."

"Hi, Ms. Muriel, my name is Ernesto Vasquez from OuNYe. My employees said you came by our truck this morning."

"Yes, Mr. Vasquez. I'm an inspector with the Department of Sanitation, we have received a complaint claiming the poor sanitary conditions of the truck made one of your customers ill. We would like to come and inspect the truck as soon as possible. Until we do so we ask you don't serve any more food."

"A complaint? I don't understand." I was not having a lot of luck keeping my tone neutral. "I've never failed an inspection. I just had one a week ago and didn't have a single issue. I take every precaution with the food I serve." I was gripping the phone so hard it squeaked in my hand.

This could not be happening right now.

"I understand, sir, but we have to respond to complaints. Unfortunately it's pretty late in the day, so I may not get to you before Monday." My phone almost slipped out of my hand when she said that. She was shutting me down. I was going to lose three days of business and possibly an investor over this.

"Please, Ms. Muriel—"

I was about to start begging her to come today when she interrupted me.

"I do see here your past inspections have been satisfactory. I may be able to squeeze you in at the end of the day." The utter desperation in my voice must've gotten to her. "I can come out around four. Does that work?"

Today would be a wash, but at least I still had a chance to do the festival. My head felt hot, from the panic of the last five minutes.

"Yes, sure. Four is fine. Thank you." I kept my voice cordial when I answered. Staying on this woman's good side was a top priority.

"Okay, I'll be there then."

I ended the call and turned to see Jude and Carmen walking toward my car. I opened the door and got out, noticing Jude's face was red and that he looked furious.

I slumped against the car as he approached me. "Someone filed a complaint against the truck, they said my food made them sick. I can't open until the inspector comes, so that means no lunch service and possibly no festival. Fuck." I stopped talking because I was about to cry from sheer helplessness.

Jude moved closer to me, then looked at Carmen. "See, I told you she'd pull something. God she's unbelievable."

Carmen looked pissed too.

"Please tell me this isn't about Misty."

Jude shook his head like he was figuring out where to start. "We just stopped by the truck to tell you about the meeting with the board, and found Ari and Yin looking frazzled. They said you were talking to an inspector about an issue with the truck." He looked so heated, even in this moment of panic, seeing him this pissed off on my behalf made my chest tighten with affection.

"So why do you think any of this has to do with Misty?" His mouth flattened at the mention of her name.

"She was in rare form at the meeting today, especially after Martha shut her down for being horrible about my presentation. She was all smug and cryptic afterwards. I knew she would do something like this. I'm going to tell Martha."

I tried to keep my cool, because I had a long day ahead and I didn't want to add a fight with Jude to an already shitty situation.

"Jude, please, I don't want you getting involved in this. I don't want this affecting your job. This has nothing to do with you." As soon as the last part came out of my mouth I knew I'd made a mistake. Jude's back went up, and he looked mortified.

Fuck.

How was I supposed to be rational when my entire future could be riding on this weekend?

I sighed. "Babe, I'm sorry I snapped at you, I'm just a little bit on edge right now." I felt wrung out from the stress of the last ten minutes. I noticed that Carmen's eyebrow shot way up when I called Jude "babe." I guess it wasn't only my people who could see right through our "just friends" charade.

I went for a change of subject before Carmen ran with my momentary slip. "I didn't even have a chance to tell you, but I got a call from Harold Sheridan, the local businessman, and he's interested in talking to me about OuNYe."

At this Jude's face softened a bit, but he was still not talking.

Carmen's eyes widened when I mentioned Sheridan. She spoke up, sounding impressed.

"Coño, Nesto, ese hombre es poderoso aquí. He's a big deal. Sheridan's the biggest real estate developer in the region. His company just built the new engineering building on the Cornell campus that cost like fifty million bucks."

My heart leaped and then sank at the information. I had no clue the guy was at that level, or how big this opportunity could potentially be.

"This is bad," I said, running my hands over my face. "He's coming to the festival to meet me and try the food. I know it's a long shot, but I really want it go well and if this inspection isn't good, I'm fucked."

Jude still looked wary, so I moved to take his hand, and to my relief he let me. "Why do you think it was Misty? The inspector said it was a food complaint."

After a second he seemed to relax and squeezed my hand. "Okay first, the Sheridan thing could be potentially amazing. He owns like half the town, and he's known for investing in start-ups and partnering with up-and-coming entrepreneurs."

Carmen nodded in agreement. "He's legit."

"About Misty, I don't know." He frowned as if figuring out what to say. "She came up to me after the meeting and was being her usual shitty self, but then talked about your truck, and mentioned bad food, in a way that just made all the hairs on my neck stand up. Now suddenly there's a complaint about your food." He inhaled as he shook his head. "She did it, she knows people everywhere, and she'll use the influence she has to do stuff like this."

Carmen was seething next to him, when she spoke

she sounded angry. "She's a fucking bully. She has connections in the city and at the state trooper's and she totally uses them to fuck with people."

Carmen was practically pulling her hair at this point. "She's done this before too. A few years ago she almost ran a guy out of town who was teaching one-on-one yoga, because she decided it was taking business from her daughter's studio." She threw her hands up in exasperation. "Her kids don't even talk to her."

A surge of fury filled me. How could this woman fuck with my business? My livelihood, because she decided it was stealing the spotlight from her kid's hobby?

Jude's brows dipped in a furrow. "It had to be her. Why would she say that today and not an hour later you're getting a call from sanitation? She's pissed my project might get funded and she can't fuck with my head anymore. And she's pissed her son's truck is a total disaster and yours has only been in town a month and is already getting all kinds of buzz. She's horrible. I'm sorry, Nesto." He squeezed my shoulder, his blue eyes dark with worry.

"If that woman does anything else to mess with my business, she'll be sorry."

Jude put his hands on my chest. "The inspection will be fine. As soon as the inspector walks into your truck, she'll see no one has higher standards than you do. This is a distraction. She won't win."

He hugged me in silence and after a few minutes headed back to his office, leaving me to figure out what to do while I waited for the inspection, which could make or break me.

I tried not to lose my shit with the inspector still in the truck, but it was really fucking hard not to walk over to that library and blow up on Misty. The only thing keeping me in check was the fact Inspector Muriel looked like she wanted to be doing this even less than I wanted it to be happening.

She'd been in the truck for about thirty minutes and so far hadn't asked a single question. I was trying not to track her every move with my death glare, so I kept updating Jude over text to distract myself. He said Misty had been walking by their office and smirking until Carmen told her to get her bony ass out of her sight.

I laughed out loud at that.

One point for the Dominicans.

I was still a ball of nerves though and was about to go in and see how much longer this would take when the inspector stepped out of the truck.

She looked at me with a bewildered expression. "Mr. Vasquez, your truck, your food, and everything surrounding it—including the trash can—are immaculate. Frankly, unless someone sold you something off, which I'm sure would've resulted in more than one person getting sick, I can't imagine these conditions causing anyone buying your food issues."

I sighed, dizzy with relief. "Does this mean we can open again?"

She nodded. "I don't see why not." She looked around and said in a low voice, "You didn't hear this from me, but I think this whole thing was just a higher-up putting pressure on one of the supervisors. There is no reason anyone should've come out here just from one random call."

Misty's stunt had cost me an entire day of profits. I'd had to turn people away and watch them go across the street to get lunch somewhere else, because Misty decided she wanted me gone from town. I wasn't in a position to lose money like that. The reality was a few more days like today could put me out of business.

But what could I do? I couldn't actually accuse Misty of trying to shut me down. She'd just laugh in my face and tell me I was trying to intimidate her. What I needed to do was get back to work.

I turned to the inspector again, grateful that she came on such short notice. "Thanks for your help, I'm glad you found everything in order, and for being so flexible about coming today. Having this truck closed for the weekend would have been a serious problem for me."

I extended my hand and she shook it, chuckling as she looked at the truck. "It was no trouble at all. If everyone kept their spaces to the same standards you do, my job would be a lot easier, not to mention a lot less cringeworthy. Take care, Mr. Vasquez."

"Thanks, Inspector Muriel."

As soon as she was in her car, I turned around and called Yin and Ari, who I tried to send home after explaining what happened, but refused to leave me to deal with this on my own. They'd sat around all day and were now at the picnic table we kept by the truck with concerned looks on their faces.

I clapped my hands and gave them a thumbs-up. "Okay, guys, we're back in business." They both perked up and stood at attention, ready to work. Their faith in me made me vow to do whatever I needed to make OuNYe succeed. This was not about just me anymore. There were people counting on me, people who loved my business as much as I did.

"We lost today, but tomorrow we have the festival. Let's get the truck back to Trumansburg and get to work getting ready for that." They both nodded, as I tossed my car keys to Ari.

"I'll get the truck and I'll see you guys at the kitchen."

"You got it, boss." Ari gave me a short nod before they both started walking to the car.

Chapter Fifteen

Nesto

"Nesto, you didn't say your guy looked like Hunter Parrish." I glanced over to where Milo was pointing and spotted Jude on the other side of the festival grounds walking toward us in the red OuNYe t-shirt I'd given him a few days ago, paired with very well-fitting navy shorts. He also had on a green baseball hat with the library logo, and sunglasses perched on his nose. The stress of the last twenty-four hours had taken a toll on me and I'd been on edge all morning, fussing about everything needing to be perfect. But as soon as I saw him walking up the path, the tension in my shoulders seemed to melt away. It was hard to stand there and not just hurry to where he was and kiss him. I tried to keep my cool though. The guys ragging on me about my thirstiness in front of Jude would not be fun.

I winked at Milo, who was still staring in Jude's direction. "He's not my anything, and I don't need to dish about how he looks to you. What are we, fourteen?"

Patrice, who was working on filling the fridge with the desserts, just shook his head and laughed. "You know Camilo, he needs to turn it into a fairytale."

Milo rolled his eyes and looked at us like we were idiots. "Please stop trying to play yourself with this 'just neighbors' bullshit, Nesto, because you're not playing us," he said, pointing at his own chest. "There's nothing neighborly about the way you were just eye-fucking him. And whatever, Patrice, just because your idea of dating is meeting some trick once a month for sex doesn't mean others can't be into the people they're seeing."

I stepped in between them before they got into something. "Okay, let's not get into an argument in front of Jude, so chill the fuck out." Patrice and Milo were arguing constantly, and yet they were the closest of all of us. Patrice even went to live with Milo and his mom while things cooled off at his place after he came out to his mom. They were tight, more than brothers, but fuck could they argue.

I lifted a shoulder as I kept my eye on Jude, who was getting closer. "What's the difference if I'm into him? Doesn't change things. I'm here for business, not a relationship."

If looks could kill, I'd be bleeding out on the floor from the one Camilo shot me. "Why can't you ever fucking relax, Nesto? You like him. He likes you, you see each other all the time. You're fucking—"

I balked at that. Camilo threw his hand up, and spoke in a low voice, his eyes trained on Jude. "Okay technically not fucking, but together all the time and by the looks of it, you both enjoy each other. Why not let yourself have this?"

Both Patrice and Camilo stared at me expectantly, but I was not getting into this now. I sighed, looking around for Juanpa, who'd disappeared a while ago. "Where's J? Please tell me he's not walking around hitting on people." They both shook their heads at me like they knew exactly what I was doing. "Fine. I'll try to relax more, now shut up because he's going to hear us gabbing about him like we're middle graders."

I was trying some deep breathing when Jude came up to the tent and gave us a little wave. "Hey, sorry I'm late. Traffic was bumper to bumper getting here. Unusual, but definitely a good sign."

I straightened from where I'd been working with Patrice and leaned over the counter. I was going to do a shoulder slap, then thought better of it and gave him a kiss.

He seemed a bit startled, but after a second he leaned in and pressed our lips together. He sighed as I stole my tongue into his mouth. I leaned back to take a good look at him, and the blush on his cheeks made my pulse race.

"Hey, you're looking fly. If I ever want to sell OuNYe merch you're going to be the t-shirt model." That blush crept down his neck and I had to go in for another kiss. I pulled back and saw Patrice and Milo staring at us with funny looks. I was about to say something when Juanpa "Mr. Extra" himself, walked up to the stand hollering.

"Damn, Nes, you flexin' so we all know you have a man? I mean that *is* your man right?"

He was dressed in his version of "Upstate Fresh." It involved a lot of white linen and Gucci slides, because he was just that fucking tacky.

"J, please tell me you have other shoes and the OuNYe shirt in the car, you're going to lose a toe in that tent wearing those things on your feet," I said, pointing at the black, green and red slides. "And you're talking to me about flexin', son? You look like a jacked-up Henny ad."

I heard Milo and Patrice busting up behind me, but Juanpa just flipped me off and kept walking to the car. Over his shoulder he waved and yelled, "Nice to meet you, Jude."

Patrice was looking at Juanpa and grinning like he was fucking hilarious. Milo just rolled his eyes and walked up to us.

"Hey, Jude, it's nice to finally meet you. I haven't gotten nearly enough information about you since Nesto can't send texts longer than two words."

I sighed and Jude laughed as he shook hands with my friend. "I'm lucky I have him in person then, because I've heard a lot about you guys. It's nice to finally meet you, Camilo. I like your hat, that's a great organization." He pointed at Milo's hat which had the logo of a place that worked with human trafficking survivors. I knew about it from all the years Milo volunteered for them. I saw my friend's nod, and knew Jude had just earned some serious points.

One down, two to go.

Then Jude turned to Patrice. "You must be Patrice." P offered his hand to Jude, smiling wide.

"It's nice to meet you," he said, winking at me. "Did Nesto force you to come work for free all weekend too?"

Jude laughed and bumped my shoulder. "Oh no, I offered! This event is a big deal, and he'll need lots of help. Especially after all the stress from yesterday. I'm so glad that got resolved."

The guys had gotten an update when they'd arrived. Thankfully, by the time they drove in, the crisis was over, but they all thought I shouldn't let it go and should file a complaint about Misty. I told them I was going to keep working.

Just as Milo was about to respond with what I was sure would be cussing and threats for Misty, I heard my mom's voice behind us. "Jude, you're here. I'm so happy you came!"

She walked up with Minerva, who was on her phone, like always. I was seriously worried we would have to have the damn thing surgically removed.

When he saw Mamí, Jude's back straightened and his eyes got a panicked look to them. I could see Milo and Patrice trying not to laugh.

"¿Como está, Señora Maldonado? Hi, Minerva." I smiled when he said my mom's name. He'd remembered she had a different last name than mine. He also pronounced my sister's name perfectly. That was one of the things I loved about him, he was never careless with the little things.

"It's good to see you," he said while offering my mom his hand. She slapped it away playfully and went in for the hug and kiss combo.

"¿Qué es eso, muchacho? Handshakes are for gringos, we're Dominican. We hug and kiss when we see each other!" Jude grinned and then blushed as my mom went in for a second kiss on the cheek. She looked over at me. "Nesto, his Spanish is so good, we need to take him with us to Santo Domingo when we go in December."

Then she turned around and took my sister's phone. "Minerva, niña, dejá ese teléfono. Come say hi to Jude!"

I rolled my eyes at her, because really? We'd barely known each other for a month and she already had us going on a family trip to DR.

"Mamí, why don't we focus on surviving this weekend before we plan any trips?" I said, trying to hustle

her back to the truck. "I'll come over there to help you
and Yin with the vegetables."

"Okay, m'ijo," she said to me. Then she turned to
Jude and fake whispered, "We'll talk about the trip
later," before going into the truck, pulling Minerva
along with her. "Don't let those boys give you a hard
time, Jude," she said, pointing to Milo and Patrice as she
walked away. I can still whoop them if they get fresh
with you. I know their mamas!"

The guys laughed as I shook my head, Jude looked
a little embarrassed, but he had an amused expression
on his face.

"Sorry about that. She's impossible."

"She's a fucking legend is what she is." Milo and my
mom had always been thick as thieves.

Jude smiled, looking amused. "I like her, and I won't
say no to DR in December." He was already getting
to work helping Milo and Patrice with the front of the
house stuff. I stood there for a moment taking in all the
activity around me. The tent was about twelve by twelve
and positioned so we could have the truck pulled up to
the back. We'd have two people cooking in the truck,
three prepping food, two taking orders and two bag-
ging and processing payments. With that plan we'd be
able to handle all the customers I was hoping we'd pull
in over the weekend.

The festival grounds were epic too. Between two of
the largest wineries on Seneca Lake, right on the shore.
The sky was totally clear today and we could see the
mountains on the other side of the lake. The blue of the
water contrasted with the green of the trees was pretty
gorgeous. It wasn't the heart-stopping view of the Manhattan skyline, but even I had to admit it had its merits.

We would work hard this weekend, but we could not pick a more beautiful spot or better weather. I was feeling good with my people at my side this morning. I decided to put the shit with the inspector behind me and focus on making the best out of the opportunities the festival would bring.

By the time I came back from working the back with my mom, I found Milo holding court while Patrice, Juanpa and Jude took a water break. "Yo, this isn't the Camilo Briggs Variety Show, your brown ass is here to work."

"Pssh, tranquilo, Nesto," Milo said, utterly undisturbed. "Take it easy. We're just taking a break before all the people get here."

Patrice nodded in Jude's direction. "Jude was telling us about his project with the library. It sounds great." His usually serious face was open and he genuinely sounded impressed by Jude's book truck. "He's planning on having a social justice section, rotating books every month. He's starting with James Baldwin and W.E.B Du Bois." And with that, I knew Jude was in with P.

Juanpa nodded. "He's got the YA hook-up too." Juanpa for all his *papito* flow, was a total young adult novel fanboy. He actually went to readings and got books signed. He'd even dragged me to a few over the years. It was sort of cute that they had that in common.

I went over to Jude and hugged him from behind. I knew I was doing too much with the PDA, but I couldn't help myself. If the way Jude leaned into me when I tightened my arms around him was any indication, he was okay with the change. After what Camilo said this morning, I felt something shift in me. He was right. Jude and I enjoyed each other.

Why *couldn't* I let myself have this? Right then and there I decided that as soon as I got a chance, I'd talk to him about how I felt.

"Did you guys figure out if you like some of the same authors?"

Jude nodded and turned around smiling at me. "We did actually, we both loved *The Hate U Give* by Angie Thomas. I might have to come down to the city and go to a reading with Juanpa when her next book comes out."

"You better watch yourself, J," I teased with my arms still around Jude.

"Well well, Mr. OuNYe, I see you've been making friends with the locals." I let go of Jude after he stiffened at the comment, then turned around to see Easton walking toward us. As always he looked like he was stepping straight out of a Polo ad. Today he was rocking seersucker shorts with a white short-sleeve button-down shirt, and a pair of mirrored aviators.

Jude relaxed when he realized who it was. Easton was a regular at the truck now, and they'd run into each other a few times. We hadn't exactly made our thing public, but I left my hand on Jude's shoulder as I shook Easton's.

"Hey, man, didn't expect to see you here today."

"And miss the biggest event of the summer? My dad's winery is sponsoring and I promised my mom I'd make an appearance." I noticed once again that his smile didn't exactly reach his eyes whenever he talked about his family.

He turned to Jude. "How are you? We missed you at the last potluck, now I know why."

Jude smiled shyly, but there was fire in those blues eyes. "There were more interesting things on my social calendar this month."

"Nesto, you better watch it. Once the word gets out, there will be a lot of single men in town wanting to ask what your secret is." Easton's grin was pure mischief.

I lifted an eyebrow and said deadpan. "The single men in town can take a seat."

Easton beamed while Jude blushed.

I turned to Milo, Juan Pablo and Patrice who were giving Easton the kind of look only a person who'd grown up in the Bronx could give. It said, "Who is this loud dude, and do we have to kick his ass?"

I waved my hand between them and Easton. "Easton, these are my best friends Camilo, Juan Pablo and Patrice. They came up from the city to help me with the truck this weekend."

"Guys, this is Easton Archer, one of the ADAs with the county, and also a big fan of the Mayimbe. The man loves his Dominican rice and beans."

Easton laughed, extending his hand to Milo. "That I do, although lately the Manno has been making me change my order," he said, flashing us with his million-dollar smile.

The guy kept up with his whitening strips applications that was for damn sure.

Milo shook his hand, and I could tell he was trying hard not to give Easton too much of a death stare. The social worker had a lot to say about mass incarceration and the legal system. Juanpa just ignored him and went back to doing something on his phone, because he had no fucking manners.

Patrice was eying Easton up and down too. P wasn't exactly throwing parties for prosecutors, but the look he was giving Easton was confusing. It was like he either wanted to punch the guy or fuck him...or both. Easton straightened when he shook Patrice's hand and did not hide in the slightest that he liked what he saw very much.

"Nice to meet you, Patrice." They shook hands a bit longer than necessary, then eye-fucked each other for a few more seconds before letting go.

Before things got out of hand, I clapped my hands to break the tension. "Ooookay, fun times are over. You all know what to do, and help out Jude if he needs a hand."

I pointed in the direction of some of the other stands. "Easton, go distract the competition, man. These guys are here to work, not socialize."

He laughed, putting his hands up. "Fine, I'll leave." His face got serious and he looked around, then spoke softly, "I just came over to ask you if you'd had any more trouble with Misty. I noticed her son's stand isn't here, and I know she was expecting a vendor pass."

He shook his head when he saw the way I reacted to the mention of Misty. "What did she do?"

I shrugged and noticed Jude had stayed behind to listen. "I'm not sure if it has to do with her, but sanitation randomly showed up at the truck yesterday saying they received a complaint that someone got sick from eating at the truck. They wouldn't let me serve until they did an inspection."

Easton's eyebrows shot up. "I wouldn't be surprised if she was behind that. Did they give you a hard time?"

"No, actually the inspector was great. She just couldn't come until late afternoon, which meant the day was a total loss. Not the end of the world, but a few more of those could really hurt me." I shifted and looked at Jude who was now standing next to us. I could tell he was itching to say what went down with him and Misty. "She did say she thought the whole thing was a little shady. Like shutting me down over a single complaint, when my last inspection had gone well, was a little over the top." At this Easton turned to Jude, who looked ready to burst.

"You guys work together, right? Do you think she'd do something like that?"

"I don't think, I'm one-hundred percent sure she did. I wish Nesto would let me talk to Martha." I was about to say "hell nah" when Jude held his hand up at me. "I know you don't want me to talk to her, but I think Martha should know what she's been up to. Misty is a bigot and a bully. The library serves everyone in our community, and someone like that shouldn't be associated with us."

By this point he had his hands on his hips and looked righteously pissed. "You know Martha, Easton. She wouldn't let Misty get away with this, no matter who she's married to. But this isn't even about the library. It's not okay for her to mess with Nesto's business."

I looked over at the counter and saw my mom and the guys all had stopped what they were doing and were watching Jude's rant. I'd never let anyone get anywhere near my business or my life like I had with Jude, but they all looked like they were totally into what he was preaching.

Easton looked at me. "Why not, Nesto? They should know she's been harassing you."

I shook my head, and then tried to give Jude a smile. "You don't know what it means that you're willing to narc her out because of me, but I'd rather deal with this myself."

From behind I heard a yelp from my mother. Without looking I held up my hand. "No, Mamí. A mí no me gusta eso. You know I don't like people fixing my problems. This lady is coming for me," I said, slapping a hand to my chest. "I will deal with her, and I don't want anyone of mine getting into something with her."

I saw Jude's eyes widen like he'd been surprised by something, and then I realized what I'd said: "anyone of mine."

Right. I was going to sidestep that for a time when we didn't have an audience.

I turned to Jude and tried not to read too much into the fact that he'd taken a step closer to me.

"This lady has the ability to mess with your project, and just from how nasty she's gotten I'm sure she'll try and fuck with you if you get her fired. Please don't say anything, and, Easton, thanks for asking, but for now, I'm going to keep my head down. This woman is not the first and won't be the last person who will see me coming up, and want to put my brown ass back in its place." I exhaled loudly. "This is not a problem I'm going to solve going toe to toe with this lady. If I go and blow up on her the *least* she'll do is say I'm hood trash trying to intimidate her, at worst she'll call the cops on me."

At this I saw Easton's face changed like he was about to argue.

"Easton, I get you think that's not how things go

down around here, but I've been walking around in this brown body too fucking long to be careless. This is not a game I can win by getting angry." I sighed, already dead tired of talking about Misty. "I have to beat her the only way I can, by being so fucking excellent, nothing she does can touch me."

Easton nodded, finally conceding my point, and Jude came up to me with what looked like realization in his face. He held my hand, those blue eyes blazing. "It's not fair. This isn't even really about you being competition. She just does it because she's mean and bored."

I sighed and squeezed his hand. "It *isn't* fair, but I have a lot of good people in my corner."

Chapter Sixteen

Nesto

We were selling a lot of burritos. The festival so far was proving to be a great place to get our name out there. It was mid-afternoon and the line had been about forty people deep since eleven a.m. People were coming by, loving our food and then bringing friends.

Jude had been a star all day too, talking up customers and keeping the guys entertained up front with insanely bad Spanish jokes. Seeing him with my friends, working together to push my business, made me so damn happy. I was staring at him with what I knew could only be described as a dopey grin on my face when I noticed my mom watching him too.

She gestured for me to come over and whispered with a smile tugging at her lips. "Your gringito seems to be doing a pretty good job of selling your food, Ernesto. And I liked how indignant he was on your behalf when we were talking to Easton before. He cares a lot about you, m'ijo."

I nodded, still looking at Jude. "I know, Mamí, I like him too." I kept my eyes on him and as I got closer I heard him give a woman information about the Marley.

"This is our Jamaican burrito, you get either jerk chicken or jerk fish, peas and rice, picklin, which is a spicy pickled slaw, and yucca straws. It's pretty fantastic and you can get it with a side of the scotch bonnet jam. I like to just put a little bit on each bite."

"How do you make the fish?"

"The fish is dipped in a Red Stripe and Jerk batter." When he said it, he actually rolled his eyes in apparent ecstasy, which was pretty damn distracting. "It's phenomenal."

The woman moaned. "It sounds amazing. Tell me about the dessert. What's in the majarete?"

He beamed at her before answering. "It's one of my favorites! Majarete is a Dominican sweet, it's like a pudding made of sweet corn. OuNYe's is topped with a passion fruit glaze that's torched, so it's a bit like a brulee. I highly recommend it."

"Okay, you've convinced me. I'll take one, an order of the tostones and the Marley with the fish. I'll have the dessert first, it sounds so good I need to taste it now."

Jude winked at her, then leaned over and whispered, "I won't tell if you don't." When he passed her the little cup, she practically tore the lid off.

I kept doing my thing, with my eye on Jude, impressed by how much he already knew about my food. The more staying here became a solid possibility, the more I wanted Jude to be part of the picture long-term. His presence in my life kept changing the script.

After a few minutes I saw the woman come back to talk to Jude. "Oh my god. This is amazing," she cried and held up the majarete. "I need to know how this pudding is made."

Jude smiled at her and said, "I knew you'd love it."

Then he started looking around until he spotted me and crooked his finger.

If he only knew how tightly wrapped around that finger I was already.

"Hey, Nesto, come over here, someone wants to know about the majarete recipe."

I walked over and smiled at the woman. "Are you enjoying it?" She nodded enthusiastically, looking like she was about to propose to the pudding cup.

"It's delicious. I've never had anything quite like this. I've had Dominican food a ton. I live in Washington Heights and there are great spots all over, but usually they have flan or tres leches. I've never even seen this before."

"Yes, flan and tres leches are more widely used in Latin restaurants, but neither of them are actually Dominican. Majarete is a traditional dessert in DR and Puerto Rico. But it's the kind of thing you usually eat at home, not so much in restaurants," I explained while she gobbled up another spoonful of the creamy custard. "I like to use my desserts as a bit of a nostalgia experiment. Make things those of us from the islands haven't had since we were kids, but with a bit of a contemporary twist, which is where the glaze comes in."

She was completely focused on what I was saying, so I kept going. "And for those who are trying it for the first time, it's a good way to be introduced to food that is part of our heritage."

She nodded. "I love that. I could tell from the name, the menu and the whole vibe of the place that you've put a lot of thought into your food, the smells from your stand attracted me as soon as I stepped on the festival grounds. I'm excited to try the rest. By the way, Jude has done a great job of telling me about the recipes and the inspiration for the food."

Jude blushed, and I squeezed his shoulder. "He's amazing."

The lady was looking at us like we were the cutest thing she'd ever seen when Juanpa handed over the bag with her order. "Thanks so much. Do you have a card by any chance? I'm in the area a lot and would love your information."

Jude was already on the case, passing her one of our palm cards. She tucked it in her pocket and waved goodbye.

I leaned over and kissed Jude on the cheek. "I had no idea you were so passionate about my food."

He rolled his eyes as he got ready to tend to another customer. "It's not like I can say it's bad! Now shoo, I need to get back to work."

"That's not the face of a man who sold almost three hundred burritos in eight hours," Jude chastised as he walked toward me with Milo and Patrice in tow.

I smiled at them as they got closer. "I was just thinking Mr. Sheridan never showed up, that's all," I said as I pulled Jude's hand, bringing him closer. Milo rolled his eyes at me as he did something on his phone.

"Nesto, it'll happen. You did so much business. You know how hard it is to get that much attention when there are so many other vendors. Yet this place was swarming with people all day." He walked over and tugged on my ear as he usually did when he thought I was being particularly dense. "The buzz is building, but you have to be patient, pa."

"He'll be here tomorrow," Jude said with certainty.

"Sheridan is known for having a good eye for business and yours is a sure bet."

"Did you just get off the phone with him or something?" I teased.

Patrice smiled at us and nodded in agreement. "These things take time, and they're definitely looking positive." He clapped my shoulder, his eyes serious. "I have faith in you, Nes, but you know that no matter what happens, we'll be here to hold you down. New York City will always be your home."

As he said that I felt Jude stiffen, then immediately loosen his body, like he realized I had noticed it.

Fuck.

I was grateful for my friends and their support, but Patrice's timing was not the best.

I shook my head and squeezed Jude tight, before letting him go. "Never mind, I'm just getting jittery because I'm tired as fuck, and I still have at least five more hours of work before I can get to bed."

Jude turned around and looked up at me with a determined expression. "I can help you." He was trying to smile, but his eyes looked sad. "Looks like Ari and Yin have the cleanup covered and the truck is ready to go. Your mom said she'd pick up more drinks tomorrow, so the only thing left is the food prep. I can drive my car home, take a quick shower and then walk over to the kitchen, it's like a ten-minute walk."

I shook my head, feeling like shit about how much he'd done for me already. Because what was I to him? I couldn't even guarantee I'd be around in a couple of months.

"Nah. You've already done too much. You guys can head home and I'll finish up at the kitchen." My hands twitched to grab him again. It was like my body only felt at ease when he was close.

Milo rolled his eyes. "Of course we'll come and help. That's why we're here, besides what do Patrice and Juanpa have to do other than troll Grindr and Tinder?" Patrice ignored him, walking to the car, and Juanpa was too busy on the other side of the tent—apparently giving some girl his number—to care.

Camilo pointed at J. "Once the man whore over there is done putting numbers into his phone we're heading out. We'll stop at our hotel for a bit and then go to the kitchen. We were there with Nurys this morning, so we're good with the code for the door."

I really was a lucky bastard. "Okay, man. I'll see you there then."

Juanpa and Milo left as Jude and I worked out our next move. "Nesto, I'll come and help. That way you can finish sooner and get some sleep. You're going to be dead tomorrow if you go to bed at three a.m."

"Are you sure? You must be exhausted. You've already done so much and I know how stressed out you were for your board meeting all week."

He looked so cute when he tried to act annoyed at me. "Yes, I'm sure. Come on, let's finish here so we can get moving."

Jude was like that, steady and reliable. He'd made this first month here so much better, and never asked me for anything, just gave and gave.

I felt his hand tighten around mine. "So, are we going?"

I smiled at him, trying to chase away my rambling thoughts. For once trying not to bring all my baggage with me. "If you're sure, but only if we can go back to your place and hang out a little bit after. I need to un-wind tonight even if it's twenty minutes."

He smiled and kissed me. "Sure, you're always wel-come at my place. We'll get the food ready and then you can come over."

"Maybe I should be a good neighbor and pay you back for all your hard work with a back rub."

He let out a husky chuckle at my leering and rolled his eyes. "I won't turn down a back rub, but I'd say that's above and beyond neighborly etiquette." We'd blurred the lines of this friendship to a point that I was afraid I was going to start getting hard just from hearing the word neighbor.

Did that stop me?

No, it did not.

I kept leering at him and made a show of rubbing his shoulders, my mouth against his ear. "I can do a lot more than your back."

He squirmed a bit. "Nesto, there are still a few peo-ple around." The smile on his face was not exactly dis-couraging, so I nipped his ear, then licked where my teeth had been.

He shivered and leaned into my touch for a moment before moving away. As he walked to his car, he called back, "We don't have time for games, Ernesto Vasquez. You've got food to make and I need a back rub, all within the next three hours."

I laughed and ran to catch up with him. I hoped that I could make this plan work: this truck, this town, and what I'd started with Jude.

Chapter Seventeen

Jude

"If I have to peel one more garlic clove, my left thumb may be in serious danger of falling off," Milo complained from his end of the long stainless steel table Nesto set us up with to chop and peel the vegetables he needed. We were working on a marinade for the meat at the moment. It was called *recao,* an all-purpose recipe used all over the Caribbean. It required enormous amounts of garlic, onion, cilantro, oranges, limes and Cubanelle peppers, which we needed to get ready for Nesto to blend.

I laughed and shook my head as I worked a paring knife around an onion. Camilo was hilarious and in the forty-five minutes since we'd started, he'd claimed he couldn't feel his forearms from peeling plantains, and that his mouth was numb from the sting of the hot peppers.

Juanpa glared at him. "Bruh, just shut up and work. Do you need to be so dramatic all the time?"

It was only the three of us, since Patrice had mysteriously disappeared with the car, saying he'd be "back in an hour." When he left Juanpa said he'd probably just go out for a drive, since he usually needed alone time after a day around so many people, but Milo had called bullshit, and said he was probably out fucking Easton. I had to say—after the multiple rounds of eye-fucking I'd witnessed between those two today—Milo's version seemed more likely to me.

I turned my attention back to their conversation to see Milo staring Juanpa down. "I'm not even going to answer that. Now all normal conversation is drama for you? Hanging out with all those jocks has gone to your head. You gotta actually leave the stadium and come see your people, lest you forget where you hail from."

Camilo was small compared to his friends, who all looked like they could be on the roster of a professional sports team. He was shorter than my own five-foot-ten by a couple of inches with the body of a dancer. His hair was a dark brown, and it was very thick and curly. He'd had it under a hat all day, but now he'd put it up in a bun. He was very pretty. His skin was a beautiful deep bronze, but what caught my attention were his eyes, which were an intense gray. His slight figure and smaller size did nothing to tamp down all that attitude, though. Of the four of them, he was clearly the one in charge.

Juanpa flipped him off without even looking up and kept on juicing oranges. "You don't even live in the Bronx anymore, asshole." A smile clear in his voice.

Milo shrugged and kept chopping, then stopped. "Actually you know what we need? Some music. Now that we have the place to ourselves, we can put some on." There'd been other people using the kitchen when we got in earlier, but they'd left about fifteen minutes before. "Here," he said, taking off his gloves and rins-

ing his hands in the sink behind us. "I have speakers
in my bag."

Milo went over to the shelf where we put our stuff
and looked through his backpack, pulling out one of
those small cordless speakers that look like a huge red
pill.

He took his phone out of his pocket, tapped a few
buttons on the screen, and after a moment the opening
sounds of Calle 13's *Latinoamerica* filled the space.
I loved that song, one of the most powerful pieces of
music I'd ever heard. Calle 13, a Puerto Rican hip-hop
duo who made very good and very political music, was
one of my favorites. I had listened to this album dozens
of times when it came out. So when the song started,
I sang along.

I muttered the lyrics as I chopped, thinking how
much I loved the words and the cadence of the voices
when I noticed that Milo and Juanpa were staring at me.

"What?" I asked, looking around.

"You know Calle 13?" Camilo asked with a look
of complete astonishment on his face. Nesto walked
over when he heard the music and grinned at Milo's
amazement.

"Yes, I do. I'm a big fan. Don't give me too much
credit on my Latinx music prowess though; I discovered them in the whitest way possible."

At this all three of them turned to me with different versions of a look that said, "Oh, I can't wait to
hear *this*."

I paused for effect, then quickly muttered. "NPR."

They all cracked up and laughed for a full minute
at my comment. I was not usually the guy who brings

down the house with a one-liner. It felt kind of good to make someone other than Carmen laugh at my jokes.

Nesto came over and bumped my shoulder, looking at me with so much affection and humor my chest filled with warmth.

"That totally counts! These two are diehard NPR listeners." He pointed in the direction of his friends. "Don't let them give you any shade for that. Milo walks around all over town with NPR totes and shit."

Milo was still chuckling and just shook his head. "You're a damn fool, Ernesto Vasquez, but at least your man has taste." I felt a thrill run through my body with the casual way Milo referred to me as Nesto's "man." I looked over at him to see how he'd react, but he just widened his eyes, pointed at himself and yelled a loud, *"Hello?"*

Juanpa was next. He stopped chuckling and with a very serious face put his hand up, as if asking for a moment of silence then said, "NPR is legit. You still get full credit." With that, he went back to juicing oranges.

Milo looked over at Nesto, shaking his head with disgust. "Of course you, Mr. No Politics, would get with the one gringo who knows all the words to a song that's essentially one of the modern Latinx rights anthems."

Milo turned back to me and pointed. "You're a keeper." Then to Nesto. *"No la cagues.* Do not fuck this up."

Nesto shook his head and laughed. "Fuck off."

I smiled at Milo. "Well, I appreciate your approval. Although Calle 13 are very well known."

Nesto came over and pecked my cheek. "I need to watch out or Milo might try to steal you, and I'm counting on your mad burrito selling skills to put the truck on the map. You were pretty amazing with the customers today."

He rinsed his hands and was now standing behind me with both of them on my waist. I had to put the knife down before I mutilated myself with all the stuff happening in my body with him so close. "It's not hard to sell your food. It's delicious and insanely cheap. How hard could it be to convince people?"

"That's it though," he said, his voice full of something which made me take this conversation much more seriously. "You're not just saying the food is good to be nice, you believe in my business and what I'm trying to do. You went above and beyond with every customer today. That woman you helped this afternoon brought back friends afterwards, and she even took photos." By now he was also nuzzling my neck.

My entire body was flushing hot and cold and the butterflies in my stomach were so intense I felt like I was on a roller coaster. I felt self-conscious that Milo and Juanpa were watching and I thought about what Patrice said earlier, that Nesto could go back to New York if things didn't work, and it felt like a stab in my gut. I knew Patrice was trying to be supportive, but just the thought of Nesto not being here, or worse, of him having to go back to New York to start over, had seriously unsettled me.

I wanted to turn around right then and ask him: *What are we doing? What happens if the thing with Sheridan doesn't work out? Am I even part of the equation when you think about what's next? Will you let me be there for you if things don't go as planned?*

I shook my head, trying to stay in the moment. Nesto's touch grounding me. Possessive and gentle at once. Feeling bold and wanting to stake my claim too, I bent my head and brought his hand up so I could kiss the tips of his fingers.

I looked up and saw Milo and Juanpa staring at us. For a moment I thought I saw a mix of worry and tenderness on Milo's face, but it was gone in a flash. As soon as he saw me looking at him, he made a show of covering his eyes.

"Pendejo, are we here to prepare the food or watch you suck on this one's neck? Vamos muevete!"

Nesto flushed, gave me one more squeeze and went back to doing whatever he was doing to an enormous amount of chicken breasts. After a few minutes I finished peeling garlic and handed the mountain of cloves to Juanpa, who was waiting to take them over to Nesto.

"Here you go." He smiled and took them.

"Thanks." He shook his head, as he looked in Nesto's direction. "Only for one of these assholes would I spend a perfectly good Saturday night up to my elbows in garlic and onions. Nesto! Where do you want this, man?" he called out.

"Is that the garlic?" Nesto asked, without pausing what he was doing. "Bring it over and we'll grind them to finish the *recao*."

Juanpa got moving and took the stuff over to the industrial-size blenders. While he and Nesto were over in the area with the food processors and the gigantic tubs of meat, Camilo and I kept working on our chopping. After a few minutes he started talking, as if we'd been in the middle of a conversation.

"I've never seen Nesto break his focus when he's working before, but when you're around, every few minutes he'll stop what he's doing and look for you. Like he's making sure you're still there."

I stayed quiet, not sure what to say. I'd never been that person for anyone. I was not the one who brought others to distraction: always an extra, never the protagonist.

I had friends and I had a life, but never that kind of connection with someone else. Even with my ex, Elijah, things had never felt intentional. More like we were trying something out with each other.

I shook my head and shrugged, going for lightness. "He's just making sure I'm doing something useful."

The annoyed look on Camilo's face told me he wasn't buying it. "No, that's not it. Nesto doesn't waste his time with people who don't know how to make *themselves* useful. He'll tell you what he needs once, if it's not done when he comes back, he'll start doing it himself. That's what I meant when I said I'd never seen him lose his focus. Nesto is a single-minded motherfucker, and he is *always* working on something. College, career, culinary school, opening the truck. He's always after something, and whatever it is, it's the only thing that matters."

He smiled and looked over to where Nesto was throwing something into a giant mixer, while Juanpa power-blended vegetables.

"And you better be ready to be iced out if you get in the way, or fuck with his plan. Other than Patrice, Nesto is the most intense guy I know, but with you, he's all soft," he said, sounding astonished. "I've never seen him like that." He lifted his eyebrows at me like he knew I was the one responsible for this change, but he must have noticed the panic on my face because he laughed and shook his head.

"It's a good thing. *You're* good for him. He needs

someone to give him a reason to stop and smell the roses a little bit. Remind him things other than his damn business plan are important too."

I looked down at the onions I was supposed to be chopping, because I was feeling too many things. I wasn't sure what any of this meant.

So far Nesto had seemed so casual, he was attentive and present when we were together, but there was no question his main priority was OuNYe. No matter how bad I may have wanted more, I hadn't indulged in fantasies of a future. Hope was a dangerous thing for me in relationships. I couldn't trust it and I certainly couldn't count on someone picking me over a dream or a conviction.

My family had taught me that lesson very well.

And that wasn't even fair because no matter how well things were going, or how close we got, Nesto hadn't made a single promise. He was here for his business.

I shook my head and said, "He's got his six months to make OuNYe a success. That's the most important thing right now."

Milo gave me one of those whole-body eye rolls I'd seen him dish out throughout the day, and said, "Oh honey, that six-month plan was just a way for Nesto to appease his control freak ways. He can't think past November because after that he'll have to make *decisions*, hard ones. He'll either have to decide the truck, which is the only thing he's ever taken a risk on, is a failure, or he has to decide it isn't, and that means leaving New York City for good. Neither of those are easy choices, and both of them require letting go of some control."

I shrugged, trying not to let Camilo in on how much this conversation was affecting me. "Nesto is driven.

I respect that about him, he works hard for what he wants."

"Oh, it's not that he won't work for it. He will grind himself into the earth's core going for something he wants, even if after he's dug himself back out, he's the only one left." He sighed and looked over to where Nesto and Juanpa were running three machines at once.

"Our mothers are lionesses, all of them. Mine, Nesto's, Patrice's, and Juanpa's. We learned to be fighters from them, they taught us working hard and getting an education were the only ways that four queer brown kids from the Bronx would ever get ahead. And we learned not just from what they told us, mind you, but from what we saw. But we also learned other things: stubbornness, and an inability to stop, or ask for help."

I nodded because he was right. How hard Nesto fought me on dealing with Misty on his own was proof of that. Camilo had more to say though. "Nurys is a great mother, she brought up Nesto and Minerva on her own. Kept them out of trouble, loved them, and was an amazing role model. When Nesto came out to her…" He scoffed, but his face shone with fondness and respect. "That woman marched into the principal's office the very next day and told him she would gut *anyone* in the faculty who gave her son a hard time, or didn't make sure the other students left him alone." He shook his head, that fond smile still on his lips.

"But." He put his hand up as if conceding a point to an invisible Nurys. "Not that she wouldn't say this herself, she's had no fucking luck with the men in her life. None."

This time I was the one looking over at where Nesto

was working, because this conversation kept getting more intense.

"Even if she would never speak ill of their dads to either Nesto or Minerva, he saw her struggle on her own. 'Men come in your life to fuck things up.' That's a lesson he learned well. So, Nesto doesn't let himself get swept away." He pursed his lips, as if trying to keep the rest of what he had to say inside his mouth. "Of the four of us, he and Patrice are the guarded ones. Juanpa and I, we get our hearts broken enough for everyone."

He finished with a sad smile on his face, and I wondered if whatever Nesto and I were doing would last long enough for me to get to know Milo better. I liked how direct he was; he just said what was on his mind. It seemed like a very liberating and very painful way to walk through life.

In that moment I felt glad for Nesto and a bit sad for myself, because he had people in his life who knew his story. Who understood the ways in which he was strong and the ways in which he wasn't, and they still loved him. Not despite, but because of it.

I'd made myself hold so much of the past inside for so long, I feared no one truly knew me, not even Carmen. I was about to say something to Milo when I heard a yelp from Nesto on the other side of the room.

"Holy shit yo! This is wild." He came over quickly while tapping on his phone screen with a huge grin on his face. Juanpa was hustling after him, with an equally large grin on his own.

"Nesto, deja eso," Milo said as he smacked him hard on the arm. "Tell us what's going on."

He held up his phone screen for us to see, still smiling wide. It was open to an Instagram account and on the screen there was a photo of a familiar-looking woman holding out one of Nesto's burritos for the person who took the photo. The caption read,

Spent the afternoon in the Finger Lakes Wine and Brew Festival and was blown away by the amazing wine, beer, and food being offered. This is me doing a happy dance before digging into my second burrito of the day from @OuNYeAfroCaribe. If you are at the festival this weekend, stop by their stand for life giving burritos with amazing Caribbean flavors.

The one in the photo is The Marley, inspired by the flavors of Jamaica, including haddock fried in a Jerk and Red Stripe batter. SO GOOD. The couple who run it are two lovely men, who had me literally eating out of their hands. If you are in the area come GET YOUR LIFE with their incredible food. #NYMagazine #OuNYeAfroCaribe #BestName #FingerLakesWine&Brew #Foodstagram #Foodie #FoodCritic

I looked at her face again and realized she was the woman I'd talked with that afternoon. She was wearing the same flowy top and Yankees baseball hat. Apparently she was a critic for New York Magazine and had over two hundred thousand followers. The photo with Nesto's burrito already had more than three thousand likes.

"Wow" was all I could say. I passed the phone back to Nesto and he immediately started tapping on the screen. After a few seconds he looked up at me, smiling. "We've had like three hundred people follow the account since she posted that." He leaned over and kissed me hard on the lips. Then looked back at Juanpa and Milo who were busy checking their phones, I assumed reading the post as well.

"That's the lady Jude helped at the stand today, bruh. I told you guys he was mad good with her." Nesto always fell back into his Bronx accent when he was happy or excited. Every time I heard it, it made me wonder about all the ways in which he'd had to adjust to fit in this country. His true self always half-hidden to deflect people's assumptions of who he was.

"Oh I don't know about that. If the food wasn't amazing, no amount of charm could've made her post that."

Nesto nodded and conceded the point, looking more than a little proud of himself. "True. True. My food is dope, but there were a *lot* of vendors there, and other than a couple wine and beer places she didn't feature anyone else from the festival, and that's huge. Babe, this is the kind of exposure we need. Stuff like this is what puts a business like ours on the map."

He leaned in again to give me another kiss. I had not missed the fact that he used the words "we" and "ours," or that the critic had assumed we were a couple, but I wasn't going to go down that rabbit hole right now either. The conversation with Camilo was enough to have me fretting for days.

Milo was still looking at his phone as he talked. "Nes, you should see the other places she's been posting about, like major foodie spots. This will bring you some attention for sure." He snapped his head up. "You need to repost this on your account, keep the buzz going a bit."

"I will," Nesto said, quickly tapping on his phone screen. "But let's get back to work. We only need a few more things prepared and can go get some rest. Hopefully we'll be doing lots of business tomorrow for when Mr. Sheridan stops by, *if he* stops by." A frown shadowing his handsome face.

Milo laughed. "Now you just want attention. He'll come by. Didn't Jude say like ten times the guy's known in town for being great to work with?"

I nodded. "That's true."

Nesto relaxed, and before going back to his station he stopped and asked quietly, "You still want to hang out afterward?" His lips lightly grazed my ears as he talked. The fluttering in my stomach was getting ridiculous.

"Yes."

"Good." After another kiss he went back to work.

I looked after him, thinking about the conversation with Camilo, and how much I wanted what he said to be true. Nesto's "we" sounded so natural.

Would I really be able to let Nesto know what I hoped for us? I had not even fully let myself in on that secret until tonight. I went back to my chopping, feeling bolder and hopeful.

Chapter Eighteen

Nesto

"So where do you want that back rub?" I asked quietly as we walked into Jude's house. It was only 10:30 p.m. With all the extra hands, we'd managed to get everything done in just a couple of hours, which meant I had a bit more time to hang out with Jude tonight. But now I was buzzing with energy, especially after seeing the post from the food critic, my adrenaline was through the roof.

Jude closed the door, turned around, and put his back against it as I walked into his arms. He ran his hands over the back of my head and looked up at me with a smile.

"If you really are going to give me a massage, you can pick." He was looking at me with such tenderness. He looked happy and tired, his blue eyes a bit hazy. He'd worked hard today. For me.

I ran my hands up and down his arms and put my forehead against his. "Couch?" I asked and he gave me another one of those lazy smiles, and shook his head.

"Ummm well, the best place is the bed." I paused at his comment, because in the weeks since we started seeing each other we'd been intimate plenty of times. I was pretty much addicted to his dick and mouth at this point, but so far his bedroom had been off limits. We'd gotten into my bed, and messed around on his couch a bunch of times, but I hadn't been invited into his bed.

I hadn't asked either. I mean I got plenty of action on his couch and at my place, so why get pushy, right? So, this casual suggestion felt like a big fucking deal. All night I'd been grappling with the feeling that today had changed something for us. I assumed it was him finally meeting the guys and how well they all seemed to gel, but now I knew he must've been feeling it too. I lifted an eyebrow in question, and asked, "Are you sure? We can do it here."

He grabbed my head, pulling me down for a kiss, as he nodded in answer to my question. He licked into my mouth, searching for my tongue.

I loved kissing him.

His lips were thinner than mine, but they were shaped perfectly. He moaned into my mouth and lifted his leg, hooking it with mine. "I want you in my bed, Nesto. I've been wanting you there for weeks, from the first night." Then he laughed and shook his head. "I don't want to wait anymore."

Oh shit.

That put my cock and every nerve in my body at full attention. In the back of my mind I thought we should probably move to the bedroom, but I couldn't make myself stop touching him. I ground up against Jude and tongued my way up his neck, while he leaned his head back against the door, giving me access to his throat. I nipped the soft skin of his neck, and worked my hands under his t-shirt, trying to get my hands on as much skin as I could.

He was making those low panting sounds, which drove me crazy. I hoped I wasn't going too far too fast, but all of a sudden I was so hungry for him. I wanted to fuck him right here against this door.

"Babe, you feel so good," I said, biting his ear. "You wanted a back rub," I mumbled distractedly as his hands went inside my shorts, grabbing my ass hard.

"Yes, we should…" He said it while opening his eyes as if he was waking up from a dream. He lifted off the door, took my hand and led me to his bedroom.

We slowly made our way through his house and down the narrow hall. He turned on the light as we walked in, and even as distracted as I was by him, I smiled when I looked around. The room was exactly like I'd imagined. The walls were an elegant sage with dark mid-century style furniture. His queen-size bed was packed with a multitude of pillows and cushions in various shades of grays and dark blues.

On the walls, he'd hung prints of vintage book covers in glass frames. Over his bed were two beautiful art deco style botanical prints. In one corner of the room I spotted a very comfortable and well-used leather chair with tall stacks of books on each side of it, and a long reading lamp tucked behind.

Everything was neat and tasteful, the only bit of disarray were the books piled all over the room. On the dresser I saw a couple of picture frames, one of him and Carmen with their arms around each other in what looked like Taughannock Falls. The other was of him, a woman and two small children, a girl and boy—which looked a few years old. I wanted to ask if it was the older sister he'd mentioned, but knew it would probably shift the mood, and right now I wanted to make him feel good.

I turned to him and saw he looked a little shy, like he was scared of what I'd think of his private space. I took his hand, and pulled him to me. He smelled a little sweaty, and I wanted more than anything to lose myself in him. I bent down for a quick kiss. "I like your room. I feel like me being here is a big deal."

He shrugged, looking embarrassed. "It's pretty boring, but I like it."

"Nothing about you is boring."

He rolled his eyes and said, "I'm so boring you're the only person that's been in this room other than Carmen and Ted when they were helping me set up the furniture. Oh and, Raj," he said, gesturing at the walls. "He helped put up the frames."

I paused at this. I knew he'd bought the house a couple of years ago. He hadn't had a lover in at least two years?

"Does that mean—" I stopped when he shook his head.

"I didn't mean I hadn't had people at the house, just not here, not in my bedroom."

I wasn't surprised, but it still made me want to take a moment and think about what all of this meant. After a few quiet seconds he smiled and got closer.

His voice husky when he spoke. "Can you touch me like you did before? Whenever I'm with you it's like my body's hungry for your hands. I've never been like this with anyone, Carmen has to practically extort me for a hug," he said, a rueful smile forming on his lips. "But when you're around I turn into some kind of needy lamprey."

I laughed. "I like that you enjoy when I touch you." I gently pushed him backward until he was sitting on the edge of the bed, with me standing in between his legs. I took his face in my hands and turned his head up so I could see his eyes. His skin was flushed and his hair messy from my hands. He threaded his fingers with mine and after a moment I brought them up to my lips. Kissing each of his palms, then I asked, "Can I undress you, baby?"

His eyes were a bit glazed and unfocused, but he said *yes* in a strong voice, then leaned back on his elbows. I knelt in front of him, my movements slow. I was hyperaware of all the places we were touching, of where I wanted to be touching him. I ran my hands up his legs from his ankle to his thighs and then slid them under the hem of his shorts, feeling his skin tremble the farther up I went. I leaned my head forward and began kissing the inside of his thighs, grazing my lips up the same path my hands had been.

I could smell his sweat, sharp and musky the closer I got to his crotch. The hair on his legs felt silky on my lips as I kissed him. Every few seconds his breath would catch and he'd say my name on the exhale, like his breaths came out of his body in the shape of my name. I moved my head up, nuzzling the junction of his thighs and breathed in still looking at him.

"Nesto, please."

"What, papí? What do you want, Jude? Tell me. I want to make you feel good. Give you what you want."

He leaned his head back and looked at me askance, like he couldn't understand what I was saying.

"Can I taste you, baby? I want to. Right here," I said, pressing my hand on his cock. Rubbing my thumb against the head. A felt little bit of moisture seeping through the fabric.

He only nodded in response, as goosebumps spread all over his body. I put my mouth over the head through the cotton and sucked. He bucked like he'd been shocked.

"Ohh that's feels amazing."

"I'm going to take your pants off now, papí. I've been dying to put my mouth on you all day. You know how much I love to play with your cock, suck on your balls."

He was moaning and thrashing at this point.

"You like it when I tell you what I'm going to do to you. Don't you, baby?" I asked as I unbuttoned his shorts and pulled them and his boxer briefs down in one go.

"Yes, I do."

He was still resting on his elbows, and he was looking at me with half closed eyes. The lights in the room were on, so there was no hiding. His cock was hard and pointing up. It was dark red, the head purple with a bead of liquid right on the tip. I leaned up and licked it off.

He whimpered, letting his head fall on his shoulders. His cock was long and slim, and I loved taking it all the way down my throat. Letting it get so far down it choked me. Seeing Jude's face when I was deep throating him was a ridiculously big turn on. I cupped his balls as I went back to his cock, taking the head into my mouth. Jude's arms gave out after that and he lay flat on the bed.

He looked like an offering.

"You look so beautiful, Jude." My voice sounded

breathless, full of emotion. He had his eyes closed, but when I spoke a smile turned up his lips. I pulled his hips so his ass was right on the edge of the bed and pushed his knees up with my hands. Spreading him open for my mouth. I looked up from where I was kneeling.

"I want to eat your ass so bad, papí, can you hold your legs up for me? I want to open you up with my hands, so I can see all of you. Play with your hole, I want to put my tongue inside of you, baby."

He was not much of a talker in bed, but the dirtier I got, the crazier it made him. As he put his hands under his knees, he babbled and thrashed his head. I could only make out a long string of *please, please, please*.

I used my hands to spread his cheeks, exposing his hole. It was pulsing, clenching like he needed me inside. I hadn't even started and I already wasn't sure how much longer I could last. Jude's t-shirt had ridden up his torso and I could see his nipples, hard and pointed. His lips were red and swollen and his hair was sticking to his face from perspiration.

He looked totally wrecked, his eyes and his body completely open to me, to my touch. I was still fully clothed and seeing him half naked and mindless with need, waiting for my hands and my mouth, was revving me up so much I felt lightheaded.

I put my head down again, licking into his ass as my fingers held him open. The moment my tongue touched him, Jude's spine lifted of the bed, his breath fast and hard.

"Oh god."

"What else do you want, baby? Tell me."

He shook his head, like he wasn't sure what I was saying, but after a moment he spoke, his voice a little slurred, "Your fingers, put them inside. Fuck me with them while you lick me."

Oh fuuuck.

I was going to come. Every time he opened his mouth my dick got impossibly harder. I didn't say a word and put a finger in as I lashed my tongue hard on the rim of his hole. I found his gland after a few seconds and pressed it as I licked him.

"Oh, oh. Nesto. I'm going to come like this. Don't stop."

I knew he was sensitive there, but to see him come with just my mouth and fingers in him might be too much for me to take.

"Este culo me vuelve loco." I smacked his ass and went back in for another lick. He was panting now, and he was so hard it looked painful. "Touch yourself, baby."

He shook his head. "No, I want to come like this, I'm so close. I can take another finger." He pushed his ass out, grinding himself on my hand. I added one more finger and I pointed my tongue, swirling it around his rim as I pumped two fingers hard into his ass.

After a few thrusts I heard his breathing change and felt his body tense. He let out a long moan as his ass started clenching on my fingers. I looked up and saw his torso lift of the bed again as one long rope of come shot out of his cock, splattering onto his stomach. I kept milking his gland until the vise around my fingers eased.

I kissed his taint when it was over and made my way up his body. I was still wearing all my clothes and my cock was so hard I would probably come just from the air touching it. I pushed him farther up on the bed and licked the come off his stomach. After his breathing slowed he opened his eyes and smiled.

"You're so hot, baby," I said, breathing hard. "I may get addicted to eating your ass if you're going to come like that every time."

Without saying anything he looked at my crotch and saw the tent my cock was making and his eyes widened like he just realized I was still dressed. He lifted his hand and started tugging at my t-shirt, and shaking his head.

"Take your pants off, come up here. I want to suck you, while you play with my hole again."

A shock went through my entire body like someone had tasered me in the neck.

"Holy shit, you're going to kill me." I made quick work of my clothes and walked up to him on my knees. Once I reached him I leaned my hands on either side of his head and loomed over him. He groaned again and reached for my cock. I moved back so I was out of reach and bit my bottom lip, letting him see how hot he made me.

"What are you going to do with it? Tell me how you're going to suck me."

He moaned and covered his face with his hands. He looked embarrassed, but after a moment leaned up on his elbow, determination on his face.

"I want you in my mouth, to take you all the way in, until I can't breathe."

I sucked in my teeth at the image. "Will you suck my balls after, baby? Put both in your mouth, play with them. Lick them," I said as I tugged them with one hand.

At this, he sat up and grabbed my cock.

We were done talking then.

"Lean against the headboard and open your mouth. I'm going to give it to you like this so I can see your lips stretched out by my cock. Then I'll turn around, so I can play with your ass when you suck me off."

I leaned over and fed him my dick in one go. He relaxed his throat, and gripped my ass to push me all the way in. I pressed my arms on the wall for balance and looked down as my dick stretched out his lips, moving my hips in a tight grind. I was so fucking close.

"Ahhh that's so good, baby." He had me panting so hard I could barely speak. "Take that dick."

My words made him redouble his efforts and within seconds I was close to coming. After a couple of hard thrusts I pulled out and turned around fast, lifting my hips so he could reach my cock with his mouth, and bent down to play with his ass. He started sucking me hard as I pressed both thumbs into his hole.

He was moaning as he sucked me. "Does this feel good, baby, or are you too sensitive?"

He made approval noises and bore down on my cock again.

As I played with his rim, he started sucking the tip of my cock and pumping me hard with one hand. I could feel the orgasm building in my groin. The sharp tug from my ass and up to my chest, like someone was squeezing me from the inside. I put my head down in between his legs and groaned, it felt so good. "Casi."

He moaned again and sucked one last time, and that was it, my brain whited out and my whole body washed hot and cold, pleasure pulsing through me. He took everything I had, swallowing me to the last drop. I slumped down on the bed, breathing hard and so blissed out, I felt like I was floating.

From far away I felt Jude's hand on my legs and ass, caressing me, and I sighed, my breathing muffled by the sheets. I turned my face so I could talk. "You're incredible. If this is you still getting over shyness, we may need to get a defibrillator for when you're full-on, because damn."

He chuckled and tugged on my leg. "Come up here." I moved so I could get at his mouth. We kissed with so much hunger, tongues lashing and our breaths still harsh. After a moment I got up on wobbly legs, grabbed a washcloth from the bathroom, and then went to turn off the light, before climbing back into the bed. I kissed him and said, "Every time with you is better than the last."

He smiled and nodded as he ran his hands through my hair. I lay on my back as he put his head under my chin, his breathing slowing down after a few seconds. I thought he'd fallen asleep when he suddenly said in a sleepy voice, "You're staying here tonight, right? Because you still owe me a back massage, Ernesto."

I laughed, not wanting to make a thing out of it, but aware this was an important invitation. "I'm a total slacker. I'll have to pay my debt to you in the morning."

He squeezed me tight and after just a few seconds his breathing slowed again. I lay there in the dark quiet room, his body so close to mine I could feel his heart beating against my chest.

For once feeling content in the stillness.

Chapter Nineteen

Jude

Nesto was rushing out the door when my phone pinged with a text. We'd stayed in bed later than we should've—for very good reasons—so now he was running almost an hour behind schedule to get to the festival.

"Is it Mami?" Nesto asked distractedly as he shoved his own phone in his pocket with a sigh. "I can't believe I forgot to charge it. I'll just do it in the truck on the way there."

I had no idea who could be texting before eight in the morning on a Sunday. When I looked at the screen I saw it was from Martha.

Sorry for texting you so early on a Sunday! But I wanted to share the good news. Looks like Tom White got his bank to commit to funding the mobile library for the first two years!!! There are a few caveats here and there, but otherwise looks like we should be operational for the fall! We'll talk more tomorrow! Enjoy the rest of your weekend.

I yelped out while typing a string of smiling face emojis and a thank-you for letting me know. After, I passed the phone to Nesto who was waiting by the door to hear what was going on. He read the text quickly and moved to give me a hug.

"Congratulations, baby. I knew you'd get the funding."

I beamed at him. "Thanks, I can't believe I'll actually get my mobile library after all."

Nesto shook his head. "They'd be fools not to give you the money." He started for the door again. "Okay, so I'll see you there around ten then?"

I nodded. "Yes, I have some chores I need to catch up on, and I'll head over around nine thirty. Text if there's anything you need me to bring."

He moved in for another kiss, as we pulled apart I could not help the big grin on my face.

Nesto was smiling too as he said, "Thanks, babe," before he rushed out the door. I waved after him, hoping the late start didn't cause any problems.

After Nesto left, I went for a run, had breakfast, and got my chores done by nine thirty. I was in the car getting ready to drive off when my phone rang. I assumed it was Carmen calling about the mobile library news, so I took the call with the Bluetooth as I pulled out of the driveway.

Before she spoke, I laughed and asked, "How long have you been looking at the phone waiting for an appropriate time to call, Carmen?"

When there was no response on the other end, I looked at the screen and saw it wasn't Carmen. The number wasn't one I recognized, but the area code was familiar. One I had not seen in a long time.

"Jude, hon, is that you?" A woman's tinny voice asked over the phone. "It's your cousin, Esther."

"Esther," I breathed out. I'd stopped the car half-way out of my drive and was now sitting there feeling stunned. Esther was one of my older cousins, our mothers had been sisters. She was the only person out of my entire family who'd told me to stay in touch when I finally left town.

She came to my house the night before I moved to Ithaca and told me she loved me and hoped I found someone who I could be happy with. She was a good woman, and I was grateful for the kindness she'd shown me, but I hadn't heard from her in the three years since. If Esther was calling, something very bad was happening.

"Hon, I'm sorry to call you with bad news, but Jesse asked me to get in touch with you." Jesse was my sister Mary's husband.

My stomach sank.

"Did something happen to Mary or one of the kids?" I asked, fearing the worst.

She sighed heavily and I felt myself starting to panic. "The cancer's back, hon." Esther always did get straight to the point. "She collapsed at home three nights ago, and they took her to Rochester. It looks like it's metastasized to most of her body. Jesse says they'll run more tests, but things aren't looking good. He thought you'd like to know."

As the information sunk in, I felt hollowed out. Mary's cancer was back. She'd been in remission for over ten years, we all thought she was out of the woods after she'd hit the five-year mark.

Mary turning her back on me after I came out had almost broken me. The hurt from her rejection was still an open wound. But hearing she was sick made me realize how much I'd missed my sister.

I sat there knowing I should say something, but nothing came out. When I opened my mouth, a sob almost escaped my throat. I took a deep breath and tried again. "Umm, where do they have her now? Did Jesse say if it was okay for me to call him?"

After everything that happened when I came out, my four siblings, using Mary as their speaker, had politely requested I never contact them again. So now I needed permission before I called to ask about my sister who was dying.

Esther's strained voice startled me. "Jude, honey. I'm so sorry for the way we treated you. I've never felt right about any of it. Your father was a damn stubborn man, and Mary..." She sighed again, and this time I could hear the bone-deep weariness in her voice. "She never was able to go against anything that bigot Paul Jones was spouting from his pulpit, even when it broke her heart not to."

I heard some shuffling and then it sounded like she'd put me on speaker. "Anyway, Jesse asked me to give you his cell phone number, and said you could call him anytime. I'm not sure if he told Mary he was going to send word to you or not."

Esther gave me Jesse's number and ended the call saying she'd be late for church. I thanked her for letting me know and told her I'd get in touch with him. Still sitting in the car, I dialed Jesse's number before I lost my nerve. After two rings he picked up.

"Jesse here."

"Jesse, it's me, Jude. Esther told me about Mary. Thank you for asking her to call me."

I heard muffled noises, like he was covering the phone and talking to someone else. After a few seconds he spoke again.

"Hi. It's good to hear from you. How are you doing?"

I almost laughed. Jesse was asking me how I was doing when his wife was in the hospital.

I suppressed a sigh and tried to keep my voice steady. "I'm good. Thanks for asking. How's Mary doing?"

He cleared his throat, but his voice came out hoarse, like he was trying to keep from crying. "It's not good, Jude." I gripped the steering wheel, dreading what he was going to say. "They're not sure it's worth doing chemo. She's been feeling off for a while, but didn't say anything. You know your sister. Stubborn." I could picture him shaking his head.

"How are the kids? Do they know?"

Their two kids had to be in elementary and middle school by now. When I left, Faith, the oldest, had just started third grade and Micah was almost five. A wave of sadness flooded me when I thought of everything I'd missed since I left.

Jesse started to answer, and I could hear him choke up. "We told them last night. They're scared and angry, but mostly they just want Mom to come home. They're staying with my brother and his wife while we're out here," he said in a strangled voice.

"She's the heart of our family, Jude. How are we going to go on without her?" I let him cry and told him again and again how sorry I was. After a minute he was back in control.

"I'd like for you to come and see her at the hospital. I'll talk to her before you come to make sure she's up to it, but I know she'd like to see you. I know it's a lot to ask, especially after the way things went with you all, but Mary has never forgiven herself for what happened. It would do her good to see you."

At this I almost lost my composure, wanting to cry for my sister, for myself. For the screwed-up way we were raised to see the world. All that black and white.

But I was long past crying over the senseless ways my family's misguided morals fucked with all our lives. "Of course I'll see her. When can I come?"

He exhaled, clearly relieved by my answer. "Thank you. They'll be doing tests on her tomorrow, but we'll be here for the next week. Can you come on Tuesday morning? She's in so much pain, she's wiped out by noon. It's better to come early."

I nodded as if he could see me. "Would ten a.m. be okay?"

"Yes, that's a good time. I'll text you after I ask her about you coming, but I know she'll say yes."

We ended the call and after I sat in my car with a thousand things running through my head. I stayed there for a long time, until I looked at the clock and saw it was almost ten and I was late for the festival.

I had to get my shit together. Nesto was counting on me and it was a big day for him. Still, I felt scared that once the door to my family was opened again, I would be tempted to go back to pretending to be something I wasn't.

And where did that put Nesto and me?

The happiness I'd been feeling this morning felt like it was someone else's, as the old feeling of helplessness threatened to overtake me. But I couldn't let it. I could no longer let other people's beliefs make me feel adrift and lost. Never again would I let someone else control the way I saw myself.

Nesto

"See you soon, m'ijo! Take the smaller road I told you about, you'll hit less traffic. I'll take the county road so I can pick up Minerva and meet you at the festival!"

"Esta bien, Mami." I waved my mother off and went back to the commercial kitchen to grab the last container of food I needed.

We were running an hour behind to get to the festival and I was starting to get antsy. Today was the last day, so if I missed my chance with Mr. Sheridan I was fucked. I wasn't going to dwell on the fact the delay started with me thirsting after Jude's ass in bed this morning. We'd gotten up with the alarm, but I couldn't keep my hands off him and ended up leaving his house at eight instead of seven like I'd planned. But whatever, if I hustled, I'd get to the festival grounds right at ten thirty. We'd start serving about an hour later than yesterday, but it shouldn't be a big deal. The crowds didn't start coming in until eleven anyway.

I shoved the bin with condiments in the back and quickly fired up the truck. The guys would meet us at the grounds and my mom was on her way there with Ari and Yin. It was just me in the truck. I took the smaller road my mom recommended to avoid hitting the traffic we'd run into on the way in yesterday. As I cruised on my way to Seneca Lake my mind started drifting to the night before and how amazing things had been with Jude.

Something big had changed between us last night and I was done pretending what we had was casual. I needed to tell him. He turned me inside out, and with the way he'd given himself to me, I knew it was the same for him. This chance with Mr. Sheridan could be the key to staying here, and now that things with Jude were part of the plan, more than ever, I needed to get my head in the game. Today could be a game-changer for me not just professionally, but personally too.

I was checking the time when I saw a young woman standing by the side of the road. Her car tire looked blown out and it seemed like she was not getting reception on her phone. As I got closer, I noticed she was young, had to still be in high school, but there was no way I could stop for this. When she spotted me, she waved frantically, but I drove past her without even slowing down.

I felt like shit for leaving her out there like that, but I was already running late, and couldn't risk any more delays. After a couple of minutes, guilt started gnawing at me, especially since I hadn't seen any other cars on the road since I'd gotten on it. My mom told me it was pretty isolated, so that poor girl would probably be there for a long time waiting for someone to help her, or worst what if whomever stopped was some creepy asshole.

The guilt was already next level about not stopping, but what made me finally snap was the thought of something like that happening to Minerva. I would want someone to stop for my sister if she was ever in trouble, and not leave her stranded by the side of the road.

"Fuck," I yelled as I turned the truck around and backtracked the few miles to where I'd seen her.

A few minutes later I pulled up a few yards from her

and jumped out. I approached her slowly, noticing she looked freaked out and more than a little pissed. She was petite, very blonde, and was wearing horse-riding gear. She had her phone in a death grip, but wasn't using it.

I didn't make any sudden movements, not wanting to scare her. I was a strange man after all, and it was just the two of us out here. "Hey, I'm Nesto." I pointed at the flat rear tire. "You need help putting the spare on?"

She looked at me for a second, like she was trying to figure out if she could take me, then stuck her hand out. "Hi, I'm Riley. Thanks for not being a total douchebag and coming back, I was starting to think I was going to be here for hours."

I chuckled as I moved closer to the car. I liked this kid. "No problem. Were you able to call a tow truck?"

She huffed with frustration, and lifted the hand clutching the cell phone. "There's no signal here." I was about to suggest we try my phone and then remembered mine was dead and like a fucking idiot I'd forgotten my charger at the kitchen.

I nodded at the tire again, and walked to her trunk. "I can help you with the tire though."

She shook her head like I had no idea how bad shit actually was. When I walked around the car I saw why she was so frustrated. Her front right tire was blown out too. She would need a tow for sure.

"What happened?" I asked, as I bent down to look at the tire more closely.

She crossed her arms over her chest with a stank face almost identical to Minerva's. "Some tool ran me off the road, and I ended up driving over these fucking spikes." She waved her hand in the direction of the road behind us. "I didn't realize they were so sharp. I got back on the road, but within a few minutes both tires were flat."

I shook my head at her story. "And that asshole didn't stop?" She rolled her eyes at my stupid question. This kid would get along great with my little sister. "Do you have anyone you can call to come? Triple A or something?"

She pointed at her phone, looking at me like she may have overestimated my ability to be helpful. "No signal, remember? My parents have Triple A, I just need to let them know to send someone."

I sighed, already resigned to the fact that I was going to be ridiculously late. "Where do you live?"

"Right outside Trumansburg."

Shit, taking this kid home was going to really mess with my already super late starting time at the festival, but I couldn't just leave her here. I rubbed my hands over my head, feeling sort of desperate and wondering how bad I was fucking myself over.

"Okay, I'll take you back. It's probably quicker than trying to get to another town and find someone to call a tow truck for you."

She gave me a suspicious look and I laughed. "I promise you'll be okay."

This time she took her stank face to another level. "Riiiight, because that isn't what every creepy serial killer says to his victims."

This kid was something else. I held up my hands and then nodded toward the truck. "You can check the truck, it's full of food. I was on my way to the Wine and Beer Festival when I saw you. I promise. No dead bodies. Just a lot of stuff to make burritos."

She perked up at the word *burritos*. Typical teenager. After a second, she went to the car, got her bag, locked up and climbed into the truck. We were on the road back to Trumansburg within a couple of minutes. After a moment Riley spoke again. "Thanks so much for doing this, really. I'm sorry if it's making you late for your job."

I smiled, keeping my eyes on the road. "No worries, and you're welcome."

She looked around the truck cabin. "I've seen your truck at the Farmer's Market but haven't tried it. What kind of food is it?"

"Caribbean food in a burrito. You gotta stop and try them. You're missing out."

I could see her nodding in my peripheral, her face very serious. "Oh I definitely will. You totally saved my ass. My mom has told me like a million times, not to take that road, because it's too lonely. But it's a faster way to get to the stable. I work at a horse farm in the summers."

She stopped suddenly and pressed her palm to her forehead. "Dammit, I'm going to be late for that."

I turned my head for a second and tried to give her a reassuring smile, and not freak out about my own lateness. "I'm sure they'll understand."

I kept my attention on the road until Riley signaled toward a huge property with a very ornate gate up the road. "It's the house on the right."

When I stopped and turned to look at her she was rolling her eyes. "My parents are too much, I know."

I smiled and extended my hand to her. "You're home safely. Good luck with the car, okay? I have to hurry back."

She shook my hand with a strong grip, a big smile on

her face. "Thanks so much for stopping, Nesto. You're a life saver and I hope you do great at the festival today. I'll come by your truck for sure."

She waved me off as I got back on the road to the festival, hoping this detour wouldn't cost me everything.

Chapter Twenty

Nesto

We were going to open almost two hours late. That was the only thing running through my mind when I jumped out of the truck and saw the whole crew eagerly waiting for me. As my feet hit the ground my mom came rushing toward me, her face in a grimace. I waved her and the guys over, so we could start unloading the truck. It was almost eleven at this point and I was starting to wonder just how badly I'd fucked myself over this morning.

"Mamí! Can you call Tía Maritza and ask if she can bring us some more water bottles? I realized I didn't ask Jude to pick some up and my phone is dead."

She took her phone out of her pocket as she reached me. "Ernesto. ¿Dondé estabas, m'ijo? We've been waiting on you for over an hour."

I moved to the back of the truck where Ari, Yin and the guys were already busy unloading stuff, and noticed Jude was nowhere to be seen.

"I stopped to help this girl who had a couple of flat tires on that back road." I shook my head as I got down to start connecting the grill to the truck's gas line.

"You know how bad phone signal is out here. She was by herself and had no way of calling for help, so I gave her a ride back to town. That set me back like forty-five minutes. I was so stressed out not wanting to get here too late, I passed her at first. But then I felt guilty and went back." I looked down at what I was doing before I continued talking. "I wouldn't want someone to do that to Minerva, you know?"

My mom's eyes immediately got that look like she was going to fawn all over me.

"But I was also freaking about not being here if Mr. Sheridan stopped by." At the mention of Mr. Sheridan my mom's face paled, and she looked like she was going to be sick.

Fuck.

I stood up feeling like someone had punched me in the gut. "Did he come?"

She didn't have to say it, the regretful look on her face was answer enough.

"I'm sorry, baby. He came by like fifteen minutes ago. We tried to call you, but it went straight to voicemail."

I turned around and slammed my hand against the side of the truck. "¡Mierda! Did he say if he'll be back?"

She shook her head again and with that all my hopes for this weekend went up in flames.

"What did he say, Mami?" I snapped, but the look she gave me made me check myself. "Sorry, but this really fucking sucks."

"Ernesto, watch your language. He didn't say anything. Just that he was looking for you and when I said you weren't here, he left." She moved to reach for me and I let her, but I couldn't even hug her back. I was

so mad at myself, the opportunity of a lifetime squan-
dered. Because at the end of the day I knew. No matter how much I killed myself, I would never be able to
take OuNYe to the next level on my own.

My mom pulled back and looked up at me, her face
fierce. "This is only a stumble, papí. A setback. You're
on your way. You can still do this." I didn't have the
energy to reality check her right now. I felt defeated,
the only thing I wanted was to put this whole fucking
day behind me.

Then I looked around and saw my friends and Ari
and Yin hustling to get everything ready. They were
here for me, to push my business forward. I couldn't sit
here and mope. "Let's get to work, Mamí." She tightened her arm around my waist and nodded. "Pa' lante
m'ijo."

As I glanced around again I noticed there was still
no sign of Jude. It was past eleven and he was nowhere
in sight. "Did Jude go somewhere?"

My mom shook her head, looking confused. "He's
not here. I haven't seen him. We figured you went back
to get him and that's why you were late."

"No, the plan was for him to come straight here. He
was supposed to be here like an hour ago." I got my
phone out of my pocket and remembered I still hadn't
charged it. "Mamí, do you have a charger? My phone's
dead."

She nodded and moved to grab her purse from somewhere in the tent. "Here you go." I grabbed the cord and
started moving to the truck where I could plug it in.

"I'm going to see if I have any messages from Jude,
then I'm going to go get started with the grill. We might

be able to start serving in like thirty minutes if we hurry."

"Okay, m'ijo."

As soon as I powered on my phone I saw I had a voicemail from Mr. Sheridan. My stomach dropped and I almost trashed it without listening to it, because I knew what he would say. Knowing it and actually hearing it were two completely different things. Once I'd heard the message then it would be real.

I tapped on the screen and closed my eyes, I could hear the background noise of the festival as his voice came on. "Ernesto. Looks like we missed each other."

That was it. No "I'll stop by later," nothing. He just hung up. For the second time in three days I felt like crying from frustration. I'd done this to myself. I lost my focus, prioritized other things and I missed a chance I would probably never get again. I looked around wanting to talk to Jude about it, and then remembered he wasn't even here yet.

I scoffed as I jumped off the truck. He was late, and now we'd be shorthanded. I needed to remember what I was here to do, and it wasn't to chase after Jude. I was here for OuNYe, I seemed to have forgotten that in the last twenty-four hours, but that stopped now.

This day had to be a test on how much stress I could handle before I finally lost my shit. On top of blowing it with Sheridan, we'd now been serving food for almost an hour and Jude was still MIA, and we needed him here to help. Despite everything, the truck was still doing great business after the boost from the food critic, and we were shorthanded.

It wasn't like him to drop off like that, but he knew

how much I had riding on this day. I was seriously wondering if something had happened to him when I finally saw him walking toward the tent. I reminded myself that it wasn't Jude's fault everything had gone to shit today and tried hard not to scowl at him as he got closer.

He looked up at me and instead of his usual shy smile, he stared at me blankly, like he could see right through me. Still I told myself, I needed to chill out, because Jude was here as a favor. Before coming into the tent, he stopped by the truck where Yin was working on preparing food and leaned close to tell him something. His already serious expression turning into a frown from whatever Yin told him, then he came toward me.

I put down my spatula for a second. "Hey, did something happen to you? I was worried." My tone wasn't exactly warm, and Jude took a step back when he got a look at my face. He seemed sad, and when he spoke I could barely hear him. "I'm sorry about Mr. Sheridan." He looked down then. "I hope it wasn't because I made you late." Seeing him like that, so full of worry, did something to me. But I was deep in self-loathing and acted like a complete asshole. I shrugged off his concern for me, and turned around as I answered him, "It is what it is."

He stiffened and moved away, then tried to smile, failing completely. "I'm really sorry, I'm late, I—"

I barely acknowledged what he was saying and spoke over him, "Well there's a lot to do, so if you're ready to help, go and see if you can give my mom a hand. She's been running the front on her own all morning." His face had paled in the last few minutes, but I didn't make a move to reach for him. In the back of my mind something niggled at me about how Jude was acting, but I was too caught up in my own misery to ask. I turned my back on him and started working the grill again. He just stood there looking a little lost, as I flipped meat with a scowl on my face.

"Hey, Jude. You made it!"

My mother. I cringed at the thought of what she'd do if she knew the way I was treating him. But at this point the people who were disappointed in me today could just take a fucking number.

"Come over here! Let me give you a hug. I heard about your library, and that the lady you helped yesterday turned out to be a big food critic from *New York Magazine*!"

Milo called out from the other end of the tent. "Congrats, Jude! Good work, man." Patrice, Juanpa and Ari all called out some encouragements too. I didn't say a word and kept working. In my peripheral vision I could see Jude walking over to my mom. She gave him a one-armed hug as she took a card from a client.

"Thanks, Mrs. Maldonado."

She shook her head clicking her tongue. "Nurys. Honey, if you have to put up with that boy over there, you can at least call me by my first name." She winked at me, then frowned when she saw my face, but kept talking to Jude in a cheery voice. "Because I know what a nuisance you're dealing with. Pobrecito, Jude," she said, and he chuckled quietly.

"He's not so bad." He looked over at me for a second, then his eyes widened like he remembered something, and his face changed into an expression I'd never seen before.

He looked brittle.

When he realized I was staring, he shook himself and pasted on a smile which would not reach his eyes.

Moving away from my mom, he said, "Let me take over for you, Nurys, sorry I'm so late, you must need a break."

"Oh, I'm fine, but if you come here, I'll go back to help Nesto with the food. Thanks, sweetheart." My mom came over to me and gave me a worried look.

I said nothing. I couldn't be bothered to reassure anyone right now.

The afternoon moved fast but things were tense in the tent. Jude forgot to put in an order and a customer lost it because he'd already been waiting for ten minutes. We apologized and comped him an order of tostones, but he left unhappy, and that's something a business starting out cannot afford to do.

Jude was flustered and apologetic, but he was more and more distracted as the afternoon went on. I was on edge already and started to feel guilty about how shitty I'd been to him all day. I was so distracted running scenarios in my head of how I'd fucked up everything, I burned my forearm on the grill.

"Dammit!"

"Ernesto!" My mom quickly grabbed the spatula I dropped. "¿Qué te pasa, m'ijo?"

She looked over at Jude who was once again looking at his phone. She grimaced and turned my arm to see how bad it was.

"This doesn't look too bad. Go and clean it up and put a bandage on. There's stuff in the truck."

"I know, Mamí. It's my truck. I put it there! Fuck!"

She put her hand on my chin, a worried look on her

face. "Ernesto, calmate. Go take a break and come back in five minutes, and then maybe you can start acting like a human being again. I know this day has been hard, but you're not helping anything by acting like a jerk to people who love you and are here to help you. Go." She waved her hand toward the water, the look on her face a mix of concern and disgust. "This tent can survive without you for that long."

"Fine." I walked out, convinced now I'd ruined things with Jude too. What if he'd been late because he'd been reconsidering things with us? Maybe the comment from Patrice about me leaving if things with the truck didn't work out had turned him off?

I should have said something about it afterward, but I got too caught up in preparing food and then when we got to his place I'd been all over him. We barely talked last night, because I had my tongue down his throat practically the minute we got to his house.

I walked to the edge of the water trying to cool myself off when I checked the time. It was already five p.m. The festival only went until six today and cleanup would be fast. If I could keep my shit together for a couple more hours then I'd talk to Jude. This day literally could not get worse. Because no matter how many times I told myself OuNYe was the only reason I was here, I knew the truth. Jude was too important to me to just walk away from. But what did I do the moment things went awry? I'd acted like an asshole to him. If he ghosted me after today I wouldn't blame him.

I was walking back to the tent when I saw Carmen leaning over the counter talking with him, a worried look on her face. I came up to them and he stopped talking. Carmen turned to me with a forced smile. "¿Y que, Nesto? ¿Como estás? Sorry about Sheridan."

I leaned over to give her a kiss hello. "Gracias." I shrugged, trying not to be too transparent about how fucked-up I felt. "Are you here for the festival? It's kinda late." My tone was a bit shorter than called for.

She looked at Jude again, he shook his head and she sighed. "Oh um, yeah. Actually I'm here because Jude is giving me a ride. Ted had to go back home early."

I was starting to get pissed, because there was obviously a problem and Jude was just sitting there like he wasn't part of the conversation.

I took a deep breath and looked from Jude to Carmen, then spoke. "Jude, if you have to drive Carmen back now you can take off. No worries."

He nodded taking off his apron. "Yeah, okay. It's not like I've been any help, I've been messing up all day." His voice was completely flat, and he wouldn't look at me.

I felt like my skin had turned into stone. "We have things covered here. Thanks for coming to help. I'll call you later, okay?" I tried to squeeze his shoulder and he flinched, so I turned around and walked off before I said or did something I'd regret.

I looked back and saw Jude and Carmen had started walking toward the car. He'd left without even saying goodbye, which I probably deserved.

It seemed like every time I felt closer to being able to confess to Jude how I felt, something happened to send me back to square one. But I couldn't dwell on any of this right now though. I had work to do.

I could fall apart later.

Chapter Twenty-One

Nesto

That night we walked into my mom's house in a heavy silence. Between the stress of the morning and Jude's strange mood, I'd been a monster after he took off. The fact that my mom, Milo, Juanpa and Patrice had even stuck around my ass was evidence of how much they loved me, which only made me feel worse. Still we'd managed to get everything cleaned and sorted out in record time. Thankfully Ari and Yin had agreed to get the food service ready tomorrow, so for once I had the morning off on a day we were serving lunch.

I was a mess. I was worried about my business, but also had the feeling that I'd missed something with Jude. That I'd fucked up with him even beyond my assholic behavior at the festival. I couldn't stop myself from running through everything I'd said and done in the last twenty-four hours. I went back and forth between regretting not just asking what was wrong one moment, and being annoyed at myself for letting all this distract me.

I had never felt this unsure of myself.

I tried to put things in perspective as I paced around

my mom's living room. Yes I'd blown it in a sense, but our sales had been amazing this weekend. Despite the setbacks, the festival had been good for business. I should be glad how well the weekend had gone with OuNYe, instead I was moping around. I had no fucking idea what to do either, not with Jude, and not with the truck.

"Ernesto, fix your face, nobody in this house did anything to you. Why are you looking at my couch like you want to rip it apart?"

My mother. Of course. No one could look pissed in her house without an immediate attitude adjustment.

Milo, Juanpa and Patrice had come by to hang out a bit before heading to their hotel since they were driving back to the city at the crack of dawn. But right now I was in such a foul mood, I knew for a fact I would pick a fight with anyone who tried to talk to me.

I ignored my mother and went to her bar to pour myself some of the rum she kept there for special occasions. I pounded the first drink, feeling the burn sear my throat, and was about to go for another one, when she got up and ripped the bottle out of my hands before I could even tip it onto the glass.

"¡Diablo, Mamí! ¿Que fue?"

¡No señor!" She yelled at me while she twisted the cork back in the bottle. "You're not going to swallow my good Barceló because you're frustrated. Nesto, you need to calm down, m'ijo. This isn't like you. Is having someone to be mad at because you hit a stumbling block with your truck really worth losing a man who's crazy about you and you're crazy about, son?"

She sounded worried, and I tried to get it together

before I scared her. I slumped at her words and sighed. "No."

"You had a successful weekend at the festival. You did a lot of business and even if things didn't work out with the investor, you got some great exposure." She stepped closer and put her hand on my cheek.

"These are good things, baby. You will get past this, your business is good and people will see that. What you *will* regret is pushing away someone who cares about you because of stubbornness. Ernesto, you were unkind to Jude today, and he didn't deserve it."

I sagged, looking longingly at the bottle in her hand. "I know. I *know,* Mamí. I was just so angry at myself for missing Sheridan. I fixated on how I got caught up in Jude this morning and made myself late." I ran my hands over my face, rubbing hard. I felt so foolish and ashamed of how I'd acted. I regretted not being more open with Jude, and telling him how I felt. I hadn't given him a single reason to believe in what we had.

"Things were so good this morning too. We had a really good night together, and now it's all fucked up." Realizing what I was implying, I held up my hands. "Sorry!"

She rolled her eyes and I looked over at the guys, who were doing their damndest not to lose their shit.

"Por favor." She flipped her hands up. "Do you think I assume you go to the houses of the men you're seeing to play dominos? Deja eso, Nesto."

She shook her head like she couldn't believe she'd birthed something so pitiful. "Ven." She grabbed my hand and tugged me over to the love seat. "Let's sit down. Talk to me, baby, I'm here, your best friends,"

She gestured toward Milo, J and Patrice. "Your brothers are here, we can figure this out."

I sighed and put my head in my hands. "There's nothing to figure out with Sheridan. That chance is gone. I don't know what that means for my future here, but I just need to get over it. With Jude—" I cleared my throat. "I don't know what to do. I feel like I should just leave it alone. That it's just going to distract me from what I came to do here, but the thought of not seeing him again, it fucking kills me, and thinking back at how I treated him today…"

I shook my head remembering how I didn't even let him explain why he'd been late. "I keep thinking something must've happened to him and I didn't pick up on it, because I was too busy feeling sorry for myself."

The look on my mother's face told me she felt the same way.

"He *was* super different today, are you sure it wasn't because of the thing with the investor guy?" Camilo piped in.

I shook my head. "I don't think it was that. I mean he seemed genuinely upset for me, but he looked so sad, and he was distracted. He messed up orders and then left early. Every time I talked to him he looked like he was going to be sick, but didn't say anything. Maybe after I left this morning he started having second thoughts about last night, and that's what he was trying to tell me when I cut him off like a fucking douchebag." I threw my hands up, feeling at a complete loss.

"It was the first time I'd slept over, and…" I exhaled. "It got intense between us, physically I mean," I said, cringing and avoiding eye contact with my mother at all costs.

"I don't know. Maybe this is for the best."

Milo's stank face made an appearance after that comment, Patrice shook his head like I was an idiot, and Juanpa just rolled his eyes. Meanwhile my mom looked like she was about to get on her pulpit.

Great.

"Ernesto Amado Vasquez Maldonado," she said in the voice she used when she was about to let me know all the ways in which I was a trifling loser.

From the couch I heard Milo whisper, "Oh shit, she used all four names. If she starts talking in syllables, we're out of here."

Juanpa had his eyes trained on the flip-flops on her feet, then muttered. "If she goes for her chancleta, you better duck, bruh."

Fuckers had to make me laugh when there was nothing funny about this.

My mom ignored our chatter and looked at me with concern on her face. "Something happened with Jude, m'ijo, and I'm sure it has nothing to do with you. If he wanted some space from you, do you think he would have made the effort to drive out to the festival to help or stayed most of the day when clearly neither of you was at his best?"

She had a point. If the issue had been something to do with us, he could've just blown off helping at the festival.

I looked over at Milo who was shaking his head. "Something was definitely up with Jude today, and you *definitely* need to grovel for acting like a jerk." I hung my head because he was absolutely right. "You're feeling this guy hard, Nesto, more than I've ever seen before, and he's *into* you. I actually think the guy's cool, and you know I hate everybody."

This was true.

"Go see what's wrong, you can make this right, m'ijo. As for the truck, you will make your business succeed." My mom's fierce belief in me never faltered. "But first go fix things with Jude, you need to learn to make your heart a priority, son. I didn't raise you to be this clueless."

Juanpa, who usually left the love advice to the other two, stood up and clapped me on the back. "Mi hermano, we're gonna make a move, because we got an early day. I'm not going to pile on because it's all been said already, but I'll tell you this. Deadass man, I ain't never seen you look at anyone the way you look at that gringo. Don't be a fool, Nes."

Damn, that was the most advice Juanpa had given me about anything, ever.

I stood up. "I'm driving over there. I hope he'll let me in, because I'm not sure I would let *myself* in," I said, closing my eyes.

"Of course he'll let you in," my mom said, sounding exasperated. "Go, m'ijo. He needs you."

I said my goodbye to the guys and quickly walked to my car. I needed to step up and find out what was happening with Jude, and how I could support *him* for once.

Jude

"Nesto's here. He's parking his car," Carmen called, startling me. I'd been sitting at home for the last two hours agonizing about my sister and wondering if my meltdown today had messed things up between Nesto and me.

"I hope that asshole came here ready to grovel. You did not deserve the way he talked to you today."

I sighed. I knew venting to Carmen about that was going to put Nesto on her shit list.

"Carmen, please. Don't say anything to him. He took the thing with Sheridan hard, and I didn't help by being late and messing up orders all day."

I was grateful Jesse let me know about Mary, but I was also resentful it was all happening now. The sad news and sudden influx of contact with my family had my emotions all over the place today, adding all that to the fight with Nesto, I was a wreck. Which only made me feel guiltier because my sister was dying, and here I was fretting because it was messing with my love life.

"Stop that, Jude. You've had an awful day and he made it worse, instead of realizing there was something wrong." She threw her hands up as she moved around getting her things. "Don't get me wrong. I like him, but he fucked up, and he needs to apologize for that."

I knew she was right, but whenever something went awry, I tended to place the blame squarely on myself.

Carmen moved toward the door when we heard the doorbell, but I stood up before she could get there. "I'll get it. I need to tell Nesto what's been going on, at least he'll know I haven't lost my mind."

As soon as I opened the door and saw this day had taken its toll on Nesto too. His usually calm and confident face looked drawn.

"Hi," I said as he stood there looking unsure.

He was quiet for a second and then moved to kiss my cheek, but pulled back before he reached me, which only ramped up my anxiety. "Hey, is it okay that I came over?"

I nodded, dying inside. "Of course it is," I said as I pulled him into the house.

We almost ran into Carmen. She was getting her shoes on, her purse already perched on her shoulder.

She smiled at me and glared at Nesto. "I'm taking off, hon, Ted is trying to make dinner and I need to hurry over there before he hurts himself or sets the house on fire. You'd think a man with three Ivy League degrees could manage making spaghetti." She shook her head, an amused smile on her lips despite the death stare she was sending in Nesto's direction. "But you'd be wrong."

"You know you love it. Now you get to go home, open a jar of sauce and boil some noodles and have him worship at your feet."

"You know me too well, friend." She looked at Nesto as she got to the door. "I hope you worked on an apology on your way here."

Nesto looked mortified and I rushed to try to rein in the situation. "Carmen!"

She ignored my horrified tone and held up her phone. "Text me if you need anything. I'll see you mañana."

She walked out, leaving us standing in the living room in a tense silence. For a moment I didn't know where to start, but Nesto spoke before I could.

"I'm so sorry."

What?

"You don't have to apologize to me. I was late and you were stressed."

He shook his head and came closer. He looked like he wasn't sure if his touch was welcome. "Today was hard, but there is no excuse for the way I talked to you. You didn't make me late. You didn't do anything. You came to support me this weekend and when shit got stressful I took it out on you."

He ran his hands over his face and he looked so tired, but his eyes were determined. "That chance with Sheridan is gone and I'll have to figure out something else, but I want to know what's going on with you, babe. You weren't yourself all day, and I know it was probably more than just me being an asshole to you."

I exhaled, and moved closer to him. I knew I should hold myself back more or play hard to get, but I couldn't. It was such a relief to have him here.

"I did have a tough morning, and thank you for apologizing. You didn't have to do that." Nesto's face fell and I took his hand.

"I did though, my behavior was at peak fuckboy today." I laughed at that, I couldn't help it. "I'm only grateful that you're ten times the better person than me, because I don't know if would've let my trifling ass in tonight."

It was useless trying to resist him, I pushed up and kissed him. We stood there for a few minutes, me holding on to him for dear life while he kissed my hair and face and ran his arms up and down my back, apologizing and soothing me. Not demanding anything, just giving me the comfort and quiet I needed. Finally, I pushed away from him and walked over to the kitchen, pulling him along with me.

"I know I need to tell you what happened, but I don't even know where to start."

That was my big fear, that I would open myself up to someone and once they heard about all my baggage, they'd realize I wasn't worth the trouble. After all, my own flesh and blood chose their beliefs over me.

I exhaled, not sure what to say, but feeling like if I didn't have him close I'd completely fall apart. As soon as I leaned against him, he embraced me in his strong arms, and immediately the day's stress seemed less daunting.

He felt so solid against me, and I was so weary.

When we pulled apart Nesto leaned against the counter, his shoulders still tense. I could tell he was trying very hard not to ask questions. Suddenly he started moving to the fridge as he talked. "Did you eat? You want me to make you something?"

Hearing that was what finally took the edge off my nerves. Nesto coming by at the end of the day and making dinner seemed so normal.

So like us.

My stomach grumbled as I watched him pull out bread and cheese, a reminder that I hadn't eaten since breakfast. "I haven't actually, but you don't have to do that. You're always feeding me."

He peered over his shoulder as he got busy shredding cheese. "I want to, please, babe. Today sucked, and the only things that make sense right now, are making food and you."

How could I say no to that? "Okay, thank you."

His face looked tired, but his shoulders loosened a bit. His hands kept moving, sure and nimble, as he worked on making what looked like a very fancy grilled cheese. When he spoke again his voice was almost pleading.

"I just want to know if you're all right, if you can't forgive me right now I understand, but if there's any way I can help with whatever was going on today, I swear I won't let you down, papí."

He glanced up then like he was searching for something in the ceiling, and started talking again. "Did I push you too far last night? I hadn't been like that with you before, and I know I can be intense in bed. Maybe I made you uncomfortable." He shook his head and turned to look at me. "I was perfectly happy with how things were. I don't want you to feel pressured or like I need more."

I almost laughed at that, because of all the things that had happened in the last twenty-four hours what we'd done together last night was definitely a silver lining. I should've known he'd worry about it. We hadn't had sex like that before, and it had been the first time I'd asked him to stay over. I had to remember my family would not even be on his radar, I'd barely talked to him about them.

I immediately made my way to him, and pulled him so we were face to face. I put my hands against his chest, then tugged his chin down, so he'd look at me. "Last night was amazing," I said, shaking my head. "I'm thirty years old and I had no idea I could let go like that."

I hugged him, wanting to get closer. "I loved it. You make me feel so good. I can't get enough of you, of us together."

I could feel him exhale and relax. He kissed me softly and I was ready to leave the conversation for later when we broke apart. "Okay, I'm glad I didn't fuck all the way up, but what happened?" He turned around again to finish my sandwich and for a few minutes I watched him efficiently prepare my dinner, thinking about how to explain today to him.

He turned on the skillet, buttered bread, placed the Monterey Jack and sharp cheddar he'd shredded and added mustard and a slice of tomato. The smell of the butter toasting the bread on the pan making my stomach grumble again.

He smiled at that and lifted an eyebrow as he worked. After a few moments, he tossed the bread onto my wooden cutting board and ran the knife down the center, making two perfect triangles. When he was done, he turned to me again, my dinner on a plate in his hands.

"Jude, I've tried to be respectful because I know it's hard for you to talk about personal stuff, but if something is wrong, I really hope you can trust me enough to say something."

I sighed and spoke in a low voice. "I heard from my family today. My brother-in-law let me know my sister's cancer is back."

"I'm so sorry." He said, his eyes widening with concern. "When was the last time you saw your sister?"

Before I answered, I moved to grab a couple of beers from the fridge, then gestured for him to follow me to the living room. We sat on my couch, each against one end, our legs stretched out and tangled together. I took the sandwich from him and bit into it, suddenly feeling famished.

"Thanks for feeding me, again."

He nodded and watched me eat in silence. I finished the whole thing in a few bites and took a long sip of my beer, as he patiently waited for me to start talking.

"I haven't really talked with anyone in my family since I came out to them about four years ago." His eyes widened, but he didn't say anything. "I told you about my sister Mary, she's the one who got me into reading."

He nodded. "Yeah, I remember. She took you to the library every week."

I smiled, of course he remembered. "Right, she basically raised me and my two younger siblings after my mom died when I was eight. Mary was nineteen and had just gotten married, but she took us home with her. She and Jesse, her husband, took care of us. My dad was never very nurturing, and after Mom died he sort of shut down."

Nesto leaned over so he could touch my face, his eyes full of concern. "I didn't realize you've been on your own this whole time."

I wanted to shrug it off, act like it was no big deal to be shunned by my family, and then I remembered I didn't have to lie to Nesto. I put my hand over the one he had on my face and nodded.

"My family, well my whole town really, goes to this church. It's ultra-conservative. I told you about the pastor before." He gave me a terse nod, as if he could already tell where I was going with the story. "It was pretty awful, but my dad's family has been part of the congregation for generations. So, when I realized I was gay, I locked all of it way down. I didn't want to lose my family, so I told myself I'd just be celibate. If I didn't act on it, I could just keep being me. In Honduras was when I realized celibacy was going to be a lot harder than I thought."

I laughed, and looked at Nesto who was sitting very still, like he didn't want to spook me.

I sighed. "Nothing even happened there, but I had the biggest crush on one of the local guys that came to the church. We just hung out and he took me around the country sightseeing and stuff. I wanted him so bad though, and I was miserable about it the whole time. After I got back, I went to a Christian college, which I actually loved in some ways, but wasn't exactly a place to explore that side of myself."

Nesto nodded as I spoke, and I stopped talking when he looked like he wanted to ask something. "Were you able to confide in anyone? You must have felt so alone."

"I didn't tell anyone. I was too scared. When I was in Rochester for graduate school, I met this guy, Elijah, he was also in school there." I closed my eyes for this part. "He was in the closet too, but we made plans to be together after we finished. I'd gotten a job in the library at the state college in Cortland, so I'd be close to my family. I could see them often, but was far away enough it wouldn't be an issue if they needed time once I came out."

I moved when Nesto patted the spot closer to him. I assume he anticipated where the story was going.

"I was convinced they'd come around. I'd waited so long, and I was the perfect kid. Good student, responsible, no drinking, smoking, church every Sunday. They had to know by then me being gay wouldn't change any of it right?"

I laughed bitterly, remembering how badly I'd misjudged my family's reaction.

"One Sunday, Elijah and I agreed we'd each talk to our families. So, I went to my dad's for dinner and I told them."

I paused then, because we both knew it had not gone as planned. I was exhausted from talking and reliving that horrible fucking day.

I felt Nesto shift on the couch. He gently took my beer out of my hand. He moved and tugged, until I was sitting with my back against his chest. Neither of us said a word, he just held me tight. After a while I started talking again.

"It was a disaster. My father just stood up from the table and told me I was no longer welcome at his house. My sister could barely look at me and said she'd never forgive me for saying those things in front of her children." My voice broke at the memory of that. "Micah, her youngest, was just five-years-old back then. I'm his godfather, you know? And my sister couldn't forgive me for saying I'd fallen in love in front of her son."

Nesto squeezed me harder and whispered in the gentlest voice I'd heard from him, "I am so sorry."

I shook my head, my eyes squeezed shut. "That's the thing, there's nothing to be sorry for. *I* had nothing to be sorry for. I didn't do anything wrong. *They* were wrong. As much as I love them, they were wrong. I had to work very hard to believe that, but I do believe it now."

I sagged against Nesto then tipped my face up to look him. "Only in the past year, I've felt more like I know who I am, of who I want to be than at any other point in my life. I love my job, my house, and it's been so good with you. I feel horrible for resenting the timing of all this, even though I'm terrified for my sister. I'm just worried this is all going to end up sending me back to a bad place." Nesto put his fingers on my face, and I realized it was wet with tears.

"Jude, you're entitled to your feelings. You had to start over on your own, and it's not selfish to want to keep the peace you fought so hard for."

"I stayed in town for a year after I came out. None

of them talked to me, only my cousin Esther and Jesse ever tried to reach out. I was like a pariah, Pastor Jones even told me to stop coming to church because it was too upsetting for my family. But I stayed, hoping they'd come around."

Nesto's face looked thunderous. "I swear I want to go fight people right now for doing that shit to you. That's just fucking wrong."

I shrugged, thankful for how fierce he looked on my behalf. "It was a long time ago. Things fell apart with Elijah too. His parents were a lot more understanding than mine, and in the end, he decided he wanted to live closer to them. I'd exploded my whole life for a relationship that wasn't going anywhere." Nesto stiffened a bit then, but the levee had broken and I couldn't stop talking.

"I'm not being fair though, because I know I wasn't really in love with Elijah. He was just a crutch, I just needed a reason to tell the truth. So, when I got the job here three years ago I left and never looked back."

"You're so fucking brave, Jude. I'm not going to say coming out wasn't rough for me, but my mom supported me every step of the way. I can't imagine what it was like to have your family turn their backs on you like that." He kissed my cheek hard. "You're amazing."

Why had I ever doubted Nesto?

I put my head back, feeling lighter, but also very much unprepared for my visit with Mary. "I'm going to go see my sister on Tuesday. My brother-in-law was updating me over text all day, and tonight he confirmed I could come and see her."

"That's why you were so focused on your phone today," he groaned. "Fuck, I had so many things going through my brain. I'm so sorry I was such an asshole to you."

I shook my head feeling awful that I'd worried him. "I was a basket case today and you were dealing with a lot too."

"That's no excuse. I saw you weren't yourself, and I should've taken the time to talk to you and ask what was wrong. I can get tunnel vision when it comes to the business."

"You're here for your business though."

He made a weird noise and kissed me again.

"Babe, do you want me to come with you on Tuesday? I have a couple of things I need to do, but I can shift some stuff around and drive you there. If you want company, I mean."

The weight of the whole day seemed to lift off my shoulders at once, and the flutter in my chest was like a drum. "Are you sure? I know things are really busy with the truck right now, and it'll be a long day. It's almost two hours to Rochester." I paused, thinking of something, but I made myself say it. "Also, I'm not sure you would be welcome, at least in my sister's room. I'm pretty sure she still won't be okay with 'my homosexuality.'"

His face hardened, but he nodded. "That's fine. I can bring my laptop and work while you're visiting with her. I'm sure they'll have a cafeteria with shitty coffee I can sit in for a couple of hours, and I have bookkeeping stuff I need to get done anyway."

I moved closer so our foreheads were touching, and whispered, "Thank you."

"Of course, anything you need."

He put his hands on my face and lifted my mouth up

to his for a kiss, then stood grabbing my hand. "Come on, baby, let's go to bed. We've had a long weekend."

I let him pull me up, feeling a bit dazed. "But you don't have clothes."

He smirked, his eyebrows dipping, giving him the mischievous look that made my knees weak.

"I have a bag in the car. I stopped at home for some clothes before I came over. I was hoping you'd take pity on me and let me in."

I shook my head. "You know I can't resist you."

He let out a long breath. "I am so sorry about this entire day. Can we start over? Go back to your bedroom where everything made sense?"

"Yes," I answered, already walking there, holding his hand tight.

Chapter Twenty-Two

Jude

Nesto's hand squeezed mine as we walked into the Rochester Cancer Center.

I was clutching a small container of Mary's favorite cookies, which I'd baked the night before, and trying to breathe through the jumble of emotions crawling up my throat. I told myself over and over this was just a visit that my life was my own, and nothing would change after seeing my sister.

Nesto stopped when we got close to the elevators. He stood in front of me, with his gaze focused on my face. The lines of his mouth tight with worry, as he pulled me to him and kissed my forehead.

"You'll be fine. If you need me, just text okay? I don't care what anyone says, if you want me, I'll be up there in a hot minute."

I nodded, trying to calm myself before going up to Mary's room. "I'll let you know when I'm leaving her room." He looked over my shoulder and pointed toward the end of the hall. "There's a cafeteria that claims to have Starbucks, I'll be waiting there." He patted the messenger bag slung over his shoulder. "I've got all my stuff for work, so I can wait as long as you need."

I hugged him again. "Thanks for coming with me."

"Of course. No big." I held on to him for a few more seconds and walked toward the elevators.

When I glanced over my shoulder, Nesto was looking at me with concern on his face, but he held up his hand and smiled. He was still there as I got into the elevator and pushed the button to the third floor. I felt so grateful for his presence. I knew he was still reeling from missing his shot with Sheridan, but he still made the time to come with me today.

As I went up, I was so anxious I felt like I was in a fog. I tried not to dwell on the last time I'd seen my sister, or the blank look on her face when she asked me not to contact the family again. Thankfully the elevator stopped before I could work myself up into a complete panic.

The doors opened, and I walked into a generic hospital wing with lots of white and bad lighting. The nurse's station was off to the right and there was a young man at the desk who looked a little too peppy given the location. As I reached the counter, I breathed again and smiled at him. "Hi, I'm here to visit my sister, Mary Connor."

He flashed me a smile and nodded. "Hi, there." He pointed at a whiteboard on the wall behind the desk and I saw M. Connor written next to her room number. "That's her room, visiting hours are open. You can go ahead." He pointed to the left. "Third room on the right."

"Thanks."

When I got to my sister's room the door was open.

From where I stood I could see homemade cards sitting on a small table by the window, and just a couple feet away Mary was lying on the bed, her eyes closed.

She looked older, but still beautiful. Her blonde hair fell over her chest in a long braid. I smiled, thinking how she and I were the only ones who'd gotten our mother's hair and blue eyes.

She was so pale, and her lips were pursed like she was hurting. I could see her chest moving slowly up and down as she took deep breaths. Her body held tightly, like she was bracing it for pain. I knocked softly on the door and she opened her eyes, turning her head toward me.

When she saw me, a huge smile blossomed on her face. "Jude, you're here." She raised her hand, beckoning me to her. "It's been so long, little brother."

I lifted my hand and walked in, trying to smile. "Hi, Mary." I sat in a chair next to her bed, the container of cookies still in my hands. I raised them, so she could see. "I made you cookies, your favorite." As I handed them to her I realized she may not be up for eating them.

She opened the lid and inhaled. The smell of chocolate and butter filling the space between us. "You were always the only one who could replicate mom's recipe to a T."

I shook my head at that. "You're the best baker in the family." She smiled again but didn't speak, just looked at me, an awkward silence settling between us.

She sighed and closed her eyes again. "I'm dying, Jude. The doctors said radiation won't help very much, so I told them I won't put Jesse and the kids through that. I want to at least be present and enjoy the time I have with them." Her voice broke and she shook her head. "Just like Mama. She was two years younger than me when she died."

I jerked my head, emotion clogging up my throat. "I know. I'm so sorry, Mary."

"Well." She laughed. "You're not alone in that. How I've missed you." She reached out and took my hand, when I closed mine around hers I almost flinched. Her skin felt so cold and papery, and I remembered how scared I'd been when she'd been sick the last time. How I'd driven from college to see her every weekend.

"You and the twins were our first kids, you know? Everyone would ask why Jesse and I waited so long to start a family. I would laugh and tell them we started raising one the day we brought you all to our house." She sighed heavily and squeezed my hand again. "We pray for you, every day. We pray you're all right, and that you find your way back to us."

As much as my heart ached from missing my sister, the thought of that, of having to go back to denying who I was, made my stomach sink. Since talking to Jesse on Sunday I feared seeing Mary would make me yearn to be in the fold of my family again. But being here with her now, I knew I could never go back.

It hurt to know she'd never see me the same way again, even though I was the same Jude she'd held and sang to every night for months after Mom died. The same young man she asked to be the godfather to her child.

It struck me how sad it was that this one thing about me could be more important than everything else. I wondered if there would ever be a way for me to explain to her or any of my family how wretched and small it made us all.

Mary's voice brought me out of all my sad thoughts. "Are you still out in Ithaca? Esther said you were working at the county library there. Always book crazy like me." A wistful smile formed on her lips.

I nodded, grateful for the change of topic. "Yes, still in the book business. It's a good place to work. I really like Ithaca too. It's a nice community." I'm not sure why I felt compelled to say that, but it seemed important to make it clear I was happy where I was. "How are the kids and the rest of the folks up there?"

"They're good. Faith is starting seventh grade this fall. She's a book nut like us, loves to write." A tear fell down her face and I could tell she was working very hard not to start sobbing.

I took her hand again. "Oh, Mary."

She closed her eyes and breathed deeply. When she opened them again the stoic mask the Fuller family wore so well was firmly set on her face.

"Micah is starting fifth grade, he's obsessed with soccer and says he wants to be a preacher. Imagine that." The thought of little Micah being indoctrinated into the ways of our church made a shudder course through me.

"Everyone else is the same, working, living, kids getting bigger. Our lives don't change much year to year. Amos's youngest just got married."

"That's great." I sighed, thinking about all the events I'd missed in the past few years. "I've missed the kids."

"They missed their Uncle Jude too. Faithy made her herself sick from crying after—"

She stopped mid-sentence, grief marring her face.

I waited, knowing she was thinking of a way to talk about what happened, to explain why she had cut all

contact with me. I wondered if it would still hurt. If the
skin on my face would still burn with shame when she
talked about "my choices."

Suddenly Mary turned to me. "Why didn't you ever
tell me you how you felt, Jude? I could've helped you."
She looked earnest and hurt. I didn't answer, knowing Mary wasn't done. "I could've prayed with you, or
gone to Pastor Jones, talked about it with him, found
a way to fix it."

There it was.

Fix it.

Fix me.

I was surprised to realize it was not so much hurt I
felt, just weariness.

I exhaled. "Mary, there was nothing to fix. There *is*
nothing to fix. I didn't say anything because I needed
time to figure things out, and I was scared of what
would happen once I said it." I laughed sadly, thinking
of all those years I spent living in agony. "I waited so
long to say something because I wanted more time with
all of you. Do you know, I knew I was gay by the time
I was eight or nine? I was certain of it, and I prayed,
and begged God to take it away, but it didn't go away.
So, I put it off as long as I could. Tried to learn to love
myself enough the way I was, so no matter what happened after I told, I could go on."

She'd put her hand on my forearm as she spoke, and
when I finished she tightened it for a second before
letting go. "I can't go against what I believe, Jude. No
matter how much I love you, and I do love you, little
brother."

"I'm not asking you to, Mary. I don't need you to accept anything. I'm here for you, to see you. If you want me here, I'll stay, if you don't, I'll go."

"No, don't go." Her voice gained an urgency then and she moved around, pulling out a book from under her pillow. I smiled at that because she'd been the one to start me on the habit of waking up and falling asleep with a book. I always had one, or my e-reader, tangled in my sheets. I learned that from Mary.

"Will you read to me?" Her conspiratorial tone finally brought back the older sister I remembered. I looked at the cover of the book she handed me, a grin blooming on my face. *Love in the Time of Cholera* by Gabriel Garcia Marquez. Mary had only ever been irreverent in one thing, books. She read everything, whether it was allowed or not by our church. If it was good, she devoured it.

"Do you have a page marked?"

She shook her head, then adjusted herself on the bed. "Start from the beginning." She leaned back on her pillow, a serene look coming over her face.

I opened the book to the first page, cleared my throat and read the first line.

It was inevitable: the scent of bitter almonds always reminded him of unrequited love.

A happy sigh escaped Mary's lips as I began to read to her.

I stayed long enough to finish the first few chapters, and for one hour we were the old Jude and Mary. Too engrossed in a good story and beautiful writing to let the outside world concern us. Mary had fallen asleep while I read, so I was sitting, watching her rest when Jesse came in. He touched my shoulder and gestured

for me join him outside. With one last look at my sister, I walked out of the room, leaving her to her nap.

When I came out to the hall, Jesse surprised me by
giving me a hug. "It's good to see you, Jude. Thanks
for coming, how did it go?"

Jesse looked older too, still tall and strong, but his
face was gaunt from exhaustion.

"It's good to see you too. Where did all your hair
go?" I teased, immediately going back to the easiness
I'd always felt around Jesse.

He smiled, running his hand over his bare head. "It
started thinning so I shaved it all off, it's easier. Mary
says it's because I'm too vain to walk around with a
bald spot." He grinned for a moment and then a dark
cloud passed over his face.

I squeezed his shoulder again. "Thanks for letting
me come. We had a good visit." I shrugged, thinking of
our conversation before she got the book. "Mary said
her piece as she usually does, but then she saved us both
by pulling a book from under her pillow."

He laughed. "She has to have her say, doesn't she?
I'm glad she remembered the book. She asked for it special, so you could read it to her." His expression changed
again; this time regret filled his eyes. "There isn't a
week that goes by without her mentioning how much
she misses talking books with you. She says you're the
only one who could keep up with her in the reading
department."

I smiled sadly at his words. "I miss talking books
with her too." I looked at Jesse and saw how tired he
was and wondered how much help he was getting from
my family. Mary had always been the one to rally the
troops. Would they step up for her now?

"Jesse, would it be okay for me to come back and visit? I'm not sure how long you'll be here, but I'd like to come again before you guys head home. I'm not sure I'll be able to go see her there."

He shook his head, and my heart sank. "We're not going back home, Jude. The doctor just told us this morning, there's not much more they can do other than manage the pain. She's being transferred to Syracuse at the end of the week, so she can be closer to home, and from there a hospice when she gets closer." He ran his hand over his mouth like he was trying to hold back a sob.

"It's summer, so the kids are still out of school. My folks are in Syracuse. They'll watch them for us."

"I'm so sorry, Jesse," I choked out, my eyes brimming with tears.

He covered his face with his hands, his voice muffled when he spoke again. "You're welcome to come and see her once we're settled there."

I nodded. "Syracuse is only an hour away from Ithaca. I can come anytime. Just let me know when it's convenient for me to stop by. And if there's anything you need, please let me know."

"Thank you, for everything. It had to be hard to come here, but I knew she'd be happy to see you."

We shook hands again before he went back into the room, and I headed down the hall to the elevator. I texted Nesto to let him know I was coming down, grateful the visit had gone better than I expected.

As I stepped out of the elevator I looked up and came face to face with my older brother Amos, who did not seem happy at all to see me there.

Nesto

I was walking up to the elevator to meet Jude when I saw some guy getting in his face. He was taller and with dark hair, but they were definitely related.

I debated for a second whether I should intervene, since I knew Jude didn't want to make waves during this visit. But when I saw him grab Jude's arm like he was going to walk him out of the fucking hospital, I got my ass moving. This asshole was not going to man-handle Jude.

I stepped up to them, so I was inches away from the guy's face and growled, "Get your hands off him, my man," in a tone which evoked a very clear "*Don't test me, motherfucker.*"

The guy turned to look at me and startled. I wasn't even trying to control my face at the moment either and thankfully he noticed I wasn't above throwing hands in this hospital lobby.

He let go of Jude and sneered at me. "Who are you?" Then he turned around and looked at Jude like he was repulsed by him. "You know what? Never mind, I don't need to know."

Jude's face was completely devoid of emotion when he looked at the guy.

"Amos, this is Ernesto. Ernesto, this is my oldest brother, Amos."

His brother.

This fucker knew Jude had just come from seeing his sister who was dying of cancer, and he couldn't take a break from being a douchebag and let him leave in peace. No wonder he'd been a mess about seeing these people again.

Amos stepped up to me like he was going to do something.

"I'll fight you right here, my dude." I was pissed and knew my body language was giving off a pretty menacing vibe.

After a moment he scoffed like an asshole and just walked into the elevator.

Jude turned toward the exit, taking my hand. He looked at his brother and said quietly, "Take care, Amos." Then he walked away. I did the same, following him out of the building.

"What's up with that guy, is he always like that?" I asked as we got close to the sliding glass doors.

Once we were outside, he smiled at me and squeezed my hand. "Looks like Amos is taking up for my dad in the excessively aggressive department. Thanks for rescuing me."

I did not like the sound of that *at all*. It also freaked me out a little how placid Jude looked. I knew all this shit affected him, so this blank stare thing must be some kind of defense mechanism, which he apparently had perfected to be around his family.

"I'm glad I was here, and if you decide to visit again, I'm coming with you. *Every. Time.* No one's going to be putting their hands on you like that again. Period."

Jude just gave me a tiny smile as we walked to my car in silence. It was midday and the sun was out in full force. I gave him time to digest how he felt about seeing his sister, hoping he wouldn't shut down again, but once we were in the car he spoke.

"I'm really glad you're here too. The visit went okay, but it helped so much to know you were waiting for me downstairs." His eyes were trained ahead, and he sounded eerily calm. "Things were a bit tense at first and Mary wanted to rehash things. Thankfully she realized it wasn't the best thing to do and pulled out a book." He smiled at that. "I read to her for a bit."

"That's good, babe." I knew he wouldn't say much unless I pushed him a little. Jude was a master at keeping it all surface when it came to the hard stuff.

I reached out to run my hand over his hair. I just really needed to touch him. "How did it feel to see her again?"

He sighed and turned his face to the window, his hand squeezing mine hard. "It was weird, to be honest. The last time I'd talked to her was about a week after I came out to them, when she told me not to contact the family."

I almost felt sorry I hadn't popped that fucker Amos on the mouth.

His face looked so bleak and sad. I wanted to wrap him in my arms and protect him from the world, take this hurt from him. "Even after that conversation I still thought once there was some distance between us, we would find a way to fix things, but we never did. Everything was too broken by then."

He squeezed his eyes closed again, his face pained, like he was trying to vanish something from his mind.

It took him a minute to speak again. "My dad had a heart attack about a month after Mary came to see me." The look of despair on his face was almost unbearable. "It was a minor one, but he never really bounced back, he'd had cardiac issues for years and never really took care of himself. He died a year after I left. I wasn't invited to the funeral."

"Oh baby. I'm so sorry."

"It's okay."

It really wasn't fucking okay, but I just let him keep talking.

"You can imagine what my family said was the reason." He shrugged again looking down at the seat. "Not that I begrudge them. It was my fault."

"Jude, it wasn't your fault."

"Rationally, I know he already had problems with his heart, and it was only a matter of time, but I can't deny reality. I came out and just weeks later he had a heart attack. The last time I saw him, he looked at me like I was the biggest disappointment of his life."

He laughed then and it sounded so hollow. "The thing is, I worked through all of this. I really have learned to accept that none of it was really about me. My family failed me, because they refused to put aside their prejudices and love me the way I was. But seeing Mary brought a lot of those feelings back, that's all. I'm still glad I came, it would've been a lot harder to hear about it after it was too late. I want to come back and see her again."

After a second he put his hand behind my head and leaned in for a kiss. I touched my lips to his and his mouth tasted salty from his tears. "Thank you for letting me be here for you."

He just nodded and sat back, looking out the window, his fingers still around mine.

Jude fell asleep almost immediately after we started driving, probably exhausted from the visit and not getting enough sleep the night before.

As we drove, I thought of what he'd done today. How he'd walked into the room of someone who had turned her back on him, scorned him, and done it because she'd asked him to, because she needed him.

There was such strength in that, in his forgiveness and grace. I thought of what it would be like to lose everyone I loved overnight.

Would I be able put aside my pride and be there for those who'd hurt me in their time of need? I wasn't sure I could.

I tended to walk away from people who disappointed or hurt me. But as I looked at Jude's sleeping figure, I felt humbled by the kind of man he was and that's when I knew; I was so full of love for this man.

I loved Jude.

I had never been more certain of anything in my life.

Chapter Twenty-Three

Jude

"Carmen told me you're not a fan of surprises, but I did something. So, don't be mad."

I smirked as I put my seat belt on. We were sitting in the car at the parking lot of the hospital in Syracuse. I'd just finished visiting my sister for the third time in three weeks. Today Jesse brought Faith and Micah over so I could see them while I was there. They were huge and surprisingly remembered all about me. Faith was just like Mary, serious and bossy, and Micah was as easygoing and gentle as his dad.

The visit had its hard parts too. Mary got weaker by the day. Every week she looked more fragile, but we'd stayed off difficult topics since the first visit and just tried to enjoy the time we had. Today I'd brought a book of poems by Pádraig Ó Tuama, an Irish priest I discovered recently, and read to her from it. Overall things had gone well, and I was in good spirits.

I heard Nesto clear his throat, and looked over at him and laughed. He was always so confident, but right now he was looking adorably unsure. I thought he was actually going to blush. I pulled him over to me and gave him a hard kiss, with lots of tongue.

"You must be joking. Why would I be mad if you did something nice for me? For the record," I said, holding my finger up, "I love surprises. What I don't like is Carmen buying me things I've told her I don't need, and then trying to force me into keeping them!"

He rolled his eyes at my griping. "You two are like an old married couple." He slipped his hand under my shirt, and ran it over my chest. "I'd be jealous if I didn't know where you've been spending most nights."

I shivered thinking about the last couple of weeks. Even as stressed out as he had been with the truck, Nesto had barely slept at his place. We'd both been so busy, but almost every night we'd gone to bed together.

"So, what did you do?"

He smiled, his confidence back in place. "I booked us a romantic getaway."

"Whaaat?" I asked in disbelief. "For when? You have a million things going on with the truck, and the mobile library launch is only weeks away. We literally have no time."

That sexy grin was on full display and he looked a little too pleased with himself.

"Now, tonight. I got a room at the Aurora Inn. I've been thinking about doing it since the festival. We both need to get away for a bit. Things are about to get busier now that I'm going to start doing dinner at Ergos again."

I shook my head and smiled at how casually he said that. Ergos had called a couple of weeks ago, begging him to come back. They told him they were sorry they'd ever invited Misty's son's truck and desperately wanted him back.

Anyone else would've gloated or given them a hard time, not Nesto, he thanked them for giving him another opportunity and didn't waste a single breath on Misty. That was the kind of man he was, and right now he was looking at me with such genuine affection I had a hard time believing it was all for me.

He leaned closer, totally focused on me. "We've been going at full speed for months now, and I wanted some time just the two of us." He shook his head, his usually smiling face suddenly serious. "Things are moving so fast, and pretty soon I'm going to have to make some decisions about the future."

My heart sank when I heard those words. So far we'd avoided discussing the elephant in the room.

He pressed our foreheads together as he spoke. "We haven't even talked about what it would mean for us." This time he did blush as he waved his hands between us. "I'm seriously in unknown territory at the moment, so please stop me if I'm acting like a fool right now."

I shook my head against the niggling feeling that said, "This is too much. You're being careless. Whatever you let yourself have right now, will make it a hundred times worse if this doesn't work out." I almost told him to forget it, that we shouldn't, that *I couldn't.*

Then I pulled back to look at him and he was *so solid.* I leaned into what *I knew*, what felt certain. I could trust what I had with Nesto right now.

"You're definitely not doing that."

Another blush.

"I asked Carmen if she'd talk to Martha about you taking today and part of tomorrow off." He put his hands up looking embarrassed. "Was that totally creepy and over the line? Martha said it was fine."

I kept staring at him with what I knew was a stunned look on my face, unable to talk. I could not believe Nesto managed to pull this off when he'd been working fourteen-hour days for the last two weeks.

He cringed, and the blush was now working itself down his neck. "I also packed us a change of clothes. The bag's in the trunk." He looked back like he was expecting the thing to jump out and slap him.

I just sat there grinning at him while he confessed.

"It's less than an hour from Ithaca, so we can both be back after lunchtime tomorrow. I took care of the truck too. Ari and Yin are handling everything without me." He lifted his shoulder this time, a very naughty smile on his lips. "I figured I'd finally pay you back for that massage I promised you."

I was having trouble deciding what to do, because there was no way I could crawl onto his lap in the limited space of his Prius. But I at least would give him a hell of a kiss. I leaned over, this time running my hand over his crotch while I bit his lower lip. He let out a surprised yelp when I tightened my hand on his hardening cock.

"Oh shit, okay. So, we're good then?"

I didn't answer right away. Instead I spent another moment sucking on his tongue before pulling back.

"We're more than good. I can't believe you did all that. How did you even get a room? That place is always booked solid in the summer."

The tip of his tongue slid over his upper lip and he preened. My Dominican man's swagger back in full force. "What am I, brand new? I got some tricks up my sleeve, papí. One of the ladies from the market, the one who runs the raw food stand, mentioned she was tight with the manager. I texted her on Sunday and she came through. They had a cancellation on a room with a lake view, so I took it."

I knew I was looking at him like he just told me he'd climbed Mt. Everest, but I couldn't help it. No one had ever done anything like this for me.

He waggled his eyebrows. "We better get this car on the road then, because I actually made us a massage appointment."

More winking.

"Start driving, Ernesto. I'm ready."

"I don't think I've been this relaxed in well…ever," I said as I heard Nesto walking onto the balcony in our room.

"I've got something to get you even more relaxed." He stood behind my rocking chair and handed me a flute of champagne. I tipped my head back for a kiss and he lowered his head, lightly pressing our lips together before sitting down on the chair next to mine.

Nesto turned his head and clinked our glasses together. "Salud. Here's to guerilla getaways."

"Here's to lovers with stealth for romance," I said smiling, and reached out to hold his hand. I leaned back, closing my eyes, and felt a little dizzy from the wine we'd had at dinner, the warm night air, the lull of the rocking chair and this man.

I knew I'd been half in love with him already, but today had been like something out of dream. From the moment we got to the inn everything had been perfect.

Our room was exquisite, with an amazing view of the lake and the most delicious bed i'd ever laid on. After a nap we'd gotten lunch in the patio restaurant and then went for a couple's massage. We took a walk along the lake before going to the dining room for a delicious dinner. We talked about books, movies we liked, the places we'd been to and others we'd like to visit someday. It was a perfect day.

He was perfect.

I turned around to look at him, and he was staring up at the sky, sipping from his glass. I took a drink from mine and sighed as I squeezed his hand again. "This is amazing. Thank you, I had no idea how much I needed it. I don't think it would've ever occurred to me to just go away for the day."

He smiled and dipped his head. "One thing we know well in the islands is that sometimes you just need to drop everything and go to the water. Recharge." He turned around, his face serious. "We needed this time."

I nodded, agreeing wholeheartedly, the doubts from earlier today a distant memory. "We did."

"Are you happy, baby?"

Occasionally Nesto would ask me that out of the blue, at random moments, and I'd say *yes* automatically, but always thought it was such an odd thing to ask.

"I am actually. I *feel* happy. Why do you always ask me that?"

He shrugged. "It's a Dominican thing I guess. We always ask each other. ¿Estas contento? ¿Te sientes bien? It's important to ask, if the person you're with is happy, if they're okay. Those things shouldn't be taken for granted."

I looked at him again, his dark eyes so intent on me. "No, they shouldn't be."

"I don't want to take you for granted, Jude. I—" He stopped talking then, his shoulders tensing like he wasn't sure how to proceed, and then he held up his finger. "I'll be right back." He put down his glass and went into the room. Then I heard him looking through his bag. I was about to go in and ask if he needed anything when he came back with a little Bluetooth speaker and his phone.

He set it up on the arm of his chair, and soon the low notes of a slow merengue filled the balcony. Nesto crouched down and took my hand.

"Baila conmigo."

I squinted up at him, trying to convey my bemusement. "I don't think I could keep up with you dancing merengue."

He took my other hand and pulled me up, then wrapped his arm around my waist, pressing us tightly to each other. "Just move with me, baby."

We started a slow sway, listening to the music. I put my head on his shoulder and we moved together in the quiet night. This was probably the most romantic moment of my life. Everything felt right. I didn't want to break the spell by asking what he was about to say before he got the music. It felt important to let him take his time.

The first song ended, and the notes of an accordion and percussion sounded over the speakers. Nesto grunted in approval of the new song, and then he put his mouth next to my ear and started singing along.

My stomach flipped, and I felt like a thousand butterflies were fluttering in my chest. His voice was a lot deeper than the man singing on the speakers, and with his mouth so close to my ear, his lips brushed against my skin as he mouthed the lyrics.

The song was in Spanish and I was feeling so addled

by the moment, I had to focus to understand the words. Nesto sang about setting a flight of kisses loose on my mouth, and painting rainbows on my skin.

I could barely keep up with the mix of his words and the things that I was feeling. Just as I started to drift in his arms, he pulled me closer and whispered a line from the song in a sure, clear voice.

"And when the roses bloom, my life, they can tell you how much I love you."

I stiffened, and he laughed huskily. After a moment he kissed me. His tongue stealing into my mouth hot and hungry, I returned it in earnest.

He pulled back and sighed, keeping us swaying together. "Remember that first day you came to the truck?"

I nodded. "Of course, how could I forget? Best burrito of my life."

"Oh, it was the burritos that kept you coming back, huh?" he asked, amused.

"Not entirely." I was going for cheeky, but it came out pretty breathless.

"After you stopped by and dropped that one liner on me before walking away, giving me a view of this delicious ass." He grinned as he smacked my butt. "My mom told me I should ask you out. She told me I needed balance. That I had to believe I could have my work and a life. My work has always been my life. I've always been hustling after something. Everyone around me was always running after something. Relationships were always secondary. Sure I dated, but no one ever made me stop and look around or think about what I was missing, what I could have with someone."

My heart was going to beat right out of my chest.

"You make me want to slow down. Because of you, for the first time in my life, happiness feels like a very different thing than business success." He shook his head like he was struggling to find words. "Jude, I don't know what's going to happen with the truck. Even though business is good, I'm still not sure if I can make a go of it, as a living you know?"

His face was so serious, like this was the most important conversation of his life, and my chest tightened, because it felt like that for me too. "All I know is, I don't want to give up on what we have."

I looked up at him. His face so beautiful in the moonlight. He'd let his hair grow out and his curls looked like a halo around his face. His nose and mouth like carved wood, handmade. I brought my fingers up to his lips and traced them.

"Ernesto, I don't want you to give up your dream for me. I can't be responsible for that."

He hid his face in my neck and let out a ragged breath. "I'm not giving up. I just want you to know that I'm not giving up on us either."

I nodded as I grabbed on to him for dear life. When he pulled back his eyes were so dark they looked almost black and his face was so open with desire for me. Suddenly all I wanted was to be grounded in the connection we had. Before going back to our lives tomorrow, I wanted our bodies to render out what we felt for each other.

I pushed my face to his and right up against his mouth I whispered, "I love you too, Nesto. You make feel so happy, more than I ever thought I could be." I felt the air rush out of his lungs, as his hips pushed up against me almost by reflex and I was done talking.

He groaned and his hands, which had been on my waist, moved down to my ass, his fingers digging into me, hips moving in that tight and hard grind that made me so hot. He was tonguing my neck and I was burning up for him, my hands running over every part of his body I could reach.

I needed more skin, to feel his body against mine. I was about to grab the hem of his shirt when he lifted me up like I weighed nothing. I wrapped my legs around his waist as he walked us back into the bedroom.

I smiled and rested my head on his shoulder, my lips brushing his skin as I mumbled against his neck, "This is by far the hottest thing that's ever happened to me."

He chuckled as we got to the room. "Wait until I have you naked on this bed and we'll see how you feel about that." The hunger in his voice made my entire body seize up in anticipation.

He put me down and quickly took care of bringing in our things from the balcony. Then drew the curtains to give us more privacy.

He walked back to where I was standing, so we were just inches apart. Without talking, I moved my hand to the hem of his shirt, and in one motion pulled it off.

We stood there undressing each other in the half-lit room, kissing and touching for what felt like a very long time. He ran his hands everywhere, his fingers digging into my skin, like he wanted to sink into it. So many thoughts were running through my head, how much I wanted this, how badly I needed to feel him inside me.

His caress was igniting, it made my blood boil under my skin. I gave him one last kiss, hurried to the bed and lay on my stomach with my head resting on my arms. I looked over my shoulder and smiled at his silence, because he usually was a lot more talkative.

"You're so quiet."

He'd come up on the bed and was kneeling with his legs on either side of mine, one hand stroking his cock and the other on his balls. He was biting his bottom lip again and looking down at me intently, like he was trying to figure out where to start. He ran his thumb over the tip of his cock and then brought it up to his mouth, making me shudder.

"I want to take my time with you, baby, tell me what you want. How do you want me to touch you?" He lowered himself, his chest hovering over my back. I could feel his cock grazing my ass and I pushed back, wanting to feel him on me. His body always felt so hot when he pressed against me.

"I want you inside, Nesto." His gasp of surprise spurred me on. "I've wanted that for so long. Please, baby."

Whenever we were together, it was as if he could tap into a part of me that only woke up for him. Feeling the touch of his arms, the dampness of his skin, a little clammy now that we were moving together, it unfurled a need in me I never knew existed. I moaned, pushing back, wanting him to know I was with him in every way.

He started moving down my back, licking at the knobs of my spine, whispering as he went. When he made it down to the dip of my ass, he bit one of my cheeks, then turned his head from side to side, his scruff brushing against my skin making me tremble.

"This should be illegal. From the first moment I saw you walking to the library, I was hooked on this ass."

"I'd never guessed you'd be so into my ass," I said, resting my head on my hands again. "But I'm not going to complain."

He ran his fingers down my cleft. After a moment I felt his thumb probing at my hole, extracting a long moan out of me.

"Push your hips up, baby. I want to make sure you're ready for me."

My breath caught at this and I moved to lift up. He used both hands now to open me and I felt the air touching the sensitive skin. His moved his hands away, but before I could complain I heard him rifle through the bedside drawer. I turned my head and saw him fish out a small tube of lube and a condom.

"Wow, someone was pretty sure of himself," I said, shaking my head at the shameless grin on his face.

"It was a calculated risk." I smiled at him again and put my head back down.

I heard the click as he opened the top of the lube and after a few seconds felt the pad of his two fingers rubbing small circles over my entrance. It felt electrifying, like he was lighting up every nerve inside me.

I moaned, caught up in the pleasure. "Feels so good."

"It's going to feel even better when I'm inside you." I shuddered in anticipation, knowing how good it would feel to have him filling me up. He pressed one finger, moving it in and out slowly, letting me adjust. I pushed out, so he knew I could take more. He sucked in a breath, and added another finger.

"Your ass is going to feel amazing on my cock."

He grabbed my cheek and bent down for another bite. "Este culo me vuelve loco."

I groaned. "Nesto, come on, please."

"¿Qué pasa, mi amor?" he asked, teasing. "¿Qué quieres?"

"I want *you*," I groaned, pushing back harder.

He kept working his fingers inside until the only sounds I could make were senseless dribble. I heard him opening the condom wrapper and after a moment he was lifting my hips up and pressing his hand down on the swell of my ass to hold me in place. He teased my entrance with his cock and pushed in slowly.

"Oh fuck, that's so good. Push back for me."

My entire body was pulsing. He leaned down so his chest was brushing my back, his arms on either side of me, and worked himself all the way in. That tightness eventually giving way to so much pleasure. He pulled back once and then started pressing into me at an angle that hit me exactly right with every thrust.

"Fuck you're so tight. It's too good. I'm not going to last long, baby." After a few more thrusts he pulled out. But before I could balk, he lifted me, so I was lying on my back. He pushed my legs onto my chest and slid back in. His hair dripping with sweat, his chest moving up and down as his breathing quickened. He kept making those circles with his hips, and after a few moments he pushed my legs farther up, so he could go deeper. I was so full, I could feel him everywhere.

"Grab your cock, baby. I want to feel you come on my dick."

I took myself in hand and started stroking. My groin and hips felt like molten liquid. After a few seconds my orgasm slammed into me with such force I lifted off the bed as long ropes of semen pumped out of my cock. I felt Nesto stiffen above me, his mouth open in exquisite agony. He had both hands under my knees and

I felt them twitch as he pumped into me with the last of his orgasm. He let my legs fall back on the bed and slumped on top of me, his breathing still harsh.

"That was amazing. *You're* amazing."

I smiled and ran my hands over his thighs. "When we're together I feel like I'm on fire. I love the way my body feels when you're touching me."

He licked the sweat off my neck and sighed. "I literally can't get enough of you."

"I feel the same way." I looked for a reason to be afraid of what I was feeling, but the only thing I felt was peace.

Chapter Twenty-Four

Nesto

Last night had been epic. We'd made love and then I'd fallen asleep with Jude warm and happy in my arms. This morning, we woke up slowly, taking our time before heading home.

Home.

I never thought I'd be okay living anywhere other than New York City, but as I looked over at Jude in the passenger seat placidly reading a book as we drove, I felt like I was exactly where I needed to be.

"Are you happy, baby?"

He looked up at me and smiled. "Very."

I smiled back focusing on the road, while Jude returned to his book. We were just ten minutes out of Ithaca, and I was going over the things I needed to do once we got back when a call came over the Bluetooth. I figured it was either Ari or Yin calling to ask something, but when I looked at the screen I gasped, startling Jude.

"Who is it?"

"I think it's Mr. Sheridan."

He laughed and gestured at the screen. "Then take the call!"

I pressed accept and breathed out. "Ernesto here."

"Ernesto, how are you doing?" He sounded relaxed, and I tried hard to match his tone.

"Everything's good Mr. Sheridan. I can't apologize enough for not being there the day you came to meet me at the festival. I'm not one to leave people hanging."

He made a sound like he was agreeing with me. "I think I have a sense of the kind of man you are, Ernesto. That's why I'm calling you today."

He sounded so serious, but before he went on I spoke up, "I just want to let you know I've got you on speaker, my boyfriend and I are driving back to town from spending the night out in Aurora."

I looked over at Jude, whose jaw was somewhere down by his feet.

I shook my head and winked at him, mouthing, "It's fine."

I don't fuck with closets, so if this was going to be an issue, I might as well know now.

Mr. Sheridan didn't miss a beat though. "No problem at all. Were you taking some time off?"

"Yeah, we just did one night at the inn there."

"Good for you, recharging is important."

"It definitely is." I looked over at Jude, a grin on my face, but he just covered his face with his hands and shook his head. I focused back on Mr. Sheridan.

"How can I help you, sir?"

"Well, I wanted to let you know my oldest grand-daughter, Riley, just bought me lunch at the food truck of the man who rescued her when she blew out both tires on the way to work a few weeks ago."

Both Jude and I jumped when he said that. "Riley's your granddaughter?" I asked, completely floored.

He laughed at my obvious surprise, it was a deep and friendly sound, making a little flame of hope ignite in my chest. "She is and since I got back from vacation a few days ago she's been raving about your food. I finally let her take me there today and your staff made me the best burrito I've ever eaten."

I felt a surge of pride thinking of Yin and Ari, those two never let me down.

"I'm really happy to hear you liked our food."

"Oh, I more than liked it." I turned and saw that Jude looked as stunned as I felt. My head pounded, as I tried to make sense of what Mr. Sheridan was telling me. "I've been wanting to open a place for a while now. Something that appeals to the college students, but is also nice enough to attract young professionals and families in the area. Sit down, but casual, good food, good drinks. A small but reliable menu, with a very strong concept and flavors you can't get anywhere else around here. I think OuNYe hits a lot of those marks."

I glanced over at Jude again just to make sure he was hearing the same thing I was. He was grinning from ear to ear, which meant this must be actually happening.

"I'd like to talk with you, Nesto. If you're still interested that is."

I had to pull over to the side of the road then, because all the blood was rushing to my head. When I stopped, I exhaled before I responded.

"I'm definitely interested." I sounded winded. Probably from all the times I'd stopped breathing during the conversation.

He laughed again. "I can meet tonight at six thirty if you'd like to talk further."

"I can do that. Where?"

"My office. It's in the Cayuga building downtown, suite A on the fifth floor."

"I'll see you there."

"I'm looking forward to it."

With that he ended the call, and I sat there for a couple of seconds digesting the last few minutes.

Jude's yelp startled me out of my stupor. "Nesto, this is huge!"

I didn't want to get my hopes up too much, but after last night, this felt like fate.

"It sounds promising." Jude was grinning, his face a reflection of my own excitement. I leaned over and gave him a kiss as I started the car, thinking about all the ways things had changed for me in the last twenty-four hours.

I arrived at Sheridan's building at exactly 6:15. Yes, I was fifteen minutes early, but I wasn't trying to blow this for myself *again*. I walked in and looked around the lobby, the inside of the building was done in an art deco style, with black marble floors. I stopped to look at some of the huge black-and-white vintage photographs of downtown Ithaca on the walls, while I tried to relax before going up to Mr. Sheridan's office. I was about to press the button to the elevator when the door opened and an older, very tall, white gentleman stepped out. He was wearing jeans and a button down shirt that looked way too expensive to pass as casual. He noticed my shirt, which had the OuNYe logo stitched on the breast pocket, and extended his hand, beaming at me.

"You must be Ernesto."

I shook his hand, trying to put on my game face. "Nice to meet you, Mr. Sheridan, please call me Nesto."

He shook his head and signaled toward the building entrance. "Harold, please. Thanks again for helping Riley."

"It was nothing." The way he lifted his eyebrow, told me he was well aware of what that detour almost cost me.

"Not nothing. You missed out on a business opportunity to help someone. I respect that." He looked down at his watch. "You're early, not taking any chances this time huh?" His tone was friendly and warm, and helped drain some of the tension out of me. I looked straight at him, trying to convey how important this moment was for me.

"No, sir."

He nodded and then started walking. "I was going out for some coffee. We can talk on the way. I'd like to hear more about you."

I walked out on the Ithaca Commons with him. The Commons was a large strip of shops and restaurants in the heart of downtown Ithaca. It was blocked off from motorists and had benches and play areas throughout. At this time, on a summer day like this, there were lots of people out. Sheridan and I walked out on to the fray and headed toward the coffee shop located a few blocks away.

After a few seconds he looked up at me and asked, "So why OuNYe?"

I straightened at his question, because this was it, right? In culinary school we always talked about "the pitch," what we'd say if we got the opportunity to make a business proposal to an investor. My ideas had always fallen in the "ethnic" category and the advice had been to neutralize as much as possible. Make it palatable. Tone it down.

I always had trouble with that though. My food was unapologetically Afro-Caribbean. The flavors of the islands my friends and I came from, were the heart of my business, and I would not push it aside to make anyone comfortable. Besides, if it turned Sheridan off, then I was better off passing on whatever this was anyways. I took a deep breath and went for it.

"I'm Dominican." I smiled, remembering Jude's teasing tone when he'd told me those two words didn't actually make a complete sentence. "I mean, I grew up in New York City, in the Bronx, but I was born in the DR. And my best friends' families growing up were all from the Caribbean too—Puerto Rico, Cuba, Jamaica and Haiti. We were inseparable, so our parents became friends too."

I paused and looked over at Mr. Sheridan who was staring straight ahead, with a smile on his face as he walked.

"They were all immigrants for the most part, and when we celebrated or something important happened, happy or sad, we cooked for each other. All our parents were trying to make it here, they wanted us to adapt, grow up like Americans, but to also know where we came from. Food was one of the ways we held on to our roots."

Mr. Sheridan nodded at this, his face suddenly serious, he stopped and quietly turned. His focus totally on me, despite all the people rushing by us.

It felt surreal to be doing this out here. I wondered

if the people passing us could tell I was having one of the most important conversations of my life.

"I remember as a kid walking with my mom to the store that had the produce she needed to make the beans and thinking, 'How can it be this important to use this one kind of pepper?' It couldn't actually make that much of a difference, you know? But it *did*, because it's what made it like home. The spices, the flavors, even the names of our food sometimes felt like the only touchstone we had. Caribbean food is full of nuance. I mean, we're all these different countries. We had different colonizers even, other than DR and Haiti we can't even get to each other without crossing the sea, right?"

The interest in Mr. Sheridan's eyes gave me the last push I needed to tell the rest of my story.

"Yet, there's this thread of common ingredients and preparations that make us more than just neighbors. Because no matter who came through each island, the men and women who were brought there from Africa as slaves made us brothers and sisters."

I turned around and stretched my hand out in the direction of the library where my truck was parked right now.

"So, when I decided to open my business I wanted a name which could convey our common roots. *Ounje*, with a J not the Y," I said, smiling, "is the word for food or nourishment in Yoruba. The West African language our ancestors brought to the islands. Of course the NY had to be at the center, because that was the place we all came together."

I dug my hands in my pockets. "So, that's how OuNYe Afro-Caribbean Food came to be. I wanted to bring my interpretation of all that beauty and flavor to the world."

We'd started walking again while I talked and were now right outside the coffee shop. I looked at Mr. Sheridan who was standing silently by the door, his hands still in his pockets, eyes focused on something in the distance. As the silence stretched, I started feeling self-conscious. I knew I'd gotten way too personal. I hadn't even mentioned the menu or profits. I had one shot and I blew it. I was about to say something just to fill the silence, when he finally spoke.

"I lived in Panama for the first twelve years of my life."

I must have done a shitty job of hiding my surprise, because he just laughed and patted me on the shoulder. "My father was an engineer with an oil company and worked all over South America, but we were based in Panama City. Anyway, we came back to the States right before I turned thirteen. I felt so out of place here."

He shook his head and looked back in the direction we'd come from.

"Imagine, after living in Panama my whole life coming to Ithaca in the sixties. It was literally another world. I mean we'd been expats there, and had a very privileged life, but I felt Panamanian too. There is something so visceral about being from a place that small, it's a completely different identity. So much pride and love, it's a constant ache in your heart." His face turned wistful as he spoke, his hand clutched at his chest, and I knew he got where OuNYe came from.

"I still follow the Panamanian baseball winter league, you know? And it still pisses me off when the Dominicans, Cubans or the Puerto Ricans kick our asses every year!" he said, feigning anger and pointing a finger at me.

I put my hands up and mouthed, "Sorry, not sorry."

He chuckled at that, then extended his hand. "Thank you for sharing your story with me."

I nodded, but couldn't get any words out with my head pounding in anticipation of what he would say.

He looked at me then and smiled sympathetically, and I realized my nerves were probably showing. "I want to keep talking about opening a restaurant together, Ernesto. If that sounds good to you."

I exhaled, lightheaded. "That sounds great. I just want to be clear on one thing. With all due respect, sir, I'm not going to be an employee. I'm not working for someone else. OuNYe is mine."

He clapped my shoulder then and laughed. "You don't beat around the bush. I like a man with confidence, and I can assure you, what I'm interested in is a partnership. I want you as invested in the success of the restaurant, as much or more than I would be."

I relaxed then and nodded. "Okay."

"Now let's get some coffee and walk back to my office so we can talk business. I already tried one of your burritos and can't wait to try the others. Hopefully that lovely woman with the silver hair who was at your stand during the festival will be there next time and can instruct me on which one to order?"

"That's my mom!" I yelped in horror.

"Excellent, when I see her I'll congratulate her on the fine job she's done with her son," he said with amusement.

My dream, what I had been after day and night for

the last two years, what I'd quit a good job and moved out of my home for, was finally within reach. This time I would do whatever it took to make sure I grasped it.

Chapter Twenty-Five

Jude

Nesto was late again.

I looked down at my phone and saw his smiling face flashing on the screen. It was a photo from our trip to Aurora three weeks earlier. The sky visible on either side of his face, the water of the lake sparkling behind him. Even that perfect blue couldn't compare with the smile that had come to brighten every dark corner of my life.

Except I didn't feel bright right now. I felt resentful and tired of waiting for him.

I exhaled and took the call, doing everything I could to erase the frustration from my voice. "Hi. Did you get tied up with the truck?" My shoulders felt tense and the smile I pasted on, which he couldn't even see, felt like it was going to crack my face in two.

"Babe, I'm so sorry. I got delayed talking to Harold. We're so fucking close to locking down this contract. We're almost there, papí. I almost have everything settled." The excitement in his voice thawed me out a little. I couldn't forget why Nesto was here, and how he almost lost his chance.

"I'm just going to stop over at my place for a minute to get some clothes, because I need to go see the lawyer tomorrow. Is it still cool for me to come over?"

His voice dipped then and I knew he was about to say something that would raze through the annoyance of the last hour like fire. "I've been thinking about that ass of yours all day. I'm gonna take my time with you tonight. I got some much pent-up energy from all this business talk. When I get my hands on you, mi amor—"

I gasped so loudly his fevered talk turned into a husky chuckle that I felt down in my gut. The irritation of earlier turning into a want so deep, it made everything else feel inconsequential. "Of course it's still okay for you to come over, but would you like me to order something? I got the stuff you asked for the lasagna, but I'm not sure I can wait. I'm hungry."

I heard him curse over the phone when I mentioned the lasagna.

He'd forgotten.

"I totally blanked on making dinner tonight. This thing with the restaurant has me so distracted. Forget me stopping by my place, I'll come straight to you and I'll whip something together in a minute. I can just go home after." He sounded flustered and exhausted.

Why was I acting like I was entitled to Nesto making me dinner? Guilting him after what had been an obviously long day. Making dinner for us was something he did to be nice. He came to my house and cooked for me after spending the day making food for other people. And now I was making him feel bad because he got busy with his business. I wanted to re-do the last few minutes.

When I spoke I tried to sound less annoyed. "No no.

I didn't mean it like that, I just meant I was hungry. I know the restaurant is the most important."

"Jude, that's—"

Nesto sounded like he was going to argue, but I wanted to be done with this, to not have caused this mood.

This *fighting* mood.

"You know what? I'll just order something. By the time you get back from getting clothes at your place, it'll be here and we can eat and go to bed. You must be tired from all these long days."

Nesto sighed on the other line and I couldn't breathe. He'd called me up happy and excited and I'd ruined it by snapping at him. "Papí, I totally fucked up and you are one-hundred percent right to be cranky if you've been waiting on me for over an hour."

I tried to say something but he just kept talking, "Here's what I'll do. I'll order a pizza at the place downstairs from me when I stop in to get my stuff. Sound good?" His voice got husky again and I felt so glad to hear him sounding normal.

"Yes. Sounds good."

"This is better actually, because that way I'll have more time with you tonight." I listened with my eyes closed, feeling a flutter of anticipation for whatever sexy and ridiculous thing he would say to get us back to being okay and in love. "I can't wait to be inside you. I'm going to fuck you so good tonight. I'm getting hard just thinking about it."

My stomach dipped and I felt a mixture of arousal and debilitating relief. We were fine.

Everything was fine.

"You're shameless, Ernesto Vasquez."

Another husky chuckle. "Just with you, papí. I'll see you in thirty."

I lifted my hand and smiled like he could see me. Aching already to have him near, to touch him.

Nothing ever stayed bad with Nesto.

"See you soon."

I ended the call determined to do whatever I needed to do to keep us in a good place. I could overlook a little lateness and forgetfulness if I got to have him with me.

"Are we walking over to your man's truck, so I can get a free burrito? Or are you going to make me pay for lunch again?" Carmen asked as we walked down to Nesto's truck after a meeting at Cornell.

I glanced at her as we waited to cross the street and I couldn't help but laugh at how serious she looked. "It's like ten thirty in the morning, and no, we're not going over there to get food. Nesto's driving me to Syracuse today. Remember I told you this week I was going on Wednesday?" I tried to keep my voice upbeat, but things were getting grim with my sister.

"They'll be transferring Mary to the hospice soon and they needed to run some tests yesterday. Jesse asked me to come today instead."

"Oh hon, I'm sorry, it must have slipped my mind. You've been going on Tuesdays for weeks now, so I just got used to Wednesdays being burrito days." Her smile was as bleak as this all felt, when she put an arm around my shoulder.

"Speaking of which, how are things with Nesto and the restaurant? From what he said when I saw him at the market, things are moving fast. It's been only like a month since he had the big talk with Sheridan."

I lifted a shoulder, before answering. "Yeah, I think he was supposed to hear some news about the location soon, but we didn't get a lot of time to talk last night."

I tried not to sound too bitter, but it was getting harder to keep a lid on my frustration with Nesto's lateness.

Carmen's face changed immediately. "Are things okay with you guys?"

I kept walking, not wanting to get into anything with Carmen while we were on our way to meet with Nesto. She had a hard time keeping things to herself when she had a grievance, and the last thing I needed was a blow-out between the only two people I felt like I could even speak to these days.

"It's just been hectic. Nesto opens the truck seven days a week now, and when he's not working he's doing stuff for the deal with Sheridan. I know this all means he'll be able to stay here for good, but I'm not feeling like I'm getting a lot from him right now."

I felt like a heel for even bringing it up. "It's not like he's completely absent. He's been coming to see Mary with me. And please don't get into any of this with him, okay? Because there isn't an issue, and I know he's trying his best."

She looked surprised, but nodded. "Of course, I would never say anything if you asked me not to."

I started talking again, hating how I felt. "I just thought he would relax a bit more about the truck now that things with Sheridan are essentially a done deal, but he's working three times harder. I don't think he's turned down a single offer for work or an invitation to an event. Instead of slowing down, he's even more driven."

I probably sounded so damn selfish. "I mean we've only been seeing each other for a couple of months, and I know him even coming to the visits with my sister is above and beyond what anyone would do after such a short time. But it's like he's doing this one big thing for me and everything else is about the truck."

Carmen tightened the arm she had around my shoulder. "Hon, have you tried to talk to him? Nesto's a reasonable man and he's crazy about you. Maybe he's not realizing securing a future is making things hard for you now."

"Yeah, I'll try. I'm just not sure I'm even entitled to demand more time, you know?"

Carmen stopped and turned, so we were face to face. "Don't do that. Nesto loves you, and I know he wouldn't want you to feel like you can't count on him."

I nodded, as we crossed the street toward the truck. "I'll talk to him on the drive today, thanks."

"Anytime, babe."

As we approached the truck we went around the back to find Nesto, but when we got there only Ari, Yin and two of the new staff were there.

"Hey, guys, where's Nesto off to?" I pulled out my phone to see if I had any messages from him. We were supposed to meet at the truck at ten forty-five to get on the road by eleven, and it was already ten fifty.

"Hey, Jude," Ari said, stepping down from the truck. "He was here earlier, but Mr. Sheridan called." He rubbed his hands and smiled. "Looks like the space is ready and Nesto went to check it out."

I tried not to jump to conclusions. Nesto had been late a couple of times, but so far, he'd kept his promise of always being there when I went on the visits. He knew this was the last time I'd see Mary before she went to hospice. We *had* changed the day of the visit, which I knew complicated things for him, so he might just be running behind schedule.

"It must have slipped his mind." I smiled at Ari, attempting a light tone and avoided looking at Carmen, who would see right through me.

I tried calling him, but it went straight to voicemail. The second time, I left a message telling him I'd drive there on my own. I ended the call and turned to Carmen.

"Hon, can you remind Martha I won't be in the office this afternoon? I'm going to go from here."

She looked at me through narrowed eyes, obviously aware I was a lot more frazzled about the idea of going to see Mary by myself than I was letting on. My anxiousness at going alone only made me more annoyed at myself, because what was my problem? Nesto wasn't under any obligation to go with me. I was an adult, and this was about my family.

"It's fine, Carmen, really. I'll text you when I get back, okay?"

She didn't look convinced, but she kissed me on the cheek and waved me off. "I'll let Martha know."

"Don't worry. I've been to visit Mary a bunch of times by now, I'll be fine," I said over my shoulder as I walked toward my car.

Chapter Twenty-Six

Jude

By the time I made it up to Mary's room it was past one. I waved at the nurses at the station as I passed them. I'd visited enough by now that I recognized some of them.

As I walked to her room, I wondered how she was doing today. She'd lost so much weight in the past few weeks, she didn't look much like herself anymore. She'd been so frail last week, I wondered if I'd only get a few more chances to see my sister.

When I got to Mary's room, I noticed there was a man in there already. He was sitting off to the far side of the room, in a chair by the little round table that held the homemade cards and flowers people brought Mary. His back was to the door, head down, like he was on a phone call, but when I knocked on the door he turned around. I almost gasped in surprise when I saw his face. It was our old pastor, Paul Jones. He was still as handsome and imposing as I remembered. He'd be in his mid-sixties now, but he could still suck all the air out of a room.

Pastor Jones.

His was a face I could have gone the rest of my life

without seeing again. The embodiment of every self-loathing thought I'd had as a teen. Every moment of absolute despair, knowing my family would cast me out if they knew the truth about me, sitting right here in my sister's hospital room.

He stood when he saw me, as if he'd been waiting for me, and my heart sank. I hoped this wasn't some kind of intervention. I wanted to believe Mary wouldn't do this to me. That she wouldn't betray my trust like this by using Pastor Jones to ambush me. I walked in hoping my unease was unnecessary.

I ignored Pastor Jones and looked over at the bed. Mary's eyes looked regretful, but I could see the stubborn set in her jaw. Whatever it was she'd planned for this visit, she was going to see it through. I let a long breath out as I got closer, knowing this conversation would wound me, but I sat down on the chair anyway. In some sick way, I felt I owed Mary this, her last attempt at saving my soul.

"How are you doing today?" I tried to keep a jovial tone, taking her hand as a tear rolled down her cheek.

"Pastor Jones came to pray with us." Just those few words brought on a coughing fit. It had a dry rattling sound. Her bony shoulders shook so violently I was afraid her IV would come out.

I gestured at Pastor Jones, who just stood there like a statue, to pass me the pitcher. I poured some water and passed it to Mary after she finished coughing. She drank deeply and slumped against her pillow, breathing hard.

She turned her face to me after a moment. "I'm so weak now, the hospice will be better. They'll be more mindful of my comfort."

"Oh Mary," I croaked, unable to say more.

"I'm getting ready, Jude. Soon I'll be with Mama and Daddy." She looked at Pastor Jones and he gave her a comforting smile, which I assumed was his way of encouraging her on whatever was about to happen. I nodded, ignoring the stare he was sending in my direction.

After a moment, he cleared his throat. "Jude, I'm here at Mary's request to talk about your salvation, son. Your sister is dying, and she's worried about the state of your soul as much as her own. She loves you and wants more than anything to see you turn away from the life of sin and perdition you're living. She doesn't want to leave this world without hearing you repent and say you accept our Lord in your heart once again."

Mary looked at me, her face pleading.

I was surprised that I could still be stunned by his words. It was like I felt everything, and nothing in that moment. I felt the humiliation of being with people who truly believed they were saving me from myself. I felt pity for my sister and me and how this last chance we'd had for some closure would go to waste. I felt rage toward men like Pastor Jones, who spent their life spewing hate and still felt entitled to tell the rest of us how wretched we were.

Most of all, though, I felt scared, because for a moment I wanted to do it. If I could just say this now and let my sister have this. Let her die in peace knowing I would not burn in the hell she was certain I was condemned to. But then I reminded myself I'd been through too much to betray myself like this, even for Mary.

I took her hand and I kissed her palm. In a strangled voice, my eyes full of tears, I shook my head and said, "I can't, Mary. And what's more I don't believe I have to. There's nothing wrong with who I am or how I live. I can't say something I don't believe is true." Pastor Jones rumbled from the side, but I held up my hand to stop him from saying whatever he was going to say.

Mary looked away for a moment and then turned her face back toward me. "Jude, I've appreciated your visits, and I hope you know how much I love you, but I don't think it's a good idea for you to come back. I fear seeing you may weaken my resolve, and I'm concerned for the state of my own soul. I can't condone your life-style, and I'm afraid I may be tempted to if you keep coming to see me."

I knew it was coming, and still it felt like a punch to the gut. Shame filled every cell in my body. I nodded, unable to talk, and after squeezing her hand one more time I stood up.

"I'm sorry, Mary. I love you."

I didn't bother even looking at Pastor Jones as I walked out of the room. As I got to the end of the hall-way I felt like my body was floating. The humiliation and hurt churning in my body like sludge. I saw a rest-room down the hall and I hurried inside. I went into a stall and just sat there, my eyes dry. I don't know how long I stayed there, but after a while I got up and splashed some cold water on my face.

When I walked out of the bathroom I saw Amos heading toward me. I was about to turn the other way, but he grabbed my arm and pushed me against the wall. "I don't care what you told Mary in there. You will never be welcome into this family again. You're an em-barrassment, coming into this hospital holding hands with that man. You're disgusting." I pushed his hand away, trying to control the tremors in my body, shaking from sorrow and anger.

"Let go of me, Amos. You don't get to treat me like this again. I don't care what you think of me." I gasped, trying to keep my composure. "I just told Mary the same thing I told all of you four years ago. I won't apologize for who I am."

With that I started down the hall without looking back. I was all right. I had been on my own for a long time, I didn't need redemption and I didn't need forgiveness. I got on the elevator, telling myself I would be fine over and over again. As I stepped out into the lobby I wished Nesto was waiting for me outside the elevator like he usually did. I stopped and pulled out my phone to call him, the need to talk with him so strong my hands shook.

It was almost two and I hoped he was out of his meeting by now. I dialed his number and sagged with relief when he picked up after two rings, but before I could say a word he cut me off. "Hey, I can't talk right now. I've got something important going on now. I'll call you later okay?"

With that, he disconnected the call.

I stood there holding the phone to my ear with no one on the other end for a long moment. Then I snapped out of my daze and started for my car.

I should have learned my lesson a long time ago, but I never did.

Nesto

It was really happening.

OuNYe was going to be a brick and mortar restaurant. The space I'd just walked through with Harold was perfect. It was an old showroom space lined with floor to ceiling windows, so people walking on the busy street in downtown Ithaca could see what was happening inside. Harold had called in one of the architects he worked with for the meeting, and the three of us brainstormed for hours about what we would do to the space.

We talked about building booths along the back and side walls and having the bar just as you came in. On the walls we'd have massive full color photographs of the islands. We'd have eat-in on one side, and take-out service in a separate area that would replicate the way OuNYe served out of the truck. The truck would stay open, of course. I'd already been approached by Cornell, asking if I could set up there during the academic year, and during the summer there was the Farmer's Market. Things were looking pretty damn good for OuNYe's future in Ithaca.

As I walked to my car, I processed the meeting I'd just left. In the end Ithaca had been a risk that paid off. Then there was Jude. Things had been hectic for the last few weeks, because I'd been working my ass off to get everything with the business on track. I was so close to being able to tell him I had a solid foundation for us to build on.

I remembered he'd called about half an hour ago when we were finishing up with the architect. As I walked back to my car, I pulled out my phone to call him back when I saw I had like ten notifications. A few missed calls, texts and voicemails. I looked at the time and saw that it was past two thirty. Shit, I was with Harold for more than four hours. I stopped at a corner so I could listen to the voicemail from Jude when a call from my mom came in.

"Hey, Mamí, I have awesome news."

"That's great, m'ijo, I was just calling to ask if you guys are on the road coming back already. How did it go?"

For a second I had no idea what she was talking about and then my heart sank. Shit, I was supposed to meet Jude to go to the hospital today. That was why he called, and I didn't even let him talk. Just barked that I'd call later and hung up on him.

Oh shit, this was his last visit before Mary went to hospice.

"Nesto, are you there?"

"Mamí, se me olvido. I totally forgot about the visit. I was at a meeting with Harold. Let me let you go, I have to call to see if he's still waiting for me."

"Ernesto." Her voice was full of disappointment. "Pero, m'ijo, it's almost three—"

"Mamí! I gotta go."

I ended the call and tapped my phone so I could listen to Jude's voicemail. Guilt flooded my chest as I played the message. It was Jude letting me know he was going to drive on his own. To anyone else he would have sounded like he was totally fine, but I could hear the flatness in his voice.

Dammit.

I tried to call him, but it went straight to voicemail.

I read Carmen's message, but she just said she was worried about Jude going to the visit alone.

Fuck, it was literally the only thing Jude asked me for in the entire time we'd been dating, and I had completely dropped the ball, after I'd promised him I'd be there for every visit. I knew I'd been slacking the last few weeks too. I'd made my big declaration that night in Aurora, but since we'd gotten back, I'd been busier and busier. Jude always pushed me to do what I needed to for OuNYe, but I knew I was going back to my old ways. Taking the person I was with for granted when work got crazy.

I started walking to my car again, feeling like a complete asshole. This visit was going to be a hard one. Mary didn't have much time left.

By the time I got to my car I'd called him four times, but they all went straight to voicemail. A feeling of dread started to creep in. If he'd missed his visit, or worse if something went wrong while he was there all alone, I'd never forgive myself. I didn't know what to do. I tried calling Carmen to ask if she'd talked to him, but her phone was switched off too. I got in the car and started driving, then called my mom on the Bluetooth.

"¿Qué paso, m'ijo? Did you get in touch with him?"

"No, I almost want to drive over there, but he's probably on his way back by now. Maybe I should go to his place and wait for him. I know I don't need to treat him like a baby, but I could tell he was nervous for this one. And I've been so busy trying to get everything on lock with the business… Mamí, I don't know what to do."

My mom breathed out on the other side of the line. "Ernesto, I know this thing between you is new, but I also know it's important. You love him, m'ijo, and I know he cares about you. You let him down."

"I know. I know. I'm going to let you go, Mamí, okay? I'll talk to you later." I cut her off before she started lecturing me again, because I really couldn't deal with "I told you so" right now.

The feeling I'd done something irreversible wouldn't quit. Jude didn't like letting others see his pain, and he didn't trust easily. I feared I'd broken what he'd given me. Not for missing the visit, because if something had come up with the truck and I'd let him know in advance he would have been fine.

What I worried was he'd think he wasn't a priority for me.

I parked my car across the street from the truck, thinking of what to do, and came up blank. I'd blown my chance to be there for Jude today, and now I had to deal with whatever the consequences were. When I thought about OuNYe and the big news of today, the elation I should've felt at being so close to having my restaurant fell completely flat.

Chapter Twenty-Seven

Nesto

"He said he'll call you tomorrow." Carmen's voice was off and she sounded worried. When I'd called earlier asking for Jude, she hadn't berated me or even told me I'd fucked up, just said she'd call me back in five minutes. Now after three tries, all she had was he'd call tomorrow.

I tried not to sound as desperate as I felt when I answered. "Can you at least tell me if he's all right? Did something happen at the visit?"

She sighed wearily. "I'm sorry, Nesto. All he said was he'll call you tomorrow."

"But why isn't he home? I came by his place twice, and he's not there."

This time her voice sounded wooden, like she was forcing herself to sound neutral. "He'll call you tomorrow. When he says he'll do something, he does."

Ouch. That fucking hurt, but I deserved it.

"Gracias, Carmen. Buenas noches."

"Bye, Nesto."

It was nine p.m. and I was sitting on my couch after hours of frantically trying to get in touch with Jude. I'd gone to his place, called, texted and got no reply. I almost went to Carmen's house, but I'd only been there a few times, and felt like I would be overstepping by showing up unannounced. If Jude didn't want to talk to me, I'd just have to wait until he was ready.

I tried to think of the last time I'd felt this helpless or scared and couldn't come up with much. This is what my mom and Milo warned me about. I got tunnel vision when I went after something and could forget everyone around me. I'd been so hell-bent on not messing up my second chance with Harold, I'd let down the person that mattered most to me.

I hadn't even gotten around to telling my mom about the restaurant space. Once I realized how bad I'd fucked up with Jude, everything else seemed unimportant. I hoped I'd get the chance to make things right with him, but I wasn't even sure I deserved it.

I was trying to convince myself Jude just needed some space and we'd be fine when my phone buzzed. I picked it up immediately, hoping it was him calling, when I saw Milo's number. Of course, Jiminy Cricket himself, calling me when I was primed for my reckoning.

"Hey." My voice sounded awful.

"What happened?" This motherfucker really did have superpowers.

"I just said hello."

Milo clicked his tongue and sighed like I was trying his patience. "You sound like someone died. I haven't heard you this fucked up since…well, ever actually. Did something happen with Jude?"

"I fucked up."

"Would you care to elaborate?"

I ran my hands over my face, thinking Milo would not bullshit me about this. He'd give it to me straight and he'd also lost his dad to cancer, so he knew first-hand what it was like to be in Jude's situation. So I gave him a rundown of what was going on.

I expected Milo to interrupt me every two words, or to call me a moron and then yell at me for being a thoughtless prick. To my surprise he just quietly listened until I was done. When I finished talking, he sighed heavily.

"You need to show him he wasn't wrong to count on you. Jude let you into his life, a very *painful* part of his life, and trusted you had his back."

I cringed at that, trying to hide from the hard truth. Again, I tried to deflect. "Maybe I'm overreacting. I don't even know if something happened at the visit."

Milo's usual snide self finally came back and he scoffed at my bullshit. "If everything was fine at the visit, do you think he'd be icing you out and hiding somewhere?"

And that was exactly where I avoided going all day. Something went very wrong on that visit, and whatever it was, Jude had to walk out of there and drive home on his own. Then when he tried to call me, I hung up on him.

"How do I make this better?"

"By showing him where he stands in your life. When I say show him, I mean it too. You've already told him you loved him and wanted to be with him, and then went right back to your workaholic ways. So, talking won't do much. You need to make changes, Nesto, and let him see for himself he's a priority in your life."

I had no clue what I was supposed to do, so I just gave him a shaky "okay."

Milo chuckled sadly at my pitiful answer. "I know you think you know fuck all about how to do that, but you have it in you. There isn't a better son, brother or friend than you. You're a good man, you know how to love right. Just be there for him, make him see how much what you guys have matters to you."

I sighed. "Gracias, Milo."

"You're welcome, pa, I love you."

After we disconnected, I went to bed thinking about what I would do if I got a chance to make things right with Jude.

Jude

"Stop looking at me like that," I told Carmen when she kept staring at me over her monitor. After the visit with Mary I'd gone to Carmen's house. I didn't want to see Nesto if he stopped by my place, but I didn't want to be alone either. This morning, I'd gotten up at five a.m. and driven home without waking her up. I'd needed a change of clothes and to be in my own space before facing the world again.

When I walked into the office with a big smile, acting like everything was totally fine, I knew I'd pushed her right over the edge.

"I'm just worried about you, Jude."

"I'm fine, Carmen. I'm going to go get some fresh air. I'll be back in a few." I walked out of the library, ignoring the concerned look on her face.

I hated myself for feeling the way I did. Discarded and let down. After Nesto hung up on me, I'd just gone to my car and sat there for hours. Eventually Jesse found me and apologized for what happened. He was so angry at Pastor Jones and Amos, and frustrated with Mary. I told him I was fine, and he obviously didn't believe me. He asked why my boyfriend wasn't with me like usual. I spluttered at that, because I didn't realize he knew about Nesto. He smiled and said he'd seen us arrive together a couple of times. When I told him Nesto forgot about the visit, the look of pity on his face almost broke me.

There I was, four years later, the same pathetic Jude who was discarded by the people he was foolish enough to love.

Before I drove away, Jesse asked me to stay in touch and promised to send me updates about Mary. I wasn't sure if I'd ever see him or the kids again. I knew I'd probably never see Mary again. I'd headed to Ithaca feeling like a husk.

Now hours and hours later, I still felt numb. I couldn't even cry.

It had all dried up.

The truth was, deep down I suspected things with Mary would end up like they did. But I'd gone to see her anyway, because in the back of my mind I was counting on Nesto to help me through it. I let myself rely on him, and in the end, he couldn't make me a priority.

And whose fault was that?

Mine.

I knew I was being unfair, that he had no way of knowing the visit he flaked out on would be the one where my family managed to emotionally eviscerate me, again. But I knew better than to let myself rely on what I felt. People who loved you could hurt you. If you opened yourself up to love, you opened yourself to pain and disappointment. I'd let my guard down once more, and was in that old familiar place again.

I got to a small park in the middle of downtown, which was usually empty this early in the day, and sat down on a bench. It wasn't even eight yet, so there was only one other person in the whole place. I looked over at the little church on the edge of the park, trying to put off the call I had to make. After a minute, I pulled out my phone and called Nesto.

He picked up after the first ring, sounding tired but alert.

"Jude."

"Hi."

He let out a long breath. "I'm so sorry, babe. So fucking sorry. It won't happen again. I know I broke my promise to be at every visit, but I swear, next week I'll be there one-hundred percent on time."

I closed my eyes at the anguish in his voice, hardening myself to it. "You don't need to worry about that. I'm not going back for more visits." I tried to keep my tone light, but it sounded fraught to my own ears.

Nesto's silence was heavy, like he was trying to figure out what I wasn't saying.

"Did something happen with Mary?" he asked, his voice hesitant.

I wanted to say nothing, keep him in the dark. To go and hide with my hurt and my shame, but the worry in his voice made me say it.

"She asked our old pastor to come and talk to me about my soul. Ummm…she's worried about my salvation, and since she doesn't have a lot of time left, she asked him to help her. Amos was there too. He let me know no matter what I said to Mary, I'd never be welcome into the family again."

"Oh, babe. No."

"It's fine. I told Mary I couldn't do what she was asking, so she requested I not come visit again. She and Pastor Jones are worried for her soul if she continues to see me." I had to stop and clear my throat because it was closing up. "You know, because she loves me so much and she'll be tempted to forgive me."

Nesto muttered a curse under his breath, as I squeezed me eyes shut.

"Jude, what they did is not okay. I get that your sister has her beliefs, but this is not about you, baby. It's not. You're perfect just the way you are. You hear me, *mi amor*?"

I almost broke down when I heard the endearment, but steeled myself to get on with why I called before it got harder.

"I'll be all right. Don't worry about me." I paused for a moment to take a breath, but quickly pushed on. "So, just to let you know, things are going to be pretty intense with the mobile library launch in a week. You know how it is. You have the party at Mr. Sheridan's too, so you'll have lots going on. Oh, and congratulations on the space, Ari said you were there yesterday." I knew I was in a hysterical ramble, but if I stopped I'd start sobbing.

"Wait, what are you saying?"

"I just need some space. I know you have a lot of important things happening, so I think it's best to part ways now."

"No, baby, please don't do this." Nesto's voice sounded panicked and like he was about to cry. I shut my eyes, trying not to let it get to me. "I'm sorry I let you down, Jude. I can fix this. I won't ever take you for granted again." That last part came out in a shudder and it took everything in me not to give in.

"Every time it's come down to your business or me, you've picked your business and I get that. It's what you're here to do," I said with finality. "I just wanted you so much, I let things slide. So I could have you a little bit longer, you know? But I'm too tired now."

"Jude, please."

My throat made a clicking sound as I worked to keep myself under control. "I understand I can't be a priority for you. I don't want to stretch this out anymore, when I know what's going to happen. How things will end for me. Goodbye, Nesto. Take care, okay?"

I ended the call and turned the phone off before putting it in my pocket.

As I walked back to my office I let the feeling of utter devastation settle into my bones. The sharp pain almost suffocating me. I would try hard to never forget how much this hurt the next time I was tempted to open myself up to love.

Chapter Twenty-Eight

Nesto

It'd been over a week since Jude ended things with me and I was a fucking wreck. I couldn't eat, I couldn't sleep, and worse, I still had no idea how to fix it. It was like he built a wall around himself.

He wouldn't see me or talk to me. I'd gone to his place the night after he called me and he told me to go home. The scariest thing was how calm he'd looked, like he felt nothing. His smile was so brittle I thought he would crumble right in front of me. I tried to ask Carmen what to do, but she told me she couldn't get involved. That Jude asked her to stay out of it. I was at a loss.

Meanwhile, things were moving fast with the restaurant. Tonight I was going to co-host and cater a dinner at Harold's house. He'd invited a bunch of high-profile people from town to formally announce the project. OuNYe would be a completely new kind of dining experience in town, and we wanted everyone talking about it. We'd also been discussing plans for the future. Harold was convinced we had the food and the concept to eventually branch out to other college towns in the region. We just needed to get the right people interested.

It seemed like a bit of a stretch to me, but it was hard not to get caught up in his enthusiasm. So tonight, there would be people there who could potentially back an expansion plan.

It was a big deal, and I should've been ecstatic. My hustle was finally bearing fruit in huge ways. Instead, I was ditching work for the second time this week, to sit on my couch and look at photos of Jude and listen to despecho songs all day. It was already noon and I had to get my shit together soon, since I needed to be at Harold's in two hours.

But I had zero fucks to give.

I thought I heard someone knock on my door, but instead of getting up to see who it was, I opened my phone again to look at the last photos I'd taken of Jude. They were from a couple of days before he broke things off. He'd just woken up and was smiling up at me, his hair muzzled from sleep, a tiny love bite under his right ear. I'd taken like five shots in a row and as I scrolled through them now, the screen showed him shaking his head at me, a big grin on his face. I missed him so fucking much.

I didn't know I could hurt like this.

"Oh my god. We got here not a second too soon, this is a full Code Red. He's listening to Selena and crying over photos on his phone. Jesus, and it reeks of Vicks in here. Patrice, open a damn window. Nesto, what the fuck are you doing? Do you have a cold?"

I looked up from where I was clutching my phone and saw my mom, my sister, Patrice and Camilo standing by the couch, looking at me like I'd lost my mind.

I sat up, wondering why the guys were here and not in the city. "Umm hey, I had a headache, so I rubbed some on my temples. Mamí, how did you get in here? Do you still have the spare key?" I pointed at Milo and Patrice with my phone. "And what are you two doing up here? I didn't know you were coming to visit."

This was apparently the last straw for my mom, because she snatched the phone out of my hand and turned off the music.

"Mamí! What the hell? I need the phone!"

"No, Ernesto Amado, you need to get yourself together. It's been over a week and you are still moping around." She waved over to Milo and Patrice. "Your friends are here because I called them. I'm worried about you. You don't answer my calls, you've barely been at the truck in the last few days, and worse, you're doing nothing to make things right with Jude. This is not like you, Nesto, you don't give up on what's important to you." At the mention of Jude I curled in on myself like she'd punched me in the stomach.

"What am I supposed to do, Mamí? He told he doesn't want me. He asked me to leave him alone. He wouldn't even open the door when I went to his house. I fucked up." I shook my head as another wave of self-loathing and regret washed through me. "I let him down and I deserve to be iced out. I—"

Someone whacked me over the head so hard I almost fell off the couch. Startled, I jumped up and saw Milo staring at me looking furious. I rubbed my head, glaring at him.

"¡Coño, Camilo! What did you hit me for?"

"Because you're a moron, that's why. Out of all of us, you've always been the relentless one, once you start something you don't give up until you get it. And now you're going to sit this one out because it's *too hard*?"

Milo's face was angry, and my mom just looked worried. Patrice and my sister were standing to the side, watching with concerned faces.

I ran my hands over my face and sat down on the couch again. "It's not because it's hard. It's because it hurts. Every time I think of how he sounded when he told me what happened with his sister. How sad and empty his voice was. It makes me sick I wasn't there for him."

Milo sighed, and my mom came and sat next to me on the couch. "M'ijo, of course you can fix it. You love him, and he loves you. Jude's a good man, but he's been hurt badly by people who should've loved him unconditionally. He doesn't know what it's like to have someone fight for him. You need to show him, you always will."

I nodded, and looked up at them, my people, who came to get my ass in gear before I threw away the best thing that had ever happened to me. As I sat there an idea started forming in my head. I wasn't sure if there was still a chance Jude would take me back, but it wouldn't be because I sat on my ass crying while the love of my fucking life thought I'd given up on him.

I stood up and started walking to the bathroom. I had work to do and then I needed to start planning. Before I went into the shower I turned around.

"I'll be ready in ten. We need to get this thing at Sheridan's done. When we get back tonight we're making plans for how I'm going to show Jude he isn't just a priority, he needs to know he's *everything*."

Jude

"I can see you staring at me, Carmen."

In the last week, Carmen had spent each second

we were together scrutinizing my every move. I knew she was trying to make sure I didn't fling myself off a bridge or something, but the constant worry on her face was starting to piss me off.

Except it wasn't just Carmen, everything and everyone pissed me off. My patience seemed to have evaporated in the past seven days. I'd been so short with people lately, I noticed some were going out of their way to avoid me.

Like I cared.

I didn't need people walking by and staring at me like I was a pathetic loser. I looked up to see Carmen still glancing in my direction and huffed, "Seriously, Carmen. I'm fine. Nesto and I were seeing each other for two months, it's not like he jilted me at the altar. Besides, it's better this way. He has important things to do and so do I. I need to focus on the launch, which is only days away."

Carmen stood up from her desk and closed the door, then planted herself on my desk right in front of my monitor.

"The launch is going to be fine, Jude. You've managed to come up with a great program, despite our miniscule budget. It's going to be perfect. You know it and I know it." She threw her hands up in frustration as I stared blankly at the wall.

"You need to let me do my work."

"No. We're talking about this right now. You're not fine, and this was not just some fling that ended. What happened with your sister was horrible and heartbreaking, and then you broke things off with the person you're in love with. None of it is even remotely fine, and pretending it is won't make it go away."

I scoffed at her words, feeling angry. "Well what do you want me to do? Fall apart? Lose it? Stay in bed for weeks? Let this despair and sadness overtake me, so I can't leave my house? Because I've done that once already. I've been there, and I'm not doing it again. What happened with Mary..." I held up my hand while I took a breath. "Even though it hurt, I forgive her, because she's as much a victim as I am in all this. Nesto—" Here I really needed to tread lightly, because this thing with Nesto would be what undid me.

"Nesto is here to build his business. That's what he needs to focus on. What we had was a distraction."

Carmen rolled her eyes to the ceiling as if looking for some guidance on how to get through to me. "What you had was a *relationship*. Nesto is just as torn up about this as you are. Nurys says he's been a wreck all week. Leaving early or missing work altogether. She even said she was going to call his friends to come from the city to talk to him."

I stared at her in disbelief, caught between wanting to throttle her for meddling *again* and pumping her for more information about Nesto.

"Why are you talking to Nesto's mother about me?"

The flummoxed look on her face was priceless. "I stopped at the truck for a burrito last week."

I almost laughed at her regretful grimace. "Traitor."

"I'm sorry! I walked by and they had the Lavoe that day. You know I can't resist guandules and pernil. Anyway, Nurys was there and asked about you and we've been in touch since. We're worried about you both. Nesto isn't doing well at all, and you've been working eighteen-hour days for the last week."

She slumped, giving me a pleading look. "Hon,

please consider trying to work things out with him. He was good for you. You were happier than I've ever seen you."

"I *was* happy, Carmen. I'm just tired of asking for so little and still being let down." I scrubbed my hands over my eyes. "It hurts too much."

Carmen put her hand under my chin and lifted my head. "Can I give you a hug?"

I huffed out a laugh and stood up with my arms wide open, she immediately wrapped me up in one of her amazing hugs, and for the first time in days I let myself let go.

"You'll work this out. Nesto is a great guy and he loves you." I didn't argue with her and just let the comfort of her presence soothe my frazzled nerves.

"Well isn't this nice? Such camaraderie amongst our staff. Very touching."

Carmen stiffened at the sound of Misty's voice and spoke in the coldest tone I'd ever heard from her.

"We're busy right now, Misty."

"You don't look busy. I'm surprised you're still here, Jude. I thought you'd be over at Harold Sheridan's place setting up for the party your man friend is catering for him. I heard they're making a big announcement. A real American success story. Very heartwarming."

Her tone was foul and she was practically spitting the words out.

I gave her the iciest look I could manage. "I'm not planning to be there, and Nesto isn't just catering. They're hosting a party to announce they're opening a restaurant together. Mr. Sheridan is very excited about the project. Not surprising, since Nesto can barely keep up with the demand."

She walked up to my desk with a shark smile on her face. "Oh, I heard. He's even had to hire more help. I've seen them there when I pass by, lots of foreigners." She twisted her mouth to the side like she was thinking of something distasteful. "Some of them barely speak English. I hope they've all got their papers in order. I've been hearing the police are going around checking for illegals. Scary times." With that, she pushed off my desk and made her way toward the door.

I walked over to the door before she could get to it and stood in front of her. "I don't know what you're scheming, Misty, but if you try anything to mess with Nesto, I'll talk to Martha."

She just lifted a shoulder, totally unbothered. "What's Martha going to do? You think because you managed to convince Tom White to give you the money for your little project you're home free? I still have control over your funds for the launch. I can make it so you won't even be able to afford a few dozen water bottles."

That was a low blow, because she knew if there was something that would make me hesitate, it was losing the launch. Then I thought of how hard Nesto had worked for this moment, and knew what I needed to do. Not being able to have the launch I'd planned would hurt, but I'd still have my project. Misty could do a lot of damage to Nesto's business if she pulled one of her stunts tonight.

"I don't care about your threats, Misty. I'm not going to let you ruin this for Nesto. You want to take the money, take it. I'll just have to go without."

Her laugh was pure vitriol. "You're not important enough to threaten, Jude. Hope your selfless act comes with a cash allowance, and if you paid any deposits for next week, I suggest you figure out how to cancel them." She tapped a finger on her cheek and widened her eyes. "I just realized I have an urgent need, and will have to put that slush fund you were counting on toward something else."

She held her arm up to me and shoved her watch in my face. "Look at the time. I've got to get moving, or I'll be late to Harold's. Don't want to miss the biggest party of the summer." The look on her face as she walked off was way too smug for my comfort.

When I turned around Carmen's face settled it. "She's going to call in a tip saying Nesto has undocumented staff working in the truck."

Carmen looked worried, but tried to keep things in perspective. "They're not allowed to just show up at a private residence like that, Jude. Unless she lies or uses her contact at the state troopers. But she wasn't kidding about the launch money, Jude. She'll figure out a way to fuck with you over this."

I knew Carmen was right, but I'd deal with that later. "I have to do something. I wouldn't put it past her to try and abuse a relationship to mess with Nesto. I should've known she hadn't given up on making trouble for him. She was just biding her time to do something that could really embarrass him, and if she wants to take the money so be it. We'll figure it out."

Carmen's was as serious as I'd ever seen her. "You know I got your back, babe."

"I know, thank you." I thought for a moment about what to do and then had an idea. "I'm calling Easton. I'm sure he'll be there tonight, and hopefully he can keep an eye out."

Carmen shook her head in disbelief. "So you're not

willing to talk to Nesto, but you're putting a call into the DA's office for him."

"I'm certainly not going to let Misty ruin his night if I can help it."

Chapter Twenty-Nine

Nesto

The party was filling up and people were coming around to the truck to get food. Everyone was asking lots of questions and sounded excited about OuNYe opening as a restaurant in the spring.

I was handing an order of our crab empanadas to one of the guests when I saw Easton heading toward us, looking pissed. I knew he was on the guest list, but hadn't seen him yet. We had a bar next to the truck serving drinks that complemented the menu, so I assumed he was gunning for it. But he came up to the counter and signaled me over. I had no idea what it was about, but the expression on his face said he was not playing, so I told the guys I'd be back in a minute and climbed down.

"Hey, man, what's up?"

He pulled my arm until we were behind the truck, away from the guests milling around.

"I just sent away two state troopers who were asking questions about the immigration status of your employees." He held up his hand and shook his head, looking even more pissed than before. "I know all your employees are authorized to work. I also told them they had no right to walk into a private home asking people for their papers, unless they had a warrant from a federal judge, which they obviously didn't."

I just stood there dumbfounded for a moment. I literally couldn't make words. Then I finally breathed out, "I don't understand"

He sighed, "Jude called me this afternoon and said Misty had come into his office making cryptic comments about tonight and about your staff being 'foreigners.' He asked if there was anything I could do to stop them. I assured him it was almost certain there wasn't much they could do, other than embarrass you and Harold, so I told him I'd keep an eye on things."

My mind was going a thousand miles an hour. Misty had tried to fuck with my business *again,* and Jude had called up Easton Archer to make sure nothing happened. I never thought one could be filled with rage and elation at the same time, but that's exactly what was happening to me.

"Jude called you?"

Easton's face softened at my question and his lips turned up a bit. "Yes, and he warned me you might be pissed at us for getting involved, but he was dead set on making sure your big night went on without a hitch."

He chuckled, an impressed look on his face. "I got to tell you, man, you bring a whole other side out in Jude. He told me Misty even threatened to take away some of the funding for his project, but he said he didn't care. I think he would've driven out here and blocked the troopers himself if I'd said no."

"He's amazing." And apparently still cares about me enough to call an ADA on my behalf.

"He's a good guy. Listen, I told Harold about what happened, and he's livid."

"What? Easton—"

I was about to go on another rant about people handling my business when I heard Misty's shrill voice yelling at someone by the truck.

"This is garbage. Is this supposed to be food?"

I walked around the side and found Patrice trying and failing to calm her down. She looked drunk and mean, her teeth bared as he quietly spoke to her.

"Ma'am, if you're not happy with this we can certainly make you something else. I'm sure there's something on our menu that'll appeal to you."

She scoffed, looking him up and down. She was about to open her mouth when I stepped in between then. "We're no longer serving this woman, Patrice. Ma'am, you need to leave."

"I'm a guest at this party. You'll serve me if I say so. I've never seen hired help this insolent."

"That's right, you're a guest here and I'm not hired help. I'm hosting this party with Harold Sheridan, my business partner. I won't tolerate you disrespecting me or my staff ever again."

She looked like she was about to start yelling again, when I saw Mr. Sheridan and another man walking over to us.

"What have you done now?" The man whispered in her direction, as he came to stand next to us.

She ignored him and turned to Sheridan. "Harold, I'm sorry to see you've lost your edge. This business investment seems beneath you."

"Thanks for your input, but like Mr. Vasquez just told you, he and I are hosting a party to announce our new business venture. There's no place here for disrespectful people. I would've hoped you were better than to behave like this, but I see that's not the case. The valet is bringing your car around. Have a good rest of your evening."

He walked right past Misty toward me, ignoring the heated conversation between her and her husband as they walked off.

"Is everything all right here, Nesto? I apologize for what just happened. That was unacceptable. I want you to know that there will be consequences for this."

"That woman's been trying to mess with my business literally since the day I got to town," I said. "But I just kept my head down and did what I needed to do, because I knew the day would come when people would see what she was about. I have no time to waste on her. We have an announcement to make."

He gripped my shoulder and smiled. "Yes, we do. Everyone is raving about the food. I've had over three people ask about investment possibilities. I'll give you a few minutes to regroup and will come back so we can formally make the announcement for the restaurant together." He clapped my back again and walked off in the direction of the house.

I turned around and saw my mom, Patrice, Milo and Easton standing by the truck, their faces serious, but looking a lot more relaxed than they'd been a few minutes ago.

I offered my hand to Easton. "Thanks for your help tonight, man. This could've gone a lot worse without you." He shook it with his million dollar smile back in place. I noticed he and Patrice were standing a little closer than what allowed for personal space, and was that P's hand on Easton's back?

Interesante.

"Glad I could help."

I turned to my two friends and my mom. "Okay, mi gente, here's the plan. As soon as we take care of things here, we need to get home, and I'm going to require all hands on deck for this one. For the next week Ernesto Vasquez and OuNYe will only have one mission: getting Jude Fuller back."

Jude

"Carmen! Did you even hear what I just said? Who are you texting?"

It was Tuesday morning and we were on our way to the first event for the mobile library launch week and I was a ball of nerves. Today we were bringing the truck to the Newfield Middle and High School campus. In coordination with the school, we'd arranged to park there for the day so students could try the library. We'd have music, prizes, and free books for a county-wide read. We'd also make announcements about all the events we'd have throughout the year. It was pretty basic as launches went, but we were hoping our enthusiasm would make up for it.

The plan was to do the same at the three other rural towns in the county. So we'd be taking our show on the road for the rest of the week. All morning I'd been freaking out, worried no one would come, but Carmen and our two interns had been furiously working our social media accounts and assured me we'd have a good crowd. After I called her name again, Carmen finally dragged her eyes away from her phone and had a huge grin on her face.

"Umm yeah, so everything is set. Just heard from Z and Roi and they said there are already a bunch of kids there, and we're not even supposed to start for another half hour."

Relief washed through my body. I'd been so on edge since Friday. Between preparing for this, and the anxiety from the debacle with Misty, I was so ready for a vacation. Thankfully, in the end, Misty's scheming didn't ruin Nesto's night. From what I heard through the Dominican News Network, which Carmen was now fully a part of, the night had been a huge success. Misty hadn't been at the library yesterday, and word was she was "taking some time off." For all of her attempts to sabotage us, she hadn't been able to undo mine or Nesto's hard work. As he'd said all along, people finally saw her for exactly who she was.

Things with Nesto were still not okay though. Friday night after the party he'd texted to tell me he knew what I'd risked to help him. I told him I didn't have any regrets, but that I needed time.

I still felt unsure.

I didn't know if Nesto could ever really make me a priority. I knew I'd need to talk to him eventually. I wanted to, but I'd been working nonstop for the last three days trying to prepare for the launch, and hadn't been able to stop by his truck. But I promised myself as soon as I was done with this on Friday, I'd go to Nesto's house and talk to him.

When we started approaching the school, I noticed Carmen shifting in her seat like her ass was on fire, and she kept glancing at her phone.

"Carmen, what's going on with you?" I asked, exasperated.

"Look ahead, Jude, you're going to hit someone." I looked up at the road as we turned onto the high school grounds and noticed there were a lot of cars there already. Then as we got closer my heart almost leapt out of my chest.

Next to our book truck, with a line forming already, was Nesto's truck. There was also what looked like a face-painting station, and a bunch of kids were walking around with tote bags featuring the library's and OuNYe's logos. When I looked closer, I saw Nesto standing a few yards away from the truck, in a spot where he had a clear view of the cars driving in. He had his head down, focused on his phone and didn't see us. Before he looked up, I quickly pulled into one of the spots farther away from the crowd and turned to Carmen, who looked ready to burst.

"Spill."

"So, your boyfriend is here with his crew, serving free food and refreshments for all the kids who come to the launch." She did a little shimmy with her shoulders and her grin was so big I could barely see her cheeks. "He also had bags made so the kids could carry any books they checked out. I don't even know how he managed that so fast! Oh, and the face painting was my idea. He's paying for it, though."

I was breathless, and the urge to leap out of my car and sprint to Nesto was so intense I was sure I'd snap the steering wheel off if I didn't let go.

"Nesto is here serving free food at our launch. How exactly did that happen?"

"Well Nurys called me Friday night, you know after you mobilized the district attorney's office to ensure

Misty didn't disrupt his event?" Another shoulder shimmy. I was going to *throttle* her. "Right, so Nurys said Nesto wanted to help with the launch by providing food and drinks. I may have mentioned we didn't have a budget for it. I told him we'd love for him to help out, so he was in."

As she talked, I glanced up and saw that Nesto was still standing in the same spot. There were kids swarming all around him, carrying bags full of books and the food his truck was serving. He didn't look at anyone though, his eyes trained on the cars coming into the lot. Remaining calm with Nesto this close was becoming more of a challenge with every passing second. "He's been working on this all weekend?"

Carmen actually clapped before she answered. "Yup! He also got a hold of some of the other vendors at the market he knew. The 'Lick your Lassi' ladies donated a bunch of popsicles." Her face looked more serious now. "The truck won't serve in town for the rest of the week. He'll be with us at the schools for the next three days."

Wait, what?

"He's closing down the truck all week *and* giving away free food? What kind of fucked-up business decision is that?"

Carmen was howling with laughter at this point. "You better go ask him yourself," she said, pointing in his direction. "Z said he's been standing there for an hour looking out for your car."

I didn't even respond. I jumped out of the car and did a sprint-walk straight for him. As soon as he spotted me he started moving too. We both came to a dead stop when we were only a couple of feet away, both short of breath like we'd run for miles. The need to touch him was so intense my hands shook as I went to grab his.

"Mi amor."

As he spoke he tightened his fingers around mine, like he was scared I'd vanish.

With him near, it was like I could see in color for the first time in days. I looked around, noticing all the kids who'd shown up for our launch. I saw Nurys and Camilo serving food, and they both waved at me when I lifted my hand to them. They were here for Nesto, but I knew they were here for me too. Somewhere in the time we'd been together, he'd made me part of his whole life.

"Ernesto Vasquez. Ven aca," I said, pulling him behind me until we were hidden in the tight space between the wall and the side of the truck. I was doing my best to look serious, but the smile tugging at my lips was going to be impossible to hide for long. Still he didn't speak, his eyes so serious, completely focused on my face. It was my call, he was giving all the power.

"So, are you just throwing money away this week or what?"

He shook his head, his eyes focused on my mouth.

"There is so much I have to say, but first, can I kiss you, baby? I've missed you so much."

He licked his lips and I pushed up because with his mouth so close, mine needed to be touching his. He gasped as our mouths met, and it was like coming home. I belonged right here, in these arms.

After a moment we pulled back, our foreheads touching. Nesto did the thing where he touched the tip of his tongue to his upper lip and my knees gave a little.

"Are you really closing the truck for the week?"

His face turned serious for a moment, and he nodded. "Yes, OuNYe follows you this week."

I stared at him confused. "But you have like a million things going on right now. How can you possibly take a week off to do this?"

He shook his head then, as if trying to get his thoughts in order. "I'll figure it out."

"Why?" I wasn't that dense, but I wanted to hear it.

Nesto pulled me to him, our bodies finally touching after so many days without his warmth. "Because what's important to you is important to me." He shook his head, looking for the words he wanted to say. "I've been going about it all wrong. I kept telling myself I needed to build something solid I could offer you. I couldn't see that I didn't have to do it alone, that all I needed was to ask and you'd do it with me." He let out a long shaky breath and pushed our mouths together, our kiss salty from tears. "I've needed to put my priorities in order for a long time now."

"And what priorities are those?" I asked, my chest swelling with hope.

He leaned in again, and licked the seam of my lips. From a distance I could hear Milo yelling at us to "quit traumatizing the children."

"Not what. Whom. And it's you and me. My priority is us. I love you, Jude."

I must have caved in, because his arms tightened around me as he went in for another kiss.

"Please tell me you'll try again, baby. I miss you so much. OuNYe, the restaurant, none of it makes sense if I can't share it with you. You're what makes me happy."

My heart was going to burst, just explode in my chest from absolute happiness.

"Te amo, Ernesto Amado. I can't even believe you did all this."

I wrapped my arms around his neck reveling in having his body so close. "So is this it? Are we finally going to spread books and Caribbean food to the Finger Lakes youth like you wanted?"

Nesto beamed at my question, then answered in a strong sure voice, "Vamos, mi amor."

Epilogue

Jude

At some point I would stop waking up with a grin on my face, but today was not that day. "How are you this awake already?" I grumbled feigning annoyance. It was still dark out, which meant it was probably before five a.m., but Nesto seemed to be fully up. He was busy running his hands up my chest and neck while he licked my shoulders.

"Because I can't keep my hands to myself when you're in bed all warm and soft next to me."

I shivered, letting the last bit of sleep melt away as my brain caught up with the effect Nesto's touch was having on my body. I turned my head to the side, giving him more access, and put my hands over his.

"Bueno Dias, mi cielo. How did you sleep?" I would never stop getting a small thrill when I heard the many endearments Nesto constantly used. "My sky" in Spanish was a new one. I shook my head and answered, "Buenos Dias," lifting his hand to my mouth.

I put his fingers in my mouth and sucked, getting them wet. I wasn't sure if I was up for much more than kissing, but his nearness had me hot and bothered. His erection was grinding up against my ass, making things a lot more interesting than any Saturday morning at five a.m. had any right to be.

"Ungh, papí. You make me so hot. Turn around, baby, I want to jerk off together. Come all over you and then lick it off." His voice was rough from sleep and arousal, and it made my entire body shudder.

I turned around so we were lying on our sides, face to face, and immediately he grabbed the back of my head, kissing me hard. Sucking my bottom lip as he grabbed both our cocks, and started jerking us together. I lifted my leg over his and started grinding against him. I wrapped my arms around his shoulders, trying to get closer while he ran his thumb over the heads of our cocks, using the drops of pre-come as lubrication. Nesto put his head down on my shoulder and let out a long moan as he stroked us faster.

"Fuuuuck that feels so good."

I ran my hands down his back to the swell of his ass. He was moving his hips so fast I could barely hold on, the muscles going hard as he flexed them. I lightly swept my fingers over his cleft, and felt him stop and then push his ass out. I took that as a cue, and quickly brought my fingers up to my mouth and got them wet.

Nesto sucked in his breath then gasped. "Yeah, finger me, that'll make me blow in a second."

I nodded and quickly ran the pad of my finger over his hole. Nesto was mumbling, so I could only make out a string of curse words, and I smiled. I was doing this to him. I was driving him senseless with pleasure. After a moment I slid my finger inside and went looking for his gland.

Nesto was jacking us off fast and hard, and I felt

my orgasm starting to build too. I found the spot and pressed down right as Nesto bit my shoulder. We came a few seconds apart from each other, making a mess of sweat, saliva and semen. As my breathing slowed I heard Nesto flop back on the bed.

"Goddamn, Jude Fuller," he said with a chuckle. "I will never ever get enough of you."

"It's a good thing you live here now, then. No delayed gratification."

His smile got so big his eyes crinkled. I loved this man so much.

We'd finally had the big talk a few weeks ago and Nesto had moved in with me just a couple days before. We'd been practically living together for months, but now it was official, and I couldn't be happier. My life was so full, Nesto had brought so much to it. That lonely existence I'd fought to protect, replaced with so much joy and laughter…and family.

I leaned in, so my mouth was against his ear. "Welcome home, baby."

He moved his face until our mouths touched, his smile wide as we kissed.

"I've been home since I met you, Jude. I love you."

"I love you too. Now let's try and get another few minutes of sleep before someone calls and starts yelling at us in Spanish."

"I'd take your comment a lot more seriously if my mom didn't call you more than she calls me these days."

I wrapped his arms tight around my chest.

"Go back to sleep, Nesto. We have a big day ahead." I could feel his grin against the back of my neck.

"We do, babe. We do."

Nesto

"It's not even 6:30 yet, why is she calling?" I grumbled while I tried to cover my head with a pillow.

Jude just chuckled and handed me the phone, which was blaring with the old-school ambulance ringtone I had set for my mom.

I grabbed it and moaned into the phone, "Mamí, it's way too early."

"Don't even act like you were still asleep, Nesto. You were probably all over poor Jude. You don't let that muchacho breathe. Yo no se come te aguanta. Jude, how do you put up with him?" She was literally yelling into the phone.

Jude was laughing his ass off into the pillow, of course. He thought she was hilarious.

"Mamí, please."

"Are you coming over for breakfast? Milo, Patrice and Juanpa asked for the Tres Golpes. They brought the salami from the city. So tell Jude we're having Dominican breakfast. I know how much he loves it."

I groaned again. "Mamí, I don't know if I'm up for plantains, fried cheese and salami at seven in the morning. We have a long day, and all I want to do is sleep after I eat all that."

Jude perked up at the mention of fried salami and plantains. The boy might be gringo, but damn, he loved his plátano. I ground into him, pressing my hard-on against his ass, just to get his attention back to the more pressing issues at hand.

"Exactly. Today is going to be really busy. So you'll need your strength. M'ijo, today is a big day. You're opening your restaurant." The pride in her voice made my face break into a huge grin. Today was the day, almost a year exactly since I'd driven the truck up from New York City. OuNYe Afro-Caribbean Food was opening as a brick and mortar restaurant, but most importantly I had woken up with the love of my life in my arms.

"I know, Mamí. We did it."

"No, m'ijo, you did it. I'm so proud of you. I told you, you'd have your restaurant within a year."

I grinned into the phone. "You sure did. You also bullied me into asking Jude out, so I guess you were two for two last season." I shifted again, tightening my arm around Jude. "Okay, mujer, let me get my man out of bed. We'll be there in an hour."

"See you soon, m'ijo."

I ended the call and pressed my lips to the back of Jude's neck, thinking about the last twelve months. Jude and I would hit our one-year mark soon too, and things couldn't be better.

The anticipation for the opening of OuNYe in town had gotten so out of control we were booked solid for the next month. Jude's mobile library was also a huge success, so big in fact, he'd been asked by the state to consult with them, because they wanted to replicate his model all over the Southern Tier.

The year did have its challenges, however. Jude's sister passed away a few weeks after that last visit, and he was never able to properly say goodbye. But his brother-in-law Jesse requested we attend the funeral and we went together. Even though it was a tense and sad affair, it was uneventful, and in the end it helped Jude find some closure. Since then Jesse had made an effort to bring the kids for visits, and it meant the world to Jude to have his niece and nephew in his life.

So, despite the setbacks, life *was* good up here in Ithaca. My six-month plan turned out to be the best decision I ever made. No, it wasn't New York City, it never would be, but this Dominican kid had found a way to live his dream.

I nuzzled Jude's neck, licking a bit of the sweat left from our earlier lovemaking.

"You up for plantains for breakfast, Mr. Fuller? Nurys is requesting our presence at her home for Dominican brunch."

His husky chuckle made my whole body light up. He turned around and ran his leg over my hip, bringing our mouths together.

"Sure. I love Dominican brunch."

I shook my head before I spoke. Sometimes what I felt for Jude seemed so big, it overwhelmed me. I moved so our foreheads were touching.

"Are you happy, baby?"

At my question I felt a ghost of a smile brush against my lips.

"Si, mi amor."

* * * * *

*Reviews are an invaluable tool when it comes
to spreading the word about great reads. Please
consider leaving an honest review for this or any of
Carina Press's other titles that you've read on your
favorite retailer or review site.*

*To purchase and read more books
by Adriana Herrera, please visit her website:
https://adrianaherreraromance.com/*

Acknowledgments

I began writing *American Dreamer* at a time when the narrative about the place of immigrants in this country had become almost unbearable for me. I set out to write a romance with multicultural characters that represented people like me, but I also wanted to write a story that honored the Afro-Latinx immigrant experience in America.

This book is my humble contribution to the rich tapestry that has been woven by those who come here ready to forge lives for themselves and their children. I am endlessly grateful to the many people who have helped me put Nesto's story out in the world.

In particular, I'd like to thank:

Linda Camacho, for being an amazing agent and support, as well as a fierce advocate for Latinx authors.

Kerri Buckley, my editor, for loving my story, for exactly the reasons I wrote it. I think we make a pretty kickass team. I'm forever grateful for the warmth and enthusiasm I've received from everyone at Carina.

My friends at RWA-NYC. I began this journey with Jude and Nesto after returning to NYC from an eleven year absence. In the process, I found a community of friends who have enriched my life in more ways than

I can say. Alexis, Harper, Kate, LaQuette and Rayna, thanks for holding me down, answering every question, and cheering on every milestone like it was your own.

My partner and my girl. Thank you, for so much love and endless support. I am so blessed.

My sister for her many smiles whenever I had a "book update."

Tiffany, thank you, friend, for telling me exactly what I needed to hear when I confessed I was working on a story, and was feeling brave enough to share it. You were the first person to read *American Dreamer*— your excitement for Jude and Nesto's love story meant everything.

Thank you to my beta readers—Tina and Elsa—for your encouragement and your generosity.

To JC Lillis for going above and beyond, and being so incredibly kind with your words, the care you took with this story, and your time.

To the authors in the community who graciously read and critiqued my story: Joanna Chambers, Johanna Parkhurst and Lydia San Andres, *Dreamer* is a much better book because of you.

Finally, thank you to all the authors of color who write romance so those of us who yearn for it can see ourselves in stories of people who get the happy ending we all deserve.

Chapter One

Camilo

"You better hurry up before I do too much damage at this open bar. Holy shit this thing is lit!" I heard a tortured groan over the phone. My coworker Ayako was running late.

"I'm on my way! Traffic is crazy. I don't know why I took an Uber from Astoria during rush hour. It would've taken me half the time on the subway. Don't drink all the champagne, Camilo!"

"I can't make any promises. Imma let you go. I see the bar, and it's not too busy."

"Okay we just passed the Brooklyn Bridge. I should be there soon."

I ended the call with Ayako as I got to the bar, and once again was glad for my finely honed fashion sense. Stopping home after work to change into a suit was the right call, because this thing was fancy. I thanked my lucky stars for my job and my boss, as I walked through the huge and beautifully decorated room where the Roi Green Center, a social services agency for homeless LGBT youth in New York City, was hosting its annual fall gala.

The event was at Cipriani's Wall Street, which was as posh as you could get in New York City, and Ayako and I each had a seat at one of the tables. The room was decorated to look like Central Park in the fall. Lots of yellows, oranges and reds, it was beautiful. Melissa, the executive director of New Beginnings, the social services agency Ayako and I worked for, bought two tickets for a thousand bucks a pop, but at the last minute had to stay home with a sick wife and kid. She'd sent an email offering the tickets to all the department directors and Ayako and I had jumped on them within seconds. Being a social worker didn't exactly pay enough to be able to do this kind of thing. So, after a very stressful week at work and some personal life fuckery, I was ready to pounce on the unlimited free alcoholic beverages.

I got to the bar and gave the bar offerings and the bartender an assessing look then leaned on the polished dark wood surface, raising my finger. "I'll have a glass of champagne please."

He winked at me and got busy pouring. Within a few seconds I had a glass of chilled Moët & Chandon. I lifted my glass to him with one hand while I put a couple of bills in the tip jar. He gave me a big smile and went to serve another customer. He was hot. Had a bit of a Jason Momoa flow going on, and I wasn't mad about it. I wondered how tacky it would be to pick up a guy at this thing. I'd only been here five minutes and already gotten in some low-key, high-quality flirting and was sipping top-shelf champagne. I was musing on how the evening was already a success even if I went home right then, when I heard a deep and smoky voice from somewhere on my left.

"I like your suit." I lifted my eyes and saw a gorgeous man smiling at me.

I answered without turning around. "That's a pretty lame pickup line."

I ran my free hand over the front of my jacket. "But I agree this suit looks amazing on me." He laughed, like I wasn't being a hundred percent serious. *I was* rocking my Topman burgundy suit with a navy shirt and tie. I'd even gone for the messy man bun Ayako always said made me look extra fuckable. I knew I was popping.

I decided to turn so I was fully facing the guy, and gave him a thorough once-over as I sipped my Moët. I had to admit there was lot to like there. He must have been a few inches over six feet, because he was a full head over my five feet and eight inches. He was big too. Dark brown hair in a short, but stylish cut and hazel eyes. His mouth was small, but perfectly shaped, and at the moment, the corners were tipped up in to a tiny grin, while he stood there letting me run my eyes all over him. I had an urge to push up and take a bite that bottom lip, just to see what he would do.

Instead I kept looking farther down his very large body, and barely withheld a sigh. He was a very good-looking man. His suit was navy blue and he had on a boring white shirt and red tie. It fit him well though, like it was painted on. Once I was done with my inspection I shrugged as he smiled at me.

"Your suit is pretty boring, but it's"—I cleared my throat—"a pretty good fit. Although I have a feeling you could wear a trash bag and you'd still look hot." I went out on a limb on that one, assuming—given the type of event—we were all family here.

Besides, he started it.

Another deep laugh burst out of him, his eyes crinkling as he shook his head. Like he couldn't believe I'd just said that. He was about to say something, when Ayako barreled in between us.

"Oh my god! I saw bottles of Moët, this is fan-saaay." After she gave me a kiss on the cheek she leaned back to get a good look at me. "Damn, you got your 'Come Fuck Me' suit on, niiiiice." She stretched out the last word as she leered at me, totally unaware she had interrupted something. Meanwhile Tall, Dark and Swole behind her was turning purple from trying not to laugh.

Ayako was wearing a short magenta cocktail dress, which looked amazing on her, and kept shaking her shoulders at me clearly fishing for a compliment. I rolled my eyes at her and complied. "You look stunning, friend."

She preened at that. "You're fucking right, I do."

"You're so modest, friend." She just laughed and kept blocking my view of "hot guy in the boring suit."

Ayako and I went way back. We were extra tight because we both had Jamaican dads, and our moms were also immigrants—hers Japanese while mine was Cuban. When we started working together we bonded over our sick love for Golden Krust and hip-hop classes. She was a fucking riot and I loved her, but right now she was totally cock-blocking me.

I tilted my head to let her know where I wanted to be focusing. "Hey, hon, I was just about to ask the gentleman behind you for his name, before you parked your luscious ass on the stool between us that is." She turned around and immediately did a double take. I could tell she was trying to do some quick math on what was going on.

But she and I had done this particular routine too many times for her to miss a beat. As if on cue, she spoke up, "Oh, pardon me, kind sir." She extended her hand, those perfect teeth flashing. "I'm Ayako, and the lovely man you were just conversing with is my friend Milo." She pronounced it in Spanish, *Mee-loh*, like I preferred, as she waved a hand in my direction.

The guy looked at us like he was starting to suspect he was being punked, but he played along and extended his hand first to Ayako and then to me.

"I'm Thomas, nice to meet you both." He winked at me, and then turned to Ayako. "Would you like a glass of champagne, Miss?"

"Yes please! And it's Ayako," she said, waving her hand at him. "It's an open bar. We'll be on a first name basis soon enough."

He chuckled at her and nodded. "Fair enough. Give me a minute." Then he looked at my empty flute and raised an eyebrow. I lifted it with a nod to let him know a refill would be much appreciated.

While he turned to get our drinks, Ayako tried to engage in a silent conversation with her eyeballs I had no hope of understanding, even as sober as I was. So I just shook my head to indicate she needed to *play it cool.*

"Here you go." He passed around flutes and lifted his own glass. "To kind strangers."

We all lifted our glasses in a toast, and drank in silence. After a moment my mind started to wonder. How was a man this hot and seemingly socially competent here by himself? He had to be waiting for someone to join him and just killing time with me. Right as I was about to inquire I heard a woman's voice call out.

"Tom! There you are. Please tell me there are mock-tails, because I'm thirsty."

Figured.

The three of us turned in the direction of the voice, and I saw a very beautiful and very pregnant woman dressed in a stunning purple silk gown walking toward us, holding hands with an equally dashing man. I noticed the matching wedding bands they were wearing, and immediately felt annoyed at the butterflies fluttering in my stomach when I realized she probably wasn't carrying Thomas's—who I had only met five minutes ago—baby.

The man in question waved over the new arrivals toward our trio. "Hey, guys! Thanks for saving me from sitting through dinner with boring rich people."

The woman came up to us and kissed him on the cheek, while the guy gave him the bro half hug back slap combo. Thomas looked over at us and spoke to his friends. "Guys, these are my new friends, Ayako and Milo." He waved his hands in the direction of the new arrivals while looking at us. "This is my best friend, Sanjay, and his *much* better half, Priya."

We did the appropriate introductions and then proceeded to help Priya figure out what nonalcoholic drink she could have, which in her words, "wouldn't make her want to stab us in the neck for drinking champagne while she drank soda." Ayako and I loved her immediately.

I was about to ask her where she was sitting to see if our tables were close by when the emcee announced that people should start heading to their tables. Thomas gave me a long look, as if he were struggling with whether to say whatever was on his mind. I was disappointed when after a few seconds he just winked and raised his hand.

"Have a good diner, Milo." He said my name perfectly. Most people struggled with the Spanish pronunciation. I wondered where he'd learned Spanish. I never got to ask because after I nodded and waved back Tom walked away.

Ayako, who knew me a little too well and could probably tell I was disappointed, gave him some side eye and mouthed "his loss." I finished up my drink and looked around to spot where Thomas and his friends were sitting. I almost choked when I saw them take their seats at a table right next to the stage. The tables I knew for a fact went for ten grand a plate. I heard a whistle from my side as I stared. Ayako was probably looking in the same direction I was.

I turned around to find Ayako, who seemed very impressed by Tom's status at the very top of the gala food chain. "Damn he was pretty low-key for a dude dropping thirty grand on Friday night dinner. He's just like you like 'em too. Huge and looks like he could fuck your lights out."

"We don't even know he's gay," I offered, prompting an eye roll from Ayako.

"I'm going to point out the facts," she said, holding up two perfectly manicured bright pink nails. "We're at an LGBT benefit and the guy dropped ten grand apiece for three tickets. If that's not commitment to the cause I don't know what is. So there's at least a *slim* chance the dude's into dick. He was certainly eying your privates with interest." She gave my crotch area a pointed look like there was some kind of indicator down there I was too dumb to notice.

I sighed and signaled to the other side of the room. "Fine, I see your point. Let's go find our seats, way back there." Ayako sipped the last of her champagne and signaled for another as I made my way to our table.

Just I was sitting down I opened my Instagram app and saw a new post from my ex, which only worsened my sinking mood. It looked like the adoption he and his partner were working on finally went through. I scrolled through his recent posts and saw photo after photo of a tired but elated couple, looking adoringly at the bundled infant in their arms.

I didn't even know why seeing the photos made me feel like someone was squeezing my insides. Paul wasn't a guy I wanted to co-parent a kid with. At least not based on how he behaved while we were dating. It wasn't even about the baby though, it was about how fast he'd found someone who he wanted to make that kind of commitment with. Yet when we were together he could barely agree to keep a toothbrush at my place.

When would I find someone who saw me as their forever person? Who looked at me and saw exactly who they wanted. Not just a warm body to pass the time with until their soul mate came along.

And *that* was my other problem, despite all the first-hand knowledge I had of just how fucked-up relationships could be, I was still holding out for some kind of fairy tale. I always jumped in too fast, gave too much, put all of myself out there, and *every* time ended up getting my heart crushed. Why were these photos even bringing all of this up? I didn't have any feelings for Paul and we'd been barely speaking when we broke things off over two years ago.

Why do I care?

"Oh no you don't," Ayako whispered as she swiftly took my phone from my hand and put it in her clutch.

"Ayako, please give me my phone back."

"Why, so you can mope over that asshole and his stupid baby? Camilo, don't you remember how much of a jerk he was to you?" She sighed, squeezing my hand. "Babe, Paul was not baby-daddy material. If you're going to feel sorry for someone, feel sorry for the poor bastard who's now stuck co-parenting with him for the next twenty years. He already looks like he wants out and the kid is only like three days old."

I chuckled at her attempt to make me feel better, but still felt annoyed with myself. Paul and I had been over and done with a million years ago. Why was I letting this ruin my night? A night at an amazing event for a cause I was passionate about, where I could drink as much as I wanted.

What the fuck is wrong with me?

I took a deep breath and tried to shake off my funk then turned around to give Ayako my best smile.

"You're one-hundred-percent right. Fuck Paul and his perfect baby. I have unlimited champagne at my disposal tonight, and two days to recover before work on Monday. So Imma put that open bar to good use."

"Attaboy!" She held up her hand then. "I solemnly swear to monitor your alcohol intake *and* phone use if you want to take your drinking to the next level. You held me down this summer when we went to that beach party in the Hamptons."

I saluted her, remembering the very wild night in question. "Anytime, babe. Let me finish this one and I'll go get myself another." I sipped from my glass, looking around the room. It really was beautifully decorated, with gorgeous centerpieces laden with lilies and roses in fall colors. Each place setting had a menu printed in a blood red card stock and gold font. On one side we could read the courses we'd be enjoying during dinner, and on the other the story of one of the young people who benefited from the center's services. It was a smart and touching way to get people to pull out those checkbooks again before the end of the night.

After a few minutes the servers started coming around with bowls of delicious butternut squash and apple soup and to pour more champagne for us, and we got busy eating and moaning over how good everything was. Gorgeous courses kept coming as Ayako and I chatted with the other people at our table. Before long dinner was over and the lights in the room were dimmed to begin the more formal part of the evening.

Between the couple of glasses of bubbly I'd had and the delicious meal, I was feeling pretty relaxed. As the speeches started to get underway, I decided to walk to the bar and get myself one last glass of champagne. As I stood up I touched Ayako's shoulder to get her attention.

"Hey, do you want to go with me to the bar for one last glass of bubbly?"

She looked up at me smiling and pointed at her half-full glass. "No thanks, hon. I'll wait for you here." She turned around and went back to her conversation with a woman sitting next to her.

When I got to the bar I found it empty again, so I got the bartender's attention immediately. He poured me another glass of Moët without asking and pushed it toward me across the bar with a flirty smile. I thanked him, but could not muster up the energy to flirt back.

I stood by the bar, sipping slowly, and listening to the person speaking from the stage.

"Still enjoying the open bar I see."

Thomas.

His voice was coming from behind me this time, and I felt a flutter in my belly. Suddenly my lack of enthusiasm was replaced by a burst of energy. I smiled to myself before turning around.

"Yes I am. How is your evening going so far?"

I gazed up at him and saw him lift a shoulder as he asked the bartender for a Zacapa on the rocks. "It's another gala. This organization's mission is particularly important to me, so I try to push through. Once you've gone to enough of these, they all sort of blend together." He took a sip of the amber liquid in his glass, his eyes fixed on me. "Nothing terribly memorable ever happens at these things."

He paused then and tipped his glass at me, a very dirty smile on his lips. "Although I must say, this year's attendants have been particularly impressive."

We stood there with a charged silence between us. Thomas looked me up and down with hungry eyes, like he wanted to rip all my clothes off and maul me where I stood. I kept sipping my glass and letting my own eyes look over whatever part of his body I wanted. I noticed a little bit of gray at his temples I hadn't seen earlier, which only made him that much hotter.

As Ayako pointed out earlier, he *was* one-hundred percent my type.

Suddenly an insane urge took over me and I grabbed his hand, pulling him out of the ballroom and toward a sitting room I'd seen on an earlier trip to the men's room. To my surprise he just let me lead him away without much resistance. Just as we crossed the threshold and turned in the direction of the restrooms, he asked offhandedly. "Where are we going?"

"To make this gala memorable for you." He didn't respond, just chuckled quietly and grabbed my hand tighter.

When we got there I walked through the door, pulling him in with me. As soon as we were both inside, I locked the door, walked over to where he was standing by the wall on the far side of the room and went down on my knees.

Don't miss
American Fairytale
by Adriana Herrera
Available May 2019 wherever
Carina Press books are sold.
www.CarinaPress.com

About the Author

Adriana Herrera was born and raised in the Caribbean, but for the last fifteen years has let her job (and her spouse) take her all over the world. She loves writing stories about people who look and sound like her people, getting unapologetic happy endings.

When's she not dreaming up love stories, planning logistically complex vacations with her family or hunting for discount Broadway tickets, she's a social worker in New York City, working with survivors of domestic and sexual violence.

You can find her on:
Twitter: *https://twitter.com/ladrianaherrera*
Instagram: *https://www.instagram.com/ladriana_herrera/*
Facebook: *https://www.facebook.com/laura.adriana.94801*
Website: *https://adrianaherreraromance.com/*